"One of the

"Full of wit, delightful characters and a unique plot, *Jezebel's Sister* is Emily Carmichael at her charming, humorous best. This is just the book to chase away the end of your winter blahs and bring a smile to warm your heart."
—*Romantic Times*

"*Jezebel's Sister* is such a delight, it's hard to put the book down. The diversified characters give us insight into the kind of people who built our country. It also shows how many were able to adapt from former lives to fit into a new society."
—*Rendezvous*

"Cass is a lively heroine and the cast of characters from the brothel are a riot."
—*BellaOnline*

"A humorous western romance that showcases the intelligent writing of talented humorist Emily Carmichael. The story line is fast-paced and vividly colorful from the start . . . No one combines amusing situations, resplendent descriptions, and fascinating characters in a cleverly designed American romance better than the unparalleled Ms. Carmichael does."
—Harriet Klausner

"A fun, entertaining read." —*TheRomanceReader.com*

"A funny historical romance." —*Columbia State*

Titles by Emily Carmichael

**JEZEBEL'S SISTER
BECOMING GEORGIA**

Becoming Georgia

Emily Carmichael

BERKLEY SENSATION, NEW YORK

If you purchased this book without a cover, you should be aware that this book is stolen property. It was reported as "unsold and destroyed" to the publisher, and neither the author nor the publisher has received any payment for this "stripped book."

This is a work of fiction. Names, characters, places, and incidents either are the product of the author's imagination or are used fictitiously, and any resemblance to actual persons, living or dead, business establishments, events, or locales is entirely coincidental.

BECOMING GEORGIA

A Berkley Sensation Book / published by arrangement with the author

PRINTING HISTORY
Berkley Sensation edition / July 2003

Copyright © 2003 by Emily Krokosz
Cover art by Tsukushi
Cover design by George Long

All rights reserved.
This book, or parts thereof, may not be reproduced in any form without permission.
The scanning, uploading, and distribution of this book via the Internet or via any other means without the permission of the publisher is illegal and punishable by law. Please purchase only authorized electronic editions, and do not participate in or encourage electronic piracy of copyrighted materials. Your support of the author's rights is appreciated.
For information address: The Berkley Publishing Group,
a division of Penguin Group (USA) Inc.,
375 Hudson Street, New York, New York 10014.

ISBN: 0-425-19101-X

A BERKLEY SENSATION™ BOOK
Berkley Sensation Books are published by
The Berkley Publishing Group,
a division of Penguin Group (USA) Inc.,
375 Hudson Street, New York, New York 10014.
BERKLEY SENSATION and the "B" design
are trademarks belonging to Penguin Group (USA) Inc.

PRINTED IN THE UNITED STATES OF AMERICA

10 9 8 7 6 5 4 3 2 1

Chapter 1

The day Georgie Kennedy's world shattered started out quite innocently. The morning sun shone warmly in a clear blue sky. The cedars and pines breathed their fresh scent into clean air. Birds sang. Lynx Creek, known by locals as the Lynx, bubbled happily along its course.

The day was July Fourth, 1870, and Prescott, former capital of the Territory of Arizona, planned a grand patriotic celebration. Because of the holiday, Georgie and her partner, Esperanza Cardenas, slept until the sun had lifted above the hills instead of rising before first light to start work. Today Georgie wouldn't strain her back shoveling stream gravel into the rocker and strain her eyes to spot bits of gold among the useless pebbles. Today Essie wouldn't do the laundry or mending, repair equipment, prepare the meals, or tend her little vegetable garden. Because today Georgie and Essie were taking the two mules and the wagon into town, and they were going to have themselves a good time. That night they planned to indulge in the unspeakable luxury of staying in town, in Georgie's new house—a real house, not the ramshackle cabin that sheltered them on the claim. This house had two rooms, real plank floors, and snugly chinked log walls with three windows. The windows didn't boast glass, but the shutters were nice and tight. Far grander houses graced the one-time capital of Arizona Territory, but Georgie, who had lived in tents, lean-tos, an occasional cave, and a few slapdash cabins, regarded her "town house" as a palace beyond compare.

When they rattled into Prescott mid-morning, the town square already jumped with activity. Long plank tables held the potluck offerings of almost every respectable female in town. (The offerings of the less than respectable females drew a good deal of business as well.) Odors of baked beans, fried chicken, and roasting chiles perfumed the morning breeze. In one corner of the square, men showed off their marksmanship skills while a crowd of onlookers called out compliments, insults, and took odds on who would win or who might shoot their own foot. Not far away a wrestling contest drew a similar crowd. Young boys chased each other through the celebrants, heedless of tripping the unwary or spattering mud on women's skirts as they passed. A few girls looked longingly at the boys' escapades from where the preacher's wife and the schoolteacher led them in games suitable for young ladies. An entrepreneur peddled cool drinks—"Almost cold as ice!" he boasted, though everyone knew there was no ice to be had in July.

"Well now!" Georgie exclaimed to Essie as she parked the wagon behind her tiny house and jumped down to unhitch the mules. "This looks like a damned good time."

Rotund Essie climbed down from the wagon and brushed off her go-to-town skirts. "Girl, you mind your mouth now we're in town. Your good father, God rest him"—and here she crossed herself, as she always did at mention of the late Elias Kennedy—"didn't do you no favors by letting you run wild as a wolf cub. In the six months since he's been in the ground, you've just got wilder."

Georgie simply grinned. She was accustomed to Essie's high-handed scolding. She had learned to ignore it years ago. "I can smell that fried chicken all the way over here. Mmmmm! I'm gonna stuff my face today, and that's a fact!"

Essie sighed and handed her a big pot of beans and bacon—their contribution to the community feed. "You can carry these, since I did all the work in making them. Put them over one of the fires to warm them a bit."

Georgie took the beans in one hand and grabbed her rifle—always close at hand beneath the wagon seat—with the other. "Maybe I'll get in the shooting contest. You could bet on me and win enough money to pay for all the provisions we're buying tomorrow."

"Ha!" Though she came only to Georgie's shoulder, Essie matched strides with the younger woman as they walked toward the square. "Last year you lost, and I bet Skillet Mahoney a whole dollar that you'd win. That's the last time I bet on you!"

"Cougar Barnes cheated. I had an itch that spoiled my aim, and he wouldn't let me shoot again."

"Don't tell me about some itch! You were trying to show off and didn't pay enough attention to your aim. You're a grown woman, *chica*. Time you started acting like it, at least in town around civilized people who expect a woman to act like a woman."

"What do I care what people expect? I'm twenty-three, and that's old enough to do what I want to do and act like I want to act. I don't answer to no one but God, and most times not him."

Georgie had no way of knowing that that state of affairs was about to change.

Once they'd reached the square with its noise and bustle, Essie drifted off to the few Mexican families who had come to join in the festivities. Georgie suspected the older woman missed the company of her own kind, though she never complained. Shortly after Georgie and her father had arrived in Arizona, Elias had hired on Esperanza to help out at the claim—to cook, do laundry, clean, and doctor the bruises, blisters, and lacerations that went along with the task of mining gold. Elias and Georgie had done for themselves a long time, but Essie's husband had just been killed in an Apache raid, and the woman had nowhere to go.

In a short time they couldn't do without her, especially Elias. Georgie had never pried into her father's relationship with the little rotund Sonoran woman. She had been glad to see him content. Essie had loved Elias. When the big, red-bearded man had started wasting away from some canker that ate him inside, Essie had nursed him. When he had died, she'd just naturally stayed on with Georgie to help work the claim, because she loved Georgie, too.

Georgie loved her back, but she wished the stubborn señora would give up the attempt to turn her into a woman. A drab sparrow could become a goldfinch more easily than Georgie could become a real woman.

"Hey there, George! You're late. You missed all the shootin'!"

"Hey there, yourself, Skillet. How ya doin'?"

"Still alive, still got my hair." He tugged on a lock of greasy, indeterminate color, as if checking to make sure it was still attached to his head. "No thanks to our Injun friends who hit me and Dooley down on Groom Creek the other day. I tell ya, the guv'mint needs to do something about those bloody savages."

"I guess they're trying."

"Not hard enough, that's fer sure." He grinned, revealing a mouth of mostly missing teeth. "I'm disappointed ya weren't here to shoot. Last year a won a bundle bettin' on ya to lose."

"Cougar cheated. I won the year before."

"Hell. Cougar don't need to cheat. He's a dead shot. 'Course so are you."

"You got that right. Where is that ornery ox, anyway? I don't see him."

Skillet jabbed a thumb toward a knot of laughing men. "Arm wrestling. He beat the Swede, and Gil Hammersmith."

"Brute strength," Georgie sneered. "No skill. Someone could take him if he used his head instead of pure muscle."

Skillet laughed. "I wouldn't bet against him if'n I was you."

Georgie acknowledged that betting against Cougar Barnes was never a good idea. The man had both brawn and brains. He was hard to beat at just about anything.

She headed toward the laden tables with Essie's pot of

beans, her nose twitching with the scent of fried chicken. She came away from the table munching on a greasy chicken leg and looking forward to a whole day of doing nothing more strenuous than catching up on the local news, playing a little horseshoes, and maybe singing along with some patriotic songs. She noticed that Lem Stucker was carrying his fiddle and Jake Settle had his horn. Those two could rattle off music all day and never pause for breath.

The crowd on this Fourth of July was a good deal thinner than it had been three years ago. When Tucson had stolen the capital for itself, Governor McCormick, the legislature and all their hangers-on had left, and so had the lawyers and some of the storekeepers. Many prospectors and miners had drifted away, also. Prescott hadn't proven to be the El Dorado the first explorers predicted. When Captain Joseph Walker and Paulino Weaver had led the first hopeful prospectors into central Arizona in 1863, they thought they'd discovered a bonanza. But few fortunes had been made. The gold was here, buried in the streambeds and hidden in quartz veins cutting the hills. But it was hard to get. Miners along the streams slaved all day washing gold from gravel and still barely made ends meet, and the hard rock prospects on the hillsides required more capital and know-how than most of these boys possessed. Many had drifted off to look for easier pickings in California and Colorado.

The Apache menace didn't help matters. The soldiers at Fort Whipple did their best to protect the miners and settlers, but fighting Apaches was like fighting the wind, with much more deadly results. The Indians appeared without warning, struck without mercy, and then retreated to hideaways no one could find. Everything and everyone was a target—travelers, settlers, miners, even small patrols of soldiers.

Georgie didn't much blame the Indians for not wanting a bunch of newcomers tromping over their territory, but she figured that was the way the world worked. She wasn't partial to losing her hair, so she carried both a pistol and a rifle and used them both with deadly accuracy. Her father had staked out two of the best claims on the Lynx. One she'd sold to Cougar Barnes not long ago. The other she worked, and she planned to stick around until the gold gave out, Apaches be damned.

"Hey ya, Georgie. How's that mule I sold ya?"

"Good, Toby. She's a damned good worker."

"Ya missed the shootin'."

"Yup. Got here late."

"Mornin', Georgie." The town marshal, Colin Tate, grinned. "Did Essie send a pot of her good beans?"

"On the table," she told him. "Leave some for the rest of us."

He rubbed his barrel-like middle. "Not a chance!"

Everyone Georgie passed greeted her, and she responded with a few words and a wave of her fried chicken. One of the things she liked best about coming into town was seeing all the folks. Sometimes out on the claim she got to feeling that she and Essie were the only two people in the world. A few years ago active gold claims butted up one against the other on the Lynx, Big Bug Creek, and Granite Creek, so close that Georgie could see her neighbors both downstream and upstream, within yelling distance if need be. These days only a few hardy souls worked the streambeds and the hills.

"Hiya, Miss Georgie!" Abe Zindler's eleven-year-old ran up, breathless. "Have you seen my dog?"

"He was over at the potluck eyeing the chicken."

"Uh-oh!" The boy waved and shot off.

"George! Good to see you! I got in that shipment of new boots you was asking about." This from Mrs. Purdy, who worked at Bashford's general merchandise store.

"I'll be by tomorrow for sure, then," Georgie told her. "That cake of yours on the table looks mighty good."

"Thank you, dear. I do make a fine cake, if I do say so myself."

George worked her way through the crowd until she found herself watching the arm wrestling. Shorty Smith and Mexican Joe—whose last name nobody seemed to know—were going at it. Mexican Joe was winning, his face red with effort, his mustachioed mouth pulled into a grimace. Shorty's arm thumped down on the table with grim finality.

"Ha-ha!" Mexican Joe crowed. "I win. Cougar, now we fight for the championship. I will bet my best mule against your new fancy saddle."

Cougar grinned his big, white-toothed grin. "Now, Mex, I wouldn't want to take that mule away from you."

Cocky bastard, Georgie mused with a smile.

"It will not be that easy, *mi amigo*." He flexed a bicep to make his point.

Also a cocky bastard. What was it with men? Georgie wondered.

Cougar laughed, a booming, bear-sized laugh. The onlookers made odds and exchanged bets as he settled himself at the little table that had been dragged out from old lady Peterson's boardinghouse. The two men exchanged grimaces and clasped hands.

After only a brief struggle Cougar slapped Mexican Joe's arm onto the table. Mex grimaced and shook out his hand.

"Guess I got myself a mule," the winner declared.

Skillet Mahoney stood among the audience, and he crowed. "Don't never bet against Cougar Barnes." He tipped a hand toward Georgie. "Isn't that what I always say, Georgie?"

"Yup. That's what you say, when you're sober enough to say anything."

"What was that you was tellin' me about brains over brute strength?" Skillet goaded. "Maybe you think you could beat ol' Coug here."

The onlookers were enthused at the propect of more betting, if anyone was stupid enough to bet against the local champion. And Georgie being a woman—of sorts—only added to the fun. They took up the call.

"C'mon, Georgie!"

"Put your money where your mouth is."

"Give us a show, Georgie girl!"

Georgie was tempted. Her father had shown her ways to use a man's strength against him, and these yahoos sorely needed a set-down.

Cougar pulled a face. "I'm not wrestling a woman."

That settled it for Georgie. The man really did need a set-down. She waved her chicken leg at him. "Scared, Coug?"

He snorted.

"Scared I might beat you, big man?"

The audience, always eager for a bit of strife, took up the call.

"I might hurt her," Cougar claimed.

It was Georgie's turn to snort.

"C'mon, Cougar!"

"Give us a chance to win some money back."

"She's askin' for it, man!"

"Just don't break her arm."

"Let her back up her mouth with her muscles."

He had to give in. Georgie disposed of her chicken, wiped greasy hands on her overalls, and swaggered to the table, knowing well that anyone, woman or man, who wanted to keep from being trampled by this herd of rowdies needed to show a good bit of boldness. As she sat down, she spotted Essie pushing through the crowd. The little woman's scowl was more daunting than the onlookers' hoots and hollers. Georgie sent her a wicked wink.

She would pay for that later, but the exasperation on Essie's face was worth the price. Sometimes her friend and partner needed a set-down, too.

"What do you have to bet, Georgie?" Cougar sounded hopeful that she might still back out.

"I'll bet a big pot of Essie's bacon and beans. Best in the territory." Out of the corner of her eye, Georgie saw Essie's scowl darken. "What do you have to match, big man?"

Cougar thought a moment, blue eyes glinting. Essie's beans and bacon were a prize, especially for a bachelor who had to eat his own cooking. "I'm not going to lose, but if by some accident I do, I'll chop you a pile of firewood."

"How much?" Georgie asked, narrow-eyed.

"Four hours' work. That should give you a pile to last a month."

"Good enough. I'll enjoy that firewood," she told him with a grin.

"Don't count on it." He eyed her up and down, narrowing on his regard to put her off balance. Georgie ignored it. She was used to men looking at her as if she were something they couldn't quite figure out. Tall and broad-shouldered, she had enough lean muscle on her frame to chop wood or shovel stream gravel for hours, walk for miles without stopping, or stiff-arm any fool who took her open-natured friendliness for improper invitation. Wearing her usual overalls and flannel shirt, she might well have been mistaken for a slender man had her braids not betrayed her true gender. But she didn't care. Feminine vanity was for women, and while Georgie certainly wasn't a man, she didn't quite consider herself a woman, either.

"Sure you want to do this?" Cougar asked. His grin was cocky. "Could be humiliating."

"For you, not me."

"Don't count on it."

"Don't you count on a mess of Essie's good beans."

"Well, I certainly don't want any beans cooked by you! I hope Essie will bide by your bargain."

"Quit flapping your jaw and save your energy for chopping all that firewood."

Ritual insults complete, they settled down to work.

Jacob Whittaker could scarcely believe that he had journeyed halfway across the continent—the more difficult half, at that—simply to deliver a letter for a client to his granddaughter in Prescott. When he had decided to study law as a young man, post delivery hadn't been among the great things he had planned to accomplish.

But Alvin Kennedy was an important client of the law firm where he'd just been made partner, and Mr. Kennedy insisted that this missive be delivered by a messenger with enough authority to enforce its demands. So to Jacob fell the unlucky task of enduring unspeakably uncomfortable trains, a ship from hell steaming down the West Coast and up the Gulf of California, the tedious steamboat ride up the Colorado River, and the dangerous trek east over the Mojave Trail to at last arrive in the territory of Arizona. Or as he had come to think of it, the stinking, godforsaken, savage-infested territory of Arizona. He wasn't at all surprised that seven years ago, the military department of New Mexico had recommended the United States Government buy out the property owners in the newly formed Territory of Arizona and give the place back to the Indians. The Apaches wanted it, and from what Jacob could see, they deserved it.

Not that the countryside wasn't attractive in its own way. The rugged mountains clad in pine, juniper, and cedar, the grassy uplands and valleys, and the almost painfully bright skies had a charm quite unlike the tamer lands in the Midwest and East. But all that charm was at the ends of the earth, peopled by savages, Mexicans, and dropouts from civilized society. Jacob held no hope the land would ever be fit for decent people to inhabit.

Still, Jacob had a job to do, and he was quite prepared to do it. That morning he had, after a day's rest from the nightmarish journey, paid a call at Fort Whipple, north of town. His client had connections in the military halls of power, and the commander had been very accommodating in sending word of Jacob's safe arrival with the military dispatches—so much more reliable than the civil post in this wild country. He had also arranged for an escort to Santa Fe, where a stage could be embarked for Denver and the railroad. Jacob didn't think he could endure another ship journey around Baja California, especially since a lady would travel with him on the return trip. Ladies were fragile things. One had to be careful of their special needs.

Before he could leave this benighted place, however, Jacob must deliver Alvin Kennedy's missive and collect what he had come to collect. He didn't anticipate any difficulty in doing the job, other than the hideous amount of travel required. Prescott, Arizona, was a mere scattering of buildings scarcely big enough to be called a village. Surely everyone here knew everyone else. Fortuitous chance had brought him here on a holiday celebration, when all the inhabitants hereabouts were making merry in the town square. His quarry would be nearby somewhere, probably mingling with the few respectable-looking ladies who tended the potluck. Even if she were sitting at home to avoid the rowdiness, Jacob could find someone who could direct him to her whereabouts.

Most of the merchants of the town had closed their doors and joined the celebration. One exception was Big Mike's Tavern, where fiddle music poured from the door and a good deal of laughter and stomping indicated a full house. Jacob ventured inside, his nose twitching at the odor of unwashed bodies and stale liquor.

"Excuse me," he said to a husky man behind a long rough-hewn bar. "Would you happen to know the address of"—he hesitated to mention a respectable woman's name in such a place, but necessity dictated—"the, uh, place of residence, or where I might find Miss Georgia Kennedy?"

The man stared at him for a moment, taking in his dark broadcloth suit and fashionable narrow-brimmed hat. His mouth stretched into a gap-toothed smile. "Miss Georgia Kennedy?" He drew the name out as if it were a joke. "*Miss* Georgia Kennedy? Hoo-ha! Did you hear that, you boys? The gent here is looking for *Miss* Georgia Kennedy!"

A round of laughter told Jacob that something was amiss, though he couldn't imagine what.

"Sure thing, mister!" A fellow in a shirt that looked as if it were made from a flour sack clapped Jacob on the back. "I'll be glad to take you to *Miss* Kennedy."

Another round of laughter. Jacob wondered what he was missing.

Five minutes later he found out.

"That . . . that can't be Miss Georgia Kennedy," he told his guide.

"Sure enough it is." The fellow chuckled and clapped Jacob on the back. "I knowed ol' George since her and her daddy came here three years ago."

"Could there be two?"

"God help us if there was!" Still chuckling, Jacob's guide left him on his own.

Jacob stood in the middle of Prescott town square and stared in consternation at the . . . the person . . . that supposedly was Alvin Kennedy's granddaughter. She was engaged in an arm-wrestling contest with a brutish-looking fellow, enduring catcalls, insults, and rude encouragement from a crowd of unwashed rowdies. In almost every respect she was indistinguishable from the shabby, rough-hewn men who populated the town. She wore overalls and a red shirt that could very well have been the top half of a set of long underwear, and none too clean at that. Her face twisted into an unattractive grimace as she glared at her opponent. Sweat dripped from the tip of her nose. The creature's hair tumbled from beneath a stained felt hat in two sloppy braids that hung halfway down her back.

"Don't make her mad, Cougar," an onlooker advised, laughing. "She's got a temper to go with that red hair."

"Show her where a woman's place is!" another urged.

"You get 'im, George!"

"Show 'im what you're made of!"

"Smash her flat, Barnes! Be a man!"

Jacob closed his eyes, as if blocking out the sight might change reality. He thought of Alvin Kennedy with his gracious mansion, his prominent position in Chicago society, his insistence upon all that was proper in both public and private life. He thought of his own long journey here, a mission of mercy to rescue Kennedy's granddaughter from a life of hardship and deprivation. Jacob had pictured Georgia Kennedy as a young woman bravely struggling to maintain dignity and gentility in a primitive land. He knew she received income from a gold claim, but he assumed she lived in town, in the most gracious and proper manner she could, while the actual mining was done by hirelings.

He opened his eyes to the real Georgia Kennedy and decided he deserved at least double his fee for this piece of work.

Georgie narrowed her concentration to her straining arm, the table, and the man across from her. On the margins of awareness she heard the calls from the crowd, even noted Essie's voice in among the others, shouting encouragement. Of course Essie would cheer for her. For all her scolding and supposed scorn of Georgie's ways, Essie was fanatically loyal. If she managed to win this contest, the little señora would brag of the feat until the whole town was tired of the story.

But to win, Georgie had to focus. Focus, focus, focus. Damn Cougar for having those twinkly blue eyes that laughed at her and made her want to laugh, too. That was cheating. The way muscles bunched in his shoulder and arm drew her attention, also. The day was getting warm, and since the ladies were out of sight on the other side of the square, some of the men had opened or even discarded their shirts. Cougar had tossed his aside earlier, then shrugged it on when he'd come to face Georgie—as if she gave a flying fig about looking at his bare chest, all those slabs of muscle furred with curling blond hair. Still, she wished he had buttoned it closed, because somehow that broad bare chest kept drawing her eyes and wrecking her concentration.

Concentration was the key to contests of strength, her father had taught her. Concentration and a bit of trickiness. She was strong. Days of shoveling gravel had honed her to whipcord muscle, but Cougar had both muscle and bulk. His cockiness lent her advantage, though, as he wasn't really trying that hard. Cougar was putting on a show for the audience, and that would be his downfall, giving her time to maneuver into just the right position.

If only she could block out all those muscles, and wicked blue eyes, the knowing grin almost hidden by a bushy wheat-colored beard. You would think she was some giggle-headed girl that way her stomach got weak and fluttery as Cougar leaned forward, bringing his face close to hers.

"You're going down," he whispered, just as Georgie found the perfect angle. With a twitch of aching muscles, she flattened his arm against the table.

Chaos erupted—cheers, catcalls, insults, hoots, hollers, and huzzahs. Cougar looked stunned for a moment. Then he shook his head, grinned sheepishly, and boomed out a laugh. "Got me, Georgie. But you know I let you win because you were nice enough to sell me the best claim on the Lynx."

"Like hell! You think I'm stupid? The best claim on the Lynx is mine. The one I sold you has the gold buried in all that quartz rock. I don't mind working a shovel in the streambed all the day long—not as long as the gold in the bottom of my rocker piles up like it does. But damned if I'm going to dig my way through a mountain with a pick."

He laughed. "We'll see who ends up taking more gold out of the ground."

She rolled her eyes for the amusement of the crowd, sticking her thumb in Cougar's direction. "He'll work as hard as an ox at that claim. Dumb as an ox, too."

Cougar just chuckled.

"I'll expect that pile of firewood before the week's out," she told him loftily.

"Boys, I wouldn't want to have this one as a boss." Cougar took her shoulder in a friendly grip and propelled her into the crowd. "It's time for a drink. I'm buying."

Georgie's shoulder tingled under Cougar's grip. The man did have a way of making a female squirm in a way that was uncomfortable and sort of exciting at the same time. Odd how he did that. Before she could reflect on the sensation, however, an unexpected call interrupted.

"Miss Kennedy. Hello there! Miss Kennedy! May I have a word, please?"

At first Georgie dismissed the demand. Then she realized the dandified little man spoke to her. She didn't recall anyone ever calling her Miss Kennedy in all her twenty-three years of life. But Kennedy was her name. She stopped. "Are you talking to me?"

"You are Miss Georgia Kennedy, aren't you?"

Georgia thought a minute. "I guess. Folks around here call me George. Or Georgie."

A frown line deepened between the man's heavy brows. The brows were the only heavy thing about him. Dressed in a dusty black broadcloth suit—a suicidal choice of garb in high summer—the fellow was soft and pale. A fancy narrow-brimmed, high-crowned hat did nothing to keep the blazing sun from his face. A starched—now rather limp—collar made his face look as though it had been squeezed from between his shoulders. "Miss Kennedy," he insisted. "I have very urgent business with you."

"You don't say?"

"Very important business." He eyed her companions with some trepidation. "If I could talk to you alone it would be best."

Georgie decided she didn't like him. She didn't like soft, or hesitant, or snooty, and this fellow seemed to be all three. "Mister, I think you must have the wrong Georgie Kennedy."

"Don't I wish," Georgia heard him mutter, but he pasted on a counterfeit smile. "You're the only Georgia Kennedy in town, I believe. I have news from your grandfather. Good news, I believe."

Five minutes later Georgie and the citified stranger who introduced himself as Jacob Whittaker settled at the table that was the lone piece of furniture in Georgie's "town house," if you didn't count the rope-sprung bed in the small bedroom. Mention of her grandfather had been more than enough to pry her away from her friends. She knew she had a grandfather somewhere in the East, but only because her father had mentioned him a time or two—not with any great charity. But she knew little of the man.

"Indeed, your grandfather has taken a great interest in your circumstances," Jacob told her. He looked around the parlor/kitchen/dining room of her house, keeping his face carefully blank. Georgie felt his contempt like a slap, but it just made her raise her chin higher.

"Where is he?"

"He lives in Chicago."

"I know he lives in goddamned Chicago! Where the hell is that?"

"Don't you know where Chicago is? It's one of the thriving cities of the Great Lakes. A hub of commerce and industry."

"Well, hooray for Chicago."

He regarded her as someone might regard the flyblown carcass of a dead mule. "Chicago is a very respectable city, Miss Kennedy, in a much more civilized part of our nation." He dug in his coat pocket for an envelope. "I have a letter for you from your grandfather." He squinted dubiously. "Can you read?"

"Of course I can read," she declared, snatching the letter. "I've read the Bible. And Shakespeare. My father's books." She didn't confide that she didn't understand a word of Shakespeare. The Bible wasn't much easier.

But she had also read books that Cougar occasionally lent her, and she could read this letter, which was written plainly in a bold hand. She read it, but she couldn't believe it.

"This can't be true—about my claims!"

"Every bit of it is true, Miss Kennedy. I have in my possession copies of documents that will verify it."

It couldn't be! Her life was over. Two pages of simple words shattered her whole world, took away her independence, her pride, and her confidence.

Worst of all, Cougar Barnes was going to hang her from the highest tree he could find.

"You let her win, right?" Cal Newman said to Cougar as they sat on the porch of Mrs. Peterson's boardinghouse.

"Nope."

Cal took a long swig from a tin mug and wiped his sleeve across his mouth. Old lady Peterson didn't permit alcoholic spirits in her house or even on the porch, but she couldn't know just how spirited a cider slaked the two men's thirst on this warm afternoon.

"T'ain't right that a woman should beat a man like that. Cougar Barnes, the man who killed a mountain cat barehanded, bested by a woman who barely comes up to his chin. It's against nature is what it is."

"She's tricky."

"She's a damned unnatural woman. My granddaddy's a preacher man in Kansas, and he says women who jump themselves up to a man's place are in league with the Devil himself."

Cougar snorted. "Your granddaddy's full of hogwash."

"Still think it ain't natural."

"Georgie's got no more acquaintance with the Devil

than the rest of us. She always tosses a coin in the pot to help folks down on their luck, strikes a fair bargain, and bides by her word. Can't say the same for some others around here."

Cal slid Cougar a suspicious look. "You got your eye on her?"

Cougar snorted.

"Well, she is a woman. There ain't that many unattached females around here. Even whores is scarce. Besides, Georgie's got the best gold claim on the Lynx, and she and her daddy squirreled a lot of the takings in a bank in San Francisco. Money can erase a heap of faults in a woman."

Cougar laughed and tossed the dregs of his cider onto the dirt street. "A man would be safer courting a rattlesnake."

The subject of their conversation rounded the corner and marched toward them, a storm brewing on her face. She halted in front of the boardinghouse, stuck her hands in the back pocket of her denim overalls, and scowled.

The men nodded a greeting. "Hey, Georgie."

She fixed an eye on Cal. "Newman, I'd appreciate your taking yourself off for a while."

Cal didn't hesitate. Even an Apache wouldn't have argued with the look on Georgie's face. When he was out of earshot, Georgie pulled a chair around to face Cougar's, dropped into it, and didn't say a thing.

"What's up, Georgie? You look done in."

"I ain't done in. Just give me a minute. I got a piece to say, and it's important. I gotta get it right."

She stared at her hands in silence, which gave Cougar a chance to cogitate a bit on Cal's comments. Cougar had known Georgie ever since her father had drifted into Prescott with a yen to dig for gold. She was wild as the wind, and about as fascinating a woman—if one could truly call her a woman—as he'd ever met. She dressed like a man, walked like a man, fought and worked like a man. But the curve of her smile and a certain shine in her eye were all woman as far as Cougar could see. He'd loaned her a book now and then from the stash he'd refused to part with when he left New York. She particularly liked Mark Twain.

Strange woman. Lonely woman, Cougar suspected. The men of Prescott tolerated her with a grain of suspicion, and the women, what few of them there were in this wild region, regarded her with utter consternation. Neither the tolerance nor the consternation seemed to matter a hill of beans to Georgie.

Her father had possessed the eye for gold, and he'd made more of a success prospecting the Lynx than most others. When he'd died six months back, the daughter had stayed on and worked twice as hard, without any signs of cashing in and moving on to an easier life. Half the men in Prescott had proposed to her, either to get her rich claim or because women were a lot more scarce than gold in these parts. One fellow she'd had to discourage with a gun, Cougar remembered. The more polite suitors she had simply laughed at and told them she was saving them from a fate worse than death.

Cougar figured she was close to being right. He counted Georgie a good friend, but he figured being hitched to the woman might resemble being shackled to the cranky mountain cat that had jumped him a few years ago. The man who went prospecting to find a woman beneath the baggy overalls, shabby slouch hat, and untamed, blazing hair was a braver man than Cougar Barnes.

Georgie grimaced and let out a sigh. "I have a piece to say," she repeated. "You're not gonna like it, but you gotta remember that I never cheated anyone in my life and I ain't about to start now."

"That twisty little move arm wrestling came close to cheating."

"Cheating, hell. I just played the game smart. Not all of us can depend on muscle to win the day."

Cougar conceded with a lopsided grin. "I give you that."

"And I'm gonna fight smart over this, too. I'm gonna settle things so that everything comes out all right."

He began to get a bad feeling about this. "You're going to fight smart about what?"

She fished an envelope out of a pocket of her overalls and shoved it toward him. "This."

He scanned the contents, consternation building. "Goddammit!"

"That's about what I thought, too. The fancified fellow who delivered it says he's got the papers to prove everything. He's some lawyer who works for my granddad. All the time my daddy and me was working the Lynx, those claims belonged to my granddad. He grubstaked us in return for the claims being in his name. I guess that's why my daddy stashed nearly everything in that San Francisco bank. He said he had to settle up things before we could spend any of the gold for ourselves. I didn't know what he meant to settle, but now I do."

"So that claim you sold me didn't belong to you in the first place."

She shot him a look. "You don't have to say it like I done it on purpose. My daddy never said anything about my granddad holding the claims. In fact, he didn't say much about the old man at all. I found his address in some of Daddy's papers when he died, and I wrote the old codger 'cause I figured he should oughta know his son was dead." Then in a mutter, "Should'a left well enough alone. Though I guess we woulda learned about it when we finally got around to taking care of the paperwork for the sale."

Cougar saw all his plans slipping away. "Damn it, Georgie! I need that claim. The gold in that quartz vein could have bought me a starter herd of prime cattle as seed stock for my ranch."

She leaned forward and thrust out her jaw. "I said I was gonna deal with it, Cougar. You'll get your frigging claim. You'd be a fool to start running cattle before the Indians are taken care of, anyway."

He got madder by the moment. He had worked a year trying to persuade Georgie's father to sell him that claim, and another handful of months working on Georgie. It was a rich hard-rock claim, one that would require more than the usual amount of sweat to extract the gold, but one that could give him a start on financing a cattle spread in a grassy valley among the granite hills north of town. He was convinced that ranching was Prescott's future, not mining, and he'd already bought a nice hunk of property and arranged for grazing rights on even more, enough to support what he hoped would be the area's largest cattle spread once the Apaches were under control.

Big plans, though, took big money, and part of that money could come from that gold-laden quartz vein above the Lynx—the claim Georgie had sold him—the claim that hadn't belonged to her.

"This is a hell of a thing! Goddammit! I had Tucker Beale all set to help me out there, even made arrangements for milling and transportation."

"You'll get your goddamned claim!"

He wanted to kick someone, preferably Georgie. But she looked so mortified that he decided to back off. "All right," he said with a sigh. "Just give me back the money I paid and we'll call it square."

She bit a lip that was already cracked from the sun. "Can't. I spent it."

"You already spent that much money?"

"What do you think I bought my house with? And the new mule?"

"Well, give them back!"

"I can't! Mr. Blackstone sold me the house and took off for who knows where. And gettin' money back for the mule ain't gonna be a flyspeck on what I owe. I'd take money outta the bank, but I guess that ain't really mine, either."

"Goddammit!"

"Cougar, don't worry. I never cheated anyone in my life, and I ain't gonna start with you. My granddad wants me to go to Chicago, and that's what I'm gonna do. And when I get there, I'll get my claims back." At his black look she grimaced. "Get *our* claims back."

"And how are you going to do that?"

"I'll think of a way. No one ever accused me of not havin' a head on my shoulders."

Cougar squeezed the bridge of his nose. All that money down the drain.

"And there's something more," Georgie said reluctantly.

"More? Goddammit, what more could there be?"

"Cougar, you gotta promise to watch out for the claims while I'm gone. And watch out for Essie. I'm gonna have her hire on a couple of men to help her work the gravel, but they'll bear watching. You're the only man around here I'd trust. I figure you're good and mad, but you ain't a lowdown sneaking snake who'd jump my claim while I was gone. And there's a passel of folks who don't much care for Essie because she's Mexican. I know Mexicans aren't allowed to file claims, but Essie ain't moved in on my daddy's claim. She just helps me out. I gotta make sure that the yahoos around here don't get on her about staying out there and working the claim while I'm gone."

When she put it that way, he could scarcely say no. Not only had he lost his claim, but he'd gained a pantload of problems that had nothing to do with him. Damn but he wanted to kick something!

She got up, looking unhappy. "That claim's yours, fair and square. I don't know how that old man in Chicago gets the brass to think he can do this, but he's gonna be sorry that he ever tangled with me. Damned if he isn't."

Cougar couldn't help but feel a bit sorry for the old man, no matter that he was an interfering bastard. He wondered if Chicago knew what was in store for it.

Chapter 2

Elizabeth Whitman hadn't enjoyed herself so much for years—two years, to be precise, since her father had passed away and left the family nearly destitute. The task of pulling the world back together and caring for her mother and sisters had fallen to Elizabeth, who had always been the "responsible" one in the family, but there was little a woman of genteel upbringing and sensibilities could do to earn a living. For two years they had made do with Elizabeth's governess' pay, paltry enough for ladies accustomed to the advantages of a genteel, wealthy life. Then just recently she lost her position. The family who employed her services planned a move to England in August, and of course they were taking their three children, her charges, with them.

This night, however, was a night of celebration, for Elizabeth had found a new position that paid much more than her former one. So tonight she had taken her mother Phoebe and sisters Claudia and Chloe to see an Offenbach operetta at the Crosby Opera House. For one night she could forget that she was merely a drab governess, firmly on the shelf with no prospects of marrying at all, much less marrying well. She could forget that three of Chicago's most helpless females—her family—were dependent upon her earnings and her guidance. She could forget the drab, lonely future that stretched ahead of her. Here at the opera house she could sink into the fantasy of Offenbach's music and comedy, pretend that she was one of the glittering society that sat above in the private boxes, part of the modern American aristocracy that had earned their wealth through enterprise, courage, and hard work.

Her father had been such a one before he lost it all, then lost his life. But Elizabeth refused to think such thoughts on this night of celebration. She would not allow reality to corrupt her fantasy.

"This is very pleasant," her mother, Phoebe, commented. "Though sitting in a box would be much nicer. I suppose the better seats were all engaged."

"Yes, Mother."

Claudia sighed. At seventeen she was at an age when a sigh preceded almost every statement. "When I marry, I'm going to come to the opera house every week and sit in a private box. And everyone who's anyone in Society will drop by to ingratiate themselves during the intermission. And I'll be wearing the grandest gown of all the ladies here. They'll positively swoon with envy."

"I'm going to positively *swoon* from having to listen to you talk such nonsense," twelve-year-old Chloe sniped. "The only man who might marry you is the fellow who delivers coal for the fire. He positively *swoons* when he sees you."

"Shut your mouth, you little brat."

"You can both be quiet," Elizabeth scolded. "If you don't remember your manners, then next time Mother and I will leave you home with Mrs. Patten to watch you."

Both girls made a face.

"Indeed we will," Phoebe confirmed. "Do be quiet, both of you. I want to hear about Elizabeth's new position, and the intermission is just about over." She smiled at her eldest. "I do think your going out into the world and employing your talents is so laudable, dear. I always have. Most girls who don't marry simply putter their lives away, but the modern woman has so many more opportunities."

Elizabeth didn't remind her mother than she had little

choice. Phoebe lived in her own world and had no notion of who paid the rent on their shabby rooms or bought coal and groceries. She had been cared for all her life by servants, family, and husband, and her mind chose not to admit the new realities.

"Did you say the position was with the Kennedy family, dear? I didn't realize Mr. Kennedy had children still in the schoolroom. He seems a bit on in years for that."

"Mr. Kennedy has hired me to tutor his granddaughter, who is coming soon to live with him. I believe she's been living in the western territories."

Young Chloe's eyes brightened. "Do you suppose she's seen an Indian savage?"

"Chloe," Elizabeth chided in a schoolteacherish tone, "not all of the West is populated by savages. There are many growing towns on the frontier that are really quite civilized."

Elizabeth herself, however, was uncertain about exactly where the Kennedy granddaughter had been living, and in what circumstances. Mr. Kennedy had told her that her charge was a grown woman. Why a grown woman would need instruction Elizabeth didn't quite understand. She hadn't questioned closely. The position was a godsend, and she couldn't risk losing it by seeming impertinent.

"I think it's very fine that you will be associated with the Kennedy family," Phoebe said smugly. "Alvin Kennedy is a leader in Society and a businessman of spotless reputation. Your father thought a great deal of him. Henry always said that business dealings reflect the true character of a man's soul."

Which might have been why her father's business misfortunes had affected his own soul so disastrously. As the second half of the operetta began, Elizabeth sighed and attempted to sink once again into the fantasy.

The production ended all too soon, and the Whitman women were swept with the departing crowd back toward the real world. In the opera house lobby the crowd was so dense that Elizabeth couldn't help thinking of a herd of cattle flowing into the huge Chicago stockyards. She smiled at the image, then yelped when a jostling nearly sent her to the floor, only to be caught and held by a sturdy set of hands.

"A thousand pardons, madam! Are you all right?"

Elizabeth looked up into the face of Alexander Stanford, and her heart skipped a beat. She and Mr. Stanford had been acquainted in her former life, before her father had died, and she'd always felt a bit giddy in his presence. Apparently such giddiness never faded, even for a sensible, practical, eminently nongiddy spinster.

"My word!" Stanford exclaimed with a smile. "It's Miss Whitman. Look here, Chris! You know Miss Whitman, do you not?"

"Indeed," said Stanford's companion.

"And Mrs. Whitman as well. These young ladies with you must be the younger Misses Whitman. How nice to see you all looking so well."

Before her mother could reply with a flurry of complaints, Elizabeth answered. "Mr. Stanford, how nice to see you again." Somehow he had forgotten to remove his hands from her arms, so she discreetly slipped out of his grasp. "We are indeed very well."

The crowd had pushed them into an alcove, like river flotsam whirled into a quiet eddy. Elizabeth's cheeks heated as Alexander smiled at her. How embarrassing to be seen in such reduced circumstances. Her gown practically screamed that it was much mended and sorely out of fashion. Her hair was done up in a plain style that she could do herself, since she didn't have the help of a maid. And her mother and sisters were in the same straits. Compared to Mr. Stanford in immaculately tailored evening attire, the Whitmans were a sorry lot indeed.

"Did you ladies enjoy the production?"

"Very much. And you?"

"It was a bit light for my taste, but then, one expects that of Offenbach."

"I must admit that I do not enjoy serious opera half so much as the comedies."

Her sisters were gaping at the poor man, and Claudia actually had the poor manners to giggle.

"You ladies do not have an escort?" Stanford asked as tactfully as he could.

"No indeed. We have become quite independent, sir. It is quite the thing now among modern ladies."

His slightly raised brow told Elizabeth that he didn't believe a word. "Mr. Johnson and I would be honored to see you safely home."

The thought of Alexander Stanford, one of Chicago's elite, seeing her family's mean quarters made Elizabeth's stomach clench. Only with effort did she keep her expression pleasant. "How kind, Mr. Stanford. But totally unnecessary. We wouldn't dream of bothering you." She threw her mother a silencing look before Phoebe could pooh-pooh her daughter's refusal.

"You are sure?"

"Absolutely, sir. But thank you."

Before they could be pressed further, she hurried her family toward the opera house door. Reality had landed once again on her life with a painful thump.

Alexander watched until the Whitman women disappeared through the lobby door. He wished they had permitted his escort. Whether it was "the thing" or not, as Miss Whitman claimed, women should not be traveling at night unprotected on the streets of Chicago. Henry Whitman, God rest his troubled soul, would be devastated to see how far his family had fallen from the rarefied circles they had once inhabited.

Christopher Johnson also followed the women with his eyes. "Lovely piece, that one. Too bad she's so shabby. There's a creature I wouldn't mind keeping on the side, I tell you. It would improve her circumstances enormously and certainly wouldn't do my love life any harm. Not quite as fresh off the vine as I like, but I'd wager she has staying power."

"Watch your mouth, Chris. Elizabeth Whitman doesn't deserve your lewd speculation."

"Wasn't it her father who shot himself a while back when his business partner ran off with all his assets—and those of his clients? A builder, wasn't he?"

"Yes. Henry Whitman was a very successful builder. An honest man who trusted a scoundrel. Unfortunately, he didn't have the courage to face his disaster, so he left his family to suffer for it. I don't know how they're managing. From the looks of them they're not managing very well."

Christopher was insouciant. "She might appreciate a man willing to keep her in the style to which she was once accustomed."

"You are incorrigible, Johnson. And you obviously don't have the discernment to know an honorable, virtuous woman from a lightskirt."

Christopher raised a supercilious brow. "Sensitive, are we, Alexander? Do you have a special interest? I didn't know you were in the market for an honorable, virtuous sort of woman. Can we expect an announcement soon?"

"Hardly that. And if I were in the market to wed again, I wouldn't choose a fragile girl like Miss Whitman. She looks as though a stiff breeze would blow her off her feet."

"As I recall, your sweet Alice was just such a one."

Not many dared to mention Alice to him, even three years after her death in childbirth. Christopher Johnson was in a very bold mood this night.

"Don't look so thunderous," Johnson chided. "It's absolutely unmanly, Alexander, the way you deify that woman." He held out a hand to ward off a blow as Alex whirled upon him. "She may have been the best woman in the world, my friend, but she's gone, and you're alive. At least keep a mistress! You're going to play the grieving widower so long that you might as well be as dead as your wife."

Alexander had to muster all his control not to lash out with a fist. "We'd best be on our way," he said with cold civility. "Or we'll be swept out of the theater with the rest of the refuse."

Elizabeth Whitman was forgotten.

Some little distance away, in the Kennedy mansion on Lakeshore Drive, Alvin Kennedy and Robert Stanford, Alexander's father, sipped after-dinner brandies and discussed the very same subject—the younger Stanford's refusal to abandon his widower status for marriage.

"I swear to you, my friend," Robert confided to Alvin, "this younger generation has no sense of responsibility at all. No family feeling. No respect for heritage. No loyalty. I blame the war. When brother fights against brother, state against state, such a battle breaks down society and breeds chaos, I tell you. Chaos is what we're coming to."

Alvin didn't take quite such a dim view, but in deference to his friend, he nodded. Robert's daughter-in-law had died three years before, and every year since the period of mourning ended, the man grew more annoyed at his offspring for his stubborn refusal to remarry.

"The situation's enough to give a man a bad heart, Alvin. I've built a shipping empire second to none in this country, and I want assurance that empire will be passed down through generations, not stop at a dead end my son put in the road. He pays me heed regarding the business, but goes his own way in what he calls his 'private life.' As if any part of a man's life can be separated from family obligations."

"Alexander is a good man, Robert. When the right woman comes along, he'll marry again. Let's just hope it's a woman strong enough to give him the kind of children who will do right by their heritage."

A disconsolate grunt was the only answer.

Alvin took pains to hide a smile, for Robert's troubles played very nicely into Alvin's own goals. For two years he had tried to convince the man that their business future was rosier together than apart. Stanford had built a respectable shipping empire in freight and transportation, an empire whose tentacles spread throughout the country, even so far as California. Likewise, the Kennedy import business traded in products from as far away as Europe and Asia and found markets for them all over the country, the country that received its goods so reliably from Stanford Shipping. What could be more natural than the merger of the two concerns? Kennedy and Stanford—no rival could challenge them.

Unfortunately, Robert's possessiveness of his empire

blinded him to good business sense. For two years he had resisted Alvin's efforts, even though the two men were close friends. Now, however, Alvin believed that he had the bait to tempt him. He twirled his brandy in his glass and stared thoughtfully into the fire. He had intended to wait a week or so before introducing this subject, but perhaps now, while Robert's mind roiled with the problem, was the right time.

"You know, Robert, my friend, I may have a solution to your problem with Alexander."

Robert looked up sharply. "How could you have a solution?"

"Alexander needs to be introduced to the right woman in the right way. What's more, he needs a strong woman, one who can give him healthy children and won't put him in mind of the delicate wife he lost to childbirth. It so happens that I might know of just the woman who would do."

"You? Know of a woman?"

Alvin grinned. "Yes, indeed. My granddaughter, Georgia. She's been living in the West, but now she's on her way to take up residence with me. She's an attractive female. My son sent me a daguerreotype about four years ago. And she's strong as an ox, or she wouldn't have survived all those years wandering with her father."

"Alvin!" Robert looked at him in amazement. "Do you mean Elias's daughter? Elias your ungrateful son who threw his heritage in your face and took off for the West those many years ago?"

"The very same. Elias was a good man, a smart businessman, and a good son, but when his wife ran off with that worthless son of . . . well, we won't get into that. It soured him on life itself. I tried to bring him to his senses, but we had very harsh words. He went off adventure-seeking, looking for a simpler, less complex world, and he took his five-year-old daughter, Georgia, with him. My heart positively quails at the thought of what the child endured, because my idiot son lowered himself to try every possible endeavor—mining, herding cattle, working on the railroad, and God knows what else."

Alvin sighed. Even now, years after Elias had stormed

out of his house and his life, the estrangement tore at his heart. But Elias had never apologized, so Alvin had never forgiven.

"I never saw him again, you know. A few years back he wrote, asking me for money to fund a mine that he was sure would make his fortune. I gave it to him for the sake of the girl. Then six months ago Elias died. My granddaughter wrote from some little village in Arizona to tell me. I'm bringing her back here to live in the manner she should have always lived.

"I tell you, Robert, she would be the perfect wife for your Alexander. After the life she's lived, she'll have no silly romantical notions about marriage, and her gratitude for my help will inspire her to do what I say and marry where I say."

Robert was skeptical. "Elias's daughter. What makes you think she's not as wild as her father?"

"She's a female, my friend. Women, bless them, are so much more biddable than men. God made them to be the light of society, the moral compass, the nurturers who bring forth our children. All they require is appropriate guidance. We protect and shield them, and in return they allow themselves to be guided by the men in their lives." He chuckled. "I anticipate having no problems with Georgia. The life she's led may have given her some rough edges, but I've hired a most excellent tutor and companion to smooth them out. I think she will be a fit match for Alexander."

Robert pushed himself wearily from his chair, crossed to the fireplace, and stared into the leaping flames. "And why would Alex be interested in marrying Georgia when he has refused to look at any other?"

"Robert! Such a defeatist attitude, my friend! We will make it happen, you and I. We will be doing both of the children a favor, and ourselves as well. How can something that's so right not work out? You need a suitable wife for Alexander, and I owe my granddaughter a secure, settled life."

Robert turned to regard his friend suspiciously. "And something else as well, I think."

With a grin Alvin conceded. "If this works, my old friend, we merge our business concerns as well as our lineages. That is the beauty of my idea. By joining our families as well as our businesses, we guarantee that both of us see what we've built pass undivided to our progeny. Our unchallenged star of commerce will descend onto the children born of both Stanford and Kennedy loins. Everyone wins, you see. You are happy, I am happy, and God willing, Georgia and Alexander are happy as well."

Robert shook his head, but he smiled, nevertheless. "You are the most persistent man I know, Alvin. And the cagiest. If the girl is acceptable, I'm willing to negotiate a merger between Stanford Shipping and Kennedy Imports on the condition that a match can be made between my Alexander and your Georgia. And if you can pull this off, my friend, you will also have my heartfelt gratitude. Not to mention my amazement."

"Never doubt that it can be done, Robert. Never doubt it." Alvin could have rubbed his hands together in glee. He recognized the challenge of his scheme, because Alexander Stanford was an independent fellow who didn't like anyone, even his father, meddling in his private life. And Georgia was an unknown quantity, though not completely unknown, for Alvin knew her heritage, and blood always won out in the end, no matter what the outside influences. As a child she had possessed her mother's beauty and her father's spirit. In Alvin's experience with the female half of the race, he'd concluded that girl children grew up without changing much for better or worse.

Indeed, he thought, Alexander would be the challenge in this scheme. Georgia was the least of Alvin's worries. He didn't anticipate any problems handling his granddaughter.

Georgie didn't think she would have a problem handling her granddad, but she hated like hell going to Chicago to set the old codger straight. She didn't know exactly where Chicago was, but it wasn't anyplace that she wanted to go.

She sat with Essie on a crude bench in front of their even cruder little cabin. The sun was rising on her last day on the

Lynx. Not her last day really, Georgie assured herself. Just her last day for a good long while. Tomorrow she and Jacob Whittaker would head east to Santa Fe with a troop from Fort Whipple. At Santa Fe they would board a stagecoach for the long, uncomfortable ride to Denver, a journey that would take the better part of a week. Then, Jacob had informed her, the train would take them north to Cheyenne, then east past the plains, over the great Mississippi River, and on to Chicago. The fancy lawyer had seemed so proud of that new railroad that he might have laid the tracks himself. These days a body could travel from one end of the country to the other on a train. Wonders would never cease!

Georgie wasn't much impressed, though. She didn't want to go from one end of the nation to the other. She just wanted to stay in Arizona, in Prescott, on the Lynx, where she knew every rock and tree, every face that came down the road,

She sipped hot coffee from a tin mug and watched the sunrise change the red-tinted streaks of clouds to glowing molten gold. Normally she would have been hard at work in the streambed as the first light touched the sky, but today there was little point in doing anything other than packing. So she hailed the sun on her last morning here. She wondered if Chicago saw such sunrises.

"I'm sorry to leave you here alone," she said to Essie. "I hate like hell to leave."

"You will be back, *chica*."

"Yup. Sure I will." Georgie tried to keep from choking up. That was a damned womanly thing to do, and there was no room in her life for such weakness. "Soon as I straighten out that old man on what's what. Sneaky ol' claimjumper is what he is."

Essie didn't seem nearly as mad as she ought to be. Maybe being a Mexican on American territory, she was used to getting tromped on. Most Americans didn't much like folks from Sonora cluttering up the landscape, even though some of them were here long before the Americans came. That was one reason why Georgie didn't like leaving just Essie on the claim.

"Cougar's gonna stop out and check on you every now

and then, and if there's any trouble, just go to him for help. He's got an interest in these claims—at least that one over on the hill—and he won't let you down."

Essie smiled and lifted a smooth black brow. "Cougar is a good man."

"He's okay."

Cougar *was* a good man. The best. They'd grown a peculiar friendship over the years, especially since her father had died. He poked fun at her, and she poked back. Often he was arrogant and bossy, like most men, but she couldn't think of a better ally in a fight, or a better friend when the chips were down and your father lay dying in a cabin two hours from town and you were crying so hard you couldn't think what to do or where to turn. He was a good man then. The best.

But Cougar nursed a hell of a mad right then, and he had reason. She owed him either a pile of money or title to that claim she sold him, and she couldn't deliver either one. She hadn't know the claims weren't her father's and therefore not hers to sell.

Cougar would keep his promise to look after Essie and the claims, though, not only because one of the claims he wanted for himself, but because he was the kind of man who kept a promise. Years of living in mining camps, railroad construction camps, and rough cattle towns with her father had taught her the value of that kind of man. They were few and far between.

Her father had not been one of them. He had promised her to settle down some day and quit wandering, but it had taken death to cure his wanderlust. Maybe Arizona would have been the place he stayed, here with Esperanza and her, even if he weren't buried six feet under in the grove of trees across the stream.

That didn't matter now, though. Prescott was the place she wanted to stay. It was the place she would come back to once she'd set matters right in a far-off place called Chicago.

Essie broke the long silence. "I think if your father had known how close he was to passing on, he would have told you about your grandfather, *chica*."

Georgia shrugged. "Maybe, maybe not. The more that I think on it, the more I think Daddy was ashamed of using the old man's money for a grubstake. He always wanted to make it on his own. He never talked about his family, even about my ma, and I hardly remember her. He said he left because he couldn't stand being hog-tied to some business so tight he couldn't breathe. He had a big fight with his pa, I think. I don't remember, 'cause I was just a little nipper then."

Essie nodded. "So, your father is at peace now."

"I figure. But my granddad isn't going to know any peace until these claims belong to me, like they should. I aim to pay him out of the stash in San Francisco, and we'll be free and clear again."

"He may think that all the money is his already, *chica*, depending on what he had agreed with your father."

"I'll make him see different, then. I will."

Essie was silent. The Lynx babbled its way over the rocky streambed below the cabin as if singing harmony with the little breeze that whispered through pine and juniper. The stream had a good flow for July. Sometimes during the dry time of year in August and September, it didn't flow at all, and mining operations stopped. With no water to wash through the rocker, the gold couldn't be separated from the gravel. From the looks of the stream, though, that wouldn't happen this year. This would be a good year for mining, and she would be twiddling her thumbs in Chicago. Damn!

A distant song joined the tune of breeze and stream, a man's voice, deep and interspersed with laughter as someone laughed at his own lyrics. Georgie recognized Cougar's peculiar brand of humor before he came out of the trees.

"Came to cut your firewood," he announced as he climbed down from his horse. "Wouldn't want you to accuse me of not paying my debts."

"Don't be an ass," Georgie said ungraciously, thinking of her own unpaid debt. "I'm gonna make sure you get everything that's coming to you."

Cougar grinned. "Did I say anything about your debts?"

"It was there, say it or not." She handed him the ax and pointed him to the pile of deadfall and broken branches that needed to be split.

Essie went into the cabin, but Georgie watched as Cougar stripped off his shirt and went to work with the ax. Big as the man was, no fat messed up his build. He was all muscle that rippled and swelled every time he lifted the ax overhead and brought it down with deft, powerful strokes.

The gal who snagged Cougar Barnes, Georgie decided, would be one lucky woman. Not only was he strong as an ox and twice as honest, Cougar had ambition. He wanted more than her hard rock claim on the hill; he wanted a future here, a ranch, a real home—hell, she'd even heard him mention politics a time or two. Georgie figured he'd choose some fancy army officer's or politician's daughter to help him on his way.

If Georgie had been an actual, honest-to-god woman wearing dresses and prancing around with a parasol, she might have been tempted by Cougar, by those sparkly blue eyes and rolling muscles and the queer little crooked smile that pulled at his mouth when he told a joke. But she wasn't an actual, honest-to-god woman. She was just Georgie, who clumped around in boots, shapeless shirts, and stained overalls. Besides, Cougar was hellfire mad at her, and she had to take off for Chicago. This was no time for silly woolgathering.

She turned to follow Essie into the cabin. Chicago loomed dark on her horizon, making the bright morning sun seem a bit dimmer. She hoped that goddamned place was ready to take her on, because she was in a take-no-prisoners mood.

Chapter 3

Today was the big day. Elizabeth had been installed at Greystone House, as Alvin Kennedy called his mansion on Lakeshore Drive, for nearly a week, helping Mrs. Bolton the housekeeper prepare for the new arrival. Mr. Kennedy wanted Elizabeth present when his granddaughter first arrived, and the timing of her arrival was in no way certain. Mr. Kennedy's agent in Denver had telegraphed when Miss Kennedy had passed through that town, traveling with a Mr. Jacob Whittaker and, of course, a woman companion hired for propriety's sake. Word had also come in from Cheyenne, but then for several days they had heard nothing. Finally Mr. Whittaker had sent a message from some little railroad stop in Iowa. They were expected to arrive this afternoon. All was in readiness. Miss Kennedy's room was prepared, a wardrobe had been assembled for her use until she could be fitted with her own, a special dinner sent tempting odors from the direction of the kitchen, and the entire staff found excuses to loiter where they might have a view of the reunion between grandfather and granddaughter. The butler and head gardener claimed to remember Miss Kennedy from when she was a child in this same house, when the house was just built and her father and mother lived together with the older Mr. Kennedy.

They awaited the anticipated arrival in the formal parlor, and Mr. Kennedy seemed to absolutely glow with excitement, though he took pains to present a calm face to the household. Elizabeth had grown to know him well enough in the last week to detect the tension in his demeanor. She couldn't help but wonder why he hadn't sent for his granddaughter long ago, for surely it was most improper for a young woman to wander the frontier with her father. And what black cloud, Elizabeth wondered, had separated father and son? Mr. Kennedy did not discuss such personal matters, of course. Elizabeth would have been uncomfortable if he had done so. But she was curious. Her instructors at the very proper Northwestern Academy for Young Ladies had ceaselessly scolded her for what they termed her excessively imaginative curiosity. Proper young women, they'd lectured her, do not pry into others' affairs. They do not even wonder about others' affairs.

But how could one not wonder about a family as curious as the Kennedys?

The rattle of a carriage on the front drive interrupted Elizabeth's thoughts and made her stomach jump with excitement. She was very anxious to meet the woman she was charged with instructing. Her new employment would be quite different from schooling children in their reading and sums and manners.

Bittles the butler stepped into the parlor, playing his part with great gravity. "Sir," he intoned. "Mr. Whittaker to see you. He is accompanied by your granddaughter, Miss Georgia Kennedy."

The lawyer Mr. Whittaker entered the room first. He looked more than a little frazzled and in need of a shave. Elizabeth wondered that he had not stopped in his rooms to freshen up before presenting himself to such an important client.

But her attention was wrenched from poor Mr. Whittaker when Miss Kennedy herself walked into the room. *Strode* into the room was a better description. Or perhaps clumped into the room, for the girl wore heavy boots that looked to have gathered the dust of every state they had crossed. The rest of her also appeared a bit dusty, from the brim of an amazingly disreputable-looking hat to the cuffs of denim overalls suited to farmers in the field and laborers on the docks. Elizabeth had never seen a female in such a garment, and the sight left her nearly stunned. Other details of Miss Kennedy's appearance were equally distressing. Her hair, a unique shade of gold-red, was messily braided and hung down her back to end in a frayed tail bound with a leather cord. Her hands were reddened and rough-looking, her skin sun-browned and coarse, her green gaze disturbingly direct. No modest downturn of the eyes for this one.

The task of instructing such a creature, to make her ready for social intercourse with the best of Chicago society, promised to be a Herculean endeavor. Mr. Kennedy might have done better to employ a lion tamer than a governess.

"Mr. Kennedy, sir," the little lawyer said. It seemed to Elizabeth that he had a slight quaver in his voice. "Here is your granddaughter, delivered as you demanded." He threw a glance toward the girl, who regarded him with an amused glint in her eye. "Good luck to you, Mr. Kennedy. I assure you, sir, that you will need it."

Alvin gave his minion a severe look. "You bring me my granddaughter in this sorry condition, Whittaker? What's the reason for this?"

The lawyer attempted to laugh, but the sound that came out of his throat sounded more like a sob. "At every turn— every sorry turn—I tried to get the baggage into civilized attire. When I attempted to take her clothing to be washed, she threatened my life, I swear. When I engaged the services of a female companion to help her through this transition, she treated the poor woman as if she were poison."

"The looby tried to get me naked in a bathtub," Miss Kennedy explained, shooting the lawyer an aggrieved glare. "I would'a caught my death."

Mr. Whittaker heaved a great sigh. "Your granddaughter, sir, is stubborn as a mule and vicious as an asp. Mrs. Terhune, the companion I engaged, walked out in a huff three days ago, saying she would rather be nursemaid to a mule. The baggage threatened my very life more than once."

"Because you were bein' a jackass," the girl complained. "This piece of horsecrap dragged me out of a fine poker game that started up between some gents on the train. I was winning good money, too. I would've laid him out then and there, but I didn't want to make a scene."

"A scene?" Whittaker nearly shrieked. "You pulled a knife, you little savage!"

"You shoulda' known better than to grab me like that. I wouldn't have used it." She gave him a positively frightening smile. "Probably."

Elizabeth saw a sparkle of amusement in Alvin's eye, strangely enough. He even went so far as to chuckle, which made Whittaker turn a deep shade of red. To Elizabeth's way of thinking, the old man should have wept, not chuckled. She couldn't imagine what kind of life this poor girl had led to make her such a mess, but a mess she certainly was. The prospect of tackling the hoyden's education made Elizabeth want to follow Mrs. Terhune's example and walk out of the room, out of the house, and return to easier, less dangerous employment. If not for Mr. Kennedy's handsome salary and her very needy family, she would have.

But Mr. Kennedy seemed in rare good humor. "I see I set you a difficult task, Jacob. I'll double your fee, if that's any compensation." He sent a look askance at his granddaughter. "I hope you relieved her of the knife."

Miss Kennedy stuck an arrogant pose that was entirely masculine. "Not hardly. That little twerp couldn't take a stick from a dog. He didn't tell you that I saved his ass from an Apache buck on the trail to Santa Fe—the fool wandered off from camp to take a private leak."

The lawyer turned an even deeper shade of red.

"It's a good thing that I shoot as straight as I do, Whittaker, or your hair would'a been the prize of the day in that fellow's rancheria. And what about that tough in Cheyenne who spotted you for an easy mark? He would'a rolled you in the gutter if not for me."

Mr. Kennedy raised one brow. "I think you can go now, Jacob. I can see that it's been a trying journey. I'll send your fee around to your office."

The lawyer beat a grateful retreat, throwing Miss Kennedy a resentful look as he left.

"Some folks," she commented, "just don't know when to say thank you." She turned a gimlet eye on her grandfather. "You must be my daddy's father, all right. You look enough like him. But blood relation or not, I have a bone to pick with you."

"Do you now?"

"You may have title to my claims, like you wrote in your letter, but you ain't got no right to jump outta the brush like a lurking Apache and drag me off to this goddamned place to straighten things out when we could'a done it just as well with me staying put where I belong."

Elizabeth winced at every epithet that came out of the girl's mouth.

"And I don't care what the law says. You ain't got no right to those claims," the girl said when Mr. Kennedy was silent. "You haven't spent the last three years hunkered over a streambed with your feet freezin' in ice-cold creek water or your brains fryin' in the Arizona sun. You haven't shoveled until your shoulders and back couldn't move. You haven't lived having to keep one eye out for wild Apaches day and night. You weren't there to watch my daddy die of a canker in the gut with only rotgut whiskey to ease his pain. You may have forked over the cash that let my daddy file a claim and buy the equipment to work it, but that ain't worth a flyspeck compared to what we put into it."

Elizabeth expected Mr. Kennedy to explode, for he had a reputation as an irascible sort. But he merely looked at the girl with heightened interest.

"My daddy and me broke our backs and risked our necks every day to wash gold from about a million tons of gravel, and now you sit here in your posh house and think you can horn in on all the work we've done. You got a right to get your grubstake back with some interest, but not to high-handed robbery. And you got no right to threaten selling my claims unless I hotfoot it clear across the country to bow at your feet."

The old man drew himself up to his full, dignified, aristocratic, silver-haired height, which was impressive. The girl fell silent, though her jaw thrust out in belligerence and her eyes spit fire.

"Georgia," he said quietly. "I am glad to renew our acquaintance after all these years. When I last saw you, you were but a little girl of five years."

She scowled.

"In some things you have said, my dear, I quite agree, and I'm sure we can settle the matter of our claims with very little trouble. The greater part of what you've said merely assures me of how right I was to bring you here, by fair means or foul. The life you have lived is no life for any gently bred woman, and certainly not a Kennedy woman. Because your father and I had a falling out, you have suffered abominably."

"It hasn't been that bad," she said suspiciously.

"I mean to make up for the injustice visited upon you, as much as possible. You deserve a settled, comfortable future with a husband, children, and a fine house with servants. All this I can offer you if you are willing to apply yourself and learn the necessary skills."

She snorted. "I already got skills aplenty. There ain't no one in Prescott a better shot with a rifle, 'ceptin' maybe Cougar Barnes. I can knife-fight like an Apache and move silent as a snake, if need be. I can shovel all day in the sun without keelin' over, or all day in the snow without catchin' pneumonia."

Her grandfather cleared his throat and kept his face carefully blank. "And those are laudable skills, indeed, Georgia, but for life in the city you will need to add to those accomplishments."

He turned to Elizabeth and smiled. Her stomach dropped. She felt as though she were about to be fed to a dragon.

"And that brings me to present Miss Elizabeth Whitman, whom I have engaged to help you develop the skills you will need. Miss Whitman comes recommended as an excellent teacher, and I've seen for myself that she's an amiable young woman. You two should do very well together, I think."

Georgia turned a dubious eye her way, and Elizabeth mentally girded herself. No matter how inadequate she felt, no matter how bizarre this Kennedy granddaughter seemed, she, the teacher, must seize the upper hand if she were to do the girl any good at all. So she straightened her spine and wiped the cowardly quiver from her lips and her voice.

"How do you do, Miss Kennedy. I'm very pleased to make your acquaintance."

The girl's eyes widened slightly as she took in Elizabeth's appearance, her plain but properly tailored gray dress with starched snowy collar and cuffs, her fawn brown hair dressed neatly in a twist of braids pinned at her neck, her hands folded quietly, as a lady's should be, at her waist. Elizabeth waited tensely for the same sort of blast the girl had aimed at her grandfather, but she got only a curious look.

"You're going to teach me to look like you?" Georgia said with a half smile.

"I believe we'll finish with you looking much better than I, Miss Kennedy. You only want a bit of polishing before you will feel very comfortable in the city."

False encouragement, perhaps, but Elizabeth told herself that a discouraged pupil had the harder time finding success.

"You don't say." The girl snorted. Actually snorted. As a horse might, or a mule.

A young wolf, Elizabeth thought, would be more easily turned into a lapdog than this wild woman turned into a society belle.

"Well, Miss Elizabeth, I'm chock full of gratitude, I'm sure. But I won't be stayin' here long enough to be turned into a fine lady like yourself. Though it's right brave of you to offer."

"We will see about that, Georgia," her grandfather inserted. "Right now I will leave you to Elizabeth to make comfortable." He gave Elizabeth a meaningful look. "And clean. I will expect you to come down to dinner at eight."

With that warning, he left them to it.

Georgie felt as if she'd fallen down the rabbit hole in *Alice's Adventures in Wonderland*, a book her father had read to her when she was small and a story she had always remembered, because often in her travels with her father, she'd been bombarded with so many new things, new places, new people, and strange sights, that she'd imagined herself to be Alice. But Chicago was worse than any of her adventures before this. As the train had chugged eastward along the tracks, the land had grown stranger and stranger. The very air felt different—heavy and wet. Grass and trees littered the landscape. The sky was white and moist instead of the pure bright blue that she loved. People crowded everywhere, the women trussed up in clothing that no one with a lick of sense would wear, the men dandified, with soft-looking hands and pale faces that had never had a good dose of sun.

Chicago itself stunk. Stockyards and meatpacking houses perfumed the air, and the crowds of people didn't make the smell sweeter. Smoke from coal and woodstoves hung over the city, and the breeze off Lake Michigan added the odor of fish and offal to the mix.

If this was the world her father had fled, then Georgie didn't blame him.

On their first meeting Georgie's grandfather had surprised her. The old codger wasn't a weak-kneed, soft, useless worm like the messenger he'd sent to pry her loose from Prescott. He was clever, this one, quick as a weasel and tough as a badger. He took the words coming out of her mouth and turned them against her. He didn't quail at her frowns or duck the barrage of her insults. Like a snake, he slipped around something rather than meet it head on. Her granddad, Georgie admitted, might be a tough nut to crack.

The woman, however, didn't look tough at all; she looked like . . . well, a woman. That was why Georgie was fascinated. When she was growing up in the mining camps and railroad towns of the West, she'd met all kinds of women. Some had coddled her to get her daddy's attention. Some had tut-tutted over the way her daddy raised her. Some had laughed at her for trying to be a boy—as they put it. Most of the laughers were whores, though, so they didn't count.

Now that she was grown, most all women, the laughers and tut-tutters and the coddlers alike, either avoided her like a pile of mule dung or barely tolerated her with pitying glances and sad shakes of the head. Most turned up their noses or whispered when they thought she wasn't looking. Not that Georgie cared. Women were strange creatures that she didn't understand, but she didn't let herself get too upset by them. Men were easier. They were either friends or enemies. They brawled, cursed, spat, got drunk, occasionally were heroes, often were jackasses. But a body generally knew where a man stood.

That Elizabeth Whitman looked like a damned proper female, but she was the first of that sort to look Georgie in the eye without flinching or sneering. Georgie had to give the woman credit for that. When her granddad left them alone together, though, Elizabeth looked like a new recruit soldier facing his first Apache. She resolutely led Georgie up the stairs and through a maze of hallways—the damned house had more twists and turns to it than Lynx Creek—flinching at the least little move she made.

"Oh, good," the proper miss declared as she opened the door to a large, dim room fit for some queen. "Rachel has prepared a hot bath for you. I'm sure you feel in need of a good soak."

Georgie halted in her tracks. "Soak?"

"To remove the grime of the road?" the teacher ventured hopefully.

"I'll pass."

"Miss Kennedy—"

"Don't call me that. Every time someone calls me that I want to bust a gut laughing."

"Georgia, then."

"Folks call me Georgie. George, if they wanna make me mad. I don't look like some soft, flowery Georgia."

"Uh . . . ah, that's something we can talk about, isn't it? Right now you should clean up while the bath is still nice and hot."

"I'll pass. You can use the tub if you want."

The woman's brows twitched upward. "Georgia, you need a bath. One does not go to the dinner table bearing an . . . an odor."

Georgie smiled. The prissy miss had some backbone. "Bathin' in a tub just don't seem right, Elizabeth. All that dirt just stays around and settles right back on you. Bathe in a river and it all just washes away."

"I'm afraid I don't have a river handy, Georgia. The tub will have to do."

Another woman came in, this one with dark hair and pimply skin. A snowy white apron covered her drab gown.

"This is your maid, Georgia. Her name is Rachel. She'll help you bathe, do your hair, help you dress, and generally look after your comfort."

"A maid . . ." Georgie couldn't quite get her mind around the idea.

"Good afternoon, miss. Is the bath satisfactory?"

Georgie blamed an overload of surprises for toppling her resistance, and once she was sitting in the tub, steam and the scent of unknown flowers rising around her face, she admitted that a hot-water bath, even if it was in a tub where the dirt floated all around a body, was a lot more fun than sitting your bare butt in icy creek water. She could get used to this kind of comfort. She surely didn't like having an audience, though. The teacher and pimply-faced maid bustled around talking about soaps and oils and generally making Georgie feel like an odd sort of bird they didn't know how to cook.

"We must wash your hair," Rachel warned just before pushing Georgie's head under the water.

What followed took all the fun out of the hot-water bath. The maid had the gentle touch of a grizzly bear in scrubbing her victim's scalp.

"Get away from me!" Georgie sputtered and struggled, sending water in all directions. "Ow! Goddammit. I can wash myself, you looby!"

Rachel pushed her head under once again, and Georgie came up choking on soap and water. "Damn! You keep away from me with that scrub rag, or I'll hog-tie you with your own ears."

"But, miss!"

"Thank you, Rachel." Miss Elizabeth was a pillar of calm as waves from the struggle crashed over the side of the tub and Georgie and Rachel scowled at each other. Georgie wanted to hit the teacher for being so adult and collected, and therefore making Georgie feel like a bratty kid. Of course, Elizabeth wasn't the one being drowned. "I can handle this," she told Rachel smoothly. "Please lay out small clothes and a gown suitable for dinner—the blue silk, I think."

"Yes, Miss Elizabeth."

Georgia suppressed an urge to send a spray of soapy water after the maid. "Where I come from"—she glared at Elizabeth—"gettin' naked and washin' ain't a group chore."

The teacher just sighed.

The torture in the tub didn't end things. Next came an attempt to dress Georgie up like some kind of a fancy lady, with fripperies and bows and lace enough to kill a bull elk. The Apaches would have loved to get hold of the corset. As a method of torture, it beat tying a body upside down over a slow fire, which was the Injun's favorite trick. Georgie wasn't about to wear the thing, and to make that point clear to Elizabeth, she grabbed a pair of scissors from the dressing table and put the corset out of its misery. Stabbed it right between the whalebone ribs—a fatal blow.

"Perhaps we're trying to go too fast," Elizabeth admitted.

Georgia smirked. "That damned corset ain't going anywhere."

They didn't go down to dinner that evening. Elizabeth had food sent up to Georgie's room. The wardrobe her granddad had assembled was too small to fit a decently muscled body, so Rachel begged two dresses off Margorie the cook, who was six feet tall and could wrestle a side of beef to a standstill. The dresses were too big by quite a lot, but Elizabeth was very clever with a needle and thread, and before the evening was through, Georgie was stumbling about the room with her legs tangled in long skirts. She paraded back and forth across the room, while Elizabeth nagged her to keep her shoulders straight, her head up, and her arms quietly at her side. The whole thing was unnatural, and Georgie told her so in no uncertain turns.

"We need to have a conversation about your language, I fear."

"What's wrong with my frigging language?" Georgie demanded.

Elizabeth sighed. She sighed a lot, Georgie noticed. Probably it was a woman thing.

Alexander Stanford knew his father and Alvin Kennedy had some scheme in mind the moment they suggested he join them for a brandy in the library of Stanford House. The two older men had spent the shank of the evening conferring about something or other, and Alex figured if the something or other involved him, then he'd better watch his back. Two slyer schemers than those old men he'd never known.

"Alexander, my boy! How are you?" Alvin greeted him effusively as Alex took a seat in one of the library's leather wingback chairs. Books lined the walls, and a huge oak desk—cleared temporarily of the paper that usually littered its surface—sat by the nearly floor-to-ceiling windows to best catch the daylight.

The desk was Alex's. Although Robert Stanford still had final authority in Stanford Shipping, five years ago Alex had taken the reins of the company's everyday business affairs. While he listened to Robert carefully regarding company decisions—after all, the old man had founded the company and nurtured it for years—his private life was his own affair, something that Robert had trouble understanding. Alex was fairly sure his father had enlisted Alvin's help on some scheme to get him married. Getting Alex safely married and planting Stanford grandchildren was a project Robert pursued with great determination.

So when Alex lifted his brandy to toast the two older men, who were smiling with complacent satisfaction, he did so with great caution.

"Alvin and I have just been discussing things that concern you," his father said. "An important matter, at least important to me and to Alvin, but I believe it's important to you as well."

"What things are those, Father?"

The look he got was challenging and pleading at the same time. "Did you know that Alvin's granddaughter has come to live with him? She arrived only today."

Alex proceeded carefully. "I didn't know Alvin had a granddaughter."

"Indeed I do, and a quite exceptional young woman she is."

This scheme, Alex thought, wasn't even subtle. He would have thought these two old foxes could come up with something less obvious.

His father avoided his eyes and looked instead into the depths of his brandy. "Alex, son, I've made no secret of my desire to see you marry and give me grandchildren. I would appreciate it greatly if you would give some consideration of Alvin's granddaughter as a potential wife."

Now this was sticky, Alex acknowledged. A direct and emphatic refusal, which was his first instinct, would be a crass insult to both his father and a good family friend. He had to find a way to frame that refusal in extremely tactful terms.

Robert held up a finger before Alex could formulate a reply. "I know what you're thinking, son. Alice was a love match. She died trying to give you a child, and that is certainly a noble thing. You still grieve for her even after three years, and the thought of remarriage makes you feel disloyal. But we're not asking for you to give your heart and soul. We're asking—I'm asking—for you to do your duty and carry on the family line."

Alvin added, "Georgia is not some clinging vine who will require constant care and nurturing, nor is she a fragile little flower who withers in the face of a woman's duty."

Alex stiffened immediately, and Alvin grimaced. "That was badly spoken of me, Alex. I meant no insult to your lovely late wife, who was surely an angel. But when a man advances to maturity, which you have, he needs to turn his mind more toward practicality than romance. Whether you desire one or no, you need a healthy wife who can give you children and who comes from stock as fine as you and your father. On my part, I have a strapping granddaughter whom I need to settle with a good man. She isn't some sighing, poetry-spouting schoolgirl covered with frills and furbelows, nor a female who will cling to a man and make demands upon his life."

Alex heard the unspoken implication that he had traveled that road and should be done with it. Alice had been all those things—fragile, romantic, poetry-loving, and in need of constant nurturing. He had loved her desperately, and her death still ate at his heart.

So now his father intended to match him up with a woman who was "strapping," healthy, and undemanding—all the things Alice had not been. The thought was almost laughable. He tried to picture this paragon of practicality and independence. "Alvin, you make your poor granddaughter sound like a pedigreed plow horse."

Alvin's chuckle sounded a false ring. "Not at all, my boy. Georgia's a beauty, in her own way. An admirable figure of a woman. All sorts of accomplishments. And smart, strong, healthy. Good teeth, too. Not often does a man get a woman with all her teeth in good shape."

The man was truly reaching, Alex mused.

"She's been living out West," his father told him.

"Yes, and she's a bit independent, I'll admit," Alvin said gravely. "But independence in a woman isn't always a bad thing. My Georgia will be a wife any man would be proud of, once her rough edges are polished just a bit. But that's being seen to by an excellent woman. In no time Georgia will be dazzling Chicago society, but I'm giving you a chance at her first, because you're a friend, and I know your father is anxious for you to find a suitable wife."

Alexander shook his head. "Alvin, I truly appreciate your consideration, but my father knows my feelings on that subject."

"I do know your feelings on the subject," Robert said testily, "and they're the feelings of a selfish boy who is thinking only of himself. I'm not asking you to fall in love or change your life in any great way, I'm simply asking you to do the duty of a mature man. Why is that too much to ask?"

In a way, Robert was right, and Alex knew it. He had spent the three years since Alice had died indulging in grief and almost reveling in loneliness. The house where he had lived with his wife was the first to go, then the activities they had once enjoyed together—sailing on the lake, walking the lakeshore promenades, socializing with their friends. The friends had gone as well, at least most of them had. He seldom went out anymore. Instead, he worked, or he rattled around his parents' large mansion, in which he occupied his old chambers. His fifty-five-year-old father had more of a life than Alex did.

Perhaps, Alex thought, he had been selfish long enough. Besides, Alvin Kennedy was not only a close friend of their family, he was a businessman one did not lightly offend. If Alex had to marry out of family duty, shouldn't he at least consider a union that would have business as well as family advantages?

Oh, yes, he knew all about Alvin's plotting to merge Kennedy Imports with Stanford Shipping, and he thought the deal would be a wise move for both concerns, though up to now his father hadn't favored the idea. Annoying as the old men's meddling was, Alex could do worse than promote such a business expansion by marrying. At least it would give the marriage some purpose.

"Perhaps there's a grain of truth in what you say," Alex admitted to his father.

"More than a grain," Robert grumbled.

"I wouldn't object to meeting the young lady." Alex tried to ignore the stunned and suddenly overjoyed expression on his father's face. "But I have a trip to Saint Louis coming up, and I'll be gone awhile. Perhaps we should plan a get-together when I return. That should be in about a month."

Alvin looked almost relieved at the delay. "Wonderful. A month." He got up and clapped Alex on the back with a force that almost spilled the brandy. "Your father was right, Alex. I was all for scheming a way for you to meet Georgia and trusting her to charm you, but your father insisted on putting the situation to you straight out. Alex is a practical man, your father told me, and sooner or later he'll see his duty straight."

Alex smiled cynically. "He said that, did he? So of course you gentlemen don't have any other plots in mind."

Both old men managed to look innocent. Innocent as wolves at a convention of lambs. He left them to their schemes, wondering what he'd gotten himself into. At least he'd only consented to meet the girl, not to marry her.

Alvin rubbed his hands together in glee when the door closed behind Alexander. "This couldn't have worked out better," he told his host. "Now I have a whole month to smooth out the girl's rough edges and make her into a woman who can tweak Alex's fancy."

Robert read between the lines. "How bad is she?"

"A diamond in the rough."

"Rough, eh?"

"Just a bit rough. Never fear, my friend. Georgia Kennedy carries good blood, and she'll clean up very nicely. Like any spirited filly, she just needs to be broke to bit and saddle."

"I won't have my son saddled with a harridan who doesn't know her place or duty."

"Rest assured, neither would I. I've engaged a very capable woman to make sure that the girl would grace any man's drawing room. In a month's time my granddaughter will shine so brightly that your son will be blinded by her charm and beauty."

Robert growled. "I don't want him blinded. I want him married."

"We'll get him married," Alvin promised, glowing.

"Well, if you do"—Robert finished off his brandy—"then you can have your merger and I'll bless you for it every day that remains to me." He chuckled. "I almost feel sorry for the poor girl, having to put up with a pushy old bastard like you. She'll be glad enough to trade you in on my son."

Alvin thought privately that Robert could save his sympathy. From what he'd seen so far, he guessed that Georgia could hold her own with just about anyone. In that way she was certainly a Kennedy. The girl just hadn't learned yet that she had met a Kennedy tougher than herself.

Chapter 4

The August sun blazed down from a bright blue sky as Cougar Barnes loosened his saddle girth and tethered his horse in the shade of a pine. The day was going to be a hot one unless the few puffy clouds in the east grew into thunderheads and swept the landscape with rain. The land sure needed rain, but Cougar would rather sweat than run for high ground to get out of the way of a flash flood.

"Ain't mining fun?" he asked his horse.

The horse whuffed and turned his head to regard Cougar with hopeful eyes. Old Dusty wanted to be shed of his saddle, no doubt, but he would just have to relax in the shade with it still on. A man didn't unsaddle his horse when Apaches might be lurking in the hills. One didn't have time to tack up when the savages decided to pay a visit, and an escape riding bareback ... well, Apaches were experts at sticking to a horse with nothing between themselves and horsehide. Cougar wanted a saddle beneath his butt.

Cougar gave the horse an affectionate slap on the neck and dragged the tarp off the storage box he'd built a couple of weeks before. Inside the box were picks and shovels and a hammer—not enough mining muscle to make a dent in the wide vein of quartz exposed on this claim, but enough to break loose some rock and at least get an assay. For the real operation, if he ever got that far, he would need dynamite or nitro. That wouldn't happen until Georgie came back to Arizona owning her claims free and clear. In the meantime, Cougar came to this hill above the Lynx once or twice a week, taking time from his own mediocre placer claim on Granite Creek to make his mark on the gold that would start him down the road to being a cattleman.

Esperanza waved to him from down on the creek, and Cougar waved back. She had a couple of Mexican fellows working for her, and Cougar made sure she had a good supply of firewood and kept the little cabin in repair. Georgie had worked on the roof before she'd left, so it was in pretty good shape. She had also chinked walls so that the breeze didn't whistle through the place like it did in most miners' cabins.

Georgie—there she was sitting on his mind again. He missed the brat. With her gone, he didn't have anyone to trade insults with or tease. Georgie made trading insults an art. No one else had her knack.

She also had a knack for being a friend. When her father was alive, the three of them had once made good money bringing a herd of horses overland to Fort Whipple from La Paz, where they'd been landed from a boat steaming up the Colorado. The Army had paid top dollar for those horses, and well they should have, because Cougar, Elias, and Georgie, along with the three drovers they'd hired, had fought off Apache marauders the whole trip. Georgie could dig in and fight with the best of them, cool and competent as any man. Better than most.

She was the damnedest woman Cougar had ever met. Still, if she didn't get back here with either title to his claim or money to pay him back the price, he was going to have her hide.

A call from across the creek got his attention. Essie waved to him from where she stood in front of the cabin. She wanted him to come down.

The little Mexican woman waved a grubby handful of papers in his face when he got down to the creek bottom. "Look here, Señor Cougar! A letter from Georgie! Only I cannot read. I've been waiting two days for you to come out here and read it to me."

Cougar looked at the envelope. "She wrote it from Cheyenne, on her way east. Let's see what she has to say."

Dear Essie and anyone else who is reading this,

I am writing to let you know that I'm still kicking, and the trip so far has been pretty interesting. I got tangled up with the Apaches a couple of days east of Fort Whipple, thanks to the weasely fellow who works for my granddad. The fool wandered off from camp, as he's sensitive about doing his business where someone might hear. The Injuns heard him all right. But I followed him, because I knew the damn fool doesn't know east from west, up from down, or which end of a pistol to point where. There were only two Apaches who jumped him, so it was a pretty fair fight. The bluecoats came running to help, but by the time they got there, I'd taken care of things and the Injuns had taken off. Damn fool weasel just pulled up his pants and huffed back to camp without so much as a thank-you.

That brawl was the only trouble we had, which wasn't much. In Santa Fe we got on the stage, and I can't say much for that as a way to travel. You get smashed in shoulder to shoulder with people who hate baths even more than I do, I'd guess. It don't take long for a body to get mighty ripe in the summer heat. Nobody was taking any deep breaths. That's for sure. The train from Denver to Cheyenne wasn't much better. Soot and smoke fly back from the engine, and the seats are hard enough to make your butt bones come clean through your behind.

Cougar had to smile at that. He could picture Georgia chafing at having to sit in one place for hours on end, breathing in the smut that spread back from a belching locomotive. He almost felt sorry for the "weasel" who had to travel with the girl.

"Don't stop, Señor Cougar. This is very exciting."

"All right. Let's see. Here she talks about Denver."

You'd be mighty impressed to see Denver town, Essie. It ain't the shantytown it used to be. If Chicago is bigger than Denver, I'd be right surprised. They've got buildings almost as far as you can see, and some of them two and three stories. It's a wonder. Cheyenne, where we are now, isn't much more than all the other railroad towns my daddy and me passed through, though it's beginning to put on airs.

From here we take the train due east to Chicago, and as fast as this monster train goes, we should be there in no time at all. Don't worry about me. I'll be glad to have this business over with, but I'm having a good time looking at the country and the people. Most are a bunch of ordinary folks, but some are god-awful snooty. The weasel lawyer hired a woman to travel with us. He says she's supposed to save my reputation, and I don't understand how she's supposed to do that. She's got enough starch in her drawers that she couldn't unbend if she wanted to. The woman has been looking down her nose at me ever since we met, and just last night at the hotel, she tried to get me naked into a bathtub. Not a bath in clean creek water, mind you, but in one of those tin tubs like the whores at Mattie Bee's use. And she was watching all the time. I set her straight right fast. At least when you nag me to wash myself in the creek, you don't hang around to watch with your mouth pursed up as tight as the drawstring on a bag of gold dust.

I gotta go now because the train's going to leave and Weasel is about to spit nails at me. Tell Cougar not to worry about his claim. I hope he's looking after you like he promised. I'll straighten that mess out first thing after we get to Chicago. Then I'll hop a train back. Maybe I can get back before the creek starts to ice up. When I get to where we're going, I'll write again. Maybe you can send me word of how everyone is doing. Get Cougar to write what you say. I worry about you, but I'll be back soon.

Your ever-loving friend,
Georgie

"This is wonderful news!" Esperanza exclaimed. "She will be back before winter, she says. In winter the work is so much harder. Luis and Jose, over there, they are good men, but the winter will be much easier if Georgie comes back."

Cougar folded the letter and handed it back. "Maybe she will, but don't count on it, Essie. Georgie's grandfather is a tough old buzzard, and when he gets his teeth in something, he doesn't easily let it go."

"Señor Cougar! You know Georgie's grandfather. Have you been to this place Chicago?"

"A time or two. I used to live in New York City, which is a long way from Chicago. But my father did business a time or two with Alvin Kennedy, Georgie's grandfather. He's a powerful man not only in Chicago, but in trade and commerce all over the country, at least the country east of the Mississippi River. He'll be a tough nut to crack, even for Georgie."

She looked at him slyly. "Maybe Georgie needs help with this man?"

Cougar laughed. "Don't look at me. I've got two claims to work and you to look after as well. Georgie and the old man should be a pretty good match-up, if you ask me. And she'd better manage to pry my claim loose from him." He glanced up to where the quartz vein slanted across the hillside like a broad white stripe. "Or when she comes back, I'm going to take the price out of her hide."

Breakfast at Greystone House took place at a painfully late hour, as far as Georgie was concerned. She was accustomed to getting up long before the sun, bolting biscuits and cold bacon left from the day before, and starting into the day's labor as soon as dawn produced enough light to see by. Chicago was a different world by far. In her grandfather's house, only servants did labor, and they went about it so sneakily that she began to think they were ashamed of good honest work. The cook—a round little woman named Marjorie—had been mighty startled to see Georgie show up in the kitchen before dawn and had shooed her away like a pesky fly. Rachel had been in the kitchen as well, and she'd dithered and wailed that Georgie hadn't stayed in bed until the maid had brought her morning tea, or some such thing. Georgie had managed to get away with a hot blueberry muffin, but that was little compensation for spending the best part of the morning wandering the huge house with nothing to do. Georgie wasn't used to having nothing to do, and she surely didn't like it.

Her grandfather and Elizabeth appeared well after the sun, and the servants immediately produced a selection of food that got Georgie to thinking that the citified life might not be all bad in some parts. The sideboard fairly sagged beneath the weight of scrambled eggs, bacon, toast, muffins, oatmeal, ham, peaches, sliced apples, and cheese. The only thing missing was flapjacks. Georgie was very partial to flapjacks. Her daddy had mixed up the best flapjacks in the world whenever they had something to celebrate, which admittedly wasn't that often. But she did love flapjacks. The food here was good enough, though, that she was prepared to forgive the absence.

Georgie tore into her food with gusto, and right away her granddad spoiled the pleasure by scolding about her manners.

"Georgia, you eat like a hog with its face in the trough. What are you thinking?"

Across the table from her, Elizabeth had turned rather pale. "Georgie, dear. You needn't use the fork as if it were a shovel. No one is going to remove your plate before you're through eating. You can take your time."

Just so they would stop whining, Georgie slowed a bit, but Elizabeth still went at her. "Hold your fork like this." She demonstrated. Her fingers barely touched the fork. A breeze would have blown it out of her hand. "And put only a small amount of food on it."

"That's damned inefficient," she told them.

"And I'm afraid that language isn't acceptable," Miss Prissy corrected.

"What language?"

Elizabeth struggled with the word, but couldn't quite get it out.

"Damned," Alvin supplied. "Damned, crap, drat, hell,

shit, goddammit, and any other strong language. There'll be no more of it coming out of your mouth."

"I'll say what I want however I want to say it."

"Not in my house you won't."

"Then I'll get the hell out of your house."

"You'll stay put and do as you're told."

Elizabeth had the guts to break in. "Mr. Kennedy, Georgia just needs some time to adjust. We will work on all these things, but you must give her time. Transformations don't happen overnight."

Alvin merely grumbled. "And where did you get that dress? What happened to the clothing we bought?"

"They were too small for her, sir. I hastily altered one of Marjorie's dresses until Georgia can be fitted with something more suitable."

"Then get her to the dressmaker as soon as possible, for heaven's sake. She looks like a scullery maid."

"I look like an idiot," Georgie said. "These damned skirts"—her grandfather scowled, but Georgie ignored him—"tangle in my legs, and the sleeves pinch my armpits. But she"—Georgie glared at Elizabeth—"had my good clothes burned."

"For which I commend her," Alvin said dryly.

"But whatever she says, I ain't gonna wear one of those corsets. I'd rather the Apaches stake me out on an anthill."

Her grandfather grew red in the face. "Ladies do not mention undergarments such as corsets."

"I don't recall that bein' on your list of don't-says."

"Don't you be pert with me, girl. That attitude will earn you nothing but a comeuppance."

Around a mouthful of eggs, she replied, "I'm shakin' in my boots."

His face got redder, but Georgie was beginning to enjoy herself. Alvin Kennedy deserved a little grief for the trouble he had caused her. "I don't see much use in you people carping like jaybirds at how I hold my damned fork, what I wear, or what I say, 'cause I ain't likely to change my way of doin' things on your say-so. I don't give a feather what you folks think. I just came here to get straightened out on this claim business, and when that's done, we can call it quits." She drew a bead on Alvin. "I don't much like your high-handed way of threatening to sell the claims unless I hotfooted it out here. I'll credit that you're owed something for grubstaking my daddy when he needed the help, but I don't owe you sittin' here and listenin' to you squawk about what I am, because what I am is just fine with me."

She figured her granddad was going to plumb bust out in flames any second, but she didn't much care.

"Miss Whitman," he said in a strangled voice. "Would you leave us for a short while? I would like to chat with Georgia alone."

The teacher looked more than grateful to leave. Now that the nonfamily was out of it, Georgie figured, the old man was going to let her have it. Not that she cared. All she wanted was to take care of business and go home.

"You, young lady, are a hoyden who lacks all respect and a person not fit for the company of civilized people!"

Georgie almost laughed. Her ears weren't exactly blown back from the force of that tirade. The man needed some practice in throwing insults.

"What's more, I'm beginning to think you don't have the brains of an ant."

She smiled. Now he was warming up.

"Don't smile that know-it-all smile at me, missy. Because you don't know nearly as much as you think. I'll tell you how it is, and then maybe we can get down to work. Your father left here on his twenty-eighth birthday, six months after your mother died. He spouted some fool notion of being free, living a life of adventure. Instead of being free, he ruined his life and yours, too. Turned his own daughter into a little savage. And while none of that is my doing, I feel like I owe you the life your father took away. You're my granddaughter, after all, and I have a family obligation to make things right."

"Glad to hear it." Things were looking up, Georgie thought. "If that's what you want to do, just hand me the title to my daddy's claims and I'll be on my way."

Alvin snorted. "Forget those stupid little claims, girl. I'm going to give you a life. A home, a husband, children, and a respectable place in polite society."

She greeted that notion with a belly laugh. "Forget that! No man is going to have me unless it's for the gold, and folks around here ain't all that interested in gold unless it's already out of the ground, I'd guess."

He looked smug. "I already have the man who will have you. He's rich, honorable, a pillar of the community, and the object of every unmarried girl's hopes. But he plans to court you, my girl, because you're a Kennedy woman, my granddaughter."

Georgie was stunned. For a moment she didn't say a thing, just stared incredulously at her granddad. The idea was so ridiculous that she didn't know whether to be angry or split her gut laughing.

"You have a month to learn how to be a lady worthy of Alexander Stanford, because that's when you will be presented to him. Fortunately, he's going out of town between now and then, so we don't risk his seeing you as you are. It's a short enough time to smooth out your rough edges, I'll admit, but if anyone can do it, Miss Whitman can. Mrs. Newmeyer told me Elizabeth worked an absolute miracle with their bratty little Prudence, and I trust she can do the same for you."

He sat back in his chair, folded his arms complacently, and appeared to expect gratitude. This fellow Stanford apparently didn't know a thing about her, and now she had to be made over into some piece of fluff that he could live with, because the actual, real Georgie would curdle the poor man's stomach, or so it seemed. The laughter drained right out of her.

"I don't the hell care about smoothing out any rough edges." She pinned the old man with her eyes, wishing she could pin him with the long bladed knife that Elizabeth hadn't allowed her to wear to breakfast—not pin him by the flesh, but maybe by his starched collar, just so he would understand that she meant business. "I like my edges just fine, and I ain't gonna be put on the auction block like a broodmare for some man to decide if I'm good enough to take home. I don't need a man to give me a good life, so you can just forget the whole thing."

"I will not forget the whole thing, Georgia. I know

what's best for you, and you'll do as I say. There is not only your happiness and security at stake here, but the expansion of the Kennedy family interests as well."

"The Kennedy family interests can just do without my help." She pushed back her chair and stood. "I don't know what stupid notion has gotten into your head to think you could peddle me around like some yahoo selling a mule, but you've got the wrong person. I'm going back to where I belong, and you and your schemes can go to hell."

Alvin stood, also, his breakfast ignored. He leaned over the table and met her eye to eye. "What will you go to when I sell those claims? There are plenty of fools with gold in their blood who would pay me good money for them."

She mentally kicked herself for forgetting why she had come to Chicago in the first place. She pictured herself telling Cougar Barnes that she'd made a mess of things and the claim she had sold him belonged to someone else. He'd take a card from the Apache deck and hang her by her heels over a slow fire. The old bastard had her by a ring through her nose, that was for sure.

Deflated, she dropped back into her chair.

"Georgia," her granddad said more gently. "What I'm offering you is what every girl longs for, hopes for, and dreams about. You're just scared, aren't you? Scared that you aren't good enough for a man like Alexander Stanford, scared to try being better than you are. I never thought a Kennedy could be a coward."

That got her back up but good. "Who are you calling a coward, you soft-livered son of a coyote? I've faced Apaches, rattlesnakes, scorpions, winter blizzards, and summer thirst without batting an eye, while you've sat here on your cushioned settees."

He shook his head and gave her an infuriatingly superior smile. "You're talking about physical courage, Georgia. I've no doubt you have that in spades. What I'm talking about is moral and spiritual courage. The courage to strive, to change, to reach out and explore new things. Think about it, my girl. Wouldn't you like to prove that you can be as good as any woman in Chicago? Do you have the guts to live up to your heritage, to become a credit to your gender? Do you have the courage to do that? Or do you snivel and slink back into the hole you've dug for yourself where no one cares how you look or speak or act?"

Georgie fumed. "I have the guts to do anything I need to do. Damned if I don't. I could become a regular fancified lady if I wanted to. But I don't want to."

"Because you're afraid."

"Bullshit!"

His brows inched skeptically upward. "Then prove it."

She made a rude sound. "I can see right through you, old man. Don't think I can't."

"Of course you can. You're a Kennedy, so you're not stupid. But you also know I'm right. You'll always wonder, Georgia, if you could accomplish this task, or if you ran away scared."

She stared at him in hot silence, her jaw clenched, her mind roiling. Damn the man. She could see her father in him. Elias had always been able to play her like Lem Stucker played his fiddle. "Even if I proved I could be a lady, you couldn't make me get married."

Alvin smiled. "I'm betting you'll want to marry this one."

"You're betting on the wrong horse."

"You haven't met him. Why dismiss the possibilities out of hand?"

She ground her teeth and turned away. Outside the window, the sun had disappeared behind a high gray curtain of clouds, and the damp heaviness of the August air hung like a warm wet blanket, weighing her down. Even here in her granddad's breakfast room she could hear the bustle of the city, the rattle of traffic, the not very distant roar of a train on its way to the lakefront rail yard. In Chicago, peace and quiet didn't exist. Bright blue skies and the fresh scent of juniper and pine were far away, supplanted by haze, clouds, and the odor of the meatpacking plants. After only a day she hated Chicago. She wanted to run away, back to the land and the people she knew. In a way, the old man was right. She was a coward.

Alvin Kennedy was smart, Georgia admitted, and he held all the cards. For a while, at least, her granddad would get his way. But if she was to hold up her head ever again, she had to come away with something.

She sighed. Why wasn't anything in life as simple as a person expected it to be?

"I'll do you a deal," she said firmly. "You can't expect me to kick over my whole life and you not give anything in return."

He snorted. "I'm giving everything in return, my girl."

"You're not giving me anything I want."

That shut him up for a few moments at least.

"This is what I'll do," she said, gaining confidence. "I'll parade myself around in dresses and learn to hold a fork and talk like a lady—if you'll sign over those claims to me. I've got to have some security for me that's separate from what you dole out in the way of food to eat and a roof over my head."

He narrowed his eyes, thinking. "You've got to genuinely try to fit into the mold of a well-bred, well-educated Kennedy woman."

"I don't do nothin' halfway."

With a slight grimace Alvin continued. "And you have to accept Alexander Stanford's attention. I assure you that he won't press you for anything improper, and of course I wouldn't expect you to compromise yourself. But you have to give him fair and courteous consideration."

"As long as he behaves himself."

"All right, then. If you apply yourself to your lessons, and you allow Alex to court, whether or not you two marry, I'll sign over your claims at the end of, say, two years."

She exploded. "Two years? Not a chance. Four months."

"Eighteen months."

"Eight months."

"One year. After one year, if you want to go back and grub in the Arizona dirt, the claims are yours, free and clear."

Georgia puckered as if she'd swallowed a bitter tonic. Finally she gave in. "One year. Not a day longer."

* * *

Georgie pounded a balled fist into the silly, frilly pillow on her bed. She was trapped like a fox in its hole with no way out, behind bars just as surely as ol' Jack Cordes every Saturday night after a bender in Prescott. Only her sentence was a lot longer than Jack's had ever been, and all because she'd let the granddad get the best of her. A string of cuss words rattled through her mind, but she didn't let them pass her mouth. It was damned painful letting those words buzz around inside her, heating up her brain, without letting them blow, but she'd given her word to start talking like a lady. Shit and goddamned, but she couldn't believe she let the old man get the upper hand.

Alvin Kennedy was a tough old buzzard. Georgie almost had to admire the man. Not just anybody could get the best of her. But she could admire him and curse his schemes at the same time. A year was an eternity. A year in Chicago was eternity spent in hell, especially since she had to sit around pretending to be someone she wasn't, making stupid small talk with a man dense enough to consider marrying her. How would she endure it? She physically ached for Prescott, for the mountains, and most of all, for her freedom, ached so much that her stomach hurt. At her little cabin on the Lynx she might not have hot water for bathing, but neither did she have someone telling her when to bathe. Essie didn't count, because Essie was easily ignored.

And then there was Cougar. She would have to write and tell him how things stood. His reaction was going to rival one of Arizona's summer thunderstorms. It wasn't right that he should have to put off his plans a year. But she was doing her best. Her heart gave a couple of jumps for his sake. Cougar was a good friend, but a dangerous enemy. She tried not to think about him too often, because thinking about him made her stomach twist, not only because she felt guilty for the trouble she'd caused, but also because she missed the big ox. He was a thorn in her side, always teasing about her wild red hair and her baggy overalls. But she got revenge, yanking that sloppy beard of his and squashing him at arm wrestling. Joshing with Cougar was fun.

But oh, my, no one wanted Cougar as an enemy. In the normal course of things, he was a pretty easygoing fellow, but if someone brought him a fight, he could be meaner than a cornered coyote. She remembered one time when she and her daddy and Cougar and four or five others had been relaxing at the old Juniper House eatery, a pack of Apaches had dropped in and raised hell. Cougar had taken on one of the bastards hand to hand. That Injun got a surprise, because at close quarters Cougar was as deadly with a knife as he was with a rifle. The buck got away, though just barely. Georgie suspected that Cougar had let him get away. Tough as the man was, he disliked killing. He'd out and out admitted it to her once. She liked it that Cougar had a soft side. Everyone needed a chink in his armor.

Georgie didn't think he'd show any soft side to her, though, if she didn't come through with that claim of his. He set big store by the gold in that quartz vein, and he'd paid top money for it. He wasn't going to wait a year while she pranced around Chicago town in fancy frills, walking out with some fool who wanted to marry her.

Damn! The very thought made her stomach heave. She wondered if her granddad had greased this Alex Stanford's palm to lure him into courting her. What other reason would a man have for cozying up to a person like Georgie? In a world that expected men to be men and women to be soft and curved, Georgie was a freak. She knew it, and it didn't bother her much, because what she was suited her just fine. People who pretended to be something they weren't just asked to be laughed at, and that was going to happen here in Chicago when she started parading about in dresses and started using fancy language. Eventually all her granddad's friends and their wives, all the snooty, mincing ladies who went to teas and turned up noses at servants, even this poor bastard who wanted to court her—all these folks would laugh themselves sick at Georgie Kennedy's expense.

And then something inside her would die. She would want to shoot them all, but a person couldn't do that and get away with it, even if you just aimed to hit a toe or a kneecap. She would just have to shower them with all the

BECOMING GEORGIA 67

cusswords she was bottling up inside and stalk off as if she didn't care.

Because she didn't care, Georgie told herself. And she wasn't going to cry. Crying was for babies, brats, and weak women. She was definitely not going to cry.

When Elizabeth heard the door to Georgia's room slam, she had debated leaving the girl alone for a time or starting right then on what was going to be a considerable job—transforming a wildcat into a well-mannered pussycat. She decided that the girl needed some time to herself. Then she heard the sound of desperate weeping through the wall that separated their two rooms. Without further debate Elizabeth rushed into Georgia's room to discover the trouble.

Georgia whirled from the window where she stood with tears streaming down her face. To Elizabeth's great surprise, the girl grabbed the nearest thing at hand—fortunately it was a pillow—and threw it at her.

"Get out of here!"

"Georgia!"

"Don't call me that. Leave me alone. I ain't cryin'."

Elizabeth found Georgie's distress daunting, that a person so confident, so spit-in-your-eye sure of herself, could weep so miserably. "Georgia, you shouldn't be ashamed of weeping. All people weep when they're upset. Perhaps if you tell me what the trouble is, I can help."

She snorted loudly, and Elizabeth hoped another missile wouldn't come her way, especially as a pewter candlestick lay conveniently close to the girl's hand.

"You must be very homesick," Elizabeth ventured.

With a loud sniff, the girl wilted. "So what? I'll be going home soon. I struck a deal with my granddad. After a year he'll give me back my claims and I can go wherever I want." She swiped the back of her hand across her dripping nose. "He thinks I'll marry this fellow he has on a leash and I'll stay. My guess is he wants those claims for himself, the old buzzard."

Elizabeth laughed. It was impolitic, but she couldn't help it. "Oh, my dear, I can assure you that isn't so. I'm sure your grandfather only wants to see you settled in a good life. I know he has a bit of a crust, but Alvin Kennedy truly is a fine man."

"Hmmph!"

"And as for being homesick, Georgia, that will pass. A year will go by quicker than you think, and maybe by the time it ends, you truly will want to stay in Chicago. Maybe even marry this man your grandfather has chosen. I'm sure he has your best interests at heart."

Georgia melted a bit, plopping down in a brocade wingback chair beside the room's cold fireplace. But she still regarded Elizabeth distrustfully. "If marrying is such a 'best interests' kinda thing, then how come you ain't married? You're the prettiest girl I've ever laid eyes on, and you talk right and walk right and smile a lot. Seems to me you're prime fodder for bein' some man's wife."

A blush heated Elizabeth's cheeks. "Marriage isn't as simple as that, dear. In society a man doesn't offer for a girl to be his wife unless she has a suitable dowry. A woman is expected to bring something into a marriage besides herself."

Georgia raised a brow. "You look rich enough."

Elizabeth hesitated. Normally she didn't discuss her personal history with anyone, but she wondered if this strange girl might be more willing to trust if she knew more of her teacher's circumstances. Somewhat reluctantly she opened the door on that dark closet inside her that hid her shame. "See how appearances deceive, Georgia? I'm actually not rich at all, except in having my dear mother and sisters. Two years ago my father . . . died. He had just lost his business and all his assets, poor man. My mother and sisters and I depend upon the money I earn teaching the children of wealthy families."

"Uk!" Georgia made a face. "Teachin' kids. I'd rather stand all day in the sun and shovel gravel. And now you get stuck with me!" This time her voice held a hint of laughter.

"I don't think it will be so bad," Elizabeth said with a smile. "I believe that I'll enjoy teaching you what you need to know to join society."

"Sure."

"I've never failed a student," Elizabeth insisted.

"Then get ready for a new experience."

Elizabeth launched into teacher mode. "All you need do is apply yourself, Georgia. You've been given a great opportunity to explore a side of life that you've never known, so at the end of a year you can make a choice of which life you really want. Your old life will still be there waiting if you want it, dear."

The girl grew gloomy again. "Maybe, maybe not. All sorts of things might happen to the claims, to my friends. The Apaches would hang all the settlers by their heels if they could. White people, Mexicans, even other Injuns—they fight 'em all. And my claims, well, there's claim jumpers crawling all around. Or Essie might get a bellyful of snakes, scorpions, and wild animals and go back to Sonora. I told Cougar to take care of her, but he can't watch every day."

Georgia's life sounded like an adventure story to Elizabeth, something made up from some writer's imagination that had no place in the real world. "Cougar? Is he . . . he a man?"

"Yup." Georgia nodded and smiled. "He's a man all right."

Elizabeth suffered a pang of regret that Alvin Kennedy had hamstrung such an exotic creature as the girl who smiled so softly when she spoke of the horrendous-sounding life and people she had left. Sequestered in the world of a proper, well-behaved woman, she had never dreamed such possibilities that this girl had actually lived. Wild animals and wilder Indians, and a man with the unlikely name of Cougar. Georgia Kennedy had lived outside the sphere that defined feminine existence. She thumbed her nose at convention, depended on no one, and consulted no one in making decisions.

Now Alvin Kennedy, with only good intentions, wanted to imprison Georgia in the walls that confined all civilized women. He would take this rare, lively creature and cage her like a lioness in a circus. And Elizabeth was to be the girl's keeper. How sad, she thought.

To combat such thoughts, she spoke with determined cheer. "You're going to like it here, Georgia. And we're going to make a grand lady of you. All Chicago will be at your feet. Just see if it isn't. You must regard this project as an adventure. Who knows what we will discover in you, what beauty, what untapped talent, what grace. Can you see the possibilities?"

Georgia merely shook her head. "Miss Elizabeth, I think you've been at the hooch."

Chapter 5

Georgie sat at the little desk in her room, looking out the window at fireflies darting through the dark night. August was passing quickly, and September was close at hand, but still the air, day and night, remained hot and heavy. Fierce thunderstorms rolled through almost every afternoon, filling the world with wind, thunder, and lightning. Georgie's own soul was filled with similar turmoil. And every day she wanted to jump into a pair of baggy trousers and walk like a human being should walk, with big, striding steps and unfettered freedom. She wanted to laugh loud (not that there was much to laugh about here), make rude noises when a situation called for a rude noise, and open up the dam on what Elizabeth called her "colorful expressions."

She didn't, however. Her granddad had pried a promise from her, and a promise was a promise, even if given only because her arm was twisted behind her back by her granddad's sneaky bargaining. Georgia really was trying to understand this strange world, the dos and don'ts, the odd behavior expected of people, especially female people. She despaired of ever fitting in and, to be honest, didn't much want to. But she did try.

Every evening, tired and homesick, she sat at the little desk in her room and wrote volumes to Esperanza, and then at the end of each week she sent them off in the post. At first, writing had been hard. She could read all right, and write too, but she'd had much less practice at the writing than the reading. With each passing day, setting her adventures onto paper became easier. Elizabeth accused her of becoming downright literary.

August 8
Dear Essie,
  You would admire the place I went today, one of the busiest places I have seen, and all women, too. I've never seen so many females together in one place. In Chicago they're like weeds.
  This place was a dressmaker's shop, because my granddad thinks I need all new clothes. The ones that were here were all too small, and so I've been wearing the cook's clothes, and I don't see nothing—anything (I'm leaning to talk and write like a lady, you see)— wrong with the cook's clothes, but my granddad says they're not suitable.
  So Elizabeth (she's my teacher) took me to the dressmaker, who's very busy. It took us days to get an appointment, so I guess most women hereabouts are too lazy to make their own clothes. Anyway, in the shop a regular army troop of women poked, prodded, and measured me for everything from underclothes to fancy dresses—dresses to walk in, ride in, eat in, visit in, and sit around in. Women here in Chicago town do a lot of sitting around.
  You should have seen the hissy fit these silly women threw just because I walked into the shop without a corset. You would have thought I walked in naked for all they carried on. Elizabeth tried to get me to wear one of those contraptions the first day I got here, but I killed it. But the dressmaker refused to sew any clothes for me without the thing, and Elizabeth took advantage and reminded me that I promised my granddad to behave. In the end I had to give in, and they wrapped me in an absolute horror of satin, lace, and whalebone. I didn't let them pull the laces as tight as they wanted,

though. I swear that these corsets fit only women who have no ribs at all. Torture, pure and simple.

I've decided that the people who make women's clothes have a lot in common with Apaches. At least the Indians give up, sooner or later, and just kill a person. Corset torture goes on a lifetime

All the poking and prodding and being bossed around got my back up but good, so I wouldn't leave the shop until the teacher got measured for a new dress as well. She got red in the face and sputtered a lot, but I won that round. If my granddad can spend money like it was dirt and fit me out with more clothes than I could wear in a lifetime, then he can fork over a bit for Elizabeth as well, and so I told him when we got home.

I have to tell you about my teacher, Elizabeth. She's a good sort, very pretty with a gentle way about her, and I like her a lot. Getting to know her makes me admit that not all ladies have their noses in the air. Hard to believe some man hasn't snatched her. In Arizona the fellows would be fighting gun duels over who gets her, but here, money is more important than anything else a woman can offer. Elizabeth doesn't have any money, so she's going to be a spinster. I'd tell her to go to Arizona, but I don't think she would like it there.

I've got to go to bed. Tell Cougar I can still beat him at anything he cares to name, even if I have to wear a corset while I'm doing it.

August 15
Dear Essie,

All my new clothes are finished, including the damned corset. I'm not supposed to let cusswords like damn and crap and shit out of my mouth anymore, and probably I'm not supposed to write them, either. But those corsets deserve a hell of a lot of cussing, believe me!

A couple of days ago I started dancing lessons with a fellow called the Dancing Master. They don't dance here like we do, but very slowly and stiffly and not touching your partner very much at all. It's very boring.

But the Dancing Master wasn't. You would have laughed at this fellow just as hard as I did. He pranced worse than one of the whores down at Mattie Bee's. And he waves his hands when he talks, with his little finger lifted just so. How could anyone dance with him in the room? I near busted a gut laughing.

Anyway, the DM got mad and walked out. Elizabeth said I was rude, but I know she wanted to laugh, too, because her lips twitched a lot. Elizabeth is good at a lot of things, but she doesn't have any kind of a poker face. I got a dancing lesson anyway, with Elizabeth's little sister Chloe playing the piano (she's really good, even though she's only twelve years old) and me and the teacher dancing together just like some hoity-toity folks at a fancy ball. If anyone had caught us in the act, they would have locked us in the slammer for either being crazy or perverted.

I'll bet Cougar would have laughed to see me prancing around with another woman like Cinderella at the ball.

August 25
Dear Essie,

I got the letter Cougar wrote out for you, and it made me so homesick I cried. Just don't tell anyone I cried. I've been in Chicago a month, but it seems like forever. When you count the weeks it took to get here, the time stretches out to damned near eternity. The July Fourth picnic in Prescott is so far back I can barely remember it. Except for beating Cougar at arm wrestling. I remember that all right. I would give half the gold in Daddy's claims to be back at that picnic, though. If I was, when I saw Mr. Weasel Whittaker coming through the crowd to talk to me, I'd run the other way. Then I'd hide in some cave where he couldn't find me. I don't think hiding from things is a good idea, but I'd hide from him.

I've never been one to do a lot of whining, but I guess I'm whining up a storm right now. Don't worry about me, though. At the end of the day I get tired and whiny, just like a snot-nose kid. The paces they put me through here take the starch out of a body faster than chopping wood and shoveling rock. My granddad and my teacher, Elizabeth, are bound that they're going to knock me down and build me back up as some kind of a lady, and that means they nag at me all day about how I walk, how I talk, even how I sit my butt down in a chair, for chrissakes. Every time a damn comes out of my mouth I get a glare from Elizabeth that could put blisters on my tongue. She doesn't like me saying "yup" either. Say I sound like a dog. And if I use the wrong fork (they've got more than one for each person at the table, would you believe? I know—you won't believe I use a fork at all). Anyway, if I use the wrong fork, Granddad calls me a savage. I can dance pretty good with Elizabeth, and once Granddad danced with me while Chloe played a waltz. The old coot is a pretty good dancer. And these days I talk like a fancy lady. Not here in this letter to you. Writing to you is the only place I can talk normal with a few cusswords thrown in to get my meaning across. Talking to anyone around here I really have to watch myself. Ladies are supposed to faint at strong language, Elizabeth tells me. Isn't that something? Even calling body parts by their proper names sends a Chicago lady into fits. This talking right is frigging hard.

Other than all the hard work learning to talk and walk and eat and dance, things are awfully boring. We have things Elizabeth calls teas, where we sit around stiff as boards, drinking weak tea and visiting. We don't visit with anyone interesting, because Elizabeth says I'm not up to being presented, but her mother and sisters come, and she has a few friends she trusts to not tell tales on me. The only people I see regular are Elizabeth, my granddad, and the house servants. Would you believe that my granddad has servants to cook and clean and weed the garden? I even have my own personal maid. Her name is Rachel, and she lays out my clothes, brushes my hair at night, and brings me rolls and tea in the morning, just like I was some kind of princess in a fairy tale. I heard my granddad one day tell her if she talked about me to anyone outside the house, he'd throw her out on the street. Poor girl.

I can't see that I'm so interesting that anyone would want to talk about me, though. Right now I'm a better kept secret than where Skillet stashes his gold.

The only thing that keeps me going here is knowing that I'll come back to Prescott, where I can get back to living like a person is supposed to live. I struck a bargain with my granddad, which was no easy thing, because he's a wily sort. The old man wants me to stay here, learn to be a lady, and marry some widower friend of his. My granddad is rich as a king, so my guess is that he's paying this guy to hitch himself to me. The fellow's name is Alexander Stanford—some business friend of Granddad's. I guess he can't find himself a real wife because he drools or stinks or something. He probably can't heft an ax, use a pick, or skin a squirrel. Granddad says I have to receive his attentions (people talk fancy around here, don't they?), but if the yahoo lays a finger on me, he'll draw away a bloody stump, so he'd better mind his manners.

Personally, I think my claims come into this marriage plot somewhere. Granddad probably wants them, but he'd feel rotten about snatching them right away from me without getting me settled, as he puts it. I am his blood and bone, after all, and he says he feels obliged. It's the only thing I can figure out. Maybe he's offered a cut to this widower fellow.

But I'm not putting up with this messing around for long. I made a deal that if I try this lady stuff for a year and still want to go home, then Granddad has to sign the claims over to me. I tried to get the time shorter, but like I said, Granddad is a wily old codger. He holds all the cards, and he drives a hard bargain. (He really thinks I'll knuckle under, but he doesn't know me very well.) I figure Cougar will have a fit, but tell him I did the best that I could. He can go ahead and work the mine (Granddad will never know) and just stockpile the ore until I can get him the papers. I hope he's watching out for you and our claims. If the yahoos there know Cougar's on the look-out, they won't likely try any funny business.,

I gotta go, Essie. Miss you a lot. I hope Cougar got those grazing rights he was after up in Chino Valley. Without me there to take him down a peg now and then, he's probably cockier than ever.

"It's damn hot for September." Lieutenant Brown quaffed a long swallow of beer and wiped his sleeve across his mouth. "Doesn't it ever get cool in these mountains?"

Leaning on Big Mike's bar beside the lieutenant, Cougar Barnes chuckled. "Two months from now you'll be wishing it was warm again."

"All right by me. I'm from Ohio. I'd rather fight in the cold than the heat any day. All during the war I was in northern Virginia. Wish I was back there now. The Rebs weren't anything compared to these goddamned Apaches."

"Sooner or later you boys in blue will get the Apaches under control," Cougar said. "Leastwise, that's what I'm hoping. I've got a prime piece of land in Chino plus grazing rights all around, and I don't dare put cattle on it until the Indians settle down."

The lieutenant shook his head. "If these savages would stand and fight like a man instead of coming out of nowhere and then disappearing into nowhere when they've done their bloody business . . ."

Skillet Mahoney, whiskey in hand, joined in from a nearby table. "They oughta send enough'a you soldiers out here to comb through these mountains and rout 'em out like fleas, bucks and squaws alike. Then they oughta shoot every last one of the bastards. S'only way we'll have any peace around here."

Cougar shook his head. "Skillet, you're drunk."

"He makes a lotta sense," Cal Newman said. "Ain't ever gonna have peace around here as long as one of those savages is drawin' breath into his lungs. Adam Nicols over on Big Bug Creek lost two mules to the Injuns two days ago. He's lucky he didn't lose his hair. I been thinkin' about goin' up Colorado way. There's a fair lot of gold in those mountains, and they don't got as many Injuns. Leastwise, what Injuns they got ain't Apaches."

"Thassa fact," Skillet agreed. "Cain't make enough to stay alive around here anyway. Gold's there, but goddamn, ya have to work for it. Best damned claims around here are ol' George's, and she turned 'em over to that Mex woman. Damned crime."

"Mexicans can't file claims," the lieutenant said.

"Yeah, well, Georgie didn't make it official," Cal explained. "She just upped and left the woman to dig the gold. Wouldn't have thought it of Georgie. But then, she did sorta double-cross you on that claim she sold you, didn't she, Cougar?"

Cougar answered grimly. "Georgie didn't double-cross anybody on anything, and there's nothing wrong with her letting Esperanza look after things while she's gone. Essie is practically the girl's mother."

Skillet sputtered. "Girl. Thas right. Georgie's a girl. Fergit, sometimes." He snickered. "'Specially when she flattens ol' Cougar here in arm wrestling. Big fella like you oughta be ashamed of lettin' a little girl beat him up like that."

Snickers from the entire saloon—all four tables—greeted Skillet's remark.

Cougar didn't laugh. He didn't like the way the talk was running. "You boys leave Georgie's claims alone, and you behave yourselves around Esperanza. I promised Georgie that I'd watch out for the claims and the woman, and I wouldn't mind knocking a few heads together for anyone making trouble."

"Don't git all huffy," Skillet said. "Hell, Georgie ain't never comin' back to dig in those claims ag'in. I wouldn't come back, if'n I could get outta here."

The lieutenant stared out the doorway, squinting into the bright sunlight. "Isn't that woman out there the Mexican you're talking about?"

Cougar followed the direction of the officer's gaze. "That's her." With a warning look at the others in the saloon, he set down his beer. "Guess I'll go out and say howdy."

Esperanza had parked her wagon in front of Bashford's mercantile. She smiled as Cougar offered her a hand down. "Señor Cougar. I was going to look for you."

"How are things, Essie?"

"Everything is going well, señor. Except that less gold is coming out of the rocker, I think. We are going to dig a new pit. I hope when Georgie comes back, her claims have not faded away to nothing."

Cougar hoped so, too. That wasn't uncommon in the Prescott area.

"More letters have come from Georgie, señor. Will you read them to me?"

He smiled. "Our Georgie is becoming quite a correspondent."

"She writes so much, I think, because she is lonely." The woman smiled. "Or maybe she knows I am lonely without her."

Cougar glanced over the pages Essie handed him. He had to admit that he missed Georgie as well, though he wasn't about to spread it about. He didn't have anyone to share the shelf full of books he kept in his cabin. Georgie did love to read. And he didn't have anyone continually trying to knock him off what she called his "high horse." He remembered getting a kick out of just watching Georgie walk down the street. Hoyden as she was, she had a sway to her walk that was pure, unadulterated female. Even her free-swinging stride couldn't hide it. And of course those overalls, baggy as they were, emphasized every lilt of her rounded hips.

God, what was he thinking? Maybe the lack of women out here had driven him round the bend.

"Read the letters aloud, Señor Cougar. Is she all right? When is she coming home?"

Cougar read, laughing in places, embarrassed in others. "Maybe you should have a woman read these to you." He could almost see the dressmaker lacing the hated corset, pushing up Georgie's bosoms. He knew she had nice bosoms, because the overalls didn't do much to hide those, either.

"There are not so many women here that I would trust to read Georgie's private words. Maybe Señorita Barton at the school, but she is busy all day."

"Uh . . . you're right." He shrugged and read on, frowning mightily over the lines about Alexander Stanford. He knew the man from years ago when they had attended the same school. And later, when Cougar had still been trying to fit into the Barnes family banking business, their bank had provided financial backing for Stanford Shipping. Cougar had traveled to Chicago more than once and had been a guest in the Stanford house. Back then Robert Stanford had run the business, and Alexander had just taken a wife.

The Alex Cougar remembered certainly didn't drool or stink, as Georgie speculated, and if something had happened to his wife, he certainly wouldn't need the likes of Georgie to take her place. He had looks, brains, and money. He would marry a woman with the same qualities, not Georgie.

Then he read further and exploded. "A year? Goddammit! If she stays there a year, she'll never come back. I'm for sure not waiting a cotton-picking year to start milling the gold from that claim!"

Essie deflated. "Señor, if her grandfather will not let her come back sooner, then what can she do?"

Cougar didn't have an answer to that one.

After Essie had gone about her business, Cougar went back to the boardinghouse where he stayed when he was in town. Georgie's letters continued to bother him. What was old man Kennedy up to, trying to match Georgie up to a man like Alex Stanford? Alex would never consider tying himself to a woman who had won the Prescott spitting contest two years in a row.

Yet, if Georgie was Kennedy's only heir, then she was rich. Her hardscrabble little gold mine wasn't a drop in the bucket of Alvin Kennedy's wealth. And weren't Alvin and Stanford close friends?

Georgie and Alexander Stanford. What a travesty. What was Kennedy trying to pull?

He had told Essie he would repair the porch steps of Georgie's house, as long as he was in town. When he got to the house, Essie was off-loading the supplies she'd picked up at Bashford's. He helped her.

"Not going back to the Lynx this afternoon?"

"I stay here tonight. It would be dark before I got home."

"Yeah. Good idea."

He started working on the steps, listening to Essie rattle around inside the house. Compared to where Georgie lived now, the treasured house that she'd bought with his money was a hovel. Would she even want to come back? Her letters rang with homesickness, but a person could get over being homesick real fast when dosed with a bit of luxury. She would probably forget all about her claims, forget about her friends here, forget she goddamned owed him the rights to that rich quartz vein. The witch.

A picture of Georgie clumping along on Alexander Stanford's arm plagued his mind. If by some miracle the man married her, she would be miserable. Maybe her head would spin at first from the comparative ease of wealthy living, but the life wouldn't suit her. Why would Kennedy want to marry her off anyway?

Then revelation struck. Maybe Stanford Shipping was in trouble and Alexander needed Georgie's money. The man Cougar remembered wouldn't have stooped to using a wife's inheritance for his own ends, but people change. The thought made him coldly angry. Stanford would use Georgia's wealth and despise her all the while, making her life a living hell.

By the time the steps were repaired, Cougar had convinced himself that he needed to travel to Chicago to make sure Georgie was all right and that no slick city predator like Stanford lay in wait for her. Not that he would travel all the way to Chicago just for Georgie. Of course not. There was the claim to consider. He had big plans for the gold locked into that quartz vein, and he would be a fool if he left the resolution of this mess in Georgie's hands.

Maybe if he approached Kennedy directly and explained the circumstances, the old man might hand over the claim. After all, Cougar had paid for it, and Kennedy didn't need it. Neither did Georgie. He mulled over the idea.

All night in his bed in Mrs. Peterson's boardinghouse Cougar lay awake, thinking about gold, Chicago, and Georgie. If he went to Chicago, he wouldn't be going for Georgie. If he ever told Georgie that she needed help taking care of herself, she would have cuffed him one, then laughed. That was her style. The thought made him grin. He did miss her. But that wasn't why he would go to Chicago, if he went.

Nope, he would go to straighten out the rights to his claim. And if he couldn't get Kennedy to hand over the claim, well, there was a lot of money in Chicago, some of it with an uncle and cousin who lived there. A lot of water had passed under the bridge since Cougar had run with the big boys in the city, but he couldn't let that bother him. He'd learned from hard living in the West that nothing comes easy. If a man wanted something, he generally had to fight Apaches, flash floods, dust storms, raging heat, and an army of rattlers to get it. He figured Chicago couldn't offer anything more daunting than that.

August had disappeared and September was well begun. In less than a week Georgie would confront Mr. Alexander Stanford at a "quiet little dinner" her granddad had planned for the big meeting.

"Putting the mare to the stud," she said with a laugh when Elizabeth drilled her in how to act during her introduction to the man.

"Georgia!"

"Well, isn't it?"

"No. Not at all!"

Elizabeth seemed a bit huffier than usual, Georgie thought.

"Alexander Stanford is a fine man, and you should work very hard to appear a lady for him."

"If he's such a fine man, how come he'd be willing to look at me for a wife?"

"He hasn't, yet!" Elizabeth snapped, then immediately apologized. "I'm sorry, Georgia. You deserve a wonderful man to marry. I'm sure Mr. Stanford will be able to see your excellent qualities."

Georgie shrugged. "I don't care what he sees. I don't want to marry. As soon as my year is up, I'm leaving this place. I'm only meeting this yahoo because of the deal I made with Granddad."

They were strolling the promenade along Lakeshore Drive, in the park where all of Chicago society seemed to take their daily exercise either on horseback or foot. Only for the past week had Elizabeth permitted her to be seen in public. After weeks of being drilled in the dos and don'ts of things as simple as walking and talking, Georgie was ready, Elizabeth had declared, to make her bow.

Release from the dull confines of Greystone House made Georgie feel like a bird suddenly free of a cage. On this day she felt like bubbling and bouncing, celebrating the sunny weather, and running in circles to mock the shorebirds that whirled in the sky above. Doing all that was pretty tough in a corset. And of course it would result in Elizabeth dragging her back to her granddad's house and clapping her in irons, or at least the ladylike equivalent of irons.

"Do you see that woman in the blue dress?" Georgie commented to Elizabeth. "She walks just like a puffed-out hen. Looks sort of like one, too."

"Shhhh!"

"She can't hear me. Oh, my! Lookee there at the fella on the gray mare. With that stomach of his, he looks like a fat little quail."

"Georgia, that is very rude. I'm sure the gentleman can't help his size." But she had to seal her lips shut against laughter. "There's Mrs. Philpott and her daughter Bernice. You'll meet them at the dinner."

"We could go say hey right now."

"No, dear. You haven't been introduced, and this isn't the place to do it."

"It feels so good to be out of the house. Look at those birds. I could just fly away with them, and wheel and dive on the water like they do." She spread her arms as if she might actually take flight. "Wouldn't everyone be surprised to see me soaring through the air?" She slipped Elizabeth an impish look. "But of course, I couldn't do that. My petticoats or . . . gasp! . . . an ankle might show."

Elizabeth tried a stern scowl, but her lips quivered from imprisoned laughter. "I think the sun has addled your head, Georgia. Let's take a little rest on this bench. The shade will be welcome for a few minutes."

Georgia objected. "You're a spoiler, Elizabeth."

"Sit. We're both beginning to perspire in the sun. You wouldn't want to stain that lovely gown with perspiration, would you?"

Georgia rolled her eyes as she dropped down beside Elizabeth on the bench. "That's right, you ladies ain't . . . aren't supposed to sweat."

"We ladies. You are a lady, also." She smiled a fond smile. "Sometimes. Someday soon you'll be finding yourself wanting to be a lady all the time."

"Not likely. I hate rules. Ladies can't sweat, stink, scratch, or talk about body parts. If you ask me, being a lady is—"

Elizabeth's quiet gasp interrupted. "Oh, my!"

"What?"

Elizabeth's cheeks flushed a rosy red, and Georgia perked up immediately. Something that could rattle her teacher was bound to be of interest.

"We have to go." Elizabeth pulled Georgia up and urged her along the path, back toward Greystone House.

Georgia shrugged her off. "You're acting like you just saw an Injun."

"Indian, Georgia. And don't be ridiculous. But I don't want you seen just now by Mr. Stanford."

"The famous Alexander? He's here?"

"Over there." Elizabeth had maneuvered them behind a crowd of children and their nurses—no one in Chicago seemed to raise their own little ones—and through the bodies Georgie could catch only a very inadequate glimpse of a tall man talking to another fellow mounted on a bay gelding.

"Is that him on the ground or on the horse?"

"On the ground."

"Oh, my!"

"Quit staring, Georgia." Elizabeth took her arm to pull her along the path. "Come back to the house."

"No. I want a closer look."

Curiosity fully engaged, she escaped Elizabeth's grasp and sauntered—every bit the lady, she believed—to a spot where she could get a better look at this yahoo who wanted to marry her. Alexander Stanford was not at all what she had imagined. He probably hadn't drooled a day in his life, and from the looks of his fine clothes and proud bearing, she doubted that he stunk. Georgia had imagined someone smaller, bespectacled, maybe, with greasy hair and a pudgy belly. How wrong her imagination had been! The real Alexander Stanford made her stomach flutter. Tall. Very tall. Broad shoulders beneath the fine cloth of his jacket. His fashionable hat shaded a straight nose and a firm jaw. From a distance she couldn't see the details, but she thought all the same that the face looked downright pleasing—the sort of face a woman wouldn't mind seeing on the pillow beside hers when she woke up in the morning.

"Georgia!" came Elizabeth's whispered reprimand. "You are making a spectacle of yourself. Staring is very rude. If Mr. Stanford sees you, he'll think you're forward."

"Better than being backward," Georgie quipped.

"You're impossible today."

"You've lost all your humor today."

Georgie reluctantly let herself be dragged away. A bright red still stained Elizabeth's cheeks. The breeze had tilted her hat askew, and she didn't seem to notice. Georgie had never seen the woman so flustered. She would have thought Elizabeth the Perfect would straighten a crooked hat even with a pack of Apaches bearing down upon her. She stole a glance back toward Alexander Stanford, wondering. Could it be that Elizabeth Whitman, self-proclaimed staid spinster, had a weak spot in her heart for Mr. Stanford?

No, Georgie decided. If Elizabeth fancied the fellow, she for sure wouldn't groom another woman to ambush him. If Georgie had ever wanted a man, she would have flattened any female who tried to crowd in line ahead of her. Not that she'd ever ever in her life wanted a man. Except maybe when she had been thirteen years old, a boy a couple of years older than she had been a mule skinner hauling stuff for the miners in California. He had looked mighty fine up on the driver's box, cussing those mules and acting every bit the man. Georgie had suffered a weak spot for him before he'd laughed at her for being a big, clumsy ox with pigtails—those were the very words he had used—and she'd knocked him on his ass. After that she'd decided that some gals just weren't meant to be real women, and she was one of them. Being one of the boys was easier than trying to make a silk purse from a sow's ear, as the saying went. She'd never suffered that kind of weak spot again.

Cougar Barnes flashed unexpectedly through her mind, but she immediately chased him away. She liked Cougar too much to get mushy over him.

But Elizabeth looked right mushy over Alexander Stanford. A man like him would have females flocking around him like hens around the feeding trough. And he wanted to marry Georgie Kennedy. Just imagine. Of course, the man hadn't seen her yet, so that likely would change. Or maybe not, now that she was frilled up, laced in, and the calluses on her hands were gone.

Georgie felt a hint of challenge warm her blood. In only a few days she would formally meet that fine specimen of manhood. Maybe the time had come to suck it in and cinch up her corset so she would look like a real woman.

Chapter 6

The great day came. Fourteen people had accepted Alvin's dinner invitation in addition to Robert Stanford and his son, Alexander—Alexander, the man on the auction block, Georgie mused with a silent chuckle. More likely she was the one on the auction block.

Three hours before the guests would arrive, she sat in Alvin's library reading a volume of poetry by William Wordsworth. Elizabeth had assigned her the reading. Georgie only reluctantly admitted to enjoying the poet's words. Poetry wasn't as exciting or entertaining as Mark Twain's stories. Elizabeth called it refined. Georgie called it hard work. Poetry made her think too hard, and sometimes the new ideas made her head fairly spin. She suspected Elizabeth had given her the reading simply to stop her pacing and nervous fidgeting.

Georgie sighed, turning a page without having read a word on it. Her nerves danced, making ladylike composure an impossibility. If she hadn't seen Alexander Stanford in the park, she wouldn't be nervous. She would be bored, impatient for the event to be over, and not at all curious about the man her grandfather wanted her to marry. But she had seen the man, and every time she thought of Alexander wanting to marry her, her stomach started somersaulting. Over the past few days she had applied herself with a vengeance to becoming a real woman, someone who might get a smile, a kiss, even a wedding ring from such a man. She had practiced talking to everyone who would hear her—the servants had started avoiding her she talked so much. She had walked a path in her bedroom floor, concentrating on small graceful steps instead of the ground-eating strides that were her natural gait. She had driven poor Rachel to distraction experimenting with hair arrangements. Even Elizabeth, perfectionist that she was, was weary of drilling her in manners and speech.

Alexander Stanford tormented Georgie by dangling in her mind like a tempting piece of bait plopped in front of a hungry fish. Curiosity consumed her, along with despair whenever she looked in the mirror and saw her garish red hair, the scattered freckles that no amount of lotion would erase, the too-broad mouth, the wide shoulders that could have belonged to a man, the waist that would never—no matter how painfully her corset was laced—be dainty. For all of Elizabeth's lessons and Georgie's efforts, the sow's ear was still a sow's ear as far as Georgie was concerned. Not that she actually wanted to marry Alex Stanford and stay in Chicago, but getting a chance to be noticed, to be admired, maybe to get a proposal from such a fine specimen might be nice, even if she turned the fellow down.

So Georgie sat in the library, nervous and restive, and awaited her big moment. Soon Elizabeth would fetch her to bathe and dress, but until then she was stuck with William Wordsworth.

"Ah! There you are, Georgia. Elizabeth told me you would be here." It wasn't Elizabeth who saved her from the poet, but her granddad. "Wordsworth, eh? Do you enjoy his work?"

"Oh, sure," she lied. She wasn't in the mood to argue—a gauge of her nerves. Normally Georgie liked nothing better than a good argument, especially with her grandfather.

"I'm glad I found you before you went upstairs to dress, my dear. I want to congratulate you on the fine transformation you've made. I see results especially over the last few days. You've worked hard, as you promised, and I admire a person who keeps a bargain."

"So do I," she said pointedly. "You've got a bargain to keep, too, Granddad." Several weeks ago she had stopped calling him "old man," at least to his face. The change signaled a truce of sorts.

"Kennedys always keep a bargain, girl. But you still might decide that living in a big house, sleeping in a clean bed, and having servants to wait upon you is a life superior to digging all day in the Arizona dirt and waiting for the Apaches to make mincemeat of you." He smiled craftily. "You have been enjoying yourself here more than you thought you would. Admit it."

Maybe she had, but she wasn't about to admit it to the old coot. She merely grimaced in answer.

He chuckled knowingly. Sometimes Georgie suspected uncomfortably that the man could read her mind, maybe because the same blood ran in their veins.

"Too stubborn to admit it," he said with a nod. "A Kennedy through and through. I am proud of you, Georgia. You've made such progress that soon we'll be able to dispense with your tutor and give you a bit more freedom. You would like that, wouldn't you?"

Alarmed, Georgie slammed her book shut. "Give Elizabeth the boot?"

"I wouldn't put it so crudely. Miss Whitman knew her position was temporary. I'll give her a very good reference to find another position. In fact, when Chicago sees the miracle she's wrought upon you, employers will be clamoring for her to train their children."

A cold lump of loneliness settled in Georgia's stomach. "Elizabeth stays, Granddad. As long as I live in this house, she stays."

Elizabeth was her only friend in a world that was still strange and hostile. Elizabeth knew her heart, shared her humor (most times), and at least tried to keep her from flying to pieces from frustration. Elizabeth was the only person in the world who could have ever persuaded her to wear a corset.

Alvin raised a brow. "No need to take on so, my girl. Miss Whitman won't want to stay once her job is complete. She'll find other employment, and you'll make friends with women of our own circle."

Georgia could have reminded her grandfather that Elizabeth had a mother and two sisters dependent upon her, but that wouldn't have moved him. She knew the man well enough to realize that his loyalty extended to family, close friends, and perhaps longtime household servants such as Bittles the butler and Mrs. Bolton the head housekeeper. Elizabeth he would discard without a thought.

"I'm putting my foot down, old man. Elizabeth stays as long as I do. If you want me to act like some frigging lady, then I still need her. If she gets the boot, then I go with her, bargain or not. Understand?"

Her grandfather drew himself up like an indignant rooster. Georgia rose, meeting him eye to eye. She was nearly as tall as he was, and she could rooster it up, she figured, with the best of them.

Alvin backed down first. He smiled and the tension eased. "Very well. I can see you've become attached to Miss Whitman, and obviously you need a bit more work on your manners. She will stay as long as you feel you need her."

"Good."

"I admire loyalty. It's a sterling quality, my dear. Just remember that there is a hierarchy of loyalty, and in that hierarchy, family comes first."

Georgie could have reminded him that for most of her life, her only family had been her father. Some Johnny-come-lately grandfather who ignored her until she was a ripe old twenty-three deserved far less loyalty than good friends. But she decided to save that argument for another time when she was more in the mood for a scrap.

"Perhaps you're right to keep Miss Whitman at hand," her granddad admitted. "She's done a fine job. You're going to shine tonight, Georgia. Alexander will be impressed, I think, and so will his parents." He smiled expansively. "And so will you, my girl. Any woman would want Alexander Stanford. He's a fine man. A fine, fine man."

Georgie couldn't argue with that. The butterflies in her stomach took off en masse.

Greystone House, usually about as interesting as a tomb, came alive that night as the cream of Chicago society descended upon the drawing room like a flock of gaudy geese. Busily honking geese—that's what Georgia pictured as she waited in her room and listened to the noise that floated upstairs.

"Stop looking like the condemned about to ascend the scaffold." Elizabeth watched critically as Rachel made last-minute adjustments to Georgie's upswept hair. "You're going to have fun tonight."

"Why can't you be there?"

"This affair is for intimates of your grandfather, not employees."

"You're more than an employee. You're my best friend."

Elizabeth smiled at her in the mirror and put a gentle hand on her shoulder. "You are my dear friend as well, Georgia. And I'll be up here all the while, praying that you're a huge success. I know you will be, my dear."

Georgie screwed up her face. "I'm damned nervous. Oops!"

"No need to be nervous," Elizabeth comforted. "You're the bravest woman I know, and those people down there are nothing compared to what you've faced before."

"I'd rather take on a whole rancheria of Apaches."

Elizabeth laughed. "Should I check you for weapons before you go down?"

"What I need is a bigger brain to store all the dos and don'ts you've stuffed into my head."

"You'll be fine."

Rachel joined in. "Look at you, miss. All your guests will be knocked right off their feet. Look into the mirror. You're pretty as a princess."

"Yeah, right." She looked into the mirror and saw a clumsy, pigtailed ox dressed up like a porcelain doll. The woman who looked back at her from the glass wasn't Georgie Kennedy, crack rifle shot, owner of the best damned placer mine in Arizona. She was someone unknown, not Georgie, but Georgia. Miss Georgia Kennedy was a person Georgie didn't know and wasn't sure she wanted to know.

Elizabeth laid a hand on her shoulder. "You're going to do just fine."

She did do fine, at least for a while. She managed to descend the stairs without tripping over her yards of skirts and tumbling ass over antlers into the glittering crowd milling in the drawing room. When her granddad announced her to the guests, she stiffened her spine, held up her chin, and smiled as Elizabeth had taught her. Every eye dissected her. The women looked meaner than Apaches as they searched for any flaw. The men's interest was even more disconcerting. Georgie was used to dealing with men, but not as a real woman.

Alvin escorted her around the room, introducing her proudly to one and all. "How lovely you are, my dear," said a woman named Mrs. Philpott. "You've been living out West?"

"Yes." She'd almost said *yup* instead of *yes*. Elizabeth hated it when she said *yup*.

"Where out West? San Francisco? Denver?"

"All over. Anywhere the wind blew."

"She's been with her father in Arizona," Alvin hastily added. "He traveled at lot. When he died, I asked Georgia to come live with me."

Subtly Mrs. Philpott eyed her, from her stylishly arranged red hair to the ridiculous little shoes that pinched her feet. Georgia felt her disguise peel away. Women were crafty creatures, almost impossible to fool. "How generous of you, Mr. Kennedy." The look she gave Georgie was full of pity, but only an eye finely tuned to contempt and pity— as Georgie's was—would have seen it.

Old biddy. Georgie suppressed the urge to make a face as the woman and her daughter drifted on. Elizabeth really didn't like her making faces.

After a few minutes Alvin abandoned her to her fate, or so it seemed. He took off to socialize on his own, and Georgie immediately felt like a pile of mule dung drawing flies, the flies in this case dressed in silk and satin, gold watch chains, and fancy cravats.

"I've heard so much about you," a gray-haired, bearded old codger commented.

"You must be very relieved to be back in civilization," a matron gushed.

"Your gown is simply stunning!" exclaimed another. "I believe I saw you at Madame Arnaud's some days ago—the dressmaker? I use the same one, you know. She is such an *artiste*."

Georgie sat stiffly on a chair (it was a sin to sit comfortably at these functions, Elizabeth had told her), drinking an overly sweet concoction that a soft-handed young man had brought her, and smiled until her lips were tired. The room was warm and smelled of hot bodies and cloying perfumes. Sweat dribbled in little streamlets down her spine and between her breasts—most unladylike, yet at the same time she was clammy cold. People lavished her with smiles only lip deep, meaningless compliments, sly digs, and nosy questions. More than one man leered. She wanted to teach them respect the way she would have in Prescott, by kicking their feet out from under them and letting them measure their length along her granddad's fine carpet. But she didn't dare. In civilization a body couldn't be straightforward about these things. Or so Elizabeth said.

So the first man who gave her the eye simply met with her blank stare. The second, a short time later, got a taste of the scowl that had made the men of Prescott quake for years. With the third fellow Georgie got impatient.

"If you don't take your sweaty hand off my arm, Mr. Soams, it's going to come up missing a couple of fingers." She bared her teeth in something that might pass as a grin.

Mr. Soams backed off with a little jump, his eyes wide. Georgie's only concession had been her quiet tone. If the yahoo touched her again, however, she would shout something unladylike for the world to hear.

She would rather crawl into a den of rattlesnakes than ever go to one of these hooplas again, Georgie decided.

Then the crowd in the drawing room parted for her

grandfather. Alexander Stanford was at his side. Her breath caught in her throat, and she forgot all about her sweaty spine, clammy hands, pinching shoes, and poking corset. The man was every bit as handsome as when she'd seen him in the park. Handsomer, really, now that she saw him up close. Where most men met her eye to eye, Alexander topped her by a good six inches. His shoulders were broad enough to swing an ax all day, his carriage proud, his face clean-shaven and carved as beautifully as a statue's.

As her grandfather presented him, Alexander took her fingers and raised them in gentlemanly salute. The hand that took hers wasn't a bit soft, though the nails were buffed and trimmed. His skin was toughened by work harder than wielding a pen or lifting a glass. He smiled and her heart nearly stopped. Even white teeth flashed behind chiseled lips, and dark brown eyes regarded her with genuine interest.

He bowed over her hand. "I am honored to meet you, Miss Kennedy. Your grandfather speaks very well of you."

Georgie and Elizabeth had rehearsed a dozen different scripts of this meeting, and Georgie had memorized an appropriate response to anything that Alexander might possibly say. An endless supply of polite responses were on the tip of her tongue, yet she could only give him a mute stare.

"Georgia . . . ?" her grandfather prompted.

A dizzy grin went along with her wide-eyed stare.

"Georgia . . ." Alvin's voice rose a bit with the beginnings of alarm. Alexander gave her a quizzical look.

Georgie breathed out hard and gathered her scattered senses. "Uh . . . hi." She could almost hear Elizabeth groan at her stupidity.

Alvin rushed to the rescue, or at least tried. "Georgia has been living out West. There they believe in brevity of expression."

"Do you think so?" Alexander addressed Georgia as well as Alvin. "Some of the most loquacious windbags I've ever encountered were in the West."

That piqued Georgia's interest. The fellow had actually been in the real world. "You've been West?"

"Colorado, New Mexico, California, Oregon—Stanford

Shipping stretches all across the country by rail and freight wagons. I've been on many of our routes myself."

"Goddamn! You're that Stanford Shipping!"

Alvin shut his eyes in pain.

"You fellas even go to Prescott and Fort Whipple!"

"I believe so." One brow slightly raised, he regarded her with his polite smile slightly askew. Other ears were perked their way, other eyes growing wide at Georgie's slip.

"Dinner," Alvin said hopefully. "Dinner must be ready."

On cue, Bittles announced the meal. The guests filed into the formal dining room to a lavishly appointed table where a servant stood behind each chair. Alvin did things in grand style.

Blushing furiously, Georgie accepted Alex Stanford's escort to the table. She wanted to kick herself. She also wanted to kick everyone else in the room, along with the furniture and walls. All the work she had done over the past weeks, and she still stepped in a pile of mule dung the minute the pressure turned on. Alexander Stanford must think she had the brains of a flea. If he had truly wanted to marry her before tonight, for whatever reason, he certainly wouldn't want to now.

Not that she cared. She didn't care at all. Alex Stanford could go stick his head in an anthill for all she cared.

She silently jeered at herself for the lie.

"Your grandfather tells me you have been living in Arizona Territory for the past few years. Did you like it?"

His voice turned Georgie's knees to water. Her ankle turned on the heel of her shoe, coming down upon the hem of her skirt, which jerked her stumbling up against the man who escorted her. A soft titter erupted behind her, where a Miss Hansen was coming into the dining room on the arm of her father. The titter stopped abruptly as Georgie recovered and locked eyes with the girl, who gave a tiny shriek.

Alvin looked as though he wanted to sink through the floor.

Georgie lifted her chin. "Arizona is heaven compared to Chicago."

"Do you think so? You don't care for Chicago, then?"

"Hell no." Everyone seemed to be listening even as the crowd settled itself at her grandfather's big rectangular oak table. Georgia detected more than one set of hackles rising. But by now she was getting mad. These people thought she was dirt beneath their feet, and the man she was supposed to impress oozed contempt from every pore. Who did they think they were in their fancy clothes, fancy homes, and fancy talk with their noses stuck so far in the air that they could drown in a good rainstorm?

She had just worked up a good steaming mad when Alexander touched her. He took her arm to guide her to a chair at the table, and her stomach did flips. In her wildest dreams, dreams she had never dared to acknowledge, a man such as Alexander Stanford might court her. But here he was, being polite even if he did think she was an idiot. She was still alive and in the fight, and Georgia wasn't one to surrender while breath still blew in and out of her lungs. All she had to do was impress the man. Nothing, she reminded herself, was impossible.

Be friendly, Elizabeth had advised her earlier. Be relaxed and natural. But not too natural, she had added quickly.

She was being much too natural, Georgia decided.

"Chicago's all right," she said once she was seated. "It's just different from what I'm used to."

He smiled at her, and that smile transformed his face from chiseled perfection to something human and very appealing. "If you've lived your whole life on the frontier, I can understand why you find Chicago a bit daunting. But forty years ago the place was little more than mud flats."

In Georgie's current mood, she thought the mud flats might be an improvement, but she summoned enough discipline not to say it.

A matron across the table seemed genuinely interested. "Are there Indians in Arizona Territory?"

Georgie snorted. "Behind every rock and tree."

"Oh!" a younger woman said. "You must have been scared all the time."

"You don't run around like a rabbit being scared. You just get your rifle and start shooting."

Everyone within hearing looked at her as if she'd sprouted feathers.

"You mean the men start shooting," the matron said with a tolerant smile.

"Hell, no. I'm the best shot for miles around." The forbidden word slipped out before she could stop it. Her nerves were thinking for her, not her brain.

"Very impressive," Alexander said with a straight face. But Georgie got the idea that he wasn't impressed.

The dinner careened downhill from there. The more gaffs Georgie made, the more nervous she got, and the more nervous she got, the more of Elizabeth's teachings flew right out of her mind. During the appetizer of sausage-stuffed mushrooms, she kicked off her shoes under the table because they pinched so badly, then discovered she couldn't get them back on. The little problem made her forget that a lady didn't eat with her fingers—especially a lady didn't eat greasy stuffed mushrooms with her fingers. As the dinner ticked on, Georgie gave her soup a good healthy blow before realizing that ladies didn't cool their food with such a hurricane. Then the soup slurped from her spoon to her mouth—not *her* fault, Georgie told herself. And the biscuit soaked in beef gravy was simply too tasty to eat with delicacy.

Glances, some amused, some horrified, some curious, darted her way and quickly bounced off. No one met her eyes, but they met each other's eyes with speaking looks. Red with both embarrassment and anger, Georgie felt like a small child trying to ape adult ways and making a mess of it. Tasks that had seemed easy under Elizabeth's watchful gaze were nearly impossible with these secretly jeering, mocking people lying in wait for her next blunder. They were storing up laughter to let loose when they were among their friends.

All that was bad enough, but the situation got nearly intolerable when her corset started itching. The added irritation inched her temper up several notches.

"Miss Kennedy, is something amiss?" Alexander's inquiry was polite, but he was clearly puzzled, as were several others sitting close by. By this time they were into the apple cobbler with rich cream, but Georgie was so busy squirming—as subtly as she could—that she'd ignored the dessert.

"It's my damned corset!" she hissed in a low voice. "Whoever invented these things should be shot."

The matron across the table gasped. She looked as if she might faint. Alexander's mouth twitched in what might have been suppressed laughter. A gray-haired gent sitting next to the matron harrumphed and gave Georgie a scornful scowl.

The Devil himself had hold of her, Georgie decided, and was making her pay the price for pretending to be something she wasn't. She didn't like being a woman. She was awful at being a woman, and no amount of teaching and practicing would change that.

Abruptly she rose, nearly overturning her chair. Throwing her napkin onto her plate, she thrust out a stubborn chin at the astonished faces. "'Scuse me. I'm leaving because I'm sick. Go ahead and eat your cobbler."

Unable to jam her feet back into her shoes, she fled without them, fled with nary a glance behind, cursing herself and every man and woman at the table. She should have known better than to even try.

Alex twirled a snifter of Alvin's excellent brandy and braced one hand against the fireplace mantel in the library.

"So Georgia Kennedy is the woman you want me to make my wife?" He was alone with his father, as Alvin had tactfully taken the other men to see his new pair of carriage horses, and the ladies were safely huddled in the parlor with their sherry.

Robert cleared his throat, clearly embarrassed. "She is a bit rough around the edges."

"Rough around the edges?" Alex repeated sardonically. "She's all edges! Jagged edges. Good god, Father! She is coarse, ill-behaved, barely schooled, and has absolutely no womanly virtue that I can discern. Her language would make a mule skinner salute in admiration."

"It . . . uh . . . wasn't quite that bad, I think."

"Nearly! I can't imagine that you are so desperate to

have me marry that you would accept Georgia Kennedy as a daughter-in-law. I'm surprised Alvin had the nerve to suggest it."

"Well, in Alvin's defense, I think he proposed the idea before he'd ever met the girl. And then he believed she would smooth out with a bit of tutoring. I never saw her before tonight, son. I'm embarrassed, I'll admit. Alvin assured me she was a woman of great beauty and charm."

Alex took a healthy sip of his brandy. He would need more than one snifter to mellow this evening. "She's a beauty, all right. I'll give him that."

Robert looked surprised. "You will?"

"Flamboyant with that red hair and those eyes—did you notice how green they were? And a stunning figure. She's beautiful indeed, but charm? Education, manners, gentility? Little doubt that she's more at home in a miner's camp than in a civilized drawing room."

"With time . . ."

Alexander snorted. "Time and polish won't do it. Father, there is more to a woman than beauty of face and form. More than even charm. The most important quality of a woman is grace of spirit." He pinioned Robert with skeptical eyes. "Did you see even a hint of that in Georgia Kennedy?"

Robert hesitated, then sighed. "The rawness of her comportment is only too apparent, but if you could look beyond that, Alexander, you might see strength of character and mind. Rough edges can be smoothed, with work, but character is something that lasts forever. Georgia is a Kennedy, an heiress, and granddaughter of a great friend who could be an excellent business partner."

"Ah!" Alexander finished the last sip of brandy and pointed at his father. "It's business you're thinking, is it? Alvin has been after you to form a partnership for two years, and now you'd like to do it."

"Possibly," Robert admitted warily.

"A merger of the two companies does not require a merger of families, Father. This is not the Middle Ages. If you want to deal with Alvin, then do your deal. I think a merger makes excellent business sense."

Robert got up and started to pace. "Perhaps it does, but it's not that simple, son. I want what I have built to go to someone who caries my blood. Right now you"—he skewered Alexander with a paternally indignant glare—"are the last of my line. But if you should produce an heir with the Kennedy girl, both Alvin and I will have a common heir that inherits our common business. Now, that makes sense!"

Alexander sometimes thought he understood his father, but at times like this, he knew that he didn't. He didn't share Robert's vision of dynasty. To him, a business was a lifetime concern. He didn't waste time worrying about who would inherit after he was dead. The issue certainly wasn't worth tying himself for life to a hoyden like Georgia Kennedy.

"Father," he said after a long pause. "I don't believe that we're ever going to see eye to eye on this. Frankly, I think you're being idiotic."

Robert huffed. "You have a duty to your family that you've ignored too long."

"Perhaps I do, but not with . . . with *that* woman. She's a disaster in every way. Her manners, her language—everything about her. A total disaster. No man with any self-respect would be seen with her on his arm, much less take her to the altar."

"So you won't so much as give her a chance."

Alexander knew the look on his father's face. The senior Stanford wasn't above trying to guilt his son into paying court to the woman.

Robert continued in a martyred tone. "I suppose I should stop troubling you with an old man's needs. The young seldom think of such things."

"Father, it's not going to work. I'd rather court an orangutan."

Perhaps that was an exaggeration, Alexander admitted. Miss Kennedy might look quite civilized beside an orangutan. But the statement got his point across. His father shot him an indignant look and stalked from the room.

Robert made his escape just in time, because no sooner had he left than a small thundercloud blew through the door. Alexander recognized her instantly, though he didn't remember having seen her at dinner—and he would have remembered. Miss Elizabeth Whitman, very attractive spinster lady. And from the looks of her, Miss Whitman was about to spit lightning, aimed directly at him.

Chapter 7

"You should be ashamed of yourself! I thought you were a man of discernment and wisdom, and here it turns out you are nothing better than a . . . a . . ."

Alexander raised a curious brow. "A what, Miss Whitman?"

"A . . ." Elizabeth searched for a word scathing enough, but nothing in acceptable vocabulary seemed sufficiently descriptive. She almost wished she had Georgia's freedom of language. "A person of shallow perception," she said huffily.

His mouth twitched suppressed laughter. "That *is* harsh."

She gave him a frosty look. "Your amusement does you no credit. I am serious."

"So it seems. But I fail to understand what I've done to earn such censure. And I'm curious to find you here in Greystone House. I didn't see you at dinner."

"I am employed here as companion and tutor to Miss Georgia Kennedy, a girl of lovely character which you obviously cannot discern because you, like so many of your gender, focus on a woman's shallower attributes. I have worked with Georgia for over a month," she told him stiffly, "so I have reason to appreciate her strength, courage, compassion, humor, generosity, and intelligence. You should be ashamed to judge her so harshly on such short acquaintance."

The other brow shot up. "Are we talking about the same woman? Red hair, tall, colorful vocabulary?"

"Sir, if you had lived your life in mining and railroad camps, surviving among the roughest element of humanity on little but your courage and wit, I doubt you would learn perfection of manners and speech in mere weeks. As I passed by just now, I heard your cruel summary of Georgia's deficiencies. You give no consideration to her circumstances, to her nervousness in her very first social gathering, or how hard she works to fit in to a world so new to her. I am surprised, frankly, that you are so lacking in charity."

Alexander regarded her in long, frozen silence, and Elizabeth wondered at her own boldness. Such forward behavior and speech was certainly not like her at all. But she had thought Alexander Stanford a better, wiser man. That he was not made her angry. Anger and embarrassment made her flush as his eyes seemed to pick her apart, and suddenly Elizabeth was aware of her very plain dress, the long thick braid of hair that hung unfashionably to her waist—she'd loosened it from where it had been coiled at her crown because the weight had made her head ache—and the little crease in her face where she'd fallen asleep reading *Oliver Twist*. She was in no state to be confronting a gentleman, but how could she let such a slur to Georgia pass?

Alexander released her from his gaze and went to pour himself another brandy. "I admire your loyalty, Miss Whitman. It's a fine quality. And perhaps I deserve to be taken to task."

She managed to breathe. Until now she hadn't been aware that she had stopped.

"Yet even you must admit that Miss Kennedy is not the sort of woman one expects to meet in good society."

"Unexpected is not always bad."

"Perhaps we're not discussing good and bad here. Merely appropriate and inappropriate."

"Mr. Stanford, I promised Georgia that you are such a

fine and fair man. You make me regret that I gave such a glowing character reference. Only the unwise pass up a precious jewel because it needs a bit of polishing."

He laughed, and his eyes warmed. "By heaven there is nothing more dangerous to society than a woman with wit. You are a danger, Miss Whitman, but I'll admit you're a pleasure to do battle with."

She flushed even deeper.

"I do not mean to be cruel to your student," he continued. "But you must realize that Miss Kennedy, no matter how laudable her basic character, will never be comfortable in society. The true cruelty would be to force such a life upon her. It would be like taking an infant raised among the wolves and expecting it to fit in among other human beings."

"You grossly exaggerate, sir."

"I think not. Civilized blood might run through Miss Kennedy's veins, but she lacks the all important early training. If you were not a lady, Miss Whitman, and therefore above such gaming, I would lay a wager on the table that Miss Kennedy will be a coarse, outspoken, overbold, graceless Amazon until the day she dies."

A quiet gasp outside the library door let them know their words had fallen on ears other than their own.

Georgia had been sneaking toward the now empty dining room to retrieve her abandoned shoes when voices from the library distracted her from her mission. She diverted to listen more closely, pressing an ear to the library door. The voices of Elizabeth and Alexander were as clear as if she stood right next to them listening to her teacher try to deny that Georgia was all the things Alexander said she was.

Each of Alexander's descriptive words struck Georgia like a blow. This was the man who supposedly wanted to court her. This was the man her granddad thought she should marry. He thought she was uglier than a toad and stupider than an ox. He didn't use those words exactly, but that was for sure what he meant. Her bumbling performance at the dinner painted her as something in the same class as mule snot.

Shoes forgotten, Georgia fled back up the stairs to the haven of her room. Fury warred with dismay and embarrassment. She wanted to throw something, kick something, rip something else apart—and if any of those somethings was that pompous Alexander Stanford, so much the better.

She picked up one of the pillows from her bed and punched it. "Take that, you fancified piece of chicken shit!" Again she punched, and again and again, until tears wrecked her aim and she hit the bedpost instead of the pillow.

"Ow! Goddamn it! What a friggin' . . ." There followed a string of invectives that had been dammed up for weeks. The air grew heavy with them. Georgia could almost see them fly around the room, sizzling and scorching, until they finally lost energy and faded, just as her anger lost energy and left her with only disappointment and misery, disappointment mostly in herself, and misery that she couldn't immediately flee to the life where she belonged.

A stranger stared at her from the mirror that hung over her dressing table. Who did she think she was, pretending to be that woman in the fancy dress? Red curls cascaded around her face. An emerald pendant hung at her throat—her grandmother's, Alvin had said. It was the same color as the dress, the same color as Georgia's eyes. The stone was worth more than Georgia could take from her claim in two years of hard work. Worth more than Georgia herself, who according to Alexander Stanford, was worth nothing at all because she didn't have fancy manners and she let loose with an occasional word that was too colorful for his delicate ears.

Georgia scowled at the image in the mirror and let loose a word that would have made his ears go up in smoke.

"Stupid clothes! Stupid hair! Stupid rules!"

She ripped off the dress in a fury that sent buttons flying. The frilly petticoats met a similar fate, along with the hated corset, itchy silk stockings, and delicate chemise. They all ended up in a pile on the floor, and if Georgia could have found a match, she would have started a frill-fueled bonfire right there in her room. Instead, she threw herself on the bed, wrapped herself in a quilt, and surrendered to weeping, all the time chiding herself to stop immediately. Georgie Kennedy did not cry like a little baby. Georgie Kennedy was tough as a timber wolf and stoic as an Apache. She hadn't cried that time a horse had thrown her into a patch of jumping cactus and her father had spent all day yanking needles from her flesh one by one. She hadn't cried when her favorite mule Murphy had become lunch for a pack of roving Yavapais, and she hadn't cried the day Cougar Barnes had promised to teach her to wrassle but ended up taking Evie Perkins from Fort Whipple on a picnic instead. Not that Cougar Barnes being smitten with Evie was important. The important thing was that Georgie had felt like crying, but she hadn't cried. She hadn't cried any of those times.

But now she cried over a bunch of mean-talking snobs looking down their noses at her, and more particularly Mr. Arrogant Ass Alexander Stanford calling her names—coarse, graceless, overbold Amazon. Georgie wasn't sure what an Amazon was, but from the tone of Alexander's other comments, it couldn't be anything good. Those pompous greenhorns and their uppity wives and daughters didn't know anything. They weren't worth crying over, Georgie told herself. Alexander Stanford certainly wasn't worth the waste of a single tear. But the tears kept flowing uncontrollably, and her sobs shook the bed.

Then Elizabeth's voice told Georgie she was no longer alone. A gentle hand caressed her shoulder as the bed creaked beneath her companion's weight.

"Georgia! Georgia, my dear, don't cry. Nothing has happened that calls for such weeping."

Georgie rolled sullenly from beneath the comforting hand. "I heard you and Alexander. He thinks I'm a pile of mule snot. And so does everybody else. Now maybe my granddad will let me go home, where I belong."

That was the one bright point of the evening. Now that she'd embarrassed her grandfather in front of his hoity-toity friends, he was bound to send her packing.

"You heard Alexander?"

Georgie sniffed loudly and wiped her eyes with the bedsheets. "Once everyone had left the dining room, I went back to get my shoes. I slipped them off under the chair and couldn't get them back on when I left. So I waited a good long time until I figured everyone had gone off to the parlor and such, and I was sneaking back into the dining room to fetch them. They pinch like hell"—she darted Elizabeth a wary look, but her tutor let the "colorful language" slip by—"but they cost a month's work back at the mine. I didn't want someone walking off with them."

Elizabeth sighed. "So you passed outside the library when Alexander and I were talking."

Georgie didn't bother to add that she'd had her ear glued to the door.

Elizabeth brushed back tendrils of coppery hair that had fallen loose over Georgie's face. Her touch was gentle, her smile a bit sad. "Georgia, dear, I'm so sorry you heard Alexander. He was being extremely rude and jumping to judgment most horribly, but you must understand that it wasn't you so much that he was talking about, but any woman who isn't quite as perfect as he believed his wife was. She died in childbirth three years ago, and he's not looked at another woman since."

"Oh," Georgie said. She was sorry about his wife, but his words still stung. "He thinks I'm a joke," Georgie said. "And so does everyone else."

"You exaggerate."

"You weren't there. I couldn't do anything like you'd taught me, and the more things went wrong, the less I could remember about how to talk and walk and which stupid fork to use. They all treated me like something that ought to be in a cage. So I got mad and left."

"So Mrs. Bolton told me. The servants were cheering for you, you know."

Georgie swiped her damp nose with the back of her hand. "They were?"

"Use a handkerchief, Georgia."

Georgia took the square of linen Elizabeth offered and snorted. "Too late now. Everyone knows I'm a savage."

"No, they don't. You were a bit nervous tonight, that's all. Society can be cruel, especially in a town like Chicago, which is still close enough to its frontier beginnings that people with pretense to society are eager to distance themselves from their humble roots. They will forgive you when they realize what a uniquely wonderful person you are. In no time you will be sought after by the very people who thought you beneath them tonight."

Georgia sat up and wrapped the quilt about her in a tight cocoon. "I don't want their goddamned forgiveness."

"Georgia . . . language."

Georgia thrust out a mutinous jaw. "I especially don't want Mr. Alexander Jackass Stanford's forgiveness. I wouldn't marry a piece of mule shit like him—"

"Georgia!"

"Well, that's exactly what he is." Anger began to heat her blood, and it felt good. It felt much better than embarrassment and humiliation. "What right does he have to judge me? Who does he think he is to call me those names and say I'm not good enough for the likes of him? Hell, every single man within a hundred miles of Prescott has shinnied up to me, and some that weren't single."

She didn't bother to add that they were after her gold, not her person.

"And they were better men than any of these perfumed, puffed-up dandies. Take Cougar Barnes for instance."

Except that Cougar was one of the men who hadn't been after either her gold or her person, but Elizabeth didn't have to know that.

"Cougar Barnes could whup Mr. Nose-in-the-air Stanford with one arm tied behind him. Hell, I could probably do that myself!"

Elizabeth stood up and propped hands on her hips. "Georgia Kennedy, I do believe you're overwrought."

"Nah! I'm just coming to my senses. Coarse, am I? Graceless? A goddamned Amazon? Someone not worth spitting on?"

"Georgia, really . . ."

Georgie threw off the quilt and bounded off the bed. Pacing, she felt energy flow back into her veins. "I'm going to show Alexander Stanford that he's not as smart as he thinks he is. I'm going to become the properest, finest lady he's ever laid eyes on. Hell! I'm going to be so goddamned proper that every man in Chicago is going to be drooling over the chance to kiss my big toe, including Mr. Hoity-toity Stanford. He's going to grovel at my feet, begging for me to notice him, and then I'm going to be the one doing the spitting."

Elizabeth had backed away a bit, as if afraid Georgie might sprout claws and fangs. She cleared her throat, then drew herself up with ladylike composure that Georgie wished she could copy. "Georgia, I'm sure you can become a fine lady and hold your own with the most demanding members of Chicago society, but to aim at humiliating someone—that is beneath you, dear. A true lady is gentle in nature, not vengeful."

Georgie grinned. "Then I guess I'll just have to bend the rules of ladyhood a little. Because I'm thinking if you can't join 'em, beat 'em. Then kick 'em in the butt."

Over the next two weeks Elizabeth was both amazed and concerned at the single-minded ferocity of Georgia's determination to transform herself. She could only guess at the depth of hurt that triggered such resolve. As each day passed and Georgia struggled with the nuances of deportment, polite conversation, dress, table manners, posture, and the other endless details of a gentlewoman's life, Elizabeth's admiration for her charge grew. Had she been the one who had heard such a scathing assessment of her worth, Elizabeth would have shriveled with shame and hidden herself away in the hopes of never having to face Alexander again. But Georgia, brave soul that she was, set about to make all of Chicago regret judging her so harshly. Far from hiding, she aimed to display herself for the benefit of the very man who had humiliated her.

Elizabeth wished she had more of Georgia's brass.

She suspected that Georgia's grandfather admired her efforts as well. He had been silent and surly for a day or two after the debacle dinner, but Georgia had ignored his pique, and the old man had warmed a bit when she threw herself into dressing and acting like a finishing school graduate. He had taken over as his granddaughter's dancing instructor, and Elizabeth's heart warmed to see a tentative friendship blossom between the crusty old man and the granddaughter who refused to be impressed by his bluster.

"Can't you walk on your own feet, girl?" Alvin complained during their first session. "Must you trample mine?"

"You're not stepping where you're suppose to!" Georgia accused.

"I'm stepping where I want to. The man leads the dance; the woman follows. Stop trying to lead!"

Geogia huffed. "Elizabeth is easier to dance with."

"Elizabeth is a woman. You must learn to dance with men."

"Well, then, men shouldn't be so clumsy!"

In spite of Georgia's complaints, Alvin was an excellent dancer, and Georgia possessed a natural grace that defied Alexander's assessment of her as a coarse Amazon. She learned very fast, and soon she moved elegantly in her grandfather's arms, bantering back and forth with him without a thought for the movements of the dance.

Almost two weeks from Georgia's disastrous debut, Alvin took them to the opera. The party included Elizabeth's mother and sisters as well. Alvin opined that the company of a variety of women would be instructive to his granddaughter, but the truth was that he knew the opera was a rare treat for her family. Elizabeth suspected the old man had a softer heart than he would admit. Grandfather and granddaughter were alike in that way, and many other ways as well, Elizabeth reflected.

They watched Gounod's *Faust*, from a private box that afforded them an excellent view. "I can't understand a word they're saying," Georgia complained with a grimace.

"That's because they're singing in French," Claudia explained. At seventeen, Elizabeth's sister thought the opera exceedingly romantic. "All the best operas are in Italian or French. Except of course Wagner, in German."

"Sheesh! Now I have to learn to talk in foreign languages?"

"My dear!" Elizabeth's mother Phoebe declared. "Every educated woman speaks at least French!"

Georgia rolled her eyes, and Elizabeth patted her arm. "Don't worry, Georgia. We'll concentrate on English for a while. Just enjoy the music, and I'll explain the story as we go along."

That approach worked very well. Georgia was enthralled with the soaring arias, the tender Marguerite, ardent Faust, and scheming Mephistopheles. During intermission, when her grandfather had gone to fetch them wine, she remarked, "That Mephistopheles reminds me of a saloon-keeper I met once in Santa Fe. Sleazy fellow. Big booming voice."

"I thought you lived in Arizona," Chloe said.

"Only for the last few years. My daddy worked all over. In Santa Fe he was a mule skinner."

"Eeeewwww!"

Elizabeth jumped in. "Chloe, a mule skinner drives mule teams."

"He doesn't skin them?"

"No."

"Then why is he called a mule skinner?"

Georgia laughed. "Sometimes you'd think he was skinning them, from all the cussing."

Elizabeth gave her charge a warning frown.

"What about this Mephistopheles that you knew in Santa Fe?" Claudia asked.

"His name was Zeke. Like I said, he had a big, booming voice like this fellow in the opera. I cleaned his saloon for him awhile, until he got the idea that the cleaning job included going upstairs with him for a little slap and tickle."

Phoebe, Claudia, and Chloe all gasped in unison. Elizabeth was sufficiently accustomed to tales from Georgia's colorful life that she wasn't even surprised.

"How dreadful!" Phoebe said. "You poor child! Of course you left the man's employ?"

"Not before I acquainted him with the business end of my knife."

Round-eyed, Chloe asked, "Did you stab him?"

"Not exactly. That would've got me hanged. Most people think that any woman working in a saloon—dancing or serving drinks or cleaning, it don't . . . doesn't matter—is fair game for a man. I carved a K in his fat belly, just skin deep. Now every time he pulls his pants down, that K reminds him that its not a good idea to mess with a Kennedy."

Elizabeth's mother and sisters were wide-eyed in mixed fascination and horror.

Elizabeth merely sighed. "Georgia, do you remember a few days ago we discussed topics appropriate for social conversation?"

Georgia gave her an innocent smile. "This isn't social. It's just us."

"Almost everything counts as social," Elizabeth chided.

At that very moment their private box became a good deal more social as Alvin entered bearing wine and a guest, none other than Alexander Stanford, who looked less than eager to be there, understandably. Alvin had grit to rival his granddaughter's, Elizabeth thought. He didn't give up easily. Beside her, she felt Georgia stiffen. Surreptitiously she squeezed the girl's hand.

"Look who I found in the lobby!" Alvin told them jovially. "He insisted on coming up to pay his respects."

Alexander shot a dark look toward his host, but for only a scarcely perceptible instant, then he recovered and gave all the ladies a quiet smile. Alexander Stanford's quiet smile was a symphony in itself, Elizabeth reflected.

"Good evening, ladies. Are you enjoying the opera?"

Elizabeth answered before Chloe could giggle or Claudia start gushing about opera in general and *Faust* in particular. "We are enjoying ourselves very much, thank you, Mr. Stanford."

He turned the smile on her, just her, and Elizabeth nearly had to gasp for breath. She squeezed Georgia's hand, more to support herself than comfort her charge. This was a fine time in her life to start melting over a man. She was saved by Georgia, of all people.

"It's nice to see you again, Mr. Stanford. Are your parents here as well?" Her voice hinted at frost, but not enough to be rude.

"My parents and I are just two boxes down."

"Ah." She raised one brow and smiled across at Robert, who observed them from where he sat with his wife, Lydia, and a man about Alexander's age. "So I see. Do you know Mrs. Whitman and the Misses Whitman?"

"Of course." He bowed briefly to Phoebe, then Elizabeth and her two younger sisters.

"Why don't you sit with us awhile?" Alvin suggested. "We have an extra seat, as you see."

Elizabeth felt Georgia stiffen, but only because she was holding the girl's hand. No one else would have noticed a thing. She was performing flawlessly, exactly as a lady should behave.

Exactly as a trained bear might behave came waltzing into her mind. An unexpected stab of regret dimmed her enjoyment of her pupil's perfection. What a shame, she thought, that someone as bright and original as Georgia Kennedy had to present herself as someone very different than who she was in order to gain acceptance.

"Do sit," Georgia seconded.

Only Elizabeth heard the tension underlying the invitation.

"For just a moment."

He sat in the one empty seat, next to Claudia, who looked as though she might faint from a sensory overload, the silly girl. Elizabeth felt a moment's sympathy for Alexander, trapped as he was with a woman he had insulted, another woman who had roundly upbraided him for it, two ingenues who might break out in fits of giggles at any moment, and a crafty old man who still schemed, obviously, to put a matrimonial noose around his neck.

"You are looking very well, Miss Kennedy. Are you enjoying your stay in Chicago?"

For a moment Elizabeth feared that Georgia might tell the truth in a descriptive burst of colorful language, but the girl held to her role.

"I'm getting used to it," she said simply.

"I would have to say it suits you." His smile was sincere. "You are blooming, if I may be so bold."

Georgia seemed taken aback by the compliment, and Elizabeth was surprised, also. Alexander's tone was genuine, though, and when she thought about it, she realized that it should be. Georgia was indeed blooming. She had been attractive on the night of the dinner disaster, but since then, her attention to the details of her appearance, posture, and speech had made her a beauty. With her gold-red hair, green eyes, and skin that had been creamed and pampered to a pearly luminescence, she was easily the most spectacular young woman in the theater. Alexander appeared to have just noticed.

Alvin looked pleased enough to float up to the ceiling.

"You're a fancy one with words, aren't you?" was all Georgia said, and her eyes were suspicious.

"Only when it's called for, Miss Kennedy."

A few moments later Alvin contrived to herd everyone out of the box on the pretense of introducing the Whitman ladies to a friend who had been a benefactor of Henry, Phoebe's late husband and the girls' father. His angling to leave Georgia and Alexander alone was blatant, but it worked, for no one had the courage to be rude to the old man, even Alexander.

Georgia felt her heart sink to her toes as the others departed. A painful silence fell, stretching into long moments of tension. Alexander's eyes regarded her steadily, speculatively, as if not quite believing she was the coarse, graceless Amazon who spoiled her granddad's formal dinner. Frantically she tried to recall the indignation that had set her on a determined road to ladyhood. She summoned the anger and hurt that every thought of Alexander Stanford burned into her heart. But what responded to her call was merely a pale reflection of the emotion that formerly had sent her reeling.

Alexander finally broke the silence. "Miss Kennedy, I think I owe you an apology."

She merely looked at him in tight silence.

"On the night we last met, you heard words that were

never intended for your ears, words that I never should have uttered. That I thought you safely in your room is no excuse. Saying such things was unforgivably cruel and unjust. What you heard was the childish tantrum of a man who considers himself ill-used by fate and unduly pressed by his parent. My words were not so much a reflection upon you as a diatribe against those who seek to interfere in my life without my leave."

Anyone who believes that would buy a three-legged mule, Georgia thought. But she merely smiled. Her indignation was heating up just enough to warm her brain. "Don't think a thing of it, Mr. Stanford. I wasn't hurt a bit. Where I come from we don't pay much mind to the opinion of jackasses."

So much for being a lady.

Surprisingly, he chuckled. "Well said, Miss Kennedy. I can see that any man who dares cross swords with you will come away bloodied. In this case I deserved to be pricked."

His self-effacement began to win her over. "I can't much fault a man who says honestly what he thinks. Keeping quiet is a lady thing I'll never learn."

"Really? Is silence a requirement for ladylike deportment? I vow most ladies of my acquaintance cluck about like hens. One can scarcely get a word in."

Her lips twitched with the beginnings of humor. "One is not permitted to be tactless, prying, overly curious, loud, or unbecomingly lo . . . lo . . . loquacious."

He smiled. Alexander Stanford had a smile, Georgie noted, that could melt the gold right out of a quartz vein.

"If that is so, then that lesson hasn't been given to most of the ladies in Chicago."

"At least Chicago ladies don't start cussing when they get nervous."

He laughed out loud. "You are an original, Miss Kennedy."

That certainly wasn't how he had described her before. Emboldened by his unexpected openness, she ventured into deeper water. "I think the word you used before was *Amazon*." For her own sake she left out *graceless* and *coarse*.

His brow went up.

"What the hel . . ." *Oops!* "What in heaven is an Amazon, Mr. Stanford?"

He had the grace to flush. "You have a distressingly excellent memory, Miss Kennedy. An Amazon, as it happens, is a formidable female warrior."

"Oh." If that was an Amazon, she didn't mind him calling her that. "Well, you were right about that."

He still deserved to sweat for the other things, though. She flashed him the smile she'd practiced in the mirror with Elizabeth by her side—not so big to be goofy, and not so small to be tentative. Elizabeth said she had a smile that could turn a man to jelly. Georgie decided that she wouldn't mind turning Alexander Stanford to jelly.

"I'm beginning to believe you're formidable indeed, Miss Kennedy."

Good. "And I know what you mean about people butting into your life without a by-your-leave. Take my granddad, for instance. You and I both know that old coot is plotting to get us hitched. I apologize for that. It's a silly idea. Granddad should know that I'm not a regular lady who's been raised like an indoor flower on somebody's windowsill. I need more than a pretty face, fancy manners, and a fat bank account in a man."

"Indeed."

The word came out a bit choked. Georgie smiled innocently. One skirmish for him, and one for her. The score in the war was even.

Or at least the score would have been even had Georgie just then not suffered a surprise that complicated her battle plans, for staring at her from a private box across the opera house was none other than Cougar Barnes.

Chapter 8

Georgie slept very little that night. How could she sleep after the evening she'd had? First Alexander Stanford makes an appearance, handsome as the devil himself with those warm brown eyes, thick black hair, and wagonloads of charm. He'd made her knees go weak again, just as he had that night of the dinner. Even after calling her names and laughing at her, he still made her knees go weak, which just went to show that she wasn't nearly the rock of steadiness that she thought. She hated that the man still made her goosey after what he'd done. On the other hand, the unfamiliar giddiness that swept her when those eyes turned her way was a kick, kind of like swallowing a snootful of Big Mike's rotgut. The whole thing was very confusing.

And then there was Cougar Barnes. Georgie lay in her bed, staring into the dark, searching her memory for the exact moment that she'd seen him. At the time she'd been sure the man was Cougar, but likely she'd been wrong. Not many men looked like Cougar, with his tall frame and ax-handle broad shoulders. Not to mention the thick mass of wheat-colored hair that always corkscrewed out of control.

The man had been across the opera house, a good distance away. She had sharp eyes that could pick out a squirrel at two hundred paces, but this time she must have been mistaken. This fellow's hair had been the familiar sunburst, but it didn't bush around his shoulders like Cougar's hair. And while the man appeared tall and broad-shouldered, what could a person really tell about size at that distance? Cougar couldn't be here in Chicago. What the hell would he be doing in Chicago?

Yet the fellow had looked right at her, and he'd smiled that cocky, familiar smile, a crooked smile that quirked up on one side and sometimes made Georgie feel as if her feet were coming right off the ground. Even across the opera house that smile had made her feet tingle. What if the man had actually been Cougar Barnes? Why would he be here? Was he looking for her? Had something dreadful happened to Essie, or to the claim, that he had to make the long journey east to tell her in person?

Then the obvious struck her. He was worried about the claim she'd sold him. He didn't trust her to straighten out the mess, and he'd come to spy on what she was doing. Her promise wasn't worth a pile of mule shit to Cougar, damn him! And here Georgie had thought they were special friends.

Not only had Cougar trailed after her because he didn't trust her, he didn't have the brass to face her up front. Instead, he sneaked about and smiled at her from a crowd of strangers across the wide gulf of an opera house, well out of her reach. Damn him, anyway! If he thought she was double-dealing him, he ought to tell her to her face.

Georgie wrenched her mind away from Cougar, forcing it back to Alexander Stanford and the opening skirmish in her campaign to bring him to his knees. All in all, she thought things had gone well. She'd called the man a jackass and gotten away with it. He'd apologized for running off at the mouth, and she'd looked into those dark eyes and stayed cool as an icicle in January.

Icicles in January—damn! That had been a romp, when she and Cougar had been looking at a new batch of mules at Sal Hawkins's corral and discovered a line of long icicles along the north eaves of the barn. Cougar had showed her how to play a tune on the things—at least it was close to a tune. More laughter than music had come from their tapping on the ice. Cougar could be a hoot when he wanted. He could also be dangerous as a mean old javelina boar. A person wanted to keep Cougar Barnes on the friendly side. He wasn't the spiteful sort, but once his dander was up, all hell could break loose.

But damn! She was supposed to be thinking about Alexander. Cougar kept butting into her mind. She would have to set him straight about trailing after her to Chicago, but right now, Georgia had other things to attend to, such as showing this lot of Chicago snobs, especially Alexander, that she could be more of a lady with one hand tied behind her back than any of the simpering, useless females who had snickered at her at Alvin's party. Hell but she would wager that Cougar's eyes had bugged out when he got a gander of her dressed to kill at the opera. . . .

And so the rest of the night went, not in sleep, not in planning her next skirmish with Alexander, but in reliving memories of the odd friendship that had grown between her and Cougar. In the small, dark hours of early morning she finally drifted to sleep, there to wrestle with dreams about the man.

Two days later Georgia and Elizabeth braved a foggy September morning to walk along the lakeshore path and listen to the melancholy sound of foghorns on the lake. Not many others strolled along the well-used walkway, but Georgia enjoyed the cool, soft damp so different from Arizona, where everything was sharp—the heat, the cold, the dry, crackling air that sucked the moisture from a body faster than a fox sucking eggs. She wouldn't want to live here where the damp was a constant wet licking at clothes and skin, blurring the horizon and even turning a clear sky a mushy white. But at times, such as that foggy morning, the moist air could be a welcome kiss on the face, leaving dewdrops clinging to eyelashes and brows. The swirling fog turned the world to mystery. Every bush and tree became a surprise, every sound magnified.

After a short time walking, a real surprise materialized from the mist. Cougar Barnes, unmistakable this time, strolled toward them smiling his crooked smile and doffing his hat just as if he were some Chicago swell. Georgia felt as though someone had whacked her over the head with a tree limb. She battled an urge to flee—the coward's way out. But neither could she continue forward. Her feet were anchored as if in quicksand.

"Morning, ladies."

"Good morning, sir," Elizabeth said cordially.

Georgia's mouth opened, but nothing came out. Her old world crashed into the new one, and she didn't know how to talk. Cougar would surely laugh at the high-toned way of speaking that Elizabeth expected of her, but Elizabeth would think she'd gone loco if she reverted to being her old self. The result tumbled her into a limbo where she was no one at all.

"Surprised to see me, Georgie? Don't I even get a hello?"

Elizabeth looked from Georgie to Cougar. "Are you two acquainted?"

"I thought we were." Mischief laced Cougar's voice.

If that didn't cap it! He was laughing at her. Georgie heard a big guffaw hidden in his voice.

The hot burn of embarrassment jerked her from limbo. "Cougar Barnes, I surely didn't expect to see you here."

Elizabeth looked a question at her.

"Elizabeth Whitman," she said by way of formal introduction, as she'd been taught, "may I present Cougar Barnes, from Prescott, Arizona and parts nearby? Cougar and I go back a ways."

Elizabeth smiled at Cougar with that particular warmth that women seemed to reserve just for him. "I'm pleased to make your acquaintance, Mr. Barnes. Georgia has spoken of you in glowing terms."

A mistake, obviously.

"I'm happy to hear it." He tipped his hat like some Chicago swell and shot Elizabeth that dazzling smile he did so well. The jackass had never bothered to shine that particular ladykilling smile on her, Georgie grumped to herself. He saved it for real women. "She's also mentioned you, Miss Whitman, in letters she sent home to Prescott."

Georgie almost gasped, remembering her references to

Cougar in her letters to Essie. She might well have sounded like she missed him. "You read my letters?" she demanded, accusing. "Those letters were for Essie."

"Essie can't read, Georgie. She had to get someone to read them to her." For Elizabeth's benefit, he explained. "Essie is Georgie's partner back home. She's keeping the mine going while Georgie's away." He turned an amused eye upon Georgie. "It looks as though Chicago agrees with you, Georgie. You're polished up brighter than a gold nugget."

He was polished up some himself, now that Georgie had a moment to notice. The hair that had scraggled down to his shoulders was now cut short to lie on his head in burnished gold waves, the neckline just brushing over his collar. His beard, once a yellow bush sprouting from his face, now was neatly trimmed, revealing the shape of a determined jaw and the curve of a frankly beautiful mouth. But no one was going to tweak Cougar about being prettier than the average girl, given the breadth of his shoulders and the size of his fists. Those shoulders, Georgie noticed, very nicely filled out the handsome tailored coat he wore, and his trousers did absolute justice to his muscular legs.

Yes, indeed! Georgie was not the only Arizonan polished up like a new penny. Georgie had to fight a sudden attack of shyness. This man was a different Cougar than the one she had known these past years.

Elizabeth saved them from an awkward silence. "Did Georgia say your name was Cougar, Mr. Barnes? That's a very unusual name, I must say."

"The real name is Cooper, Miss Whitman. Cooper Barnes. Originally from New York City. I earned the soubriquet several years ago when I got jumped by a cranky mountain lion down on Hassayampa Creek south of Prescott."

"Oh, my! Were you badly hurt?"

"I came away from the fight better off than the mountain lion."

"Gracious!"

Oh, my! Gracious me! In her mind Georgie mimed the breathless, overwhelmed female clutching her hand to her heart. Elizabeth was entirely too impressed with Cougar. You wouldn't ever catch Georgie swooning like an idiot over a man just because he'd killed a lion with his bare hands—or maybe he'd had a knife. She didn't remember. It just went to show how little she was impressed by such things. Hell, she could have probably performed the same feat, given a bit of luck.

"Mr. Barnes, you aren't by any chance related to *the* Barnes family of New York—Trevor Barnes, of the banking empire?"

"Indeed I am. Trevor and Margaret are my parents. But since I was not inclined to take my place in the family business, I'm afraid I'm considered a bit of a black sheep."

"So you prefer the mountain-lion-infested wilds to the shops and theaters of New York City?"

"You would be surprised to discover how rewarding frontier life can be, Miss Whitman, and I don't refer to monetary gain, though of course fortune is a reason that many people venture there."

"I wouldn't be surprised at all, Mr. Barnes, as Georgia has filled my head with tales of the West. It must be truly beautiful. I believe I would like to see it someday, if I could work up the courage to venture so far from civilization and safety."

Cougar chuckled. "I'm sure you have courage to spare, Miss Whitman. I sometimes think that city living takes more courage than braving the frontier."

His gaze swung her way, and Georgie endured a confused mix of emotions. *She* had never known Cougar was the son of some rich family in New York, despite their years of acquaintance. *She* never got that sort of gentlemanly behavior from him—the hat-tipping, the respectful conversation, the compliments. Their conversations had always consisted of jibes and teasing, with absolutely no respect attached. Cougar would never dream of telling Elizabeth that her hair was red enough to set her brains on fire, or that she sounded like a braying donkey when the spring pollen gave her a runny nose and sore throat.

"What are you doing here?" she demanded, not caring that she sounded rude. If he'd come trailing after his mining claim, then they could have it out right here before Elizabeth became so impressed with his gentlemanly act that she ended up a steaming puddle on the path. "You promised to look after Essie and the claims, so why aren't you in Prescott?"

"Georgia..." Elizabeth's tone was a warning about manners, but right at that moment, Georgie didn't care.

"Elizabeth, Cougar and I need a few minutes to hash something out."

Georgie could almost see Elizabeth pray for patience.

"Georgia, that really wouldn't be proper, even if you are old friends."

"Well, then, if you've got to stay, close those delicate ears, because there's going to be some cussing going on."

Elizabeth's back stiffened, but she stayed. Georgie turned her vexation upon Cougar. "Well, Coug, answer the question. Don't you know it's rude to keep a lady in suspense?"

His eyes—as blue as the Arizona sky—actually twinkled with amusement, which sharpened her vexation. "And here I thought a single, footloose fellow didn't have to answer to a woman's demands."

"You came looking for me, Cougar. I didn't go hounding after you."

He smiled. "Well, now, you caught me out, Georgie." He threw up his hands in mock surrender. "But I'm not hounding after you, girl. To tell the truth, I'm in Chicago to visit my uncle and cousin. Uncle Theodore is big in the railroad business, and he's looking for advice on conditions in Arizona for railroad expansion. And just incidentally, the burden of having too much money weighs on the man's soul. He just might want to invest a pile in a nice ranching venture in Chino Valley." He gave her a sour look. "Since my mining prospects look pretty dim, I thought I should be on the lookout for some other source of funding."

Georgie felt a blush rise, along with her temper. She glanced sidelong at Elizabeth, who was trying hard not to look curious, then back at Cougar. "I thought we were friends. Don't you trust me to take care of that?"

With an irritating shrug of ax-handle shoulders, he replied, "Trust has to be earned, Georgie. In this matter, you have a ways to go."

"You're a fine one to talk about trust. You promised to stick around and look after Essie and the mine."

"Essie's fine. She's got Jose Gutierrez and Luis Oliveras helping her out at your claim, and every man-jack in northern Arizona knows that if they mess with them, I'm going to make them sorrier than hell. Jake Settle is digging just enough on the hardrock vein to keep the claim good, for which I'm keeping him in food and liquor, I'll have you know. So if you don't get this mess straightened out soon, you're going to owe me even more than you do already."

"The mess is straightened out. If you'd been paying attention to the letters I wrote Essie, you'd know that I struck a deal with my granddad. The claims are mine free and clear after a year of me jumping to his tune in Chicago."

He shook his golden head. "A year's a mighty long time, Georgie. It occurred to me that I might be able to move things a little faster."

She bristled. "Keep your nose out of my business, Cougar." Here she'd all but sold a year of her life to make good on getting that frigging claim to Cougar, and for him that wasn't good enough. Naturally he thought he could arrange things better.

"The way I see it, this is my business as well as yours."

Her eyes narrowed. "I can't take you down like you deserve, because my friend Elizabeth is here and she gets upset when I don't mind my manners. Bloodshed isn't her idea of ladylike behavior."

Cougar had the nerve to grin. "Georgie, I've never seen you accused of ladylike behavior."

Elizabeth dived in to save the day. "Mr. Barnes! I take offense at your manner—or should I say lack of manners!"

Georgie threw him a smug look. Now he was going to learn what *she* endured day in and day out.

But Cougar immediately came to heel, touching his hat deferentially and with a certain amount of chagrin. "I beg pardon, Miss Whitman. Georgie and I have a road that goes a long way back, and we've gotten accustomed to speaking frankly with each other."

"No matter how far back your road goes, it's no excuse for rudeness to a lady. And Georgie is every bit a lady. She deserves due courtesy."

So there! Georgie scorched him with snapping eyes. *Take that!*

Elizabeth continued in a milder tone. "We were out taking some exercise, Mr. Barnes. If you'd care to join us, you're certainly welcome." She gave her pupil a cautionary glance, but strolling the path with Cougar was just fine with Georgia. She'd show him just how fine of a lady she could be. Maybe he'd show her some of the respect he gave Elizabeth.

They walked on in company. The fog was lifting, the day growing warmer, and a few more strollers were taking the air. Cougar and Elizabeth talked of socially acceptable inconsequentials—the weather, the new buildings going up in the town, the Cincinnati Red Stockings, who were touring the country with baseball players actually paid to play the game, an innovation which had very little chance of catching on, Elizabeth opined.

Georgie had little interest in such talk. She wanted to show Cougar how wrong he was in disparaging her ability to act like a lady. After all, if she couldn't impress the hell out of her friends, then how could she hope to impress Alexander Stanford?

In a daring opening move, she threaded her arm through Cougar's, as if she was so damned ladylike that she couldn't walk without assistance from a man. The muscles beneath the fine fabric of his coat caught her a bit by surprise. She was becoming accustomed to soft living and soft men. A fellow didn't grow muscles like Cougar's sitting behind a business desk by day and attending musicales by night.

Cougar looked down at her, startled.

"The fog has turned the path slippery, don't you think so, Elizabeth?" Georgie said by way of excuse.

"It is a bit slippery."

Georgie made sure her steps fit the lilting, feminine gait

that Elizabeth had drilled into her, not the mile-eating stride that let her keep up with any man, no matter how long-legged. She hoped Cougar noticed what a graceful, swaying reed she was. Those were the very words Elizabeth had used to describe how she should move.

He didn't appear to. She stifled the urge to bump against him with the feminine sway of her hips, because that would probably be carrying things too far. Instead, she tried to think of something to say, something clever and light, flirty but still proper. Elizabeth had told her many times that men did not approve of ladies talking of interesting things such as how President Grant was doing during his first few months in office, or the business troubles of the opera house's entrepreneur, Albert Crosby. Women were expected to be entertaining but circumspect, and while Georgie could be entertaining, circumspect was certainly not one of her strong points.

"Did you enjoy the production at the opera house the other night?" She couldn't get much safer than that.

"I did. And you ladies?"

"Tremendously," Elizabeth answered. "Mr. Crosby, the manager, often brings rather inappropriate entertainment to his theater, but this was true opera—a treat for both eyes and ears."

Now why couldn't Georgie think of something fancy like that? "It was a very genteel entertainment," she ventured, then added, "Alexander enjoyed it as well." Just to let Cougar know that as a lady, she had made a very high-class association with a true gentleman. He didn't need to know that Alexander had hardly considered her a lady on their first meeting.

A small frown creased his brow. "That was Alexander Stanford I saw you with, wasn't it?"

Georgie put a bright smile on her face. Let Cougar wonder if she and Alexander were a couple. "Yes, it was. The Stanfords are close friends of my granddad. They've been ever so nice to me." She nearly simpered.

"Do you know Alexander, Mr. Barnes?" Elizabeth asked politely.

"We were together in school for a time in New York,

and his family and mine did some business before I left to go West."

"You should get reacquainted," Georgie advised. "He could introduce you to all the best families in Chicago."

Both Cougar and Elizabeth cast her quizzical looks.

"But then of course, so could I."

Elizabeth frowned.

"I met a whole pack of very nice people at a dinner my granddad gave me." That was an exaggeration in more than one way, but it was Cougar's fault she was forced to stretch the truth. "If you're going to be around for a while, I'll ask Granddad to invite you to the next party he gives, and of course your uncle and cousin, too."

He raised a brow ever so slightly. "I may want to call upon your grandfather before he gets around to giving you another party." For Elizabeth's benefit, he explained. "Georgie and I had some unfinished business when she left Prescott."

Georgie sighed. They were back to the damned mine. The man was as single-minded as a mule headed for a bucket of grain.

Cougar had walked the promenade along the lakeshore every morning since he had arrived in Chicago, even though the fashionable pathway was a half hour's ride from his uncle's home in the Lincoln Park area. Discovering where Alvin Kennedy lived was no trouble, as he was a well-known man in the city, both socially and in the business world. He could have directly sought an interview with the man and put the problem of the claim before him. His uncle had a certain stature in the town and could have arranged matters easily enough, but Cougar wanted to see Georgie first. Going to her grandfather before talking to her would have seemed too much like going behind her back.

So, knowing that most of fashionable society strolled regularly along the lakeshore, he made it a point to walk there every day, sometimes several times a day. And here she was on this foggy morning, sashaying along as though she were truly part of Chicago society, and the first sight of her made Cougar feel as though he'd been kicked in the head by a mule. Who would have thought that Georgie Kennedy would have cleaned up to look like a high-toned heartbreaker? If not for her distinctive gold-red hair, she might not have been the same girl who had been all but dragged away from Prescott by her grandfather's lackey lawyer. Her face had lost its tan, and the rough, weather-reddened skin now was smooth and unblemished as a pearl, colored only by a slight flush of—was that embarrassment or a delicate application of rouge? Georgie using cosmetics? The very notion was as unlikely as old Skillet Mahoney putting on a dress and dancing a jig on Big Mike's bar. And her figure—lord above! He'd always known Georgie would look like a woman if she would trade her overalls for a dress, but no one could have suspected that she would look so much like a woman.

But for all the changes, there could be no mistake. This was Georgie, with the same emerald eyes and the curvy too-large mouth that could dazzle with a smile or spit out a curse that would curl a mule skinner's hair. The watery Chicago sun hadn't banished the sprinkle of freckles on her nose and cheeks, and Miss Whitman's schooling hadn't rid her of the way her chin thrust forward when she was annoyed. And she did seem annoyed to see him.

The quick burn of temper that flushed her face during his small talk with Miss Whitman was vintage Georgie, as was the demand that he explain his presence, as if she now owned the town and he was an interloper. In the years he'd known her, and probably in the years before she and her father had come to Arizona, Georgie's life had been a struggle—a struggle against the hardships of frontier living and also against the hard-edged people of the frontier who could make life hell for a woman who didn't quite fit into any accepted mold. She wasn't a proper female, yet neither was she one of the loose women who made a living off the woman-hungry men of the West. No one knew quite what Georgie was, but that didn't stop nearly everyone from either making fun of her, trying to reform her, or in the case of some of her more narrow-minded sisters, pointedly crossing the street rather than encountering her in town.

The result was a Georgie who was rather hard-edged herself, quick to defend herself, and equally fast to strike out if she felt threatened. Chicago hadn't softened her a bit, and somehow, Cougar was grateful to see it, because he knew the bluster defended a wealth of humor, courage, and warmth. He'd known her too long to believe her saber-rattling. Nevertheless, the Georgie he walked along the lakeshore in Chicago wasn't the same woman as the girl who'd crowed about her victory when she'd beat him arm wrestling nearly three months past. Gone was the straightforward, down-to-earth ragamuffin. Gone was the brash, devil-may-care attitude, the bold humor, the laughter in her eyes. After a flash of the old Georgie, an unfamiliar woman rose to the surface, mincing and posturing like a society belle, flirting, putting on airs. The little idiot was allowing herself to be made over into the insipid mold that society thought was ideal womanhood, a pasteboard cutout of a person not worthy to wear the same skin as the real Georgie Kennedy. The very idea made Cougar boil. He didn't care much for society's ideals and molds. That was why he had left a secure future in New York for a very uncertain future on the frontier.

He could tell that Georgie was steaming, also. Georgie liked to do everything herself, and she got her dander up when someone horned in on what she claimed as her job, her business.

Well, that was just fine, Cougar told himself. Let the little besom throw a fit. Maybe it would knock her off her feminine, flirty high horse.

He continued with the ladies until they circled around to reach the imposing stone mansion that was the Kennedy home. Throughout the little stroll, Georgie had wavered between showing off her new self and reverting to the Georgie he knew. Reference to the mining claim that should be his put a crack in her new polish, and Cougar was glad to see it. The old Georgie was there beneath the smooth, pearly skin, fancy clothes, and newborn feminine wiles.

When he deposited the women at their doorway, Cougar touched Georgie's arm. "A word with you?"

Miss Whitman, ever vigilant, frowned a warning. She seemed to be a lady with a good head on her shoulders, but what she didn't realize was that all her tutoring and watchfulness were unnecessary. Georgie and he had slept together on the ground next to a campfire, they'd huddled together with Essie on Georgie's bunk the time he'd been caught at the cabin by an unexpected winter storm—using body heat to keep warm. Compared to past improprieties, what was a few minutes alone on the stoop of her grandfather's house?

He spread his arms in a gesture of innocence and promised the pretty watchdog, "We won't move from plain sight, Miss Whitman. Just a few minutes?"

"Of course. It was lovely making your acquaintance, Mr. Barnes. I'm sure Mr. Kennedy would welcome your calling any time." Still looking uncertain about leaving her charge with no protection, she left them in privacy.

Cougar didn't give Georgie opportunity for the first attack. "What the hell are you doing?" he demanded.

She stuck her freckled nose in the air. "A gentleman doesn't cuss around a lady."

"Cut it out, Georgie. You're no lady, no matter how fancy you dress and talk, and I gave up being a gentleman years ago. I want to know what you think you're doing."

"What do you mean?"

"I mean look at you! You're simpering like Gold Dust Gertie on the make, bragging about all your rich friends and parties, acting as if the only thing on your mind is your hairstyle." He snorted in disgust, getting madder the more he talked. "The way I remember things, you left Prescott saying you were going to give her grandfather hell, straighten out the matter of the claims, then come back to Arizona."

"That's still the plan."

"Doesn't look like it to me."

"Well, that shows how much you know, doesn't it? For your information, these sorts of things take some delicacy and smart thinking. A body can't just barge in like a cranky bear and start making demands, especially when my granddad happens to hold all the cards."

"Delicacy?" Cougar was madder than he ought to be, but he didn't stop to wonder why. He swept his eyes scornfully over her expensive walking dress and useless frippery of a hat that perched on her blazing hair. "Three months ago you were digging through gravel for a living in between the times you weren't fighting off Indians and wildlife, cussing out your mules, or skinning squirrels for your dinner. Now you talk about delicacy?" He just barely stifled the urge to spit. "Excuses is all I'm hearing. I thought you were strong enough to stay true to yourself and your friends, not get sucked under by a lot of soft living and fancy doings. Guess I was wrong."

Hands on hips, she looked as if she wanted to kick him. The old Georgie would have without giving it a second thought. "You miserable lamebrained jackass! You've got no right to get after me, and anyway, you've got it all wrong! I'm coming back."

"Really, Miss I'm-A-Goddamned Lady Now? Are you going to work your claim dressed in petticoats and satin slippers? Maybe fight off Apaches with a hat pin?"

"It ain't your business if I do!" Her face flamed at the slip. She corrected herself through gritted teeth. "It isn't your business if I do."

"Wrong, Georgie. You and everything you do are very much my business until I have the claim I paid for."

"If you read my letters to Essie, you know I talked the old man into signing over the claims if I stay here a year. So what are you whining about?"

"A year! You call that fixing the problem? In a year I could take enough gold out of that quartz vein to buy a starter herd."

"What difference does a year make, you piece of mule shit? You're a fool if you start running cattle before the Apaches get their hash settled."

"That's my call, not yours."

"Well, tough potatoes! That's the way it is. I've said all I'm going to say, so I'm going in. I don't want to see your ugly face around here bothering my granddad."

He put a hand on her arm to stop her from turning toward the door. "I'm going to talk to Alvin, Georgie."

She bristled. "Don't you dare come around here, Cougar Barnes! You'll make me look like a fool, and even maybe get the old man to change his mind about handing over the claims."

"Georgie—"

"Just have some patience! I'd have patience if it were you in this mess. You know I would. What about the time my father pulled you out of that sinkhole up by Big Bug Creek? Did I let go of my share of the rope just because my hands had a few blisters? No, I didn't. I held on, even though it hurt. And what about when I kept Ted Riley from stealing your best mule that time he got so liquored up he didn't even know his name? Don't you owe me for that one?"

He shook his head. He wanted to stay angry. Anger was a defense against something else he might feel at the sight of her. Cougar wasn't sure just what that something was, but it was dangerous.

"And here you think I'm going to cheat you out of your goddamned claim? You ought to be ashamed to think I was that kind of a low-down snake."

Cougar tried to answer, but Georgie was working on a full head of steam. "And who are you to laugh at me for dressing and acting like people expect a woman to dress and act, you two-faced skunk? I've seen you sashaying around with Evie Perkins. And with Louisa Rawlins up at Fort Whipple when Captain Rawlins isn't looking. Louisa wears enough petticoats to choke a sow bear, and her giggle is enough to tempt a person to turn her over to the Indians, I swear. So where do you get off sneering at me for acting feminine for a change? For your information, you jackass, I *am* a woman. I always have been a woman, and I always will be, even if I am better than men at most things. If you're too thickheaded to realize that, it's not my problem!"

With an indignant sniff, she shrugged off his hand, marched into the house, and slammed the door behind her. Cougar stared after her, feeling a bit stunned. Then he couldn't help but smile. Her tirade ate away at his anger. Staying mad was too difficult, because this was Georgie, indeed, the Georgie he knew and . . . and what? He was relieved to find her still alive and kicking beneath all the feminine fripperies and newborn manners. That jolt of relief made him wonder if he had really come to Chicago seeking his right to the claim, or even to persuade his relatives to invest in his ranch. Had business just been an excuse?

For a moment he felt off balance. Of course he had come here on business. Seeing Georgie all gussied up had shocked him into pure confusion. That was the problem—all that clean creamy skin and bright shining hair, and that dress showing off eye-catching curves. Maybe, he thought, he could get used to Georgie in a dress, as long as she didn't bury the genuine gutsy Georgie where he couldn't find it.

Feeling more lighthearted than he had since Georgie had left Prescott, Cougar whistled his way toward the lakeshore path. For now, he would do as the little troublemaker asked and stay away from Alvin. But only for now. He would stick around and keep track of things, especially keep track of Georgie, just to make sure that no one was taking advantage of her and that her grandfather was treating her right.

After all, they were friends, and what were friends for?

Chapter 9

Georgie stayed mad for a week. She was mad, of course, because Cougar threatened to pester her grandfather about the claims when he should be thanking her for sacrificing a year of her life to get the matter settled. She was not mad because he failed to be impressed by the new Georgie, no, the new Georgia. A boy's name hardly fit the woman she saw reflected in the mirror these days, not Georgie, but Miss Georgia Kennedy, dressed fancy like a picture in one of those ladies' magazines, with smooth skin, pinned-up hair, and ladylike demeanor. From now on, Georgie vowed to think of herself as Georgia, because that was who she was. Georgia—a member of the fairer sex, feminine, proper, and deserving of respect from gentlemen.

Cougar said she was putting on airs and getting sucked in by soft living, but what did Cougar know? Nothing! He didn't know anything. He was living high and rich in New York when she was a kid getting dragged through every mining camp and railroad outpost in the West. Now he made fun of her for trying to be better than he thought she was. The jackass! The skunk! Who would have thought that Cougar Barnes would turn out to be such a goddamned poor sport?

But she wasn't mad because Cougar didn't appreciate

BECOMING GEORGIA   135

the new Georgia. That would mean she cared what he thought, and she didn't. She was learning ladylike ways to impress Alexander Stanford and Chicago's snobs, not Cougar Barnes. No, she was mad because the snake might go to her grandfather and reveal the mess she'd made. Not that the mess was truly her fault. Still, the old man, an astute businessman himself, might use it as an excuse to say she couldn't handle her own affairs and back out of their deal.

So Georgie—no, Georgia—fumed, fretted, and watched out the window for Cougar to appear. When he didn't, she became madder still.

"What are you watching for?" Elizabeth asked her on a gray Saturday five days after their encounter with her past. Georgia stood at her bedroom window, which overlooked the front gardens and portico.

"Nothing."

"Then why have you been keeping vigil at your window these past days like Rapunzel waiting to let down her hair?"

Georgia didn't like the note of amusement she heard in her friend's voice. "I'm just looking at the . . . the outside."

Elizabeth smiled as Georgia very deliberately came away from the window. "I know you're not waiting for Alexander. He called two days ago and you seemed less than excited."

"I was excited. He's taking the bait, and when he gets all the way in the trap, I'm going to dangle him by his tail until he cries uncle."

Elizabeth's smile turned wry. "Now, there's an attractive image."

"After what he said about me, he deserves that and more. One thing I've learned in my life: if a person lets herself get tromped upon without tromping back, the trompings just get harder."

Elizabeth refused to be diverted. "You still haven't told me who you're watching for. Might it be that handsome fellow we met on the path some days ago? The fellow with the intriguing name of Cougar Barnes?"

"He'd better not show his face around here," Georgia said, nose in the air. "I warned him."

"From everything you've told me about the man since you came to Chicago, I thought the two of you were good friends." She cocked her head. "Of course, I also got the impression that he was older, cruder, and sort of shaggy-bear ugly."

"He cleans up all right, I guess," Georgia admitted cautiously. "Cougar's a good enough man to have beside you in a fight, but right now he's acting like a jackass. I think half his brains ended up on the floor with his hair when he dandied himself up. I warned him to stay away from here, and he'd better listen."

Elizabeth chuckled but persisted. "And he is the one you're watching for, isn't he?" She raised a finger in warning. "Don't fib, Georgia. I don't know why you're so vexed with him. He seemed to me to be a very appropriate caller for you. A bit forward, perhaps, and rough-mannered. But he's not used to treating you as lady, is he? He's well-enough mannered when he wants to be, handsome, and from a very good family. The unmarried ladies of Chicago will consider him quite a catch, you know."

"Cougar? A catch?" Georgia started to laugh but thought better of it. She directed a suspicious look at her friend. "If *you're* considering him a catch, Elizabeth Whitman, just haul in your traps. A city girl like you doesn't want to take up with the likes of Cougar Barnes. Even if he does clean up to look like a gentleman, he's not."

Elizabeth merely smiled. "I came up to tell you that your grandfather is waiting for you in the drawing room. I believe he wants a game of chess before you have to get ready for the gala tonight."

"The old coot wants to get whomped again, does he?"

"He seems to enjoy it." Elizabeth followed her out of the room.

Georgia, still worried, warned her once again. "You heed what I said about Cougar, hear? I want your promise."

The knowing twinkle in Elizabeth's eye made Georgia want to squirm. But she was thinking of her friend, she told herself. It wasn't as if she were jealous.

"Don't worry." Elizabeth took her arm companionably

as they went down the wide staircase. "I'm so firmly on the shelf, I'm stuck like glue."

"On the shelf?"

"Ambling down the road of spinsterhood," she clarified.

"You're not a spinster. We're practically the same age."

"Yes, dear, but you are an heiress. Heiresses are never on the shelf."

Georgia humphed. "As if I care. Besides, that doesn't seem quite fair that some man might want to marry me because of what I have, not what I am. You'd make any man a much better wife than I would."

"It's the way the world works, Georgia. Make it work for you."

With a firm thrust of her jaw, Georgia replied, "Maybe I'll just make my world work the way I want it to."

That night her world worked just exactly the way she wanted it to, thank you very much. Georgia, Alvin, and Elizabeth attended the gala farewell to the year's boating season. Elizabeth attempted to demur, but Georgia threatened to "twist her tail in a knot you'll never forget" if her companion didn't keep her company.

"Hold your hand is what you mean," Elizabeth accused while they argued the point. She had given Georgia's corset strings an extra yank for good measure.

Georgia gave a pained grunt. "I don't need anyone to hold my hand, you looby. I just want to show off what I've learned. I want you to be proud of me."

"A better goal is to be proud of yourself," Elizabeth declared.

"Listen to your own words," Georgia advised with sudden insight. "Quit hiding in a closet declaring yourself a spinster. It's been how many years since your father shot himself—three? He was the one with the scandal, not you."

Elizabeth went pale at the harsh words, but Georgia refused to regret them. A snake in the brush had to be called a snake. Insisting the snake was a fuzzy little chipmunk always brought more harm than good.

In the end Elizabeth donned a sedate but very fetching

party dress and came with them. She could hardly refuse since Alvin had wrangled invitations for her mother and Claudia to attend, while Chloe stayed at Greystone House in the charge of the long-suffering Mrs. Bolton.

The yacht club celebration had originally been planned to begin in the midafternoon with boat races on Lake Michigan, but the weather was nasty enough, with off and on rain and a cold, blustery wind, for the organizers to cancel the outdoor activities and go directly to the dancing and dining at the huge mansion of Harold Calhoun, who owned one of the largest meatpacking houses in the city, not to mention one of the largest yachts. The mansion's huge ballroom sported blue and white silk festoons, various paintings depicting sailing yachts of every description, and even several photographs of Chicago yachtsmen standing proudly beside their boats. On a raised platform a small orchestra played quietly, waiting for the ball to be formally opened by the Grand March.

Georgia stifled the urge to gawk when Alvin escorted them into the already crowded ballroom. This shindig made her grandfather's dinner party look like small potatoes indeed. And the little social gatherings—the musicales and poetry readings that Elizabeth had dragged her to, were mere social pinpricks compared to this event. She felt like a minnow who had just unexpectedly swum from a small puddle into a large lake. How had she believed that she, gawkish, clumsy ox in pigtails, could ever be on equal footing with these people in their silks and priceless jewelry, people who truly belonged in this ornate room filled with fancy frills, polished marble, and more food than the town of Prescott could eat in a year. Even Claudia's jaw dropped at the sight before them, and Elizabeth's sister was a part of this world in a way that Georgia could never be.

Then Elizabeth squeezed Georgia's hand and smiled at her. "No one here has had half the adventures you've had or knows nearly as much about the real world as you do. And no woman here holds a candle to you, Georgia Kennedy. Get that chin up and take them by storm. Just be yourself, dear, with polish."

Georgia winked at her. "And don't forget the polish, right?"

Her tutor's eyes sparkled with humor. "And please don't forget the polish." She inclined her head in the direction of the crowd. "Here comes someone who appears to be seeking your attention. Be kind," she warned in a more serious voice.

Alexander Stanford broke free of the crowd and walked their way, looking extremely handsome in his superbly tailored dark burgundy coat and black trousers. The eyes of more than one lady, old and young alike, followed his progress. It was no wonder, Georgia thought, with his chiseled features, thick black hair, and broad shoulders. He was a sight to melt any woman's heart.

But not hers, she reminded herself, thinking of his cruel dismissal on their first meeting. She was the spider, Georgia told herself sternly, and he was the fly. If she wanted to retrieve her self-respect, the fly was going to have to learn his lesson.

"He is *so* handsome," Claudia whispered on a sigh.

Her sister hissed her silent, but Georgia grinned. "He is, isn't he?"

"Good evening." Alexander bowed politely to the ladies. "Alvin, how are you tonight?"

"I'd be more fit if this young woman hadn't thrashed me at chess this afternoon." He nodded toward Georgia, his aggrieved tone belied by the proud shine of his expression. "What's the world coming to when women can outmaneuver a man on the chessboard?"

"Indeed," Alexander agreed. "But I believe perhaps this young woman is a unique female. Brains as well as beauty. And I was hoping to partner her in the Grand March, if her card is not filled completely."

Georgia glanced at her dance card, which so far was completely empty. Not that she would tell him that. "You're in luck. I have the Grand March free." She looked to Alvin for permission—something that never would have occurred to her two months ago. Only when he nodded did she take Alexander's proffered arm. Out of the corner of her eye she caught Elizabeth's encouraging smile and returned it with a saucy wink, not caring who saw. Manners could only go so far.

"You are truly a fancy-talking gent," she told Alexander as they took their places in the line.

"I'm much better known as a reticent bore with the ladies, I fear. But you are looking especially lovely tonight. That provides inspiration."

She grinned, enjoying herself. "There you go again."

Georgia knew she looked spectacular, so she wasn't about to modestly deny it. Her grandfather had purchased for her an absolutely stunning evening gown in a shade of green that matched her eyes to perfection. It also molded her shape in a subtle fashion that managed to suggest rather than display. It was exceedingly proper at the same time it teased with sensuality.

She'd had to let Elizabeth lace her corset painfully tight in order to pour herself into the gown, but once it was on, one look in the mirror had told Georgia that, on the outside, at least, she was more than a match for any fashionable beauty in Chicago, despite her raucous red hair and unladylike freckles that refused to hide beneath a dusting of powder.

"It's too bad the boat races had to be canceled," he said. "I'm sure you would have enjoyed them. Perhaps when the weather warms again, you would find it entertaining to come out onto the lake on my boat. It's a thirty-five-foot ketch. Quite safe, I assure you."

The socially accepted reply, Georgia knew, would be a maidenly but obtuse reference, slightly flirtatious and with just a hint of innocent suggestiveness, to the safety of her virtue aboard his vessel, never mind the safety of her person. But even for the sake of acting ladylike, she couldn't bring herself to such inane protestations. She grinned at him. "Safety has never been on the top of my concerns, I'm afraid."

He looked amused. "Your grandfather would be included in the invitation, of course. To make things proper."

"Of course we would have to make things proper. But then, warm weather is a long ways off, isn't it? By then I might be gone, or be a married lady. There's no telling." Let him chew on that for a while, she thought. "One thing I've learned in my life is that life itself is very uncertain. No one promises us tomorrow."

"A very weighty philosophy for such a lovely lady on a festive night."

She gave him a full force of her smile, slightly mysterious, a hint of intimacy, but overlaid with a bit of chill. "But I am not quite like the other ladies in the room, Mr. Stanford. I think you noted that before."

One of his brows inched upward. Obviously the man didn't know if she was flirting or reprimanding. Stewing in a bit of confusion would do him good, Georgia decided, as long as she herself knew where she was going. Trouble was, she wasn't absolutely positive that she did know where she was going, at least not where Alexander Stanford was concerned.

Once the Grand March ended, Georgia had no more time to toy with Alexander. She was besieged by prospective dance partners, and her dance card filled completely, with only one other dance assigned to Alexander. The other eligible gents in the room, seeing him partner her in the Grand March, apparently reached the conclusion that she was safe game. They flocked around her like turkey buzzards eyeing a piece of raw meat. Georgia noted her grandfather gloating and Elizabeth's pleased smile. She was winning this game, she told herself.

Not only was she winning the game, she was having fun at it. Trying to act like a lady was boring, but after she got in the swing of things, it was also surprisingly easy. The encounter with Alexander, a triumphant one, as far as Georgia was concerned, eased her nervousness and thawed her brain. She didn't make the language slips that would have made people think her a freak. She didn't tread on her partners' toes—her grandfather's ceaseless drilling during their dance lessons in the parlor had seen to that. She talked chattily about nothing, as all her swains seemed to expect. She smiled brilliantly, glorying as they melted right before her eyes. She accepted their compliments and artfully dodged their claims on her future attentions. And all the while she got more exercise, whirling around the dance floor, than she'd gotten since she left Arizona.

Everyone else in her party was having a grand time as well, Georgia could see. Several times she glimpsed Elizabeth dancing with attentive-looking fellows, at least once with Alexander Stanford. For all that Elizabeth repeatedly recommended Alexander as a fine man with a good heart, Georgia thought she looked uncomfortable with him, her eyes fixed uneasily on his silk cravat instead of his face and her movements nervous, as if his hands burned her where they touched her in the dance. It was no wonder that Elizabeth was a spinster, Georgia thought, if she reacted to men in that way.

Elizabeth's family also was doing well. Alvin danced several times with both Phoebe and Claudia and introduced both mother and daughter to his circle as friends, so that society matrons who might have turned up their noses at the family of a man involved in such a nasty scandal—even three years ago—were forced to smile, socialize, and allow their sons to compete for young Claudia's dance card. Georgia noted it all with an almost fond feeling for the man she'd once thought of as an interfering old goat. Alvin was tough in many ways, but his heart, when you came right down to it, was mush. He was a sucker for a hard-luck story, especially if the hard-luck cases were women.

The evening got even better when their hostess, Mrs. Evelyn Calhoun, sought out Georgia to introduce her to a special friend, a white-haired man with a ramrod-straight spine and light blue eyes that seemed to constantly look beyond the room full of people to seek the distances beyond.

"Mr. Finley is a hero of sorts," the woman said proudly. "At least we who know him think so. He scouted for the railroad for years when he wasn't scouting for the army and fighting Indians. As a young man, back in the thirties, he was one of the pioneers who saw the potential in this area." She smiled indulgently. "That was before he moved on to even wilder climes. But I knew that he would particularly like to meet you, Miss Kennedy, since you have lived your life in the wild places that are next to his heart."

"Mrs. Calhoun told me you've recently come from Arizona." Mr. Finley's eyes weren't seeking distances right now. They were alight with interest. "I passed through that area only once, in '56, when it was still part of the Territory of New Mexico. Back then most folks opined that the whole of it was only fit for giving back to the Indians."

"There's folks that would tell you the same today," Georgia told him. "But once the Apaches have been corralled, Arizona's going to shine. And when the railroads finally get there, well, there won't be any holding it back."

Their hostess, satisfied that she'd done her social duty, left them to it.

Georgia immediately felt at home with Everett Finley. He was the same species of explorer/pioneer/adventurer who had populated her life from her earliest memories. Tough, self-reliant, too restless to stay in one place for very long, he had settled finally in Chicago because stiffening joints and other ailments of age would no longer allow him to live the life he loved.

"This mudflat by the lake holds some good memories for me," he confided to Georgia as he escorted her to the buffet table. "I was here as a young man, before it became such a boomtown, and I still have friends here—men who have been here since the beginning. But the West—ah, the West, with its bright skies and endless spaces. There's the place to be. Do you miss it, Miss Kennedy?"

Did she miss it? Oh, my, did she! Georgia told him about Prescott and the men who made their homes in the surrounding hills, dodging Apaches and trying to grub a living from the streams and hillsides. She told him of the other places in her heart, also—Colorado, with mountains that soared straight up from the plain to touch the sky; Wyoming, Montana, New Mexico, and California. He listened avidly to stories about the ranches, railroad towns, and mining camps where she'd grown from a child to a girl, from a girl to a woman while following a father, who was much like Mr. Finley himself, restless, footloose, with eyes always seeking the horizon and a heart eager for the next adventure.

Miraculously Georgia was able to tell the tales and talk

of her old life without once drifting into the rough speech that Elizabeth had tried so hard to drill out of her. She sounded downright civilized, in fact, even when telling Mr. Finley about the time she and her daddy had been treed by a grizzly bear in Wyoming or the brawl she had started in El Paso, Texas. Mr. Finley was rapt, and he showed her such respect and admiration that those around them began to look at her in a new light. Georgia could tell from the way they gathered around the table where she and her new friend talked and ate, until the two of them and their conversation about the adventuresome frontier had gathered quite a crowd.

Too soon Georgia was claimed by a dance partner, but Mr. Finley promised to call soon at Greystone House to continue their reminiscences. His patina of hero-adventurer had rubbed off onto Georgia by then. Women shot her envious looks, and men sought her out even more than before. When Alexander claimed his second dance, he commented on her success.

"You're taking the place by storm, Miss Kennedy."

"Do you think?"

"You definitely have everyone in the palm of your hand. Everett Finley is a bit of a legend in this town—a hero, of sorts, and a very well-liked fellow. He seems very taken with you, which means that everyone else is equally taken."

"Does that include you?" she asked coyly. Damned if this flirtatious bit wasn't beginning to come naturally!

He grinned amiably. "I generally try to not be swayed by crowd opinion. But I believe I've already expressed my admiration. You truly are a unique woman."

"Unique in a coarse, overbold Amazon sort of way?"

He visibly winced. "You are never going to forgive me for those rude words, are you? Even with the consideration that I was in a wretched mood, angry at both Alvin and my father, and thought you were nowhere within earshot."

"I'm not the unforgiving sort. Not completely, anyways. But I will admit that its a handy little sticker to prod you with when I feel the need."

Ruefully he smiled. "I suppose I deserve every prod."

She merely lifted a brow.

He wanted to claim the next dance as well, even though a spindly, middle-aged bachelor by the name of John Safford was on her card. She reveled in refusing him, even though she had to admit that being held in his arms, even in the most proper manner of the dance, felt amazingly good.

"I couldn't do that," she demurred. "People would talk, and I know you don't want that to happen. How embarrassing that would be for you."

He gave her a look, and she reveled in his perplexity as Mr. Safford came to claim her. What power women had! Georgia had never dreamed that men were such putty. And look at her, the belle of the ball! All her life she had dressed, talked, and acted like one of the boys, fearing secretly that she would only look foolish as a woman. Wrong! So wrong! She felt almost dizzy with the sudden knowledge of power.

John Safford was a bad enough dancer to make Georgia dizzy without any help from her inflated mood. She excused herself before the dance was over. If she hadn't, she might not have been able to walk for a week. But when her next partner claimed her, she wished fervently she was back with Mr. Safford. Cougar Barnes grinned down at her as he led her, half resisting, onto the dance floor.

"You aren't on my dance card!"

"I bought this dance from the fellow who was. Paid handsomely, too. Seems your value is pretty high right now."

"You bought me?" she squawked, outraged.

"Like a mare on the auction block."

"A jackass buying a mare. Fancy that." She huffed unhappily. "How did you get invited?"

"I came with my uncle."

"You'd think these yacht people would have better sense than to let you through the door."

"If you'd known I was here, of course you would have saved room for me on your card."

"I wouldn't have. And I think this dance has gone on long enough." She gave him the haughty, superciliuous look she'd seen other ladies use to great effect on unwanted gentlemen. "I feel the need to sit this one out."

"Fine by me. The dance floor's too crowded, anyway."

She attempted to pull away, but his arms wouldn't let her go. The strong hand at her waist steered her effortlessly, as if she weren't subtly struggling every inch of the way. He didn't release her until they sailed through the French doors that led to the Calhoun's famous gardens.

"This is better," Cougar declared. "I never have liked crowds. Get too many people in the same room and, no matter how fancy the room, it begins to smell worse than a stockyard."

"You can stay out here if you want, but I'm going in. In case you haven't noticed, it's freezing."

"Hell, I can remember when a little cold weather didn't bother you a bit, Georgie."

"Georgia," she corrected with a sniff. "The name is Georgia."

He chuckled. "Okay. Georgia. I've always kind of liked that name, anyway. But up until now, Georgie fit you much better."

She shot him a glance that could have turned the drizzle to sleet, but he just smiled. Georgia wanted none of his smiles. "Goodbye. Have a nice time. But don't you dare get cozy with my granddad."

Before she got a step, he grasped her arm. "Hold on there. This is my dance, bought and paid for."

"We're not dancing, dunderhead."

"Doesn't matter. Until the orchestra stops, you're mine."

"Bullshit."

"Now, is that a ladylike thing to say?"

"There is no ladylike way to deal with you."

"True enough." He tugged her toward the greenhouse. "I don't belong in polite society, and neither do you. Here. Shelter from the weather. See what a gentleman I am?"

Georgia shook out her damp skirts. "I can't believe you got invited to this gathering. My grandfather said that only the best people—"

"Only the best people . . ." he mocked. "Listen to you."

Georgia frowned. Much as she hated to admit it, Cougar had a point.

"For your information, Princess, the Barnes are considered among the very best people. These folks around here just haven't found out yet that I'm sort of a black sheep."

She fisted her hands on her hips in challenge. "Why are you being such a jackass?"

"Why are you so angry at me? I've been pretty much of a jackass all the years you've known me, and suddenly it bothers you?"

"You should have trusted me to take care of things with my grandfather. Instead, you—"

"Oh, cut the crap! That's not why you're mad." He leaned against a table of colorful marigolds, folding his arms across his broad chest in an annoyingly knowing way. "You're mad because you're bound and determined, for some reason, to become just another empty-headed decoration on some man's arm, and I'm hanging around here, a walking, talking reminder of who you really are."

Her jaw dropped. "You are so full of bullshit!"

"Am I?"

"You don't have a rat's-ass notion who I really am."

"I think I do, *Georgia*. Have you set your cap for Alex Stanford?"

"What do you care?"

"Alex is an acquaintance of mine, sort of. His family knows my family and all that. He's a good man, but not a good man for you."

Georgia felt her face flush. "You don't want your friend to get stuck with an ox in pigtails, I suppose!"

His brow wrinkled, and for the first time he looked perplexed. "Is that what you think you are?"

She advanced, finger pointing in accusation, jaw squared and ready for a fight. "What do you care what I am or what I do? Once you get title to that frigging claim, you'll go galloping back to Arizona to play with your gold mine and your cattle. What becomes of me is none of your concern."

He met her head-on, not intimidated by her vehemence. "There's where you're wrong. So happens I'm a guy who hates to see gold turned into brass. I hate the waste of it."

"What the hell do you mean?"

"You're gold, Georgie. Pure gold. And I don't mean the dirty stuff you grub out of the gravel. I mean the cleaned-up, glowing in the sunlight kind of gold. At least you were."

The intensity burning in his eyes took her aback.

"The girl I knew in Arizona was honest through and through. She didn't take shit off of anyone, but she'd give you her last biscuit if you were hungry and didn't have the scratch to come up with a meal of your own. Hard work didn't bend her. Danger didn't intimidate her. She always had a ready laugh and a warm smile. Best of all, that girl knew exactly who she was and what she wanted, and she wasn't ashamed of it."

His voice pounded on her heart. "Quit it, Cougar! You have a trumped-up notion of who I was."

"Who you *are*," he insisted.

She made a rude sound. "You ought to be grateful I'm willing to knuckle under to my granddad to get the claims back. And here you are braying nonsense about gold and brass and what I'm supposed to be. What you are is an ungrateful sack of dog droppings!"

The intensity in his eyes almost made her fade back. "Those claims aren't worth you doing this to yourself. Go back to Arizona, Georgie, where you belong, and let me talk to Alvin about the claims."

Suspicion reared its head. For a few minutes she'd actually been flattered that Cougar was concerned for her, maybe liked her old self enough to work up all this steam. But just like the Prescott men who had been so eager to woo her, Cougar regarded her as a walking gold mine. He wanted to shoo her back to Arizona while he cut his own deal with Alvin. The disappointment that hit her was unexpectedly bitter.

"Now I understand!" Accusation laced her voice. "All this nonsense about me preserving myself is just about your frigging claim, isn't it? Why can't you just admit it, Cougar? I wouldn't have thought that you were so sneaky."

"To hell with the claims."

"What a load of mulefriz you're spouting. You'll get the claim I sold you, Cougar, when I've taken care of matters myself. And just so you know, I'm not turning gold into brass. I'm just taking a raw, dirty nugget and polishing it up some. If I wanted to get myself hitched to Alexander Stanford, he would be lucky to have me," she said pugnaciously. "*If* I wanted to. And I'll do what I want, without asking your say-so about it. So you can forget convincing me that banging around in dungarees and spending my days shoveling dirt made me some kind of hero."

Though wearing overalls and flannels had been a hell of a lot more comfy than the cursed corset currently digging into her ribs. And spending her days outdoors in the fresh air, whether that outdoors be bright, warm sun or cold gray rain, was a more satisfying life than sitting in a house with genteel needlework and poetry.

But she would throw herself into quicksand before admitting that to know-it-all smirking Cougar Barnes.

"Butt out, Cougar. Go sweet-talk your uncle into buying you some cows, or convince him to build a railroad through Arizona. Or something else useful. Just leave me alone to do what I want."

"You don't know what the hell you want, you blockhead." It was Cougar's turn to shake a finger in Georgia's face, and his finger, she admitted, was a good deal more intimidating than hers. "While you let this glitter go to your head, all your common sense is leaking out. You have no idea of the restrictions that polite society places upon a female. Marry Alex Stanford, or any of those yahoos in that ballroom who seem so taken with you, and you'll wake up one of these days trapped in a life you hate."

"I know plenty about female restrictions! Haven't I worn a goddamned corset almost every day since I got here?"

For a moment he was taken aback, then he threw back his head and laughed. "There's hope for you yet."

Embarrassed, she turned huffily and walked out the greenhouse door. This time Cougar didn't stop her. He'd already done all the damage he could, she thought resentfully. Why was it every time she saw him, all her new manners flew to the wind and she became the old Georgie, even though she tried hard to be the new, polished Georgia?

Back in the Calhouns' ballroom, her grandfather quizzed her about where she'd been. Her dance partners had been searching for her, he complained.

"I needed a breath of fresh air," she lied. She wouldn't mention Cougar Barnes to Alvin, because her grandfather would ask for more of an explanation than she wanted to give. She needed quiet time to think on what Cougar had said, to wonder if maybe he wasn't right. If she was painfully honest with herself, she would have to admit the possibility. Her blossoming success might be making her just a little heady, a little drunk with the discovery of the power a woman could wield over a man—except Cougar Barnes. Georgia couldn't imagine Cougar falling prey to any woman's wiles, and if he did, he would know exactly what he was doing and why.

After just a few moments of the next dance, she excused herself, needing to escape the stuffy ballroom with its close, crowded heat. She fetched her wrap from a servant.

"Tell my grandfather that I've gone home, please."

"Shall I have your carriage brought around, Miss Kennedy?"

"Thanks, but I'll walk. I need the fresh air."

"But, miss . . ."

She brushed the servant aside, desperate to be alone. "I'm going home."

The servant frowned at the ornate front door that shut behind her. He shook his head at such female foolishness, then sighed. "Such a bad idea."

Chapter 10

Cougar Barnes was not having a good time at the Yacht Club celebration. Over the past years he had dreamed occasionally of spacious mansions, sumptuous food, beautifully gowned women—all parts of the life he left behind when he was nineteen and longing for adventure. Waking from those dreams in a crude log hut, or perhaps looking at the stars from a bed on the ground, he thought he missed all that. But he didn't miss it. The reality was just as dull as he remembered. The men were soft and narrow-minded, their vision never extending beyond their own familiar daily routines. The women, for the most part, hid any spark of intelligence behind vapid smiles and innocuous chatter, a model that Georgie Kennedy was trying hard to emulate, the little fool.

And that, Cougar admitted to himself, was why he despised so-called civilized society with a passion he hadn't felt since he was nineteen. These overdressed, perfumed, self-satisfied slugs had taken a naturally beautiful woman like Georgie and remade her into a pasteboard cutout on the same design as every other woman in the ballroom. The process wasn't quite complete. The old Georgie—straightforward, outspoken, spontaneous, and sharp as a scorpion's tail—boiled out of the new Georgie given sufficient provocation. Cougar just couldn't help giving that provocation whenever he had the chance.

It was just possible, Cougar admitted reluctantly, that he had come to Chicago not to straighten out the rights to his claim and talk to his uncle about investing in his ranch. Those served as likely excuses, but he'd spent little time thinking about them since arriving in Chicago. Most of his time he had frittered away looking for Georgie, then once he'd found her, irritating Georgie.

He missed her, dammit. Prescott had seemed empty without her, the air not as fresh, the mountains not as high, the grass not as green. Georgie was unique, vibrant, and despite the thorns she sprouted to defend herself from friend and foe alike, she brightened any corner of the world she occupied. In the few years he'd known her, Cougar had grown attached. He would admit it. He was mighty attached. And here was Georgie bent on turning herself into just another lady mincing down the narrow, confined path that society allowed its women. The very thought made Cougar want to kick something, preferably her grandfather, followed shortly by Georgie herself.

Cougar's black reflections came to a halt when the Calhoun's butler, distinguishable from the other servants by the superjcilious look on his face, walked up and sought his attention.

"Pardon me, sir."

"Yes?"

"If I may be so bold, sir . . . earlier I saw you dancing with Miss Kennedy. I cannot find her grandfather, and I thought someone should know. She left the house quite suddenly, the doorman tells me, without escort, leaving word for Mr. Kennedy that she intended to walk home alone. The doorman says she refused his offer to have her grandfather's conveyance brought around. Given that Miss Kennedy has not lived long in Chicago, perhaps she does not realize the risk of a young woman traveling unescorted at night."

Privately Cougar thought that anyone trying to assault Georgie Kennedy was in for a rude surprise, but second thought reminded him that she had no weapon, and city dangers could be just as deadly as anything the frontier could offer.

"What did you say?" came a new voice into the conversation.

Cougar turned to find Alexander Stanford confronting the butler.

"He said that stubborn she-mule with red hair and a nitro temper has taken off alone onto the dark streets of Chicago."

Alex's eyes narrowed. "By God! It's Barnes! Cooper Barnes."

"Hello, Alex."

"I haven't seen you for . . . for . . ."

"A decade or so."

More, in fact. The last time had been at a dinner the Barnes family had given for Robert Stanford, who'd brought a good deal of business to their bank. Before that, Cougar and Alex had attended a New York school together when they were sixteen. Like interests and intelligence had made them friends during that year.

But Cougar didn't have time for pleasantries. He turned back to the butler. "How long ago did Miss Kennedy leave?"

"About thirty minutes past, I'd think. It took a while for the doorman to gather enough courage to express his concern."

Cougar muttered a word that made the butler flinch. "Have my horse brought around. I'll see to her."

"Thank you, sir. If I find her grandfather, I'll tell her you've gone to serve as escort."

Alexander frowned. "Wait a minute, Barnes. I should go after Miss Kennedy. I feel responsible for protecting her."

"Georgie seldom needs protecting. If you knew her, you'd know that. This time, however, she might need a little help."

"*You* know her? Other than that one dance?"

"For years. I went to Arizona prospecting for gold in the northern mining districts. Georgie and her father came a couple of years later."

"Indeed." The frown deepened. "What a coincidence. For now that she has returned to civilization, I have ... made her acquaintance." The emphasis on *acquaintance* so obviously implied so much more. "Queer that she's never spoken of you."

Cougar hated, had always hated, the subtle undertones of civilized conversation, where enmities, insults, and challenges were conveyed around the words, not through them. God forbid you should say what you actually meant. Someone might label you as brash. "I doubt she talks much about things that mean the most to her, because few here would understand her world. She's only here for a short while, until she comes up with a way to return where she belongs." A surge of possessiveness took Cougar by surprise. "So don't count on getting too ... *acquainted*, Stanford."

"She hasn't indicated to me any desire to return to her former life."

"No, I doubt she would talk frankly to you."

The two men bristled at each other, boyhood camaraderie forgotten, until the butler cleared his throat. "Gentlemen, shouldn't someone be going after Miss Kennedy."

"Damned right," Cougar agreed.

"We'll both go," Alexander declared.

"My horse has already been brought around." Cougar grinned. "When I find her, I'll let you know she's safe."

Twenty minutes later, however, Cougar was getting nowhere with Mrs. Bolton when Alexander drove up to Greystone House.

"Miss Kennedy is not at home," the Kennedy housekeeper informed Cougar stiffly.

"I know that she's not supposed to be at home. But she left the Calhouns', and I need to know if she made it back here."

"That's nonsense. She wouldn't leave without Mr. Kennedy and Miss Whitman."

"Well, she did, and she might be in trouble. Are you going to search the house?"

"Pure silliness! Of course not. Oh, hello, Mr. Stanford."

Alexander tipped his hat. "Good evening Mrs. Bolton.

I'm sorry to tell you that Mr. Barnes here is telling the truth. Something upset Miss Georgia and sent her flying from the celebration. Could we bother you to make sure she is not in the house?"

"Well, of course, sir. Do come in."

Alex gave Cougar a condescending smile. "I'm a frequent caller."

By this time Cougar was too worried to play the one-upmanship game. "Just find her."

Georgie's room was unoccupied, Marjorie the cook and Daisy the scullery girl, sitting at the kitchen table polishing silver, hadn't seen her since that afternoon.

"She's at the grand boating party," Marjorie informed them.

"That's the trouble," Cougar said. "She's not. If she comes in, send word to her grandfather at the Calhoun mansion."

Brows lifted at that, but both men started toward the door before anyone could ask questions.

"You'll need a horse if you're to cover any territory," Cougar told Alexander. "I'm sure Alvin won't mind if you take one of his."

"Right."

They could argue later over who had rights to the lady. First she had to be found.

Georgia confessed to herself that leaving the party alone had been less than smart. Normally she didn't like to admit to such a thing, even to herself. After all, a person had to keep her confidence up to meet the challenges of life, and brooding on a stupidity here and there certainly didn't give a boost. This time, however, she might have deliberately put her foot in a mule pile.

Who knew Chicago at night would be so confusing? She knew better than to wander around the mountains and prairies after nightfall unless she knew exactly where she was going, but a civilized city, with streets and buildings and lights, shouldn't be hard to navigate—you'd think.

But Chicago was hard to navigate. Impossible, in fact. Things looked different, smelled different, felt different in the dark. Buildings seemed all the same. Street signs, when the streets had signs, hid in the night, indecipherable. Lights were few and far between.

"So you're lost," she told herself as she turned down yet another dark street hoping to find a familiar avenue, or at least the lakefront. "It's not the first time. You and your daddy got lost that time in Colorado without food or water and one knife and a shotgun between the two of you. Compared to that, Chicago is a cakewalk."

Except that wasn't precisely true. The wilderness held plenty of dangers for the unwary, but Chicago boasted its own dangers. Georgie could feel them in the darkness, nothing specific, but a vague shadow of ill feeling. She didn't like this city, and it didn't like her. Stupid as a greenhorn stepping into a bear trap, she had stepped out into the night without a thought of caution.

The whole thing was Cougar's fault, Georgie told herself. If he hadn't hung her out to dry about trying to be a lady, she wouldn't have had to climb aboard her high horse and trot out of the party. What right did he have spoiling her fun, carping about her turning gold into brass, as if the old Georgie Kennedy in messy braids and stained overalls was anything to brag about?

Not that she'd been ashamed of who she was. No, indeed. All her life she'd been true to herself and her friends, and anyone who could say that had nothing to be ashamed of. But in the very darkest corner of her soul, the fear had lurked that she could never be a real woman. She didn't possess the looks, the grace, or whatever else made a woman what a woman was.

Now Georgia knew better. She could be damned good at being a woman, just as good as she was at shooting, knife-throwing, arm wrestling, or any other useful talent. And surprise! She'd discovered that women were powerful. In a woman's presence, men turned stupid, went mushy, and lost every ounce of sense they possessed, or at least a lot of them did. Men would turn somersaults to please a pretty woman. They would make fools of themselves, turn themselves inside out, remake themselves from the toes up.

Except Cougar. He didn't fall under a woman's spell; he

just scolded her for trying to do what she was supposed to do, the jackass! Why did he have to spoil her fun?

Thinking about it got her good and riled, so riled she almost missed the narrow street where a breath of damp lake rode the breeze. The lake! Once she found the waterfront, all she had to do was turn south to find her grandfather's house.

The lakefront where she emerged, however, was not the familiar lakefront where people strolled up and down the shore and looked across the railroad tracks to the water beyond. This area was far different. It smelled of rotting garbage and dead fish. A very few gas lights barely touched the darkness, which was heavy and felt like a cold, damp blanket.

Georgie uttered a word that didn't fit with her new ladylike image. What she would give for her long-barreled Remington, or even a big skinning knife. She turned south along the side of a warehouse, telling herself she was simply borrowing trouble. If Cougar knew she'd turned so chicken-livered, he'd scold her even harder. Where was the girl who had fought her way through Apache raids and once laid out a grizzly bear who'd just about had her father for lunch?

That girl was somewhere else, Georgie admitted when she spied four figures lounging against a building at the next intersection. They had seen her, for two came to their feet and a third hit the fourth on a shoulder to get his attention. One of them hooted with glee. Georgie thought of turning and running, then thought better of it. They knew the ins and outs of this place, and she didn't. Besides, running only showed weakness, and she was far from weak. Far better to bluff her way through, or in the worst case, show these fellows that an Arizona woman wasn't a creature to meddle with. Her hands balled into fists at her side.

Cougar hated cities. He'd always hated cities, but just then he hated Chicago in particular. You couldn't track a stinking elephant through Chicago with all these wooden walkways and hard-trampled streets. Noises bounced off buildings every which way and could be coming from any direction. The best he could do was backtrack the route between Alvin Kennedy's residence and the Calhoun mansion, hoping to spot some sign that Georgia had taken a wrong turn somewhere. Emmett Four Toes, a half-breed Pinal-Mexican and the best tracker in Arizona Territory, couldn't have found Georgia in this jumble of wood and brick, at least not without a healthy helping of luck.

He had spent thirty minutes peering up dark alleys and listening for telltale signs, wondering if Alex, who was searching a parallel route, was having better luck, when Cougar's ears pricked up at the sound of a pained grunt. His horse didn't want to explore the dark street where the sound had originated, but Cougar set his heels to the gelding's sides and headed down the narrow passage toward the waterfront. In just moments he saw struggling shadows against the glow of a dim gas light. One of the figures wore skirts.

Cougar wasted no time. He flew off his mount and launched himself into the fight, noting even as he did that Georgie was holding her own even at odds of four against one. Trained in the school of survival fighting, down and dirty, she used anything she could—fists, feet, mud, fingers, and knees—to bring down her attackers. But she was taking as well as giving. These toughs didn't have any gentlemanly hesitation about hitting a lady, and they were spitting mad. What they'd taken for a tempting little pussycat had turned out to be a tigress, and they weren't happy about it.

Cougar diverted a hefty fellow who was about to grab Georgie from behind, spinning him around and introducing his face to a big fist. The man grunted in pained surprise, but didn't go down. Chicago bred them tough. He came for Cougar like a bear, fists flying. Cougar stepped aside to dodge the rush, crashing into Georgie as he did so. She grabbed him and, before he could recover his balance, threw him hard on his back. When she recognized him, her eyes grew wide.

"Thanks a lot," he groaned. He himself had taught her that particular move two years ago. "Watch out behind you!"

She turned in time to deflect a blow from a weasely little man who looked tougher than jerked beef. When he whirled and came at her again, she thrust her knee into his groin. Cougar winced in fellow feeling. The guy was as tough as he looked. He reeled from the low blow, as any man would, but came back fighting.

By this time Cougar had recovered his feet and came up swinging. He and Georgia fought back to back. If the would-be assailants hadn't been so fighting mad, they might have had the good sense to run, because Cougar and Georgie back to back were more than a match for four Chicago toughs, no matter how mean the city bred them. When Alexander found them and joined the fray, victory was assured. Their gentleman ally made the mistake, however, of trying to push Georgie to the sidelines for her own safety. Very gentlemanly, but the ill-conceived move showed how little he knew about the woman he courted, because he met with the business end of her fist before she pulled back, gave him a heated glare, and dived back into the fray. Alex shook his head and followed. Cougar noted that Stanford could more than hold his own with his fists, and he had a left hook that could flatten a mule.

Their new ally didn't have much time to prove himself, though, because the gang of four, bruised, bleeding, and with at least one broken arm in the bunch, took off for safer climes.

"Pissant sons of bitches!" Georgie called after them, her blood obviously still running hot. Then she clapped a hand over her mouth and regarded Cougar and Alex—more especially Alex—with a rueful grimace. She was tattered and bruised. A thin stream of blood ran from her nose and one eye already had started to swell. "I just scotched my new ladylike image, didn't I?"

Alexander gazed at her in awe. "You are the most amazing woman I've ever met. Incredible, really. There's not one frail fiber in your entire being. You break all the molds, Georgia Kennedy."

She swayed a bit. "I feel as if all the damned molds just got broken over my head."

And with that comment, she sank to the dirty street in a ladylike swoon.

* * *

The family parlor at Greystone House bustled for so late a night. Alexander brooded as he helped Cooper Barnes worry a path in the carpet. He was tired, confused, and most of all, worried. Alvin Kennedy sat in his favorite wingback chair in front of the fireplace looking grayer than age had made him. Mrs. Bolton hurried in and out the door like a cuckoo clock gone mad, asking if they needed refreshments, dashing out to fetch coffee and tea, then dashing back in when her distracted mind realized that she hadn't really heard what the men had said.

"What could have possessed the girl?" Alvin wondered aloud. "Walking the streets on her own—pure foolishness! It's only by God's good grace she wasn't murdered."

Cooper, who was evidently now known by the colorful soubriquet "Cougar," shot the old man a resentful look. "Georgie's accustomed to looking out for herself. She's not one of your frail, defenseless flowers who automatically seeks someone else's protection."

"Just the same, she should have had more sense. What on earth made her want to leave the festivities?" He pinned Alex with a look. "Did you say something else to upset her, young Stanford?"

"Something else?" Cooper demanded.

Alex gave the men look for look. Alvin Kennedy he respected, but he had no fear of him. If the cranky old Kennedy patriarch wanted someone to blame for Georgia's unhappiness—if indeed she was unhappy—he could look to himself. He'd let the girl languish in miserable circumstances until it suited his purposes to pluck her from the only life she knew and throw her at a world that was both harsh and unwelcoming to uninitiated newcomers.

Cooper he was not so sure of. In fact, he was unclear just where Barnes fit into Georgia's life. The Cooper Barnes he'd known in New York during the year they attended school together had been a strong, smart, and honorable lad, but restless and dissatisfied with his life in a way that set him apart from the other students. They had been friends, drawn together by a love of good horses and a disdain for learning Greek and Latin.

Alex knew that Cooper had gone West shortly after graduating from school, and that his father had been livid. He'd heard nothing else, and wondered at finding him in Chicago, somehow laying claim to Georgia Kennedy's attentions. He knew nothing ill of the man, and in school had thought quite highly of him. But he was irked, surprisingly so, at the sudden competition for a woman Alex considered his for the taking, if he wanted her. He fell short of admitting jealousy. Jealousy would imply too great an attachment to Georgia Kennedy, whom he was coming to admire more and more but whose claim on his regard was by no means certain.

Still, the thought of Georgia lying upstairs unconscious and injured, no one knew how severely, ate at his mind like a canker. And it had the same effect on Alvin and Cooper, judging from the expressions on the other two men's faces.

"She didn't look that bad off to me," Cooper claimed, glaring at Alex as if he were somehow responsible.

Alex agreed in a mild tone. "No, she didn't."

"What is your connection to my granddaughter, Barnes?" Alvin demanded. "More than just that one dance, I'd wager."

"We're good friends. And we have some common business interests in Arizona."

Alvin scowled. "Business interests?"

"If you want the details, then ask Georgie to explain."

"Was it you, young scalawag, who sent her running from the party?"

"No one sends Georgie running, Mr. Kennedy. If you knew her at all, you'd know that."

Alex regarded Cooper closely. The man was far different from the boy he'd known. He possessed a touch of arrogance and a swagger that hadn't been a part of the young Cooper Barnes. And there was a certain dangerous air about him. Despite his very correct, nicely tailored evening clothes—or they had been nicely tailored before the brawl—he filled up a room with his presence, and he had the same restless mien that marked so many men who wandered the frontier.

Alex had met other men with the same presence, not in New York or Chicago, but on his travels west of the Mississippi with the Stanford freight wagons. He'd been the length of the Santa Fe Trail and the old Oregon Trail, and most of the roads in between, getting his hands dirty with the actual business that had made the Stanford family rich. Alex didn't believe a man could run a business without knowing all the ins and outs of it.

So he recognized in Cooper Barnes the mark of one of the restless souls who would rather brave the rigors of the frontier than the humdrum of the city. He recognized that quality in Georgia as well. But unlike a man, a woman was easily molded. The more he thought about it, the more he believed Georgia was worth molding. But if she fixed her affections on a man like Cooper, she would never escape the life her father had condemned her to.

"So you and Miss Kennedy are friends," he said to Cooper, wanting clarification.

"Good friends," the man said somewhat testily. "Close friends."

The implication was clear. Barnes thought he had some kind of a claim on her.

"Strange that she hasn't mentioned you."

Cooper smiled, somewhat snidely, Alex thought. "She's mentioned *you* a lot."

The tone implied he hadn't exactly gotten a good character from her. Alex wasn't surprised, considering their first meeting. That was changing, though.

Shortly after midnight Alvin retired. He hinted broadly that perhaps the two younger men should retire as well—to their own residences—but neither consented to budge until they knew more about Georgia's condition. Left alone with his rival, Alex eyed the other warily. Battle lines separated them. Yet a strange bond had grown between them that had nothing to do with their past friendship. They both worried about the same woman. They both wanted the same woman, apparently. Mrs. Bolton broke the mounting tension when she came through the door with a tray of steaming coffee. Still dithering, she glanced toward the hallway staircase, where there was still no appearance of the doctor attending Georgia or of Elizabeth, who helped him.

"Poor lamb." Mrs. Bolton sighed. "Imagine, one of our own, attacked in the streets. What's the world coming to?"

"Do you suppose she's badly hurt?" Alex asked once the housekeeper had left.

"I've seen Georgie kicked by a mule and an hour later go back to work at her sluice box." Despite his confident tone, his eyes were anxious.

"I tried to push her from the fight," Alex told Cooper, "but she wouldn't have it. In fact," he remembered with a rueful grimace, "she hit me."

Barnes laughed heartily. "Don't get in Georgie's way when she's in a temper. She doesn't have that red hair for nothing, and her punch packs the kick of a mule."

Alex shook his head. "A remarkable female." In so many ways, he added silently. Most of them good. Most of them downright fascinating. "Absolutely intriguing."

"Don't get too intrigued," Barnes warned crossly. "Georgie may look like a ladybug, but she has the sting of a hornet. You might not want to learn about that firsthand."

Alex just smiled. There was nothing like a little competition to make a man appreciate the worth of a prize.

Just then the sounds of footfalls on the hall stairs brought them both alert. The doctor walked past the door to the parlor without stopping. Elizabeth followed him. They conferred briefly at the front door, and then the physician left. Elizabeth came into the parlor and regarded them both with a less than charitable look. They threw questions at her at the same time.

"How is she?"

"What did the doctor say?"

"Is she awake?"

"Can I see her?"

She quelled them with a stern tightening of her lips, a clear signal that she wouldn't say a thing until they regained their manners. Like chastened schoolboys, both fell silent.

"I'd like some tea, please, Mrs. Bolton, if you don't mind. With honey. I've need of some restorative sugar."

The housekeeper fluttered her hands in sympathy. "Of course you do, dear. Right away."

"And as for you two, no, you cannot visit Georgia. Rachel is sitting with her now, for she needs to be watched. She's had a very nasty bump to her head and has been bruised in other parts. Right now what she requires most is rest. Seeing either one of you would overset her, I have no doubt."

Barnes replied with a skeptical snort, as if he doubted that much of anything could overset Georgia Kennedy. But Alex didn't argue. Elizabeth would know better even than the physician what Georgia needed at such a stressful juncture. Women had frailties that only other women understood, and Elizabeth seemed to be very competent in her role as nurse.

She looked at both of them sternly. "Which one of you was the cause of Georgia dashing from the gala, gentlemen?"

Alex had no notion what the woman meant, and if Cooper did, his answer was forestalled by Mrs. Bolton's entrance with Elizabeth's tea. When the housekeeper had left, Elizabeth focused a suspicious glare on Barnes. "Were you rude to her again?" she demanded.

"Again?" Alex rounded on his onetime friend, putting all the frustration of the evening into one burst of annoyance at the man who didn't have a right to be here, messing in an already complicated situation. "What is this, rude *again*? What did you say to her?"

He earned himself a reprimand from Elizabeth. "Alexander Stanford, you've little cause to berate Mr. Barnes. He is certainly not the only man in this room who feels free to abandon manners where Georgia is concerned."

Alex clamped his jaw tight on a testy reply, because she was right. But he sent the other man a look that promised they would settle this when they weren't under a lady's eye. It was bad enough that he had wounded Georgia. He could, he hoped, repair that damage to the poor girl. But he wouldn't stand for someone else making the same mistake. Elizabeth had every justification for scolding.

Barnes eyed the both of them, looking mightily displeased. "You will let me know, Miss Whitman, when Georgia may receive visitors?"

"I will, Mr. Barnes. And I must thank you for coming to her aid. Georgia is very dear to me."

Barnes clamped his lips on something left unsaid. Was it an assertion that the girl was dear to him as well? Alex suffered a pang of resentment.

"I should leave," Cooper said. "But I hope to hear from you soon."

Alex watched Elizabeth usher the other man to the door. Closing the door behind him, she turned toward Alex expectantly. "Well, Mr. Stanford?"

Plainly she expected him to go. And he should. Exhaustion had put shadows beneath her eyes, and the gown she had worn to the gala hung limply on her rather attractive figure. Yet she had that peculiar glow of a woman who was at her best during a crisis.

"I must thank you, Miss Whitman, for your care of Georgia. She is fortunate to have a friend such as yourself."

She gave him a bland smile. "What kind of person would not care for someone else who has been hurt, sir?"

"That is not what I speak of. Your determined efforts have made a true difference in her life. That has become clear in just the short time since I first met the girl. You have worked very hard to polish her virtues and turn her into a lady worthy of her family. I do believe you're a miracle worker."

Instead of accepting his compliment with gracious thanks, as he had expected, she bristled.

"I did nothing but put a bit of polish on a piece of gold, Mr. Stanford. You see miracles only because you lacked the discernment to see the gold that was there all along."

He winced. "Ouch! I suppose I do deserve harsh words on that account."

Her mouth curved with a twitch of humor. "And I'm sure Georgia herself delivered a few of those."

"To be sure. As she should have. You are very fierce in

defense of your friend, Miss Whitman. I hope she appreciates such loyalty, for it is rare in today's world. A friend of your quality is a precious commodity indeed."

He meant the compliment. Elizabeth Whitman, he mused, deserved more than empty phrases men tossed toward women with such practiced, thoughtless, ease. She was an exceptional woman. And so was Georgia Kennedy. As unlike as two women could possibly be, they shared a certain fire that drew a man to their warmth. Elizabeth's fire did not possess the blazing brilliance of Georgia's, but in a quiet way, it was just as attractive. Perhaps a number of men had missed seeing the gold in Elizabeth Whitman just as Alex had missed it in Georgia.

He must be tottering tired to be thinking such thoughts, Alex mused. But before he could announce his intent to leave, Alvin appeared wrapped in a silk dressing gown.

"Ah! I thought I heard your voice, Miss Whitman. What news on my granddaughter?"

"She merely needs a few days' rest, sir."

"Excellent! Nice to see such a sturdy girl, isn't it, Alexander? Have you talked to her yet?"

Elizabeth jumped in. "She is certainly not up to having visitors tonight, Mr. Kennedy."

"Nonsense! Seeing Alexander will cheer her. Bound to. Unless she's asleep?"

She hesitated, then admitted reluctantly, "No. I don't believe she's asleep, though she should be."

"We'll only stay a few moments," Alvin said airily. "Come on Alexander. You rescued the girl from her folly. She'll be wanting to thank you, I'm sure."

Elizabeth didn't look too sure of that at all, and the weight of her disapproval followed Alex as he trailed the older man up the stairs.

Chapter 11

Georgia's head pounded. Every part of her body ached, some parts more painfully than others. The only time in her life she had hurt this much was after a springtime snowbank had given way beneath her weight and sent her tumbling to the bottom of a steep hill, tail over teeth. She had been twelve years old, and her father had dragged her to the mountains of Colorado to look for gold and silver, but what she'd found that spring had been a broken leg and a dislocated shoulder.

She was definitely getting soft, Georgia decided. The twelve-year-old Georgie had recovered from her injuries with a lot less fuss than the tea-sipping, fancy Miss Georgia. Imagine fainting dead away on the street like that, just because someone had caught her a fist to the head sometime during the brawl! And now she lay in a feather bed with everyone in the house wringing their hands as if she were turning up her toes and ready to be shoveled under. Rachel sat in a chair beside the bed, regarding her as if she might stop breathing any minute. It was enough to convince a person to start planning a funeral.

Damn, but turning into a lady certainly undermined years of toughening up!

"Georgia, are you sleeping?"

She turned her head on the pillow—not without paying a price in pain—to see her grandfather tiptoe through the door, followed by none other than Alexander Stanford.

"No, I'm not asleep. I'd like to know how I could sleep with that doctor poking and prodding, not to mention Rachel and Elizabeth fussing over me like I was laid out and ready for praying over."

"Ah," the old man said noncommittally. "It's good to hear your spirit hasn't deserted you. I've brought you a concerned visitor."

Alexander didn't look the fine dandy he'd looked at the gala. His expensive coat had a rip in one sleeve and a smear of what looked like blood on the lapel. He'd taken a swipe at the dirt on his face, but enough remained to give him an uncharacteristically raffish appearance. Probably he'd been reluctant to scrub too hard because of the swelling that was turning an interesting shade of purple on his jaw.

"Hello, Georgia. Are you feeling better?"

Hell no, she wanted to say. She felt as though she'd been run over by a team of mules. But of course that wasn't the ladylike answer he expected. "I'm fine," she croaked.

Alvin rubbed his hands together. "Excellent, excellent! I'll just leave you two together to visit for a bit. It's late, and an old man needs his rest. Rachel, why don't you go down to the kitchen and catch something to eat while Mr. Stanford and Miss Kennedy visit for a bit?"

Georgia watched her grandfather bustle Rachel from the room, amazed that he would do such a thing. Alexander looked equally stunned.

"Sneaky old man," Georgia said. "You ought to just follow him right out the door, Alexander Stanford. According to the rules everybody in these parts live by, I don't think you're supposed to be alone with me in my bedroom in the wee hours of the night."

He smiled down at her. The man did have a very nice smile. "The thing about society's rules is this—they don't count unless someone catches you breaking them."

She laughed, even though it hurt. "Except that my

grandfather would like nothing more than to trap you into marrying me, you poor man." Georgia hadn't given up her need to get even, but Alexander had just pulled her fat from the fire, so she owed him a warning, at least. Fair was fair.

"I doubt the man who marries you needs such sympathy, my dear. And I'm much more concerned with your condition than with propriety right now. I've been very worried"—he grimaced—"actually, both Mr. Barnes and I were very worried that you'd been seriously hurt."

"Well, don't worry. The world can't get rid of me that easily. Back in Arizona you wouldn't find me lying around in a soft bed just because I got a few bumps here and there. It's nice of you to worry, though. I can't remember the last time someone worried about me."

"Surely that's not true."

"True enough." She made a face. "Is that knot on your jaw from my fist?"

He ran a hand gingerly over the swelling. "Most likely. I don't think anyone else got through my defense quite as well as you did."

"Looks like I whacked you good. Sorry about that. In a fight, a body's blood gets heated up, and sometimes you do things without thinking about them."

He chuckled. "My guess is you're not *that* sorry you landed a good one. You still haven't forgiven my boorish behavior when we first met."

"I'm thinking about it," she conceded with a small smile. "You aren't a bad sort to have around in a brawl, and you did come to my rescue, after all. Not"—she added hastily—"that I truly needed rescuing."

"Of course you didn't," he agreed dryly. "But maybe now that you've rearranged my face, we could call things even?"

"Like I said, I'll think about it. But speaking of being rescued, is Cougar okay?"

He frowned. "Cougar? Oh—Cooper."

"Is that his real name?"

"You didn't know his real name?" His eyes narrowed. "Cooper implied you were great friends."

Georgia snorted. "If we're such great friends, why isn't *he* here worrying about me?" An odd fear assailed her. "He wasn't hurt, was he?"

"He's fine." Alex hesitated, then shrugged. "He was here, wanting to see you, but Miss Whitman shooed him away. She did her best to oust me, also, but your grandfather intervened in my behalf."

"Oh." The fear mellowed to disappointment. Silly to feel disappointed, she told herself. She didn't want to see Cougar anyway, except maybe to thank him for helping her with those yahoos who'd jumped her.

Alexander took a deep breath, as if, Georgia mused, he were getting ready to plunge into deep water. "I would have left when Miss Whitman advised it," he said, "but I did particularly want to say something to you, Georgia. I don't want you to feel bad about what happened tonight, as far as your indulging in fisticuffs like a street rowdy, I mean."

Georgia supposed that she had truly scotched the ladylike image she was trying to perfect.

"Certainly I don't hold it against you, and if anyone remarks on it within my hearing, I'll certainly stand up to defend your reputation."

That was big of him.

"I've come to realize that you are a unique woman, Georgia, and perhaps the strictures we apply to more ordinary women shouldn't apply to you."

"Unique meaning one of a kind?" She wasn't sure she liked that after working so hard to be like other women. "You didn't think unique was such a good thing when we first met."

He tried to charm her with a chagrined smile. "You've changed since that night, Georgia."

"I have?"

"And perhaps I've come to appreciate unique."

"You have?"

"So much so that I'd like to ask your permission to call upon you. Your grandfather gave his consent long ago, but I wanted yours as well."

Probably a big concession, Georgia reflected, considering that in these parts, females were rarely consulted about anything. She looked up at him. Tension tightened his face as it had vibrated in his request. This was it, she realized. She had wanted the man to grovel—well, this was probably as close as he got to groveling. He stood there suffering the humiliation of supplication, begging for her consideration, reaching for her approval just as she'd once reached for his.

Victory was at hand, Georgia thought. Now was the time to spit, to show the snobby, nose-in-the-air pig how much rejection stung. Revenge would feel good. It might even take away the pounding headache and aching ribs. And yet . . .

Georgia tried to steel her heart by reminding herself of his contempt. Coarse, he'd called her. Graceless. Overbold. An Amazon.

And now he wanted to come courting. He was all but down on one knee, the poor man. And she had the power to dose him with the same treatment he'd given her.

Except that as he stood there looking down at her, he didn't seem like the poor supplicant she'd imagined, the image that had spurred her on during dancing lessons, corset tightenings, and Elizabeth's endless drill on how to walk and how to talk and how to lift a teacup without looking like a . . . well, an Amazon. She had imagined Alexander groveling, and he wasn't, really. Nor was he particularly worshipful, moonstruck, or humble.

He had too much pride for that, she realized. She knew him better now than on the night her grandfather had introduced her, so disastrously, to society. Then he'd been a handsome paper cutout of a man, respected, educated, wealthy—and destined to be hers, Alvin had assured her. He was a star that had suddenly and unexpectedly come within reach, and when she'd reached, the star had spit on her.

But Alexander Stanford was no longer a paper cutout. Now he was a real man with a manipulating father and a dearly loved wife who had died young. Alexander Stanford was a man who worried enough about her to hang around her grandfather's place in the small hours of the night just to make sure she was all right. And he was so eager to come courting that he had to get in his bid before leaving. He was a man who had, several times, humbled his pride enough to apologize for his cruel words and admit that he'd been wrong. He was a man who hadn't hesitated to come to her rescue on the dark streets of Chicago, a man who could make a wry joke about her hitting him in the face—which had been an accident, she told herself virtuously.

The need for retribution no longer burned so hot in her blood, Georgia realized with a certain regret. Becoming a lady had turned her to mush.

Alexander still waited patiently, looking down at her with a peculiar smile on his face—half hopeful and half baffled, as if he himself didn't quite believe what he was doing.

"So, you want to come calling, with my permission?"

"It would be my honor," he said formally.

What the hell? Let the man hang himself with his own rope, Georgia decided. "Okay. Call all you want. Just give me a few days to put myself back together. Right now I couldn't cinch . . . uh . . ." A complaint about cinching herself into a corset with bruised ribs almost slipped out, but she caught herself in time. She'd just given a civilized gent permission to court, which was almost as serious as getting hitched. So from now on she was truly committed to be a lady. "Uh . . . I couldn't stand upright if my life depended on it."

His smile told her he'd known exactly what she was going to say, but he didn't scold her for it. "It's been cruel of me to keep you awake." He lifted one of her hands and brushed the bruised knuckles with his lips. "Until we meet again."

Before he reached the door, she queried him. "Unique, am I?"

He chuckled. "Indeed."

She liked the sound of that, Georgia decided as the door closed behind him. Before coming to Chicago, she'd always thought of herself as plain and—okay, she would admit it—rather coarse, a hopeless hoyden. Unique was better. Unique had class. She could live with unique.

Or maybe that blow to the head had scrambled her brains.

Elizabeth didn't have the fortitude to keep Georgia in bed for a week, as she would have liked. The task would have taken more than fortitude. It would have required sturdy chains and perhaps a whip, she confided to Mrs. Bolton, who just shook her head and said fondly, "She's a toot, that Miss Georgia. That she is."

A half day's bed rest was all the girl would tolerate, though she was quieter than her norm once she insisted upon getting dressed and going downstairs. Unless Elizabeth occupied her with lessons—Georgia was striving to learn fine needlework, and together they were reading aloud Louisa May Alcott's novel *Little Women*—Georgia knocked about the house aimlessly, reading poetry, writing letters to her friend in Arizona, or sometimes simply staring out the window at the dreary autumn sky. The quiet introspection was so unlike the Georgia she'd come to know that Elizabeth almost called in the physician once again. But when questioned about her mood, Georgia just laughed and shook her head.

"Have you ever come to a place in your life when you knew life was never going to be what it once was," she asked Elizabeth, "no matter how much you would like to go back?"

The awful day her father had been found dead, his own gun lifted to his head, flashed through Elizabeth's mind. The memory had lost none of its bitterness. "Indeed I do. Is that what has you melancholy?"

"I'm not melancholy. I'm just . . . just trying to think things through. My life has been sort of a reaction to things thrown at me. Indians carry off your mule to roast over a fire, you get a new mule. The wind blows a tree onto your cabin, then you fix it. Some yahoo tries to dam up the creek above your claim, you knock his dam down. There's never been many choices, really, no forks in my road where I had to decide which way to go. There was only one way to go because any other way would put you six feet under."

Any change to what Georgia described would be a positive change, to Elizabeth's way of thinking.

"But it looks like I might have some real choices coming up," Georgia said with an uncharacteristic sigh. "I don't have much practice in thinking things through."

Elizabeth smiled and laid a hand on her friend's arm. "I think you have more practice than you think. But you're right. Even when life changes for the better, change can be upsetting. We can never make things go back to the way they were, even if we want to."

Georgia sighed yet again. "It's strange that Cougar hasn't been around to visit. I warned him not to pester me and my grandfather, but usually he listens about as well as a rock. And after he jumped into that fight . . ."

Maybe this wasn't really a change of subject, Elizabeth speculated. Could it be that all this quiet introspection had something to do, not with Alexander, as she'd suspected, but Cooper Barnes?

"Not that I want him to come around," Georgia said with more of her characteristic force. "It's about time he started to listen to what I say."

"No doubt he thinks it too soon for you to have visitors, dear. I'm afraid I was quite stern in sending him away after the doctor saw you."

That sternness had not discouraged Alexander, though. Every day he had either sent a note or flowers, or come himself to Greystone to pay a short and mannerly visit. Alvin, of course, was delighted. And Georgia seemed to have softened toward him considerably. The pair would sit chatting and drinking hot chocolate, cider, or tea while Elizabeth or Alvin kept them company for propriety's sake, though Alvin certainly hadn't concerned himself with propriety the night he'd taken the man up to Georgia's bedroom.

Georgia seemed much more comfortable with Alexander since that awful evening when Alexander and Mr. Barnes had carried her into the house unconscious and battered. Somehow she seemed more comfortable with herself as well. The girl was perfectly polite to her caller. Amiable, even. And Alexander seemed to truly enjoy Georgia's company.

Alvin, of course, did everything he could to foster the courtship, talking constantly of Alexander's virtues, the advantages of marriage to a man of such sterling character. Even Elizabeth, who admired Alexander tremendously, tired of hearing him praised.

On a chilly evening in the first week of October, Georgia and Alvin faced each other across a table in the back parlor while Elizabeth sat before the fire reading a collection of Longfellow. Alvin had shouldered the task of teaching his granddaughter the game of whist. Her impatience with the intricacies of the game threatened to overwhelm Alvin's determination to teach her.

"Why can't we just play poker? It's fast, fun, and all you have to think about is if the other guy is bluffing."

"Poker is a crass game for crass people. It's certainly not a game for gentle ladies."

Elizabeth had to smile at Alvin's comment. Everyone in Chicago knew that Alvin enjoyed his poker as much as the next man and had been known to drop considerable sums of money playing the game.

"You think everything fun is crass," Georgia complained.

"That's because I'm an old man. You might be happier answering to a younger, more liberal man." He gave her a sly smile. "Such as Alexander."

"I don't need to be answering to anyone."

"Everyone answers to someone, girl. Learn to live with it. If you could settle yourself with Alexander, I'd give you your precious mine, and then you can probably prevail on the poor man to let you do whatever you want. Women generally end up getting their way, after all."

Georgia smiled with mock innocence. "I'll get the mine anyway if I wait out your year—that is, if you keep your word."

Her grandfather snorted. Accustomed by now to his snorts, Georgia just smiled. The two enjoyed baiting each other, Elizabeth mused. They were more alike than either would care to admit.

"Enough of this useless chatter," Alvin said. "Back to the rules of the game. If you would only concentrate, girl, then—"

"I concentrate just fine. But it's a boring game."

"You have no head for strategy."

"Twaddle. I'm an expert at strategy. Just last year when I was driving my wagon back from Fort Whipple, a lone buck Apache started trailing me. He had his eye either on my mule or my scalp, I don't know which, but I wasn't much in favor of giving up either one. I just plain outstrategized him. That's what I did. I ducked into a big shallow cave that hardly anyone but me knows about. My daddy and me used to stash supplies there because it was nice and dry and cool, and no one, even the Indians, ever found the stuff. Anyway, I drove right into this big cave and hurried back to brush out my tracks before that fellow made another appearance. Then I hotfooted it over the hill to where Mac and Charlie Downs were working in the next valley. We all three took after the Indian—Mac and Charlie like it when the odds are in their favor that way—and surprised the hel . . . uh . . . surprised him."

Georgia told of the chase in colorful but quite proper terms. As Elizabeth listened, she found herself wishing that she had even a small part of Georgia's spirit. Women weren't supposed to take on the world without the help of a man. Such ability labeled one as exceptionally unfashionable, but Elizabeth found Georgia's self-reliance one of the most attractive things about the girl.

"We didn't get the sneaky so-and-so, of course. He was way better at losing himself than we were at finding him. But he didn't get me or my mule."

She nodded with satisfaction. "Now, that's strategy."

"That, young woman, is why I will never quite forgive your father for taking you away from Chicago in the first place."

They were saved an argument by Bittles, who appeared in the doorway to announce, "Mr. Alexander Stanford has come calling, sir."

"Ah! Excellent. Bring him back, and have Mrs. Bolton bring out some of that cake and a good bottle of brandy."

Elizabeth shared a speculative look with Georgia. Alexander had been a faithful caller for the past ten days, but he called during the day. A more formal evening call might signal a new stage to his courtship.

Alvin welcomed the younger man warmly. "Alexander! Good to see you, boy. What's this I hear about you getting a new horse that beat everything on four legs on the East Coast?"

"Actually, sir, my father is the culprit. If you're fishing for a race with that gray of yours, you'll have to talk to him."

"I might do that. Sit down, sit down. Georgia and I were discussing whist. Now that you're here, we can actually play. You can partner Georgia, and I'll partner Elizabeth."

Alex made a bow to the ladies, then turned back to his host. "Thank you, sir, but I fear I'm not much of a whist player myself."

Georgia chortled. "Poker?"

If Alexander was shocked, he didn't show it. His eyes twinkled with amusement as he answered. "I'm wise enough not to play poker with you, my dear. I'd lose my shirt, I fear."

She laughed. "I'd do my best to take it. Grandfather says you're one of the richest men in town, so you could afford to lose a bit."

Elizabeth winced. Georgia was simply never going to learn the intricacies of polite, acceptable conversation between the genders. At least she had stopped cussing.

"My purpose in calling, other than paying my respects, is to invite you to dine with a small party at my parents' home three days hence. Miss Whitman as well, of course."

If any other family had invited her for an evening of socializing, Elizabeth would have accepted. But spending the evening in the Stanford home, watching Alexander do his best to win Georgia's heart, was not to her taste. Not that she didn't wish them well. She certainly did. But some small corner of her heart ached at their growing affection.

"We accept with pleasure," Alvin proclaimed.

Elizabeth decided that a raging headache would begin, conveniently, three days hence.

Alvin prevailed upon Alexander for a game of chess. Georgia, who regularly beat her grandfather at the game, stood behind her suitor's chair like a good girl and watched.

How different this Georgia Kennedy was from the girl Elizabeth had first met, the raw, loud, awkward, ragamuffin who tried to hide her fear—though she would never admit it—behind bravado. Elizabeth hoped that Georgia's goals had changed along with her appearance and manner, hoped the girl's softened manner toward Alexander Stanford meant she had abandoned her scheme to get revenge. Georgia had proven her point, after all. The man who had once scorned her, the most eligible and elusive bachelor in Chicago, now paid court.

That should be enough for her. Alexander had been rude, but he was a good man. A very good man. He didn't deserve Georgia's cruelty any more than Georgia had deserved his. What he deserved, in fact, was a loving wife, a good woman who would make him happy.

Georgia was certainly a fine woman, Elizabeth acknowledged of her friend, but in spite of her acquiescence to Alexander's courtship, did the girl truly care for him? What a crime it would be if, because of Alvin Kennedy's schemes, two wonderful people ended up in a commitment that suited neither one of them.

If Elizabeth were as wealthy, beautiful, and spirited as Georgia . . . But she refused to think on such impossibilities. Such dreaming always brought heartache.

"Ha!" Alvin crowed. "Fell into my trap there, my boy. If you don't get your head in the game, I'll have you checkmated in no time."

"Take his knight with your rook," Georgia advised over Alexander's shoulder. "Then he'll have to move his bishop to protect the queen."

Both men shot her annoyed looks. She shrugged eloquently. "It would work."

That wasn't the point, Elizabeth knew. No man appreciated unsolicited female advice, especially in an arena as masculine as a chess game. It was one of the social subtleties that Georgia would never understand.

"Your pawn!" Georgia offered five minutes later, squeezing poor Alexander's shoulder. "Use your pawn."

Elizabeth stepped in before both men upended the chessboard over Georgia's head. Putting aside her collection of poetry and taking Georgia's arm, she guided her away from the battlefield. "Do you suppose we could persuade Mrs. Bolton to bring some hot chocolate to my room? I've started a new drawing, and I'd like your opinion of it. I'm sure the gentlemen won't mind if we retire for the evening."

She thought Alexander shot her a grateful glance as she guided Georgia toward the door, but she wasn't sure.

"She's a good girl," Alvin told Alexander as Alex followed Georgia's advice and used his pawn, placing Alvin's king in check. Alvin grimaced. "And a better chess player than you, my boy."

"Most everyone is a better chess player than I," Alex told him with a smile. "I haven't the patience for the game."

Alvin nodded. "I'm glad, however, that you have the patience to pursue my granddaughter." He raised his eyes to meet Alexander's. "She is a good girl. She'll make some man a very good wife."

"Indeed," Alexander replied noncommittally.

He knew very well that the older man was after a firm declaration, but he wasn't about to give one. He was taken with Georgia—fascinated by her, actually. Elizabeth had polished the girl until her differences intrigued instead of grated. No man with eyes could deny her beauty, though a rather rowdy sort of beauty it was with the gold-red hair and jewel-green eyes. Her smiles, her gestures, her graceful, athletic walk—all were unstudied. Natural beauty was a rare thing in a hectic world that worshipped artifice.

But beyond the physical attraction, Alex liked her intelligence, candor, and independence. If she were a man, Alex would be proud to call her friend.

"She has her heart set on returning to Arizona," Alvin

confided. "But women, bless them, change their hearts easily, especially once their fancy is focused on some man. The best thing for a woman is a good man, I always say. And the best thing for a man is a good woman."

"I don't think anyone would argue with you there, Alvin. I suppose the trick is matching the right man with the right woman."

"Ah." Alvin moved a bishop to block Alex's threat to his king. "My contention, I suppose, is that within reason, any woman can become the right woman, and any man the right man."

"Hm." Alex pondered his next move. A possible checkmate was only three moves away. Somehow, he would hate for the older man to win this particular game. "I think I disagree with that notion, having once been married to a woman who was so right that heaven itself couldn't have planned a better match."

Alvin nodded. "Your Alice. She was a lovely girl, true." He raised his eyes from the chessboard and caught Alex in a somber gaze. "I felt about my dear Ellie much the same as you felt about your Alice. She died young, also, died giving me my son, Elias. Grief consumed me. It consumed me so completely that I moved through life in a spiritless daze, neglected my son, my friends—everything. I buried myself in memories so that my woe multiplied, finally robbing me of all the important things left in my life. When I finally came to my senses, it was too late. I had lost Elias, dear friends had wandered away, my business was nearly bankrupt.

"Your father helped me salvage my business, good friend that he is. And Elias—well, I have Georgia. She is all that remains of Elias."

Alexander didn't know how to react. Hearing such a personal confession made sympathy war with embarrassment.

Alvin smiled wryly. "I don't tell you this to gain sympathy, my boy. I'm long past needing sympathy. I tell you this tale so that it doesn't happen to you. I don't believe your lovely Alice would like that."

There was a thought that had never occurred to Alex. It rather stunned his brain. When he didn't answer, Alvin raised a knowing brow. "Worth considering, my friend, is it not?"

> *October 5, 1870*
> *Dear Essie,*
>
> *I'm sending this letter to Miss Barton, the schoolteacher, because I know she can read it to you, and she's a decent sort who won't be squealing everything I say to the whole territory. I know Cougar's not there to read you my letters, because he's here in Chicago making a pest of himself. Or at least, he was making a pest of himself, threatening to go to my granddad about the claim I sold him and scolding me about just about everything—what I wear, how I walk, who I talk to, and so on. I always thought Cougar was the best friend a person could have, and maybe he is, but put city clothes on him and he turns into a real pain in the backside.*
>
> *I haven't seen him for a while—not since he pulled my bacon from the fire when a gang of no-goods took it in their heads to jump me one night. I thought for a while that he got smart and went back to Prescott, but probably not. I figure he won't give up until he pries either that claim or his money from me one way or another.*

Georgia chewed on the end of her pen and pondered what to say. She wasn't going to tell Essie that she missed having Cougar around, because of course she didn't. The jackass was nothing more than a bother. She did owe him for coming to her aid in that fight, though. If she was honest about it, she had to admit those yahoos were getting the best of her when Cougar jumped in. But since then he'd ignored her as if she were a gnat or a flea, something too insignificant to rate his attention. The rat.

She sighed and continued to write.

> *Cougar told me you have two good men working the claims and they're looking out for you all right. I think of home and how beautiful it is on the Lynx this time of year, with the leaves turning yellow and the cool air*

feeling so good against your skin. Here it is not beautiful. The sky is usually gray, and when the wind blows, it feels cold even if it isn't really. Everything is damp. Chicago gets more rain in one month, I think, than all of Arizona Territory gets in a whole year. I wish so hard I was back with you in our cabin, listening to the coyotes howl and sitting in front of our little fireplace. Except probably the weather isn't cold enough there to need the fire except for cooking. The Good Lord certainly did make some places better than others.

Well, now she was really homesick. Prescott was starting to seem like a faraway dream. A few months' absence softened the hardships of her life there and sharpened the memories of brilliant blue skies, warm sun, fresh, clear air, good friends, and a sweet feel of freedom—something she didn't have here. Not all the hot baths, fancy food, and beautiful clothes could make up for a loss of freedom. But then, there was Alex . . .

You won't believe this, Essie, but I'm being courted by the fellow I told you about. He's doesn't drool or stink or any of the things I told you before. He had a wife once that he loved a lot, but she died, and he doesn't really want to marry again, I think, but everyone expects him to marry me. He is a very nice man. Handsome, rich, mannerly, and clean.

Cougar cleaned up pretty well, too. You wouldn't recognize him, because he trimmed his beard, cut his hair, and wears clothes that are almost as pretty as mine. But he doesn't have manners, that's for sure. Or if he does, he doesn't use them on me.

What was she doing talking about Cougar when the man she intended to write about was Alexander? It just went to prove that thinking too much about men addled a woman's brains. She tried to push them both from her mind.

I'm still planning on coming back to Prescott next summer, but I think I've gotten so soft that I couldn't shovel gravel all day long or cut a load of firewood or get the best of those ornery mules. Putting up with my grandfather, though, might keep me in shape to deal with the mules. You'll have to whip me back into shape, or you'll catch me moving my things to the house in town and trying to live the life of a pampered lady.

Would she ever really return to Arizona? Georgia wondered. What would she answer if Alexander Stanford proposed? The longer she stayed in this place, with these people, the less suited she became for the life she had left. The realization frightened her, because she still had no confidence that she could truly measure up to being a part of Chicago society.

And how did she really feel about Alexander? She had told him to come courting, abandoning her plans to give him the set-down of his life. Did that mean she actually liked him? Or more than liked him? He was handsome, smart, rich, and occasionally made her laugh. When he looked at her a certain way, her stomach got a case of butterfly wings, and once or twice she'd gone so far as to wonder what it would be like to kiss him.

Damn but she wished her frigging grandfather had never found her. She'd still have a simple, uncomplicated life where all she had to worry about was Indians, mountain lions, starvation, and freezing to death. Life had been so simple then.

Chapter 12

"Cooper, my boy, I'm glad we have you in the family." Horace Barnes laughed as if he'd made a joke. "Every family needs their adventurer."

Translate, Cougar thought, adventurer to black sheep.

"Every family needs to breed a wanderlust every now and again. No shame in it. Proves our blood still has a bit of gumption in it. Just glad it happened to be my brother's son instead of mine. Heh, heh!"

Cougar sat with his uncle Horace and cousin James in the library of their house in Lincoln Park, enjoying an after-dinner brandy. The brandy was good, but the company left something to be desired. Horace looked very much like Cougar's father, and the brothers' way of thinking was similar as well. They were solid, conservative businessmen. Barnes men sought to take what they were given and build bigger, better businesses, make more money, and stick with the tried-and-true. Only fools and children pursued the shine of something unseen but tempting lying just beyond the horizon. When Cougar had left to slake his wanderlust, he'd been nineteen, and his family had thought him a child indulging childish dreams. Now that he was nearing thirty, they thought him a fool rather than a child.

"I haven't wandered much of anywhere since '64, Uncle. Arizona is where I'll stay."

"Well," Horace said expansively, "at least you had the sense to stay out of the War."

Cougar didn't bother to tell Horace that he'd been with General Carleton's California Column, which fought the only pitched battle of the War Between the States to take place in Arizona Territory. That was when he'd first discovered the place and come to love it. "Prescott is where I want to settle," he said. "The area has potential for more than just gold. As soon as the Apaches are settled, ranching is going to open up, and the first ranchers to run cattle and horses to supply the army in the region are going to make a fortune. The market will stretch all the way from Santa Fe and Albuquerque to California and the Mexican border."

"Hm." Horace swirled his brandy and seemed to search its amber depths for the answer to the problem of his nephew. "I can't deny that you may be on to something there, boy. James is in agreement with me."

James was in agreement with his father about nearly everything. He worked alongside his sire in the railroad construction business, had married the girl his family had all but handpicked for him, lived in a somewhat smaller house only a half mile from his parents, and would call the sky green and the grass purple if his father told him to. His was the very fate Cougar had seen in store for himself in New York when he'd made a bolt for freedom.

"The question is this, though, my boy. Success in business takes more than recognition of an opportunity. It takes steadfastness and determination to see a thing through, thick and thin, through dark days and bright ones. You've spent the last ten years flitting from one thing to another, left a perfectly solid business where you could have slipped into your father's shoes and proven yourself a true Barnes, wandered God knows where for God knows what reasons, and now show up here after only very sparse communication with your family. And here you wax enthusiastic about a ranch and a new land and some fly-by-night gold-mine deal that was supposed to earn you your start-up money. The whole thing doesn't sound very well thought out to me."

To his uncle's way of thinking—and his father's—no venture that lacked a board of directors and a formal prospectus was a well-thought-out enterprise. He should have remembered that before taking the trouble to travel all this way.

"Right you are, Father," James echoed. "Not that your scheme lacks potential, Cooper. But you have a bit to learn about business."

Horace and James didn't know squat about the West or the kind of men who made the frontier thrive. Cougar didn't know why he had expected anything different.

"And this gold mine that you hoped would provide funds . . ." Horace shook his head with condescending sympathy. "I've made some inquiries here and there—discreet, of course. You should have known better than to have business dealings with a female, Cooper boy. According to your aunt Alicia, Alvin Kennedy all but has the chit married off to Alexander Stanford. I doubt Stanford will be interested in any errant deals his wife made through ignorance of the legal status of those claims. He's a bit of an adventurer himself, if you ask me, and likely he'll want to go have a look at them himself once they're under his control. You might as well sing for your money as go to Alvin Kennedy or Alexander Stanford, if you ask me."

"Georgia isn't going to marry Alex Stanford. She has too much sense."

"She'll probably do what her grandfather wants her to do," James said smugly.

"And Stanford can have her and be welcome," Horace commented. "For my money, the girl is too flashy to be proper. Though Kennedy's going to settle a good sum on her when she marries, I hear, and she is his sole heir."

Cougar had to keep a tight rein on his tongue. The idea of some man merely putting up with Georgie because she had money stuck in his craw, and the notion of Georgie being "flashy," well, that was annoying as hell. Maybe she did burn through a man's brain rather than simper around the margins of his mind, which was what society expected of a woman. But damn, there was more to Georgie than flash.

"Whatever is happening between Georgia and Stanford has nothing to do with me. She's a good friend and a straight shooter. She'll see the business good on the matter of that claim."

Horace and James exchanged a look. Cougar knew what they thought. The family black sheep had to be tolerated because he was still, after all, family. But tolerance only went so far.

Horace poured them all another brandy and gave Cougar a small, tight smile. "Well, Cooper, as I said before, there's nothing wrong with a bit of adventurism in the family, or in business, either. It keeps us from going stale, eh? I can't answer for your father, of course. You'd have to talk to him as well. But I'd be willing to invest in this ranch of yours, under certain conditions. I'd want a controlling interest, simply because you haven't really proven an ability to manage something like this, my boy. And you'd have to come up with at least half of the start-up money. That would go a long way toward proving that you've settled down to be a real businessman. And I'd advise you to look into something more conventional than some pie-in-the-sky gold mine that appears to be pulled out from under you like a rug."

Cougar raised his glass in mock salute, though he suspected that the mock part of the salute went entirely over his uncle's and cousin's heads. "Uncle Horace, James, when I drum up something reliable and conventional, we'll talk about this again." Which meant the subject was closed for all time as far as Cougar was concerned. His uncle would try to manage a cattle ranch in the barely civilized frontier from behind a desk in Chicago, much as he managed his railroad business. He didn't know a steer from a bull or gramma grass from locoweed. He had no notion of the country, the climate, or the market.

But knowledge and enterprise wasn't required, in his opinion. Only stability, reliability, and the ability to knuckle under to convention and make such a surrender seem a virtue.

Cougar thought again how lucky he had been to escape this trap. When he'd first left New York, his new life had been a mere lark. Soon enough, though, he'd discovered a genuine love for freedom, for making his own way, difficult as the way sometimes was, rather than doing by rote what his family expected of him. Once free of the harness of polite society he had discovered how chafing that harness was.

Did Georgie know what she was doing by letting herself get sucked into this life? he wondered. Or did she merely see an overwhelming feast of things she had always lacked—comfort, wealth, security? He had to admit, she made one hell of a woman, one who could rock a man's senses like a lightning storm coming over the mountains in Chino Valley, where someday his cattle—his very own one hundred percent controlled by Cougar Barnes cattle—would graze.

Suddenly Cougar realized that all those cattle roaming through the lush grasses of Chino wouldn't be enough for him, not with Georgie in Chicago discovering to her horror what a mistake she had made. If she weren't in Arizona with him, the claim he'd wanted for three years was merely an empty hillside of rock. The ranch that was his future was a meaningless dream.

Damned if he hadn't gone and fallen for the girl. This trip to Chicago wasn't about money—not the money he'd forked over for the claim nor an investment in his dream ranch by his family. He'd come to Chicago for Georgie, and the time had come to admit it.

But he was losing her, even as he admitted to loving her. Since the night they'd brawled together, he had tried to see her nearly every day. The fellow who posed as a butler for Kennedy was as good as any prison guard, keeping Cougar out of Greystone House, and perhaps keeping Georgie in as well, for Cougar had also haunted the fashionable walking path on the lakeshore with no luck at seeing either Georgie or Elizabeth.

If he could spend more time with Georgie, Cougar was almost sure he could remind her of who she really was.

She would come to see that she and Cougar belonged together. They were the same sort of people. Their souls were made of the same stuff. To hell with the stupid mining claim. Let her grandfather have it. Together they could find a way to build a life in Chino Valley, where they were both free to be what they were.

But if Georgie stayed barricaded in Alvin Kennedy's mansion, she would never know that he wanted her, not her frigging claim. He needed a plan, Cougar decided. He needed a plan worthy of a man who had survived Apaches, rattlesnakes, desert heat, winter blizzards, and one very cranky mountain lion.

Not an easy task, Cougar admitted. The high Rocky Mountains were easier to negotiate than the barriers society could place around a woman.

"Headache, my foot!" Georgia declared with a snort. "You need a better excuse than that to get out of going to this dinner."

"That sound is so very unladylike," Elizabeth scolded.

"This one?" Georgia snorted again.

"Yes, that one."

They were in Elizabeth's small bedroom, and Georgia was going through the wardrobe to select a dress for Elizabeth that looked "gussied up" enough for that evening's small gathering at the Stanford house.

"That sound is one of the few noises you've left me. I've given up cussing and yelling. So don't complain."

"You sound like a pig."

"Come on, Elizabeth. I'll bet you've never heard a pig in your life."

"You sound like I imagine a pig would sound, then."

"A pig sounds much worse. Really."

Miffed that Georgia wouldn't accept her tactful withdrawal from the Stanford dinner, Elizabeth felt a bit like snorting herself, but she was too much the lady to indulge.

"Why don't you want to go to the dinner? Tell me."

"Georgia, I've told you many times that prying into people's private feelings is rude."

"Rude is not one of the things I've given up. Do you know that sometimes you're so proper you forget that you're human?"

"I'm all too human, I fear."

"You're dodging the question, Elizabeth. Why don't you want to go to the dinner?"

Elizabeth glared.

Georgie pointedly ignored her. She picked out a rose gown from the wardrobe. "This looks very nice on you. You could wear this."

"Georgia, I really am getting a headache."

"I'm told I can do that to people. You still have to go."

"You no longer need me at your side every moment."

"I want you there. Some of the other guests will be the same people who came to the disaster dinner. They're going to be waiting like vultures for me to do something wrong. I need you to kick me under the table if I slip into being the real me."

"Georgia, the real you delighted absolutely everyone at the Yacht Club gala. And Alexander is very taken with the real you. Just be yourself, the lovely woman that you've learned to be."

"I need you there. And you need to have some fun. If you don't go out and yahoo it up sometimes, you'll grow mold on your soul. Then you really will be a spinster."

Elizabeth suspected that Georgia's "need" for her to attend the dinner had more to do with a misguided plot to draw Elizabeth back into the social circles her family once frequented. She didn't have the understanding of society to realize that Elizabeth, along with Pheobe, Claudia, and Chloe, would never again be accepted on equal footing with the likes of Alvin Kennedy and the Stanfords. Georgia's gaffs, which had decreased in frequency to only occasional, were not nearly the disadvantage that Elizabeth's family tragedy was.

Georgia pulled another dress from the wardrobe. "I've never seen this one! It looks like pure gold, just like the lights in your hair when the sun hits it. You'll look beautiful in this."

"It's old, from before . . ." Before her father had shot

himself. Before the world had changed. "... before I became a governess."

"We have time to make it look a little more fashionable."

"Now you're an expert on women's fashions?"

"I'm just applying what you've taught me."

Elizabeth couldn't help but laugh. "I never taught you to be so pushy."

"Nope," Georgia admitted. "That just comes naturally."

So Elizabeth wore her gold dress, a remnant of her former life, and attended the Stanford's dinner, even though she had been invited more as a matter of good form than any desire for her presence. The party was a small one, with only twenty or so guests. Included in their number were both Mrs. Philpott and young Miss Hansen, both of whom had gloated so when Georgia had tripped over her own tongue, as well as the heels of her shoes, at her grandfather's dinner party. Elizabeth hadn't witnessed the scene, but from Georgia's recounting, she could certainly imagine it. She was only too well acquainted with the irony of females being called the "gentle sex."

The Stanford gathering, however, saw a far different Georgia than the awkward girl who had fumbled her society debut. The same spirit bubbled beneath a more polished surface. The same devilry shone in the green eyes, but it had mellowed from wildness to a delicious hint of the wicked. Georgia didn't truly have a wicked bone in her whole body, but somehow the red hair, curvaceous build, and snapping eyes projected *unconventional*. And in society's eyes, *unconventional* translated to *suspiciously wicked*.

Those who hadn't met the evolved Georgia fumbled for words at their surprise. Elizabeth sat beside her protégée in the small ballroom where a string quartet serenaded the guests during the hors d'oeuvres. She watched men compete for Georgia's attention. She watched Miss Hansen and the two other young unmarried women who had accompanied their parents whisper among themselves and cast jealous looks at where the new red-haired queen sat enthroned upon the Stanford's fainting couch. And she watched Alexander Stanford watching the whole scene, his saturnine face unreadable. Try as she would, Elizabeth couldn't imagine Georgia as Alexander's wife. He was obviously taken with Georgia's appeal—what man alive wouldn't be? And Georgia had to be impressed with Alexander. What other man had such charm, steadiness, wit, intelligence, and strength?

But the strong, quiet Alexander Stanford locked in matrimonial bonds with equally strong, effervescent, volatile Georgia Kennedy? Elizabeth tried not to quail at the thought.

She also tried not to envy her friend's good fortune. Envy was an annoying sin, but it popped up now and again no matter how a person tried to squelch it.

"Good evening, Miss Kennedy. How nice to see you looking so well." This from Mrs. Philpott, one of the stone-throwing crowd at Georgia's debacle. "And . . . Miss Whitman, isn't it?" The little smile she gave Elizabeth could have withered an oak tree. "I hadn't expected to see you at such a gathering."

Elizabeth could feel Georgia stiffen beside her, and knew it was for Elizabeth's sake, not her own. She tried to stem an outburst by cordially ignoring the woman's rudeness.

"Good evening, Mrs. Philpott. I'm employed by Mr. Kennedy as Georgia's companion, as you probably know. The Stanfords were courteous enough to invite me along with the Kennedys."

"Ah. Employed." She pronounced the word with disdain. "Of course. It is a shame how the touch of scandal clings for so long. Unjust, really. But Georgia, dear"—she gave Georgia a searching look—"I've been hearing of your stunning success at the Yacht Club gala. Chicago is positively buzzing with it. But would you believe the gossip that circulates? I heard the most unlikely story about your brawling on the lakefront like a bawd! Can you imagine?"

Georgia shifted her stance to attack. "I don't fight like a bawd, Mrs. Philpott. I fight like my daddy taught me to fight: to win, with kicks, punches, knives, clubs"—she smiled scathingly—"or words, if need be. The world isn't a very friendly place. Even a lady needs to defend herself now and then. I learn fast, and I don't knuckle under to anyone."

The rather dumpy Mrs. Philpott drew herself up, evidently taking Georgia's warning. But Georgia crooked a beckoning finger to bring the older woman closer, so she could tell her quietly. "By the way, missus. I have a friend out West, a Mexican woman by the name of Esperanza, who mixes up a dye that would color that gray hair a lot better than whatever you're using. If you want, I'll write her for the recipe."

Mrs. Philpott huffed, turned red, and sputtered a bit as she left.

"That was cruel," Elizabeth chided her friend.

"She deliberately reminded you of what you didn't want to remember, and she all but called me a bawdy woman in a voice loud enough to carry to the whole room. Mentioning her dyed hair hardly compares to what I should have done. Silly woman."

"Admirably done," said Mr. Finley. The ex-frontiersman from the Yacht Club celebration was standing close enough to hear. "That fixed the old bag."

"You are both incorrigible," Elizabeth told them, but she had to smile.

The dinner itself went smoothly. Alexander partnered Georgia, which was a public enough announcement of his interest to discourage other bachelors at the table with ideas of their own. Elizabeth was escorted to the table by the entertaining Everett Finley, whom she liked very much indeed. Something of the same spirit that shone in Georgia's eyes resided in Mr. Finley's as well.

"Your friend Miss Kennedy is a remarkable woman," Finley told her.

"She is."

Remarkable, indeed. Georgia held her own amazingly well during a rather stilted meal, ignoring the pressure of her grandfather's expectations, Robert and Lydia Stanford's scrutiny, and Alexander's measuring looks. The girl had become more than Elizabeth had created, gone beyond deportment lessons and drills in speech, dancing, and conversation. She had blossomed into her true self, a unique combination of originality, freshness, and unfettered spirit tamed and polished just enough to entertain rather than overwhelm. Her table manners, thanks to Elizabeth, were impeccable, but her conversation was just different enough to add spice to otherwise bland fare. She no longer feared recounting stories that had colored her life—the tale of the bear cub that once wandered into her cabin in a pounding rainstorm elicited chuckles of amusement from both men and women—but she instinctively toned down the accounts for ears unused to hearing of such adventures, especially from a woman's mouth.

Nothing could have told Elizabeth with more certainty that Georgia's need for her had ended than watching her at Stanford's table that night. Her student had surpassed every goal Elizabeth had set for her. She was her own person, and soon, Elizabeth knew, she would fulfill her grandfather's dreams and forge an alliance with the Stanford family.

She would start looking for new employment, Elizabeth decided as the dessert course was served. Georgia would want her to stay with her simply out of the goodness of her heart. The girl knew how Alvin's generous wages eased things for her family. But Elizabeth had not yet fallen to the point where she could cling like a leech to feed off another's bounty.

After dinner the men and women separated, as was only proper, for after-dinner conversation was reserved for sports, politics, business, and brandy for the men, domestic issues, matrimonial concerns, and sherry for the ladies—spiced with tidbits of gossip, of course. The gossip was limited a bit this night, however, for the one most would have been gossiping about sat with them in the drawing room.

"Miss Kennedy," Lydia Stanford said, setting a polite tone, "I don't believe I have ever seen hair quite the color of yours. It is . . . quite lovely, really. Striking."

"Well, certainly most of the menfolk seem struck by it," Alice Cromwell commented dryly.

A hesitant silence followed the remark as the women waited cautiously for Georgia's reaction to something that might have been construed an insult.

But Georgia just laughed. "An old Indian hung around a

mining camp in Colorado where my daddy and I spent a year. He used to say that I'd been marked by the sunrise."

"What a beautiful thing to say," a young miss sighed. "Imagine a savage coming up with something like that."

Instead of conversing about proper female topics such as housekeeping woes, servants, entertainments, and social alliances, the talk that evening in the ladies' withdrawing room was of miners, cowboys, soldiers, and Indians. Less than forty years before, Chicago had still felt the threat posed by the uncivilized people who had inhabited the land before the white man came, but most of the ladies in the room had never seen an Indian, and they thought of the "red savages" in terms of flamboyant adventure stories and penny romances, not gritty reality. But then, Georgia's stories tended to be on the flamboyant side. Elizabeth suspected that she doctored them a bit. Still, the tales of Colorado, Wyoming, and Arizona, Indians, soldiers, miners, and cowboys made Elizabeth long to escape the dull confines of her life, made her wish, almost, that she were a man so that she, too, could go adventuring.

But then, Georgia was not a man, and look at the life she had led.

"Did he really pick up the snake and wrap it around his neck?" a breathless lady asked Georgia.

"Just like a collar, that snake was."

"Oh, I think you're spinning a tall tale," another said.

Before Georgia could answer, a servant burst into the room. "Madam!" he nearly shouted at Lydia Stanford. "Mr. Stanford has collapsed! We fear he is at death's door!"

Alexander Stanford was not often at a loss, but when his father turned deathly gray and collapsed in the middle of a vehement diatribe against President Grant, he didn't know what to do. Robert Stanford had always been the pillar of his family, a granite monument to strength and obstinacy, and though Alex had long been his own man, seeing his father topple came as a blow to his stable world.

He did have the presence of mind to send for a physician, but beyond that, he felt helpless. The guests left with hasty expressions of concern and sympathy. His mother called for smelling salts and had to be half carried to her room by her maid. Garner the butler hovered, but he and Alex were alike in having no idea what to do, whether to move his father or leave him on the library floor where he had collapsed, whether to try to force water down his throat or leave him be until the doctor arrived.

Fortunately, an angel of mercy came to their rescue. Elizabeth Whitman swept into the library, took in the men's confusion, and assumed charge in the manner of a general marshaling his troops. With great care she searched for Robert's pulse, observed his pallid color, and lifted a lid to look at his eye.

"If your man had exaggerated less in his announcement, your poor mother might not have been sent into such a tizzy, Mr. Stanford. Your father is most definitely not dead." She gave the long faces in the room a sympathetic smile. "Come, come. It is not as bad as all that. He breathes well and his pulse is steady. But we must get him off this cold floor to where he can be more comfortable. Mr. Stanford, if you would be so kind as to loosen his neckcloth, he could breathe more easily."

Georgia, who had also come into the room, shook her head at Alexander. "You'd better do as she says, Alexander. When Elizabeth's in this mood, she gets cranky when people get in her way."

Elizabeth was not at all cranky, as a matter of fact. An air of quiet command served her well in getting people to do her bidding. Before many minutes had passed, Robert was in his bed, the servants were building up the fire to warm the room, and Elizabeth was gently urging her patient to accept a few swallows of water. Except for the Kennedys, the other guests had departed. While Alvin and Alex worried a path in the bedroom carpet, Georgia assisted Elizabeth with Robert.

Georgia's calm in the emergency came as no surprise. The life she had lived included death and illness in many forms, Alexander had no doubt. But Elizabeth's response was unexpected. Alexander had mistaken her quiet, modest mien for frailty. Quite possibly, he mused, Elizabeth had depths few suspected.

Only an hour passed before the physician arrived—Dr. Davis, the same man who had treated Georgia.

"Shoo, shoo!" He whisked them from the room. "Do your worrying elsewhere, please, and leave the patient to me." But he did not chase Elizabeth away as he did the others. Alexander looked back as he left the room, and they were in serious discussion.

Twenty minutes later Dr. Davis and Elizabeth descended the staircase together and met Alexander and Alvin in the drawing room. "Alexander, your father will recover, I'm fairly sure. His heart is the culprit here, but with rest and an effort on his part not to worry so over the least thing, I believe he will be restored to health. For a week or more he will require nursing care. I believe you must engage a woman, for I looked in upon your mother, and I do not believe her constitution is up to the task. Caring for an invalid—especially your father, if you don't mind my saying so—is not suited to the sensibilities of a delicate lady such as Mistress Stanford. Actually, the best I could recommend is Miss Whitman, if she could remain for a few days. She is extremely competent, and in fact probably saved your father's life by taking charge of his care before I arrived."

Elizabeth had all but collapsed on the settee next to Georgia. Weariness gave her an ethereal quality, but Alexander was beginning to realize that the spirit beneath the slight frame was steel through and through.

"Miss Whitman, I hesitate to impose, but I would be most grateful if you could care for my father at least until I can engage someone. If Alvin and Georgia can spare you, I would see you well compensated for your time."

Elizabeth sighed, and he couldn't quite interpret the look she gave him. It was almost fearful. Then she straightened her spine and squared her delicate jaw. "I would be happy to care for your father, Mr. Stanford, with Mr. Kennedy's leave."

Alvin waved a hand. "Of course, Miss Whitman. We don't need you anymore in any case."

Georgia's eyes flashed at her grandfather. "We do so need her!" Then she looked an apology at Alexander. "But of course she should stay as long as she is needed here. I'll have her things sent over as soon as we arrive home."

"Thank you, Georgia."

Alex couldn't help compare the two women as they sat together. They were like earth and fire, Georgia burning bright even at this late hour of the night, and Elizabeth quiet, solid, with resources buried deep and out of sight.

Alexander shook his head to clear it. He was thinking nonsense, plainly too tired to be sensible. He had planned this gathering to become better acquainted with Georgia, to observe her in the setting of his family, and then ended the evening with Elizabeth dominating the scene.

Long after the Kennedys had gone and Elizabeth had settled into a room close to his father's, Alexander's churning mind denied him sleep. He took refuge in the kitchen, a kitchen full of boyhood memories of snitching fried pies cooling on the big worktable and the cook Elsa threatening to switch his hand if he laid a finger on one of the tasty treats. In truth, though, Elsa, long retired, had always cooked one or two little pies more than she needed, knowing the young master would make off with at least one.

The kitchen had been his favorite retreat, always warm and bright, no matter how gloomy the weather outside, with tantalizing smells and cheerful conversations. Sitting there made the past seem like yesterday.

His father's sudden frailty struck a harsh blow to Alexander's idea of how the world should be. Somehow he'd thought his father was a permanent fixture in life, the stern taskmaster he'd tried to please when growing up, the man who had taught him the value of hard work, honesty, education, and enterprise. Robert Stanford was often exasperating, but always solid, always there.

But that wasn't so, Alexander now realized, and with that realization came an awareness of how much he owed the older man, how much he would miss him when he passed on. God willing that would not be in the next few days, but tonight had certainly been a reminder of mortality.

"Oh!" came a startled feminine exclamation. Elizabeth stood in the kitchen doorway, wrapped in a robe. Fawn brown hair, still kinked from being braided, trailed down her back to her slender waist. "I didn't know anyone was down here. I'm so sorry to intrude."

"You're not intruding. Come have some tea and milk. Or do you prefer coffee?"

"Tea, thank you. I couldn't sleep, so . . . well, I'm afraid I didn't have much of an appetite at dinner. I came down to raid the larder, I confess."

"As did I," Alex admitted with a grin. "I believe there's some cheese and Joannie's good bread we can lay hands upon."

He fixed them both tea while she sat at the table, looking rather diffident about being alone with a man in only her nightclothes, though certainly any form she boasted was hidden beneath the voluminous folds of the dressing robe his mother had loaned her.

"I checked on your father before I came down. He is sleeping quite peacefully. I'm sure a bit of rest and the tonic the doctor left will have him right in no time."

Alex set the tea on the table and sliced bread and cheese to go with it. "I am very much in your debt, Miss Whitman, for the part you played tonight. You kept your head when everyone else, including myself, was fussing and fuming and running about like beheaded chickens. Just as you did the night we brought Georgia in from the night, carrying her like a sack of potatoes slung over Cooper Barnes's shoulder."

"I only did what was necessary, Mr. Stanford."

"Please call me Alexander. And I think I will take the liberty of addressing you as Elizabeth. Formality seems rather out of place in a kitchen during the small hours of the night."

She smiled. It was a quiet smile. He could well imagine it on the face of an angel.

"You did much more than what was necessary. You were sensible and levelheaded, and somehow you knew just what to do. What's more, you had the courage to wade in and take charge over a pack of blathering fools who are, nonetheless, quite intimidating fools. For that I am forever in your debt."

She colored slightly, and he smiled, wondering if anyone cared for Elizabeth as well as she cared for others. Everyone seemed to turn to her for support, even Georgia, and she gave without holding back. An exceptional woman, surely.

"Your father seems to be a strong man," she said. "He will bounce back from this, I'm sure."

"Probably," Alex admitted. "This time. My father's brother died ten years ago of a weakness in the heart. He lived only three years after the first signs of illness. My father has always been so active and hearty, we all thought the ailment had passed him by."

In the silence that followed, they sipped their tea. Alex could almost see Elizabeth marshaling her thoughts, searching for something to say to him that would balance optimism with reality. She impressed him as a lady who could face reality. He had never run from reality himself. His father might have years left. Or he might have only weeks.

Alexander had been indulging in selfishness, neglecting his family responsibilities, and that had to end.

Chapter 13

Georgia's father had once told her that straddling a fence never got a body anything but a bunch of splinters. A wise person chose a side and stayed there. He didn't spend his life with one leg trying to walk on one side and another leg walking on the opposite.

She maybe should have listened to her daddy, Georgia mused, except never in the world did she believe that she, Georgie Kennedy, would have a fence problem like the one she'd met here in Chicago. It was a hell of a fence, with Georgie on one side, Georgia on the other, and both nagging from her respective side.

Georgie wanted to hotfoot it back to Arizona as soon as she could, wipe the Chicago mud from her boots, burn the frigging corset that even now, as she sat in her grandfather's fancy drawing room reading in the weak afternoon sunlight, poked into her ribs and made breathing a chore. Georgie longed for the freedom to do what she wanted when she wanted. She was tired of watching every word that came from her mouth. She was tired of sitting up straight, walking with a graceful, measured stride, and sitting by like a frivolous decoration while someone else provided her needs. Making your own way in the world, while it might be wearisome at times, at least afforded a person some pride.

Georgia, on the other hand, loved soaking in hot baths and wearing silk next to her skin. Regular tasty meals had gotten to be a habit, especially desserts. The mirror had become a friend rather than an enemy. It showed her a woman whom no one could call an ox in pigtails. She liked the opera and plays, the musicales where everyone pretended to actually know something about the music presented. The way men looked at her made her glow inside, and the sometimes envious glances of women made her want to laugh.

Georgie squirmed with restless energy and the desire to put her life back to what it once had been. Georgia, however, wasn't so sure she wanted to go back to sleeping on a hard pallet on the dirt floor of her cabin and washing in the cold water of the Lynx. She wasn't so sure she wanted her hands to turn once again to hard leather and her hair to a wild mane of red straw. Essie's beans and tortillas—good as they were—didn't hold a candle to the meals conjured up by Marjorie, her grandfather's cook, and neither did fresh-shot rabbit or squirrel. And though Georgie resented the time it took to dress, comb, brush, and primp each morning, Georgia thought the effort might be worth not having to wear coarse denim day in and day out.

So here she was, truly straddling, one leg walking toward Chicago with its soft living and luxuries, the other headed for Arizona, independence, and freedom. And her daddy had been right. She was headed for some mighty nasty splinters.

Cougar would say she deserved them—if he had come around to say anything. Apparently he was so disgusted with her for being an "empty-headed decoration," as he'd put it, that he figured she was a lost cause. Likely he'd headed back to Prescott.

Not that she missed him at all. He was a thorn in her side, a totally unreasonable nag. He didn't know the first thing about the decisions facing her.

She closed her book—Jane Austen's *Sense and Sensibility*—with a snap, wondering if she herself knew the first thing about the decisions facing her. She had let Alexander come courting because, well, she liked him. And she wanted to please her grandfather. In spite of being a pushy, manipulating skunk, the old coot had grown on her. Somewhere in the middle of beating him at chess and stepping on his toes in their dancing lessons, she had grown a need to have him proud of her.

Then there was Elizabeth, her very best friend. Elizabeth had labored hard—hard as any prospector with a pick and shovel—to turn her into some semblance of a lady. She wanted Elizabeth to be proud of her as well.

"Excuse me, miss." Bittles appeared at the door of the drawing room. "Mr. Stanford is here wishing to see you. Shall I send him in?"

Georgia's heart lurched. She hoped this wasn't bad news about his father. "Yes, of course. And fetch my grandfather, please."

"Mr. Stanford asked to see you privately, miss."

At that, her heart nearly stopped. Surely he wouldn't... Not right now! Not so soon!

But he was going to. She could see it on his face when he came through the door.

"Good afternoon, Georgia. You're looking lovely today."

"Thank you," she said stiffly.

"Elizabeth sends her regards. I've hired a woman to care for my father, but right now he is querulous, and Elizabeth is the only one who can get an ounce of cooperation from him. I hope you don't mind if she stays a few days longer."

"No. Of course not. Tell her I miss her, though."

"I will." He pulled up a satin-upholstered chair and sat down just across from her, not close enough to be improper, but near enough to tell her that the Day, supposedly the most important day in a girl's life, had come. She felt a bit like cursing.

"I haven't come here to bear you tidings of Elizabeth and my father, however. I think you must know, Georgia, why I asked to speak privately with you. We have become well acquainted over the past weeks, I think, and I have been forthright in my admiration of you." His eyes twinkled with just a touch of the humor that Georgia had come to appreciate. "I've also tried hard to compensate for my wretched beginnings with you. I hope I've succeeded."

Georgia was at a loss for words, and she didn't like it. Ready comebacks, sassy and challenging, had always been her first line of defense against uncertainty, but the looming question that Alexander was about to pose robbed her of speech.

He took her hand in his, and she didn't pull back. Her hand felt good in his—warm, secure, comfortable. "Georgia, I have too much respect for your intelligence to ply you with words of romance, for you know as well as I that our relationship is not the stuff of songs and fables. But I care for you greatly. I respect you enormously. And I would be honored if you would become my wife."

She choked—perhaps not quite the response he had hoped for.

"My proposal cannot come as a shock to you. I think I've made my attachment known to you, and certainly your grandfather and my father have been warming up the altar ever since you first arrived in Chicago."

"No . . . no." At the look on his face, she explained. "I mean, no, it doesn't come as a shock."

"I would try my utmost to make you happy, Georgia, and I think I have the ability to do that. You would lack for nothing, and I would not expect you to conform to all the social niceties that are expected of a woman in our rather stilted world. Your uniqueness and spirit are things I admire greatly, and I have no desire to suffocate you with strictures you can't endure."

She gave him a half smile. "It wouldn't do you much good."

"But I will be honest with you, my dear. I know you long to return to Arizona. I have no objection to traveling there to settle your property once the Apaches are taken care of. I have a fondness myself for the West. But our permanent home would be in Chicago, where we can raise our children in safety. I think you will come to love the city.

And I hope you will come to love me as well. I will do everything I can to make that happen."

Georgia's heart pounded in her chest, almost as if she'd run two miles with a band of Indians chasing after her scalp. Here it was, the Big Decision. And she didn't have a notion of what to say. Feeling stupid and confused, all she could do was stare at him blankly.

"Georgia, I'll get down on one knee if you like, if that would convince you how committed I am to your happiness."

"Uh . . . no. That isn't necessary."

"The advantages to our union are legion." His smile was almost endearing. "Our pushy relations have worked out all the business aspects, of course. But you and I can create much better reasons to wed. I want children, and I believe you would want children as well. I want my father to be happy. You need a husband who can appreciate you for the very special woman that you are, without trying to mold you into something you can't be. You will get your property back from your grandfather, and I will allow you to handle the proceeds from that property without my interference."

"Such a deal," Georgia said dryly. "You're a good pitchman, Alexander. But I have to ask you—why would you want to marry me, other than my nosy grandfather and your father wanting us to wed? Don't mistake, I know my own worth. I'm a pretty good tracker, a dead shot with a rifle, and I work a shovel as well as any man. And if I say so myself, I don't clean up bad. But in spite of your pretty words like *unique* and *special*, I'm not the sort of polished-up, shiny woman that someone in your position marries."

He shook his head and squeezed her hand. "Obviously, you only think you know your own worth, my dear Georgia. Clean up well? I should say. You've lit a fire beneath every man under ninety who's had the pleasure of seeing you. You not only look like a goddess, but you have humor, intelligence, and honesty, which men value more than women know."

Her mouth slanted wickedly. "Is a goddess anything like an Amazon?"

With a shake of his head, he wagged a scolding finger. "You also hold a mean grudge."

"See?" she said with a smile. "These things would irritate you." Then she grew serious. "Alexander, you've got to know that every mother in this city is busy setting bait for you, hoping to reel you in for her daughter. You could have any girl that you wanted. Rich, beautiful girls. Dainty girls who dance well and always know the right thing to say."

He looked quite fetchingly earnest. "I want none of those girls, Georgia. Only you will do." He stood, drew her up into the circle of his arms, and pled his case with a kiss.

Georgia had been kissed before, once by a Prescott suitor who had been quicker than her fist and planted one on her lips before she could drop him, and once, long ago, by a boy she'd thought hung the moon and stars. The boy had kissed her as a joke, then laughed with all his friends about how he'd duped the "freckle-faced stick-girl" (that had been before she sprouted up front) into thinking he actually liked her. The Prescott suitor had puckered up more for the gold she'd stashed in a San Francisco bank than for her dubious charms.

So she had been kissed before, but admittedly her experience was limited. She suspected, though, that Alexander Stanford's kiss would measure up against just about any romantic hero. He started slow and gentle, holding her lightly, lips brushing hers, soft as a breath of warm air. Slowly he drew her closer and tasted her more thoroughly. His body warmed hers, hard muscle against her more yielding pliancy. The press of his hips made her feel watery inside. The demand of his lips left her breathless, her pulse racing.

But then the kiss ended. She might have fallen like an axed ponderosa but for his sure grip on her shoulders. Gradually she regained her balance and he eased his hold. His eyes searched her face. "I can make you happy, Georgia. Please let me."

The only thing that came out of her mouth was an inarticulate whimper.

He took the hint, backing off with a sigh. "I can see you need time to make a decision. Certainly I'll give you all the time you want. But it would please me to be married as soon as practicable. I will wait anxiously for your answer."

"Alexander!" She stopped him on his way to the door. "You do me a great honor. Really. And I will not delay long in answering."

He merely smiled at her and left.

The evening meal came and went. Georgia didn't talk to her grandfather about Alexander's offer. She knew he would start celebrating before celebration was due, and she hadn't yet made up her mind. The old man did inquire about her lack of appetite.

"It's a female thing," she told him, which, after all, was quite true. But she had found that using "a female thing" as an excuse made men drop a subject faster than a red-hot coal. The trick came in handy.

"Bittles told me that Alexander called this afternoon."

"Yes. He wanted to borrow Elizabeth for a few more days. His father is being a jackass, he said, and only Elizabeth can keep him in line."

"Hm." Alvin regarded her narrowly. "I'm thinking he didn't use quite those terms."

"That's what he meant."

"Ah."

Her grandfather's *ah*'s could mean a host of things. This one, fortunately, signaled the end of the conversation.

Later that night, sleep wouldn't come. Georgia could think of no decision that wouldn't leave part of her unhappy. The logical path was to revel in matrimonial triumph—the ox in pigtails had won the most eligible bachelor in Chicago. No woman could ask for a better match. She would live the rest of her days in comfort. She would have children to love, a handsome, kind man at her side, and Chicago society at her feet. Quite a step up from grubbing through the dirt and waiting for the Apaches to make a trophy of her red hair.

On the other hand, she ached to once again see blue skies and listen to the song of the coyote, to feel the hot sun beat upon her back and to move with unfettered freedom afforded by men's overalls, sturdy boots, and best of all, no corset. And then there was the grinning image of Cougar

Barnes that formed insolently in her mind. Cougar had no bearing on her decision, Georgia told herself sternly. None at all.

But he chased through her mind like a skulking thief, joining with her other doubts to rob her of sleep, until the sky in the east turned from black to gray and her head ached. Her very blood was heavy as lead moving sluggishly in her veins.

Fresh air was what she needed, Georgia decided. Fresh air helped any problem, cleared cobwebs from the brain, and poured energy into the soul. She'd had far too little fresh air since coming to Chicago. She got up and donned clothes she had squirreled away when she had first arrived, what seemed an age ago. The sturdy flannel shirt and baggy trousers felt wonderful. No corset bound her. No skirts tangled in her feet. Someone had made off with her work boots, but the moccasins she had brought with her from Arizona still lay in a corner of the wardrobe.

At this early hour of the morning, slipping from the house was simple. Her grandfather still snored in his room. Marjorie and her helpers rattled about in the kitchen, and she heard Rachel's and Mrs. Bolton's voices in the kitchen as well. Bittles was nowhere to be seen.

In the stable behind the house Tom the stablemaster's son fetched her grandfather's black mare without question. If he was surprised at Georgia's odd dress, he didn't comment.

"Don't bother with a saddle," she told the boy. "I'll ride her bareback."

That drew a look of concern. "But, miss . . ."

"Don't worry."

"If you fall, my pa's gonna skelp me."

She grinned at him. "Then I won't fall. I'll be back before the house awakes."

Georgia didn't want to go far, just along the path that followed the lakeshore, where she'd often walked with Elizabeth. Elizabeth, bless her heart, would be scandalized to see her riding astride and bareback in the gray dawn, dressed in clothes that any proper female would scorn to touch. But Elizabeth was at the Stanfords, so she couldn't see. She was with Alexander and his father.

And that brought to mind Alexander. Alexander, who wanted to marry her and live with her in Chicago.

Georgia started out at an easy walk, but soon urged the mare into a gallop, leaning low over her glossy neck. The cold wind of their passage stiffened her face, and the mare's mane whipped into her eyes, bringing tears that streamed back into her ears and hair. The tears were from the sting of the mane, Georgia told herself. She had no reason to weep, because she was the luckiest woman in the country. Just about any girl in Chicago would gladly step into her shoes—well, maybe not the moccasins she wore right that moment, but certainly the fancy slippers in her wardrobe at Greystone House.

The sun crested the horizon to the east, a dim glow buried in the fog that blanketed Lake Michigan. Georgia reined the mare to a halt and stared out at the lake. Gray water stretched as far as she could see. Dampness beaded her face and made her clothes feel clammy—so different from Arizona, where water was scarce and the air dry and clear. She tried to recall early mornings on the Lynx, the cool, crisp air, the sky so clear that even as the day became gray with the dawn, the stars and moon still shone brightly. Every hill and tree carved the sky with sharp clarity. Arizona had no morning mist to soften edges. If Georgia climbed the hill to the claim she had sold Cougar, she could see for a hundred miles and more. Every mountain would be etched in bold purple, the distant ones just as clearly as the near.

Cougar—there he was again, tromping through her mind. *Go away,* she told him silently. *You only care about your stupid claim and your stupid dreams of a ranch. While everyone else thinks I make a fine lady, you scold me for turning gold to brass. You're a jackass and an idiot, and I don't even like you anymore.*

Well, maybe the last wasn't true. It was hard not to like Cougar when he was charming, which he hadn't been of late. A few times back in Prescott, she'd even wondered what it would feel like to kiss him. Back then he had worn that ratty bush of a beard, so he hadn't been anywhere near as kissable as Alexander Stanford. Still, she couldn't help wonder if kissing Cougar would have been anything like kissing Alexander.

If she'd tried it, Cougar probably would have wiped his mouth, gargled whiskey, and claimed he'd been kissed by a mule. He thought she was so out of place acting like a woman—wouldn't he be surprised to see Alexander smooching her and her smooching him back?

Georgia and the mare walked on. The path ended, and they picked their way over a rocky beach. The sun had burned through the fog and beamed brightly down upon them, diffusing the October chill with a measure of warmth. On some days, Georgia reflected, Chicago could be quite pleasant—blue skies, blue water, and greenery everywhere, more green than Arizona would ever see. Chicago wasn't so bad, she told herself. Maybe she could get used to it. Not everything here was unpleasant. Alexander wasn't unpleasant.

In fact, kissing Alexander had been pleasant as hell. Warm, pleasant, almost exciting. Her stomach had flip-flopped, her heart had raced, and she'd had the strangest sensation of falling. Maybe that was falling in love. Maybe that feeling was what all the songs and poems were about. If it was, then those songs made a hoopla out of very little. It was all very nice, but jumping off suicide rock into Granite Creek was more of a thrill.

Still, Alexander would make a first-class husband. Once they were married, her grandfather would sign over the mine, and Alex, being a very honorable man, would just have to honor her debt to Cougar, either by giving him back his money or handing over the claim.

And there was Cougar again, poking his way into her ruminations. The jackass. Once she married Alexander and got him his stupid claim, he'd be sorry he hadn't trusted her. When he saw how beautiful she would be in her wedding dress, he'd be just plain red-faced embarrassed about thinking she wasn't a born and bred lady. Just see if he wasn't.

The mare came to a halt on her own, and so did the progress of Georgia's thoughts. Had she decided, then? Listening to herself think, it sounded as if she had. And the hollow feeling in her stomach came from missing breakfast, not dread of what she was about to do.

She turned the mare back the way they'd come, then kicked her into a gallop, trying to forget that this might be the last time she felt so free, with the wind in her hair and her movement unrestricted by the clothes and contraptions that society deemed "decent." She was being smart, Georgia told herself. She was being wise, and mature, and doing what any sensible woman would do. Besides which, after all this soft living, she probably wasn't fit to live the life she once had loved. Yes indeed, she was being very smart.

And when she got used to the idea, it wouldn't seem so wrong.

"Palming me off on that damned harpy, are you?" Robert Stanford grumbled to Elizabeth as Alexander eased him into a chair in front of the library fire. The "harpy" in question, a stern widow woman by the name of Mrs. Cotter, glowered from behind the tray of steaming tea and sweet rolls she had brought from the kitchen. She was no more intimidated by Robert's surliness than Elizabeth and Alexander were.

"You're just cantankerous because Mrs. Cotter won't knuckle under to your bullying any more than I will," Elizabeth said with a tolerant smile.

Robert glared. "The lot of you should have to spend a day being spoon-fed thin soup and treated like a babe who still wets his nappies."

"Father, mind your manners."

"And scolded as if I were still in short pants. By my own son, of all things."

"You're a terrible patient," Mrs. Cotter commented mildly, setting tea and rolls on the table beside him. "But we'll get along, sir. I've tended everything from screaming babes to old folks who can't do anything but drool and piss." She folded arms across an ample bosom and gave

Robert a look that plainly challenged. The "harpy" could obviously get as cantankerous as the old man.

"That tea smells like horse piss. I want coffee."

"The doctor says you're to have tea," Alexander reminded him. "No coffee."

Robert snorted. "I hope some day you have a son who treats you like you treat me."

Elizabeth chided him. "Now, Mr. Stanford! Alexander is the best son a man could hope for."

"Hmph!"

They compromised on hot chocolate, and Mrs. Cotter hurried away to fetch some.

"You're a much better nurse," Robert complained to Elizabeth. "Why do we have to put up with her?"

Elizabeth fluffed a pillow to put behind him. "You have to put up with her because I'm not a nurse. I'm a governess." She twinkled at him. "And you do have to be in short pants to require a governess."

"Balderdash! At least get this blanket out from beneath me. It's all rucked up and digging into my legs."

She tugged at the offending blanket. "You'll have to rise up just a bit, please."

Alexander leaned over his father to help him lift his weight from the chair at the same time Elizabeth bent to remove the blanket. Faces only inches apart, their eyes locked for a moment of startled contact. Alexander suffered a jolt of recognition that Elizabeth Whitman was actually very attractive in a demure way. He had never before fully appreciated the beauty of her fine hazel eyes.

Robert's querulous complaint broke the odd spell. "Are you going to remove that blanket, girl?"

Elizabeth started as though she'd been slapped. "Oh! Of course. There. Would you like it spread across your lap?"

Robert gave them an astute glance. "No. It's plenty warm in here, I think."

Just then Garner bustled in bearing a silver tray with a note. "For Mr. Alexander."

Alexander read the missive with strange calm, considering the note was from Georgia requesting that he call, no doubt to receive the answer to his proposal. He longed for that answer to be yes, of course. Marrying Georgia was the sensible thing to do. Their marriage would allow two stubborn old men to consummate a business deal they should have concluded years ago, give him heirs—if he and Georgia were fortunate—and give Alexander a wife who was so full of life and independence that she was unlikely to leave him with the heartbreak and loneliness that Alice had.

"It's from Georgia," he told them with a half smile. "I'm invited to call."

Elizabeth's face paled a bit, Alexander thought. No doubt she was uneasy that he'd treated her with unseemly familiarity since she'd been here—midnight conferences over the kitchen table and just now mooning at her as if he were a lover bent on seduction.

"Since you are going to Greystone House," she ventured, "perhaps I should pack my things and go with you. Since I'm not really needed here any longer, I owe Mr. Kennedy a timely return."

Alex ignored his father's scowl. "If you wish. I hope you know how grateful we are for the help you've given."

"It's been my pleasure, Mr. Stanford." She smiled. "Both Mr. Stanfords."

Such a damned shame that Harold Whitman had dragged his family into his own unhappiness and misfortune, Alexander mused. A warm, competent girl such as Elizabeth should have a husband and family to love her, but attractive as she was, her chances of making a match were impossibly small. And Alexander should have had more discipline and respect than to treat her with improper familiarity. Truly she was right. Elizabeth should leave.

"Elizabeth!" Georgia greeted her friend with the enthusiasm of open arms. "I'm so glad you're back!"

Elizabeth smiled fondly at her, then exhaled an "oof" as Georgia engulfed her in a hug. "This place has been soooo boring without you. No one to tell me to sit up straight and quit fidgeting. No one to correct my grammar. No one to scold me for walking like a man."

"Gently, my dear! Leave my ribs intact, please. And I hardly think you need me around to crack the whip over your head any longer. And see"—she skewered Georgia with her "mind your manners" look—"who has come to call on you, straightaway after your note arrived."

Alexander came up the porch steps with Elizabeth's two small carpetbags in his hand.

"Alexander! Oh, my! Well, hello, and do come in."

"Where is Bittles?" Alexander asked, looking faintly disapproving at the informality of Georgia answering her own front door.

"When I saw Elizabeth out the window, I all but shoved the poor man aside to get to the door first. He retreated in a huff, probably complaining to my grandfather in the library."

"Well then, I will leave you ladies to your greetings and search him out to deposit your bags, Elizabeth."

Georgia winced as he left the room, bags in hand. A few days without Elizabeth and she was already backsliding into what her grandfather called her "wild ways." "I can't imagine why he wants to marry me."

Elizabeth bit her lip. "He did propose, then? I suspected as much." Her brow furrowed with an expression that Georgia couldn't quite interpret—probably worry that Georgia would carry out her threats to make the man grovel and then kick his arrogant butt out the door. Elizabeth did constantly fill her ears with what a fine man Alexander was. She would naturally think that refusing his offer would be stupid. "Did you accept him?"

"No, I mean yes. I had to think, and I nearly fried my brains, I thought so hard. But I'm going to say yes this very minute. At least, the very minute he returns." She tried to make her smile as yell-your-head-off happy that she pictured a bride should be. And she *was* happy. Happy as a bear with honey. Happy as Skillet Mahoney with a new bottle of whiskey. Really, really happy.

"Alexander is a fine man, and you're a wonderful woman, Georgia." Her kiss on Georgia's cheek seemed more fit for a funeral than a hitching, but maybe that was how fine ladies and gentlemen reacted to such things. "All my best wishes, my dear friend. I hope you'll be wildly happy."

Just then Alexander came back into the room. Elizabeth smiled a bit tremulously and whispered, "I'm so very happy for you." Before Georgia could reply, she fled the room.

"You must have worked her too hard," Georgia told Alexander. "I don't think I've ever seen her look so tired."

Alexander sent a long look after Elizabeth's retreating figure. "My father is a difficult patient. It was very good of her to put up with . . . with both of us, actually."

He turned toward Georgia, a seeking on his face, one brow slightly raised in a way that made him look arrogant and disdainful, like one of the gods in a book of Greek legends she and Elizabeth had found in Alvin's library. Too lofty to be quite human, he could look down from Mount Olympus upon inferior mortals who would never have his money, his education, his confidence, his knack for eating the messiest sort of food and staying clean, the sort of food that just naturally wanted to slop onto Georgia's bodice.

"Shall we sit?" he asked.

"Oh, sure, of course. Sit."

He waited for her to sit first. Gentlemen did not sit in the presence of ladies who stood. Stupid rule, Georgia mused, then tossed thoughts of stupid rules from her mind. Chicago was full of stupid rules. She'd better get used to it.

"How nice of you to call." The words came out of her mouth awkwardly. Her mind was going numb.

"Georgia?"

The quiet question in his voice brought her back into focus. Of course he'd come to call. She'd asked him to call, and he knew exactly why he was here. He wanted his answer. Her stomach churned.

Then he smiled, and the haughty image mellowed into the man who'd so sweetly kissed her just the day before. Alexander was kind, and handsome, and witty. He'd seen her at her worst—well, maybe not quite her worst. He hadn't seen her up to her yahoo in muck trying to pull a mule from a mud hole. But he'd seen her make a fool of herself more than once, and he still wanted her. Even though he still mourned a woman long dead, he still cared for her.

Georgia was trying to form her mouth around a big fat "Yes, I'll marry you" when Cougar sauntered into her mind, pushy as usual. She could see him clearly, regarding her with blue eyes that said she ought to know better, turning gold into brass. Mentally she gave him a good kick, and not with the dainty slippers she wore now, but with the heavy work boots she'd worn in Prescott. Gold into brass indeed! Alexander thought she was gold just the way she was.

She was doing the right thing, Georgia told herself. But before she lost her courage, she had better get the thing over with. Pushing Prescott, Arizona sunshine, gold mines, freedom, and Cougar Barnes—most of all Cougar Barnes—right out of her mind, she screwed up her courage and took the leap.

"Yes, Alexander, I'll marry you," she blurted with no preamble. "You proposed, and I'm saying yes. I hope that makes you happy." Feeling as if she'd taken the suicide leap into Granite Creek with the cold water rushing up to meet her, she came off her chair and launched herself into his arms.

Chapter 14

Cougar threw his things into the poke bag on the bed and drew it shut. He had two changes of clothes and an extra set of boots. Where he was headed—where he belonged—he didn't need the fancy clothes he wore at his uncle's house. Most of his sturdy work clothes were folded away in his cabin up on Granite Creek. The claim wasn't worth spit, but the cabin he'd built was home.

Lord but he would be glad to get back to a place where he was Cougar, not Cooper, back to a place where men said what they meant, be it evil or good, challenge or friendly greeting. He was tired of so-called civilization, so tired of it that he could have kicked something, or someone.

His uncle was a good candidate for that kick, and so was his cousin. But they hadn't really done or said anything that Cougar hadn't expected. They weren't risk-takers. Putting everything on the line for glory and adventure just wasn't in them. If the truth be known, putting anything at all on the line for glory and adventure wasn't in them. Then again, probably Cougar was the only one in his family who would regard a cattle operation in a risky land and a risky market to be glory and adventure.

The someone he really wanted to kick was Miss Georgia Kennedy, belle of Chicago society, or so she thought to be. The idiot girl. All that flaming hair had fried her brain. Show her a bit of soft living, dangle a rich prospective husband in front of her nose, and she forgot her friends, her life, her standards—everything. She so feared a reminder of who and what she was that she'd holed up behind an army of servants for the last two weeks, refusing to see him. Cougar wouldn't have believed that Georgie Kennedy could be a coward. But maybe she was someone he didn't really know.

Well, he wasn't much less a fool than Georgie, Cougar admitted. He'd come all this way to check up on her—no, he'd come to get her, and that was the bare, honest truth. Her leaving Arizona had torn a hole in his life. It had taken a good while for him to admit it, that a freckle-faced, shovel-wielding, arm-wrestling hoyden could hog-tie his heart like a cowhand bulldogging a steer. But it was true. Georgie's leaving had left him empty.

So he'd come after her. His excuses for traveling to Chicago were little better than lies to himself. He'd come for Georgie, and what a surprise he'd been handed. Seeing Georgie all gussied up had been a shock. She had seemed like a different person than the one he remembered until she opened her mouth and started putting him in his place.

He smiled at the memory. Even in lace, silk, and perfume, Georgie was still Georgie. He should have dropped his pretenses and wooed the girl, but because the changes made him mad, he had scolded and carped. Instead of lending support against the people who used her, he'd nagged her about that stupid claim and made fun of her attempts to be a lady. So now he went home empty-handed, his tail between his legs.

"Hey, Cousin." James stood in the doorway of Cougar's room, holding the morning newspaper in one hand. An echo of his father, he wasn't quite as narrow and staid as Horace. Cougar even liked him a bit. It was a good thing to like at least one person in his family. "Getting set to go, are you? That all you're taking?"

"It's all I came with. This other stuff I bought here. Uncle Horace is sending it to my father in New York. Who knows? Someday I might go back there and collect it."

James grinned. "Quite the wild man, aren't you, Cousin. I guess I envy you a bit, though. Making money can be a dull business."

Cougar grinned. "Not if you make it the way I want to."

With a laugh, James agreed, then held out the paper. "Did you see the morning news? There's a notice about your girl Georgia Kennedy."

"She's not *my* girl."

"Obviously."

Cougar read the notice that James indicated and felt acid churn in his stomach. "Damned if that little fool isn't going to marry the guy."

"They're in a rush. Wedding's set for November. If you stay a few more weeks, you'll get to go. I'm sure we'll be invited. Father has business ties with both the Kennedys and Stanfords." He chuckled. "As for that, probably anyone who is anyone in Chicago will be invited."

Cougar felt like crumpling the paper in his hands, ripping it to bits, and setting a match to it. Either that or stuff it up Alexander Stanford's . . . he let the idea drop before it became too tempting.

"Thought you'd be interested. Actually, this might be a good break for you. If old Kennedy gives over those claims to Stanford, you might get your money out of him. He's less tight with a penny than Kennedy, and everyone says he leans over backward to be fair. It would be worth a try."

"I'll think about it." *When hell freezes over.*

James took back his newspaper and left Cougar to his thoughts, which grew hotter by the moment. Georgie had caved. She'd chosen the easy path over being true to her own nature. His anger had nothing to do with his frigging claim, the one she'd sold him when it wasn't rightfully hers. She'd get that for him somehow, Cougar knew, for in spite of how he'd scolded her, he knew she wouldn't cheat him. No, not Georgie. She would get her new husband to honor the sale and then shed herself of Cougar, going on to spend her life as a parlor decoration.

The claim be damned. The waste of it all made him furious. Georgie was a once-in-a-lifetime sort of woman. That realization had taken a long time getting through his thick skull. Alex Stanford would probably never see it, because even if they were married for thirty years, he would never know Georgie the way Cougar knew Georgie.

Seething, he threw his duffel into a corner, pulled on his jacket, and strode out the door to the stairs. Damned if he wasn't going to tell her exactly what he thought of her wedding plans. If any of the Kennedy servants or Kennedy himself tried to prevent him, then woe be to them. Alvin Kennedy had set everything against his granddaughter. He had isolated her from every influence that might have reminded her of her past. He had stuck his nose into a life that wasn't his to nose around in, manipulating things that were better left alone. Cougar couldn't believe that left to her own mind, Georgie really wanted to tie herself to Alexander Stanford and put up with the strictures of living in "polite society." If she had told him that while sitting on a bench in Prescott's town square or sitting on the porch of the little house she'd bought with *his* money, he might have believed her. But not this way.

In the middle of marching resolutely to the stable to fetch a horse, a solution popped into Cougar's head. He stopped in his tracks. This was one hell of an idea. He should have thought of it before. He'd been in Chicago too long, Cougar concluded, and he'd forgotten how to fight. Nothing worthwhile ever came easy. The West had taught him that. Life's treasures were usually guarded by burning deserts, scorpions, towering mountains, or angry Indians. A man learned fast on the frontier that he had to knuckle down and fight for anything worth having.

And Georgie was damned well worth having.

The stable boy regarded him curiously from the stable doorway. "Sir? Did you want a horse or sumpthin'?"

"Not yet. Later, though."

The boy looked worried. Probably his old self had blossomed on Cougar's expression, the Cougar who had killed a mountain lion with his bare hands, the Cougar that gamblers didn't dare cheat and troublemakers avoided. He felt a wicked grin spread over his face. Georgia wasn't going to take kindly to him doing her this favor, but some day she would thank him. Thank him or shoot him, one or the other. Only time would tell.

"A promise made is a promise kept." Alvin signed the paperwork with a flourish while Georgia watched him from across the library desk. She should be happy, because the claims she'd always thought were hers were now hers legally, and so was the gold she and her father had stashed in that San Francisco bank. She could formally sign over to Cougar the claim she had sold him. That should make the jackass happy. Then they both would be happy. Hoorah.

"You see now that I'm a man of my word," Alvin told her with a smirk. "I've signed over your precious gold claims even before you take formal vows. Accepting Alexander's proposal is good enough for me. You're a very smart girl, Georgia. I always believed you were. How could you be my granddaughter and not be smart, eh? I don't mind telling you that you've made me very happy. And of course you've made Alexander the happiest man in the world."

"Well, he should be," Georgia said with a wry smile. "It's not every man who gets a wife who can shoot and fight Indians as well as do needlework and dance a minuet."

Alvin's laughter was hearty and good-natured, now that he'd gotten his way. "I knew Alex would come to his senses. He's a good man. Before you make any decisions on selling these claims or hiring laborers to work them for you, of course you'll want to speak to Alexander about it. After all, you're as good as married."

She didn't tell him that she'd already discussed her assets with her soon-to-be husband. If Alexander hadn't agreed to let her make the decisions about her property, the engagement would have been off. He hadn't objected in the least, though. That was one reason she liked him. He, unlike every other male in the country, didn't believe that wearing skirts deprived a person of smarts.

She gave her grandfather a smile, reminding herself that the old coot had really treated her much better than he might have. "Are you sure that you don't want a repayment on your grubstake—with interest?"

Alvin laughed softly. "My dear, do I look as though I need it?"

"Well, no."

"Then we won't talk any more about it."

Georgia nodded. "So now you'll get your merger, I guess."

"Yes, I will, and Robert is as happy about it as I am. That stubborn old goat just needed an excuse to do what he knew was sound business."

Georgia didn't point out that the "old goat" was at least fifteen years younger than Alvin.

"The man can be difficult to deal with," Alvin told her, "but mostly he's all bluster." He smiled. "Much like me, I'm afraid."

"You old coot! Saying you're all bluster would be like calling a skunk a pussycat." Her fond smile took any sting from the words, and Alvin chuckled.

"You are a smart woman, Georgia." He came around the desk and sat in a chair close beside her. "When it comes to family, though, I am more like that pussycat. My primary desire through all of this, my dear, was to see you settled with a good man, because that is a woman's key to happiness. Alexander Stanford is the best, and I don't say that just because his father is my good friend. This marriage assures you the life your heritage entitles you to. No woman, especially a Kennedy woman, should have to grub in the dirt for a living. I can forgive Elias everything—his renouncing the business, the family, his heritage, but I can't forgive him for dragging his daughter through hell."

"It wasn't hell," Georgia denied.

Though at times, she remembered, life with her father had seemed like hell, especially to a young girl who could never put down roots, never find close friends, and grew up learning to be a man instead of a woman. But her father had loved her, for all that he loved the far horizon more, and she had survived.

"It was certainly no life for a female," Alvin insisted.

"Maybe not."

Even when she'd put down roots in Prescott after her father died, life had been hard, Georgia remembered. The work was backbreaking, and danger from Indians, wildlife, and the elements made the future a thing to hope for, not count on. But life had been good as well. Arizona was in her soul. The clear, sharp vistas gave her heart wings. The sunsets took her breath away. The mountains—well, she had to agree with the Indians that the mountains were holy places. How could anything so beautiful not be holy?

And the people—Essie seemed more like family than Alvin ever would. Skillet Mahoney, Mrs. Peterson at the boardinghouse, Lem Stucker, who had once tried to teach her the fiddle—all those were family, too. And Cougar . . . No, she wouldn't think about Cougar.

Alexander had said they could visit Prescott, but things wouldn't be the same. Maybe when something was left behind, willingly or unwillingly, that thing, that place, was impossible to find again. Georgia's world had shattered on the Fourth of July, and the shards had fallen into a new pattern. A better pattern, she told herself. She should be grateful.

She *was* grateful. Of course she was grateful.

Cougar had no trouble navigating through the night. Low clouds reflected the city's gaslights in a general glow that was almost as good as a bright moon in helping a skulker find his way. He left his horse behind the Kennedy barn, but far enough away that the beast wouldn't be tempted into conversation with his fellows in their snug stalls. Cougar would find someone else to deliver the horse to Horace's barn when he was through with this night's work, because he had no intention of returning to his uncle's house.

He slipped into Greystone House through the kitchen. It

was locked, of course, but the lock was no impediment to a man of Cougar's varied talents. Silently he made his way into the dining room, the connecting parlor, then into the hall from which the main stairway climbed to the upper floor. One by one, cautious of creaks that might give him away, he mounted the stairs. He knew the location of Georgia's room from when he and Alexander had brought her here, insensible, after she was attacked. It was down the long upstairs hallway in one corner of the house.

For a moment he stood before her door, listening. A tiny, delicate snore sounded from within. That was Georgie, all right. He'd slept often enough with her in the same camp or the same cabin to recognize the sound. Once he'd told her she snored like a mouse. At the time she hadn't been amused.

Time enough for reminiscing later, he told himself. Get the job done and get out. He put his hand on the doorknob. The easy part was over.

Georgia had not slipped easily into sleep. Once upon a time, long ago, falling asleep had been as easy as falling off a log. The questions and decisions of the day hadn't invaded her rest. Once answered, the questions faded. Decisions were made, one way or another, and that was an end to it.

Not so in her new life. She was sure in her mind that she was doing the right thing in marrying Alexander. He made her stomach flutter, and didn't that mean she was on her way to loving him? He cared about her. He was a good kisser, which probably meant that sharing a bed with him wouldn't be too much of a chore. Sex wasn't a mystery to her. Living among men in mining camps and railroad towns, sometimes when the only women there earned their way in cribs and bawdy houses, Georgia had learned young what happened between men and women. She never had understood, though, why anyone lusted after the so-called forbidden fruit. From what she understood, it was both messy and awkward.

So that was another question that wandered through her restless sleep. Any man who had ever gotten gropey with her had gotten her elbow in his gut or an iron skillet over his noggin. The thought of having to grit her teeth and let someone get away with that sort of thing didn't sit well on her stomach—sort of like a sour apple.

Still, with all that running around her head, Georgia had managed eventually to get to sleep. When something brought her abruptly and prematurely awake, she wasn't happy about it. In a moment's confusion she thought morning must have come and her uneasy dreams had made her twist in the bedcovers, because she couldn't move. She could hardly breathe.

Then alarm pushed every tendril of sleep from her head. A hand covered her mouth, and her inability to move was no accident, because Cougar Barnes was all but sitting on her. Even in the pitch dark there was no mistaking him. She knew the scent of him, the horny calluses of his hands, the unyielding resistance of work-hardened muscle.

"Mmmmph!" she objected.

The hand that wasn't slapped over her mouth raised a finger to his lips. "Ssssshhh! I knew you'd wake up spitting like a wildcat, but just calm down. It's just me."

She tried to bite him, unsuccessfully. "Hmmphfz!"

"Keep cussing like that and you'll plumb ruin that ladylike image of yours."

She glared.

"Now, Georgie, I'm going to tell you, quiet-like, what's going on. So open your ear-holes, girl. I've been trying to get in this mausoleum to see you ever since I saved your bacon down on the waterfront, but you've got a guard around you that could turn back Sherman's army. Now I hear you're determined to up and marry Alex Stanford, and I knew I had to save your butt once again, not to mention poor Stanford's. He's no match for you, Georgia, and Chicago is a place that's going to kill you. That's if you don't kill Alexander first. So I figure to do you both a favor by giving you some time to think about what else you could do with your life."

"Dmmzzzt?"

"There you go cussing again. Pretty rude, when you

consider I've come to offer myself at the altar, if you're that determined to get hitched. I'm a better man for you, Georgia, and I've decided that it's time I took a wife, anyway. We'd do well together, you and I. You make life interesting, and I figure you're about the only woman I know who's got the guts to put up with me."

She managed to free one knee from the covers and brought it up into his back.

"Now, stop that, you little—ouch!"

He sat on her harder this time. Georgia had always admired Cougar because he was a good man in a fight and knew how to use his bearlike strength to good advantage, but now that he used it against her, she didn't find it so admirable.

"You're not going to win," he warned. "So calm down."

Recognizing the truth, she complied.

"I'm going to uncover your mouth, Georgie, but if you scream or yell for help, this is going to get ugly. So don't."

Her eyes narrowed dangerously, but she nodded. As soon as her mouth was free, she hissed up at him. "Snake! Settle down, my frigging ass! You'd marry me to get your precious claim, and my gold as well, you weasel! Only woman tough enough to put up with you? You mean I'm the only woman with claims on the best gold property in Prescott, don't you?"

"Language, Lady Georgia! Last I heard, your greedy grandfather still had your goddamned claims." His smile infuriated her. "But I'll take you anyway."

"Like hell you will, you lying sack of dog shit."

He chuckled, low and deep, and the sound sent a peculiar tremor through her. She'd never seen Cougar quite like this. "That's my Georgie. At least I'm going to take you somewhere away from your fast-talking grandfather and all this fancy living to a place where you can make up your mind fair and square who you want to be. Get up now."

Suddenly she was free of his weight. Her instinct was to fight, but the air of quiet power about him made her cautious.

He lit the lamp, and she saw he was dressed for travel,

not in his gentleman clothes, but in plain denim trousers and a wool shirt. After the night's darkness, the single lamp seemed bright. Georgia wrapped her nightdress modestly around her, but for a man who had just declared his intention to marry her, he seemed little interested in her improper attire.

That, Georgia thought, was because he didn't want her, he wanted the gold.

"You need to write a note. Tell your grandfather you're eloping with me. He's to let Alexander know that you're very sorry, but you've realized that you love me and not him."

"That's a load of bullshit. Besides, I don't have any paper."

"What's that in the little desk?" He pointed to a stack of stationery sitting on the little secretary under the window.

"You can't make me marry you, Cougar."

"No, but I can take you somewhere that will remind you of who you are. And I can try along the way to convince you that you and I would be good in harness together."

She snorted skeptically. He handed her a pen. "Write, Georgie, or I will. And there's no telling what sort of things I might write that might come back to haunt you later."

She glared. He just smiled and pointed toward the desk.

Seething, Georgia made a blotched mess of the paper. Cougar folded it neatly and placed it on her pillow, where Rachel would find it the next morning.

Then things got ugly. Georgia decided that she'd taken just about enough of being pushed around by the likes of Cougar Barnes, whom not too many months ago she had beaten at arm wrestling. She could take him, she decided. Or if she couldn't, then at least she could make enough noise to fetch help. When his back turned to put the note on her pillow, she launched.

In a split second she discovered her mistake. This was no game with rules and tricks that could turn an opponent's strength against him. This was battle. She landed somehow on the bed, pinned by Cougar's hard body and looking up into glinting blue eyes. His face was close above hers, close enough that the pale laugh lines etched in a sun-bronzed face stood out with startling clarity. She could almost feel the muscle twitch in his jaw, and the slight quiver the curled-up corner of his mouth signaled either a laugh or a good yell coming on. That mouth of his—he should have trimmed back his beard a long time ago to show off that mouth. Any woman would be proud to have a mouth that gorgeous, a mouth that made someone think of things like nibbling and kissing. Not that it was a feminine mouth at all. Oh, no. Cougar's mouth was gorgeous in a very masculine way. Strange that she had never before noticed.

But then, she had never been this close. It so fascinated her that she plumb forgot to scream.

Cougar seemed in no hurry to move off her. Far from it. He seemed quite comfortable with odd parts of his body poking into unmentionable parts of hers. Those blue eyes seemed to drink in her face in a most peculiar way. She began to wonder if Chicago had made him lose his mind.

"Did Alexander kiss you?" he suddenly asked.

"What if he did?"

He smiled. She didn't much like the smile.

"And a whopper of a kiss it was, too," she said pugnaciously. "That man can kiss. When Alex and I are married, I'll bet he kisses me every damned day."

Cougar's tone was dangerous. "I don't think Alexander Stanford is capable of kissing you like you ought to be kissed."

"Get that look right out of your eye, Cougar Barnes."

"You ought to know better than to issue me a challenge, Georgia."

"You . . . you get your lousy carcass off me. And don't even think of doing what you're thinking of doing!"

This was her own fault, Georgia told herself frantically as his mouth came closer to his. She should know better than to tweak the lion's tail especially when he had her pinned down and was eyeing her as if she were his next meal.

She desperately did not want Cougar to kiss her.

Alexander kissing her had been no big thing. In fact, curiosity had made her welcome the adventure. But Cougar kissing her . . . ? Some danger lurked in the very thought—some threshold that she didn't want to cross. She wasn't even sure what that threshold was, but once crossed, suddenly everything would change.

His lips met hers. His were warm and surprisingly gentle. Hers were rigid as ice. His were persuasive, hers cringing. She tried to sink into the bed to escape, but the mattress pressed her from below as Cougar pressed her from above.

Gentle persuasion gave way to insistence. His fingers threaded through her hair. His body moved against hers, ever so slightly, but enough to send a jolt of lightning through her nerves. Somewhere below her stomach a warmth began to grow and spread. In spite of herself, Georgia softened. Her mouth opened to better taste him. Without realizing she did it, she lifted her hips against his. A deep, throaty groan vibrated between them. Georgia didn't know if it came from Cougar or from herself.

By the time he released her, she ached through and through, as if she'd climbed a mountain without stopping to rest. Her blood ran hot. It heated her skin, her mouth, her breasts, and other places she didn't want to consider. It thrummed through her ears in a savage drumbeat.

Cougar grinned down at her. "Now, that"—he smirked—"was a kiss."

She should have screamed right then, Georgia told herself later. Or at least she should have brought up her knee and damaged some parts of him that would have turned the tide of battle. But for some reason she didn't scream, which gave the jackass time to roll her in a blanket, throw her over his shoulder, and carry her off like a sack of flour. He didn't even let her dress, and there wasn't a thing she could do about it.

City living had surely turned her soft.

Hours seemed to pass before she got out of the blanket. Cougar climbed aboard a horse, threw her across his thighs, and they clopped off to some unknown destination—an uncomfortable experience Georgia hoped she could treat him to some day. Then he carried her through ugly smells—burning coal and hot grease—that she recognized from her days in railroad camps. Shortly after he plunked her down on a hard surface, loud blasts of puffing steam and the strident screech of metal on metal told her they were on a train.

She struggled to get free and met with the same results as her previous struggles. Cougar's hand landed on the top of her head in a strangely gentle touch.

"Stay put," he warned. "And be quiet."

As if anyone would hear her scream over the noise of the train.

A few minutes passed while she pictured the various grim retributions she could take once she managed to get the advantage, which of course she would just as soon as her kidnapper finally unwound her cocoon.

He did just that once the rhythm of the track had increased to a regular, speedy *clackity-clack*. Georgia came out of the blanket like a tiger, only to get tangled like a kitten in a skein of yarn. Her voluminous nightdress nearly tripped her. Cougar caught her. Gray morning light came through a crack in the freight car door to reveal his devilish grin.

"You . . . you . . . you . . . !" For once in her life Georgia couldn't find a cussword ugly enough to describe what he was.

"You don't have to thank me. What are friends for?"

"You are . . . you are . . . not going to get away with this!"

He let her go and pulled some clothes from a bag on the floor. He barely straightened in time to avoid her kick, which he ignored. "You might feel more like yourself in some real clothes." Trousers and a shirt dangled from his hand. "I had to estimate the size, but they should be better than that tent you're wearing."

"This isn't going to work." She yanked the clothes from his hand. "You are going to be so goddamned sorry."

His grin taunted. "The fit shouldn't be that bad."

"You know what I mean, you dungworm!"

"Tch, tch. Ladylike manners fade so fast, don't they?"

Then he sobered enough to sound downright scary. "Don't count on getting the better of me, Georgie. If I can handle a mountain lion, I can handle you."

Her eyes narrowed. "Don't you count on it, Cougar Jackass Barnes. You thought that poor frigging wildcat had sharp claws? You haven't seen anything yet!"

Chapter 15

Elizabeth's hands trembled as she read the note Rachel had brought her.

"It was on her pillow, miss."

"Did you just now find this?"

"Just, miss, when I brought her morning tea. She's flown the coop, hasn't she?"

"She will be back," Elizabeth assured the girl, though her own stomach was sinking.

Elizabeth hurried to Georgia's room, not knowing quite what she would find. The bed was mussed, but the rest of the room was tidy, as it always was. Georgia despised clutter and kept her things neat as a pin. Her dresses hung undisturbed in the wardrobe, and her shoes lay side by side in good order. If Georgia truly had eloped with Cooper Barnes, then she'd done so in her nightgown. She'd packed nothing that Elizabeth could see, not even underthings.

"There is definitely something wrong here," she told Rachel. "Please don't say anything to anyone, anyone at all, until we learn what has happened."

"I won't, miss! I never gossip at all."

Elizabeth knew that certainly wasn't so, but gossip right now was the least of her worries. She had Bittles rouse Alvin from his bed. When the old man came down to the parlor in dressing robe, rumpled hair, and a cranky mood, she handed him Georgia's note. His face turned pastier than it already was.

"I don't believe it, Mr. Kennedy, and neither should you. Georgia wouldn't accept Mr. Stanford's proposal of marriage and then flee in the middle of the night with another man. She's a woman who is true to her word. Even if she decided to back out of her commitment, she would face Mr. Stanford and tell him rather than sneaking off."

"But . . ." Alvin held out the note with the helpless look of a man baffled by women. He dropped heavily onto the settee. "She's gone! Where? Why, if not an elopement?"

Elizabeth paced the length of the fine Persian carpet. "Cooper Barnes is behind this. Did you know that she calls him Cougar?"

"Cougar? This is the same man who figured so prominently in so many of her outrageous stories?"

"The same man," Elizabeth reminded him, "who helped Alexander rescue her from those street toughs."

"Ah, yes. Him. Cougar, eh? Very strange name. He made a pest of himself while Georgia was recovering, and I left Bittles orders that he wasn't to be received."

Elizabeth gave him a questioning look. "He was a friend of Georgia's from Arizona."

"All the more reason to keep them apart. I knew Alexander was the man for my granddaughter, and this man could only have been a distraction. Besides, I did a bit of investigation. He's Horace Barnes's nephew, and Horace tells me he's the wild fruit on the family tree. Just like Georgia's father. I was only thinking of Georgia's own good."

"Perhaps that was wise," she conceded with a sigh. "Every time Georgia talked with the man, or even saw him, she ended up fretting and restless. But now . . ."

"Now she's eloped with the fellow!"

Elizabeth stopped her pacing, knit her fingers together, and tried to think. "I don't believe it. Georgia does not do things in such an underhanded way."

"Georgia is a female!" Alvin replied testily. "No offense, Miss Whitman, but there isn't a female alive who isn't more than capable of being underhanded. My granddaughter is bolder and more straightforward than most, but she is still a female. The little fool was uncertain about her marriage to Stanford. I'm astute enough to know that. Perhaps she took a case of female hysteria and fled to a man more familiar."

With mounting frustration, Elizabeth shook her head. Alvin was so convinced of general female duplicity that he swallowed this ridiculous note without a single doubt. "Please believe me, Mr. Kennedy. I'm sure that isn't the case. Georgia might have been a bit nervous about her coming marriage, but all women facing marriage entertain a bit of uncertainty. I believe she was afraid of Mr. Barnes for some reason. She seemed particularly concerned that he might make some contact with you."

"Georgia afraid? Really, Miss Whitman! I've never seen my granddaughter afraid of anything!"

How little he knew the girl, Elizabeth reflected. "Surely you will send someone after them, sir. What if Mr. Barnes has taken her against her will? What if the man is a fortune hunter and believes he will get a piece of Georgia's inheritance?"

That hit a nerve. Alvin had grown fond of Georgia, but a threat to his finances got his attention much quicker. He cleared his throat, expressions chasing across his face as he balanced anger with concern.

"You truly think she might be in some danger?"

"Truly I do," Elizabeth said firmly.

"Then we must retrieve her before irreparable harm is done. Bittles! Where is that man? Bittles!"

The butler appeared immediately. Elizabeth had little doubt that the brief delay had been caused by him unsticking his ear from the other side of the door.

"Bittles, send round to Stanford's house. Robert and Alexander should both be apprised of what has transpired. So send round to both of them and ask them to call immediately."

Georgia awakened to the glare of sunrise streaming through the freight car door, which was slightly ajar. After a night sleeping on the hard wooden floor, she had aches in places she didn't know could ache. Sleeping in a cushy bed every night and doing nothing more strenuous than lifting a teacup every day certainly had turned her soft.

For a moment she couldn't remember where she was, and then memory woke. Cougar Barnes, her former friend, the man she had trusted more than any other man in Arizona, had actually carried her off in a blanket like a pile of dirty clothes. Worst of all, she'd let him. She'd been too surprised, too puny, and too frigging female to stop him.

"Awake, are you?"

She gave him a look much colder than the October breeze swirling into the car.

"Yup, you're awake. I can tell from the murderous glare."

He leaned against the side of the car only a few feet from where she lay cocooned. The unrepentant grin on his face reminded her of yet another offense—he had kissed her, and the kiss the jackass had laid on her had been much more than a kiss. Or at least, it had seemed that way at the time. A kiss was no big thing, after all—a smack, a smooch, a brief lip-lock. But this kiss had involved more than just lips meeting. She had felt that contact—lips, breasts, belly, and legs—from her skin clear down to her bones. They had melted into each other, somehow, mixed together like milk and sugar. Once that mix is stirred, no amount of straining, boiling, or freezing will ever separate the two. The milk will always be a bit sweeter. The sugar will never recover all of itself.

Georgia wanted to pinch herself for thinking silly thoughts. Cougar had a lot to pay for; kidnapping her for one, kissing her made two. She was going to make him sorry for both. All the milk-and-sugar business just plagued her because she was hungry. Alexander had kissed her and made her stomach fluttery. Cougar's kiss didn't even compare. She didn't want to kiss him again; she just wanted to eat.

"Where are we?" she asked sullenly.

"Galesburg, Iowa. The train stops here for a bit. And here we're turning into legitimate passengers."

"Do legitimate passengers get food?"

"I'll get you something to eat, along with some clothes that won't catch the eye of everyone in sight. I'm afraid you're going to have to go back to wearing a dress for a while."

Just don't put me back in a frigging corset, she almost told him, but that would make him think he was liberating her rather than abducting her. She wouldn't give him the satisfaction. No indeed. Still, the trousers and shirt she wore reminded her of just how uncomfortable female clothes could be.

Then realization kicked her in the head. They were leaving the freight car, going out into the crowds where she could give Cougar the slip. She truly had gone soft in brain as well as body. The old Georgie would have anticipated this and had a plan in place.

The old Georgie, a smirking voice from the back of her mind told her, would have boxed Cougar's ears before letting him kiss her like he had.

"So we're going out to get tickets and some clothes? Wonderful. And I need to find a place to pee."

He smiled at her. "I just knew all that ladylike delicacy would slough off like old dried snakeskin."

"What? Ladies don't pee?"

"That's what they would have a man believe."

"All right. I don't have to pee. I simply need to inspect the outhouse. So let's go."

"Sorry. You'll have to hold it for a few minutes. You're staying here while I buy us some tickets and find a dress for you. You'll draw too much attention to yourself in a shirt that comes down to your knees and trousers that look as if they could fall off at any minute."

"What do you care who looks at me?"

"We're still too close to Chicago to get careless. Someone might have taken a notion to follow."

"That stupid note you made me write said we were going to New York."

"Your grandfather might be gullible enough to believe that, but I doubt Stanford will."

Georgia didn't argue the point. Staying here was a better plan anyway. Even if Cougar somehow locked the car door, she would find a way out. She would kick a hole in the side if she had to.

"Okay." She shrugged, putting what she hoped was just enough truculence into it. "I'll stay here. But you'd better get back soon or I'm going to explode."

He chuckled, then from a dark corner of the car produced a rope. "Good try, Lady Georgia, but I'm not quite that dumb."

She noted the glint in his eye and growled. "You are going to be so sorry."

Unperturbed, he advanced. "Georgie, let's do this the easy way. What do you say? The quicker we get this over with, the sooner you get to go out and . . . inspect the outhouse. Be sensible."

Georgia didn't feel like being sensible. She felt like knocking Cougar's teeth down his throat. How charming would his smile be then? But when she tried it, he caught her arm. He was more agile than she remembered, or else she was slower. Before she knew it, the rope looped around one wrist.

"You weasel!"

"Just calm down."

In trying to extricate herself, she somehow let him grab the other arm as well. But she still had fingers.

"Stop trying to poke out my eyes!" he growled.

"I'll show you sensible, you bag of pigshit!"

"You're just making this . . . ouch! Dammit!"

She landed a knee in his gut and grinned at his very satisfactory explosion of cursing. But her grin turned into a grimace when she landed hard on her behind.

"Glad to see Chicago hasn't taken all the fight out of you." He sat on her, ignoring her curses and quickly trussing her like a calf ready for branding.

The only thing she could do was slash at him with her eyes. "I am going to make your life a living hell."

"In a lot of ways you already have, Georgie girl. The minute I figured out you were an honest-to-god woman, I've been roasting over a spit. And I'm not letting you gallop back to Alex Stanford until you have some time to get reason back into your brain. Trust me, he wouldn't know what to do with you."

"Alexander Stanford is a gentleman!"

"Which is exactly why he wouldn't know what to do with a woman like you." He stuffed a gag into her mouth. "You're rusty, Georgie. I expected more of a fight. But I imagine you'll get back into practice."

Cougar closed the door of the car and left Georgia stewing in her own frustration. A smile lifted one corner of his mouth. Georgie was getting back to herself quick as a grass springing back to life after a winter snow. Three months ago he would have had a hell of a time bulldogging her like he'd just done. He hoped by the time she had all her fight back, she would have realized that he was doing her a favor. Cougar didn't want to fight her. He wanted to treat her like the woman he knew she was—a smart woman who was beautiful without corsets or frills and furbelows, strong with a capacity to be gentle, lighthearted without being frivolous. Not to mention having a great right hook. Fortunately, he was still faster and stronger than she was.

He had until Prescott, Cougar figured. If Georgie hadn't seen the light by then, he would have to let her return to Alexander and Chicago, ruin her own life, and savage his as well. His life probably wasn't the only thing she would savage, given a chance.

Purchasing their tickets took almost all his money. After buying Georgia a dress and other incidentals, he had barely enough left to buy bread and cheese for breakfast, and certainly not enough for expenses during the remainder of the trip. Fortunately, he had a bank account in San Francisco that could cough up enough to see them through. He headed to the telegraph office to wire for a bank draft. This was taking longer than he wanted it to, but they couldn't go on without money. If he hadn't been in such a hurry to get out of Chicago, to get Georgie back to where she could be Georgie once again, he might have planned better.

The best laid schemes o' mice and men
Gang aft a-gley.

Robert Burns—a tattered book of poetry on a shelf in

his cabin. Georgie had borrowed it a few times and commented that the man spelled his words worse than she did. He smiled at the memory. Georgie was enough to make any scheme go "a-gley."

He was just leaving the bank when he saw her.

"Goddamn!" he muttered. Georgia was supposed to be tied hand and foot, and gagged to boot, in the freight car, not sauntering down the main street of Galesburg looking like an overgrown urchin from *Oliver Twist*. With the baggy, rumpled clothes and her hair stuffed into a disreputable hat—probably rescued from some trash heap—she looked like a down-on-his-luck youth in search of a meal, which she probably was. She disappeared into a bakery.

Cougar got to the bakery door just in time to hear her offer to cut wood for the kitchen stove in exchange for a loaf of bread.

"There you are, you scamp!"

At the sound of his voice, Georgie turned to run, but he grabbed her by the back of her collar.

"Shame on you, running off to play your pranks while Mother is frantic with worry." He gave the shocked shop woman a rueful look. "My kid brother. Not quite right in the head. Runs off all the time. Pretends he's a starving orphan."

"He's kidnapping me!" Georgie shouted, flailing at him with her fists. "Don't let him take me. Call for help!"

"Never been right since the day he was born. Midwife dropped him on his head."

The shop woman gave him a sorrowful look. "God be with you, sir, for looking after the lad."

Cougar smiled manfully. "He's a trial, but he is family, after all."

With the woman looking on sympathetically, he dragged Georgie out the door. "Don't!" he warned her before she could kick up another ruckus. "Don't even try. Look at yourself first."

"What?"

"Look at yourself."

She glanced down at the shapeless shirt and trousers, the oversized boots he'd borrowed for her from his cousin.

"Do you really think anyone is going to believe you rather than me, no matter what story you tell?"

With withering eyes she surveyed his neat attire, shiny boots, and short, well-trimmed beard, then moved to her own ragamuffin self. She grimaced at the truth of his statement. "Too bad people can't see what a dungworm you really are."

He had to respect her for trying to escape. She wouldn't have been the Georgie he knew without trying. "I bought you clothes." He tried to placate her as he urged her along beside him back toward the train station. "Doesn't that always put a woman in a better mood?"

She simply snarled.

"How did you get out of the car, by the way?"

"You tied the knots too loose."

"I was trying not to hurt you."

"Yeah, well, don't expect the same from me when I get the drop on you."

He just smiled. She could spit, snarl, and threaten all she wanted. But he knew Georgie too well to believe the performance. If she had truly wanted to escape him, he never would have caught sight of her after she left that freight car.

"'My kid brother.'" She mockingly reprised his little act all the way back to the train. "'Never was right in the head, poor thing.' *You're* the one not right in the head, Cougar Barnes. You are asking for such a lump!"

"Keep trying to convince yourself, Georgie. You know you're grateful to me."

She snorted. "Truly not right in the head."

Elizabeth was packed and ready to go, but it remained to be seen where she would be going. She had waited above stairs, like a proper lady staying within her own sphere, listening to voices float up the stairs. Alexander had spent hours the day before, the day that Georgia had gone missing, closeted in the library with Alvin, and today he was here again. At dinner the night before, Alvin had told her that Alexander agreed that Georgia had likely left under duress and that every effort should be made to rescue her. He knew Barnes from years ago. The man wasn't the brutal sort who would force himself on an unwilling woman, but he did believe in taking things into his own hands. He wasn't one to sit by and watch something he wanted slip away. If he wanted Georgia, then he might take charge to make sure that he got her.

Elizabeth didn't have Alexander's faith in Cooper Barnes's character. The man was enormously attractive in a dangerous sort of way. He had been perfectly polite to her the few times they had met, and at first she had thought he might be a good match for Georgia. But his manners and pleasant presentation hid a rather frightening nature, Elizabeth thought. When Cooper Barnes walked into a room, the room suddenly seemed too small. Out-of-doors he somehow drew the forces of nature to him. It was a ridiculous fantasy, Elizabeth acknowledged, but had made her uneasy around him from the very first, when she and Georgia had met him walking by the lake. She hated the thought of her friend being in that man's power.

Then again, her trepidation about Barnes might simply be her timid nature coming to the fore. She had spent an ugly day and night and now another day frustrated at her indecision, at her inability to help Georgia when Georgia had so often helped her.

Elizabeth knew very well that Alvin Kennedy had planned to end her employment as soon as Georgia had the rudiments of manners and social skills, but Georgia had threatened to leave, giving up her precious mines and her grandfather's regard, if Elizabeth were turned off. She had all but forced Alvin to include a decent wardrobe as part of her employment, encouraged him to include her mother and sisters in their outings, and made her a part of the family more than a paid companion and tutor.

If Elizabeth had ever been in danger, Georgie would have flown to her rescue no matter the risks or difficulties, while Elizabeth sat back and waited for the men to decide what to do. Her helplessness, the waiting and waiting without knowing what was being planned—all that finally broke through the dam that stoppered her spirit, the years of proper education and upbringing. Elizabeth knew very well that gallivanting off to the rescue would be the height of impropriety, but for the first time in her twenty-four years of life, she also knew that the proper thing was not always the right thing. She was finally of an age to tell the difference.

So when Alexander left the library and headed for the front door, she went after him. She caught him just as he was stepping into his carriage.

"Mr. Stanford, please. I must have a word with you."

"Miss Whitman. Certainly." He spoke to his driver. "I'll be just a few minutes, John."

"I . . . we should speak out here. I don't want to bother Mr. Kennedy with . . . with what might be a heated discussion."

He regarded her quizzically. The air was chilly and a damp mist rolled in from the lake, unlikely conditions for a gentlewoman to favor over the comforts of a parlor, but "As you wish," was all he said. A gentleman through and through.

"You are going after Georgia, aren't you, Mr. Stanford?"

"Most certainly I am." A grim note crept into his tone.

"I want to go with you."

That sent his brows soaring upward.

"Really. I want to go with you." Just in case he hadn't heard the first time she said it.

"Miss Whitman . . . Are you joking?"

"No."

"I'm afraid your going along with me is quite impossible. This isn't a jaunt that a woman would enjoy."

"Enjoyment has nothing to do with it, Mr. Stanford. Georgia will need a woman to comfort her as only another woman can, sir. God only knows what that scoundrel has put her through. I realize that you are her fiancé, and that you . . . you care greatly for each other. But she will need a woman to console her and to make the journey home bearable. Mr. Kennedy agrees with me. He is willing to finance the expense of me accompanying you." Only after she had told him that Alexander himself had solicited her help, which was the primary reason she didn't want Alvin overhearing their discussion.

"Indeed." His tone was cautious. To Alexander's credit, he at least was listening. Listening, but not convinced. "Strange that Alvin did not apprise me of this plan."

"I asked him to allow me to put the idea before you."

"Did you now?" He sounded dubious. "I don't think that either you or Alvin realize the hardships."

"I do."

"No, I don't believe you do, Miss Whitman. We are assuming, with good reason I think, that they headed not for New York, but for Arizona. The journey to Arizona Territory is not an easy one, even in this modern day. Railroads haven't penetrated that far into the frontier, and considerable distance must be traversed either by ship or stagecoach or on horseback. It is no place for a woman."

"There are women there, Mr. Stanford. Georgia spent her life in such places."

"The women there are not gently born and raised, and they do not look as if a stiff wind would blow them off their feet." His voice hardened with impatience, and Elizabeth had to gather up all her courage to go on.

"I believe you are wrong. I have read accounts of courageous women from all walks of life making the journey West, even in the days before the railroad crossed the continent. And if it seems to you that a stiff breeze will knock me off my feet, sir, I can assure you that I can pick myself back up. I will not slow you down nor be an inconvenience."

He opened his mouth to rebut, but she didn't give him the chance.

"Georgia Kennedy has shown me that women can undertake adventure and adversity as well as men. Can I be less courageous than she? I would shame myself if, for fear of the unknown and reluctance to risk myself, I refused to help when she most needed me. And she will need my help, Mr. Stanford. I'm a woman, and I know. What's more, her reputation and yours as well will need the protection of a chaperone on your return journey."

He gave her a long assessing look. "And what of your reputation, Miss Whitman? What you propose outrages propriety."

She saw that only utter frankness would satisfy him.

"Sir, you know my family's story. My reputation is beyond repair through no action of my own. Reputation, for all its importance in our society, is an artificial measure of a human being. Knowing Georgia has taught me that."

"Tongues will most certainly wag, you know."

"I've lived my whole life ruled by those wagging tongues," she told him ruefully. "No more. Mr. Kennedy has kindly offered me a position of housekeeper when I return, as Mrs. Bolton desires to live in the country with her daughter. So I have no need to depend upon reputation to find work."

His eyes, chill and implacable, regarded her assessingly. "If you delay me, or distract me from my goal, I will buy you a ticket and send you back, and no amount of objection from you will make it otherwise. Do you understand?"

Elizabeth's heart soared. She had won. She had pitted herself against convention and a determined male and won. Actually, two determined males had fallen to her persuasion, for Alvin had not been easily convinced that she was needed.

"Thank you, Mr. Stanford."

"You might not thank me before this journey is through. Tomorrow morning at six o'clock I will pick you up, and I expect you to be ready and waiting. And now, Miss Whitman, good night." Looking mightily displeased, he left her standing by the porch steps.

As she stared after his retreating carriage, Elizabeth's smile slowly faded. Tomorrow at six she, Miss Elizabeth Whitman, proper, modest, very unadventurous spinster, would embark upon an escapade that would make some men's hearts quail. What in heaven had she just done to herself?

Chapter 16

Georgia sank to her neck in tub full of hot water—an outrageous luxury in the hotel where they stayed. Omaha, Nebraska, was a booming town, thanks to the railroad, but it wasn't a genteel town, especially this close to the train depot. She could hear the noise of the railroad yard as she sat and soaked away the dirt of the last two days—two cold days of sitting on hard seats, putting up with smoke and cinders, swaying with the peculiar sickening motion of the cars. The passenger car was little better than the freight car, as far as Georgia was concerned. Give her a wagon behind a team of mules any day.

Still, she hadn't complained about the cold and discomfort; a few months in Chicago hadn't turned her that soft. She had complained about everything else, however—more to annoy Cougar than to vent her own dissatisfaction. The dress Cougar had bought for her fit poorly. The shoes pinched. The bonnet was an abomination. And he hadn't bought her a corset. The only good thing he'd gotten her was a wool cape that just barely kept her warm on the train.

"Have you drowned in there?" Cougar asked from the other side of the door.

"Quit complaining. If you're nice, I'll let you use the bathwater after I'm done."

She heard a snort.

"If you don't hurry it up, the dining room will close without us getting dinner. Do you want to go hungry?"

"The dining room doesn't close for two hours yet. Why don't you go buy me some decent clothes. And don't forget the corset."

"I'm not buying you one of those whalebone torture contraptions."

"I'm not leaving this room without one." Which was purely silly, she admitted. She hated corsets, and the freedom of going without one was downright seductive. But that stupid "torture contraption" had become the symbol of her conversion to being a lady. Miss Georgia Kennedy, like any other genuine woman, wouldn't dream of parading around with her actual curves hanging out for just anyone to see. It was Georgie who insisted on the freedom to move and breathe. And it was Georgie that Cougar tried to lure to the surface. He laughed at her new polish and propriety, thought she was incapable of being a true and actual lady. Well, she—Miss Georgia Kennedy—would show the arrogant jackass.

"I need at least two more petticoats," she told him. In Galesburg he'd only gotten her one—positively indecent! "And gloves, and a hat that doesn't make me look like I'm crossing the country on a wagon train."

"Get out of the bathtub, and you can buy your own frigging clothes."

"Tut tut! Language!"

Georgia laughed softly to herself and sank beneath the water to wet her hair. What did the neighbors think about this conversation between Mr. and Mrs. Gilbert Rainey from Pittsburgh? If Cougar thought that adopting false names would throw off pursuit, he underestimated her grandfather. How hard would it be to follow a woman with blazing red hair and a man who towered over ordinary men and acted as if he owned the whole world?

Not that she was going to wait for someone to rescue her. Any time now she was going to escape. She just had to find the right opening. Yes, indeed. She was going to escape and go back to Alexander. Handsome, gentlemanly

Alexander, who truly cared about her and wanted to care for her the rest of her life. Alexander wanted her for herself, because she was "unique," and he thought she would make a dandy wife. He hadn't tried to sell her some bull about love and desire. He'd been honest, and Georgia admired that in a man.

On the other hand, Cougar—the lying sack of mule shit—claimed to love her while he only wanted those gold claims. Apparently the one claim she'd sold him wasn't enough. Now he wanted the other one as well. Somehow he'd figured out that Alvin had signed the mines over to her, and that had given the low-down skunk a notion that he should just marry her. The rat. And he thought she was gullible enough to believe him! Ha!

Yes, indeedy! Any time now she was going to leave the man in her dust. He would be mighty sorry.

A voice carped from the back of her mind. As a lying sack of mule shit, Cougar had a lot of company. Who did she think she was fooling with this escape business? Herself? Cougar? How hard had she really tried to get away? Had she gone soft, or just stupid? If she wanted to, she could just climb out the window, shinny down to the street, and disappear into the crowds of Omaha. If she wanted to . . .

And maybe she would do just that, Georgia told the voice.

Right—leave Cougar and return to Alexander, whose image she futilely tried to call into her brain after only two days of separation. The details of his face wouldn't come, because all she could see in her mind was Cougar Barnes, with his broad, irritating smile and eyes the color of an Arizona sky. Cougar Barnes with windblown, sun-colored hair and ax-handle shoulders.

Cougar filled her mind because he irritated her past tolerating, Georgia told herself. And she was heading back to Alexander and Chicago, she truly was, just as soon as the right opportunity presented itself.

"If you're going to stay in there until the cows come home, then I'm going out to get you some clothes," Cougar said through the door. "I'll be back in time for dinner. And

I'm locking the door. So don't get any ideas that will get you into trouble."

The bolt snicked home, and his footsteps pounded down the hallway until they faded. That right opportunity practically tapped Georgia on the shoulder to get her attention. Cougar was gone, foolish man. The window beckoned. By the time he got back, she could be sitting in the marshal's office setting the law on Cougar's tail, or at least she could be telegraphing Alvin for money to buy her passage home. No, not home. Passage to Chicago. How long would it take to think of Chicago as home?

Are you escaping yet? the caviling voice inquired. *Or are you sitting there in the tub whining about Chicago not being home? You said you were waiting for a chance. This is it. Put up or shut up. Pee or get off the pot.*

Just simmer down, Georgia told her conscience. I'm escaping. And this time I'm escaping all the way back to Chicago.

She got out of the tub, hastily scrubbed herself dry, and reached for her clothes. But her clothes weren't where she'd left them. Where were her frigging clothes? She wrapped the towel around herself and tore the room apart without finding so much as a pair of drawers. The wardrobe mocked her with its emptiness. Beneath the bed was only dust. The room was small. Few places could hide the pile of clothing she had peeled off before stepping behind the screen and into the tub. Even her shoes were gone.

Cougar had taken them, the scummy rat. He had sneaked into the room while she bathed behind the screen and had stolen them away. No wonder he had walked off confident that she would be here when he returned. She couldn't very well escape jaybird naked, now, could she?

Nice excuse, the voice mocked. *Some escape.*

"Oh, shut up!" she told herself, then climbed into the bed naked and imagined ways she could get even—once she got her clothes back, that is.

So far, Cougar congratulated himself, his scheme was a rousing success. He and Georgie had gotten out of Chicago without a hitch, the law hadn't closed in upon him for kidnapping, Georgie hadn't managed to wriggle out of his grasp, and right now they were eating a grand dinner and looking forward to a soft bed in Omaha. Though Georgie was the one who would get the soft bed. He could kidnap her, pester her to marry him, tie her up, steal her clothes, and even steal a kiss, but there was a limit to how far he could push without pushing the hellcat over the edge. And the bed was definitely the limit.

"Good steak," he commented. "How's yours?"

"Good," she said sullenly.

"Still mad because I took your clothes?"

A sharp swipe from her eyes answered a resounding yes.

"Come on, Georgie. How stupid do you think I am? If I'd left your clothes in that room, where would you be right now? Probably halfway to Chicago in some boxcar. You'd be cold and hungry, trying to sleep on the hard floor, wondering how you'd been so stupid as to leave a man who loves you and is trying to do you a favor. Instead, you're sitting right across from me eating a fine, juicy steak and drinking good wine."

Resentful silence was her only answer. It might take a while, Cougar figured, for Georgie to get past the notion that he had no right to carry her off, but of course he'd had the right. What were friends for if not to help out friends who were galloping down a dangerous path?

"Did I tell you that ol' Skillet Mahoney is making eyes at Mrs. Peterson up at the boardinghouse? Wouldn't surprise me a bit if they were hitched by the time we got back. It's the time of year for getting married. All the songs and poems about spring is just so much nonsense. It's when winter's coming that a man starts wanting a woman by his side. All those long cold nights coming up."

"You're so full of bullshit."

"Hell no, I'm not. When I get my place in Chino Valley built, I'm going to put a fireplace in the bedroom so we can lie together on those long cold nights. Firelight always makes the dark seem warm. You'll be nice and comfortable while I show you just how much I love you."

She looked mighty uncomfortable at the thought, which just went to show that she was thinking exactly the same thing he was about lying on that bed together.

"Keep dreaming," she advised with a sneer. "You don't have a house in Chino."

"I will soon enough."

"Not with any money you make off *my* gold claims."

"I don't want your gold claims. I want you."

"One comes with the other, you weasel. Do you really think you can get me to believe such nonsense about wanting me for just me? As if the two best claims in the district don't come with me?"

"Unless something's changed, those claims belong to your grandfather. And I'm not about to marry him for them." He gave her a disarming grin. At least, he hoped it was disarming.

She replied with a skeptical snort. "You expect me to believe you don't know that he signed the claims over to me when I said yes to Alexander?"

"Did he?"

"You know he did. Why else would you want me?"

Cougar didn't strain his mind to understand. Georgie was, after all, a woman. A man who tried to understand the ins and outs of a woman's mind would end up howling at the moon. Instead, he tried to explain. "Georgie, I wouldn't be low-down enough to marry a woman for a couple of pieces of dirt, no matter how much gold is buried beneath it. There's easier ways to get money than to chain yourself for life to a woman you don't really want."

"Marriage is the same as being chained, is it?"

"Not if you marry someone you love. I love you, and that's no song and dance. It's the truth."

She snorted again. "You could make a fortune selling snake oil, Cougar. I didn't know you had such a golden tongue."

He chose to ignore her crankiness. "Charlie Vann has asked me a couple of times to help drive his supply wagons across the Mojave Trail to Ehrenburg. The pay is sky high. I can earn what I need there."

"The pay is sky high because he can't find men willing to do it. They're too attached to their scalps."

She didn't seem too concerned about *his* scalp. "It's not that bad. I've been back and forth across the Mojave Trail five or six times, and you did it with your father a couple of times. You just have to stay alert and watch for signs of ambush."

The beginnings of concern creased her brow. "You're not really thinking of driving Charlie's wagons, are you?"

"A half year's work added to what I've already saved could buy me a starter herd. Within a couple of years the Apaches won't be on a rampage any longer, mark my words. There's too many people wanting to come into Arizona and New Mexico and settle—respectable, hardworking people who want to put down roots here, raise a family, go to church, and spend their Saturday nights at an ice-cream social or a barn dance. They don't want to be looking behind every bush for some Apache warrior who wants their scalps, and they don't want to worry night and day about their wives and kids being safe. One day soon the government is going to wise up and send us an Indian fighter who's as smart as the Indians, and then we'll see peace. When that happens, running cattle in places like Chino will go from bust to boom overnight, and I'm going to be one of the first. I intend to set down roots so deep that they'll last me the rest of my life. No more wandering. No more searching out a better life over the horizon. I've found the place I want to be, and I've found the woman I want to be with."

For a moment she seemed to soften, as if she wanted to believe him. But then her gaze narrowed and hardened. "You should save your pretty speeches for Captain Rawlins's daughter."

That caught him by surprise. "Louisa?"

"Louisa?" she mocked in a syrupy tone.

He hadn't thought of Louisa Rawlins since Georgie had left Arizona, and he doubted the belle of Fort Whipple missed him. She enjoyed flirting with her father's officers and casting out lures for the local men whom she considered worthy. Louisa Rawlins was fool's gold, where

Georgie was the genuine treasure. And the treasure had nothing to do with her goddamned claims.

"I won't be making any speeches to Louisa. She isn't what I want."

Georgie dropped into silence as she stabbed at her peas, one by one. He could see her mind chewing on something.

"You don't need to be jealous of any woman, Georgie."

Her head jerked up. "Jealous? Ha!"

Cougar grinned. "But it is nice to know you care."

She looked ready to spit. "I don't care a hoot who you keep company with. You keep forgetting that I landed the catch of the century in Chicago. He's probably chasing after us right now. The only way you're going to save your ass is to send me back, tuck your tail, and find a place to hide."

The suggestion sounded halfhearted at best, Cougar thought. He was making progress.

"Send me back, and I won't hold it against you that you carted me off like a sack of flour." She regarded him closely from beneath dark gold lashes. "And I'll make sure you get your claim. So don't go doing anything stupid like taking that job from Charlie Vann."

She did care. She truly did. With a satisfied smile he told her, "I'll send you back if you want."

Was that a flare of disappointment in her eyes?

"I'll send you back when we get to Prescott and you tell me to my face, swearing on the Good Book, that you still want to marry Alexander Stanford and live in Chicago. Then I'll send you back. So until then, we can just enjoy each other's company."

"I'd enjoy a polecat's company more," she growled.

Cougar merely grinned and lifted a glass in salute. "One day we'll tell our children about this and laugh."

The prospect of someday getting a start on those children sent a flush of desire through Cougar's blood. Clean from a soak in the tub, dressed in the new dress he'd just brought her, Georgie was the next thing to irresistible. Thinking to minimize temptation, he'd purchased the most severe costume he could find, but its plain lines only emphasized her soft curves and flamboyant coloring, the red-gold of her hair, the emerald of her eyes. Her sharp tongue couldn't disguise the soft flush that colored her cheeks when they traded words, or glances, or during the silences when she couldn't quite meet his eyes.

Her mouth said one thing, but everything else about her said something else, that he was winning, that Georgie was about to put Georgia on the mat for the full count. And Georgie, bless her, wanted him.

The question was if he could live until the battle was done. The woman didn't know what she did to him every time she touched him, every time those eyes of hers flashed in his direction. When she subtly squirmed inside the stupid corset, his heart went into his throat and his blood rushed to his groin, leaving him with an ache he couldn't assuage. Not yet. Not until she knew that she loved him. Pray God that she did love him.

Sometimes Cougar wished that the little hellcat was right, that he had pursued her for the sake of that damned mine, because wanting Georgie's gold would be so much easier than wanting Georgie herself.

Georgia blamed the push-pull of her emotions on the wine she had gulped down at dinner. But she knew, in the part of her that insisted on rock solid honesty, that the wine wasn't to blame. She blustered at Cougar and sliced him with scornful words, boldly demanding to be sent back to Alexander, and yet when he'd seemed to agree, her heart had jumped into her throat, and not from joy. She tried to scorch him with indignation, and instead, she had melted from the heat of her own confused desires.

She wondered if a weak will was part and parcel of being a lady. A perfectly sensible person donned a dress, and boom, out went pride and independence, in came a spine that turned to mush for the likes of Cougar Barnes, who had the brass to think he could use her for his own purpose. And did she stand up to him with action, with spunk, with brass that matched his own? No! She threw puny little words at him, all the while allowing him to drag her farther from the man she had decided to marry. She let him laugh at her ladyness without giving him the kick he so richly deserved. She listened to his nonsense about wanting her and almost believed it. She wanted to believe it so much that the wanting robbed her of any real will to get away.

"You don't look so good," Cougar told her when he opened the door to their room. "Dinner not sitting well on your stomach?"

"You're the one who doesn't sit well on my stomach!" she snapped. Words again. Useless, lying words.

"Tsk. Ladies are expected to be calm and polite at all times. You could use a little improvement there."

"Ladies aren't expected to be ladies when they're traveling with jackasses." She slipped into the room as soon as the lock turned and tried to slam the door in his face. "Good night!"

"Good night to you, too." He pushed his way through the doorway. She tried to hold it against him, but the big ox hardly noticed. "We'll flip for the bed. Loser takes the chair."

"You are not staying the night in my room!"

"*Our* room, Mrs. Rainey."

"In name only, *Mister Rainey*! It's indecent."

He laughed, sending her ire an inch higher. "Georgie girl, we've slept together in your cabin, on the ground by a campfire, and once I even bunked in that little house in Prescott you bought with *my* money for the claim I never got."

"You'll get your frigging claim," she gritted out from between clenched teeth.

"And most lately we slept together in a cold freight car."

"We did not Sleep Together." She emphasized each word separately, so that he could focus his weasel brain on the notion that sleeping together was not nearly the same as Sleeping Together. Bunking side by side in a prospector's cabin or the hard dirt ground was far different than sharing a hotel room for the night. Sharing a hotel room, in the eyes of society, was definitely Sleeping Together, an indecency unpardonable for unmarrieds. "Ladies do not so much as look at a bed when a person of the male persuasion is in the same room."

This time he bellowed his laughter, making her want to

shut him up with her fist. "Well, last time I looked I was definitely of the male persuasion, but I think you're mistaken about the nature of a true lady."

"What would you know about being a lady?"

"Quite a bit. My mother was a lady. So was my grandmother and both sisters. But they were ladies in their hearts, not because they followed some set of silly rules made up by old biddies who don't have anything better to do than to make other people's lives difficult. Now, we'll flip for who gets the bed."

"Barbarian!"

Cougar ignored the slur, which took most of the fun from it.

"And then you might want to get out of that whalebone cage you call a corset, because your face is looking like it might explode. I did buy you some nightclothes along with that dress."

"To think I once thought you were one of the best men I ever knew."

He smiled at that. "You don't say!"

"Now that I'm downright educated, I can see you're more like something that crawled from under a rock."

He laughed, digging in his pocket for a coin and deftly flipping it into the air. "Heads or tails for the bed?"

"Heads."

"Tails it is."

She snorted fire.

"But being a genuine gentleman, I'll cede you the bed. I don't suppose you'd care to share?"

She put an end to his mocking grin by throwing the hairbrush that lay on the dressing table. Her aim was true, as usual, and he oofed as the missile hit him square in the chest.

"Guess not," he grunted.

She only wished she had something heavier to throw.

The night went downhill from there. Georgia suffered a miserable attack of self-consciousness as Cougar blithely prepared for sleep. First he pulled off his boots, then his coat and waistcoat, his collar, and then one by one unfastened the buttons of his shirt. Georgia had seen Cougar

Barnes stripped down to his longhandles a time or two, but somehow, that had been different. On one of those occasions her father had been there. Elias, Cougar, Georgie, and two other prospectors had spent three days repairing a cabin on Granite Creek belonging to Bess Hurley, a recent widow, who ran it as a hotel of sorts. They had camped a short ways from the cabin, and everyone, as usual, had treated Georgie the same way they would have treated another man. No one had watched their language or hesitated to strip down as far as they wanted before crawling into their bedrolls.

Georgie had thought nothing of it, except perhaps her eyes had been drawn just a bit by Cougar, who took off just enough to fuel her imagination and prick her curiosity.

Then there had been the time when Cougar had gotten caught in an unexpected January snowstorm a mere month after Georgie's father had died. He had barely made it through the blizzard to her cabin on the Lynx, where he had holed up for the night with her and Essie. Georgie remembered Essie giving him the narrowed eye when he started to peel down in front of the fire. Before he'd shown his all to Georgie's interested eyes, Cougar had needed reminding that a young woman was in the room. The memory made her flush with embarrassment, not because of the broad bare chest that had caught her eye that night, but because of the reminder of all those years when she had dressed, thought, and downright acted like a man. She really hadn't been that interested in Cougar's display of naked male skin, Georgia told herself firmly.

No, indeed. And she wouldn't be interested now if he peeled down to his bare skin. The man could be a Greek god and still be a slinking coyote, as far as she was concerned.

"Are you going to sleep in that getup?" he asked.

Georgia tried to avert her eyes as he shrugged out of his shirt, leaving only a brief undershirt that didn't hide the roll of muscle in his shoulders or the powerful breadth of his chest. "At least have the courtesy to leave on your clothes," she snapped irritably.

A wheat-colored brow inched upward. "Why? In the

morning they'll look like I slept in them. Hand me one of the blankets from the bed?"

She complied, staring helplessly as he stepped out of his trousers. He wore cotton knit longhandles that stretched across corded thighs and clung to every muscle. Georgia felt a humiliating flush heat her cheeks. The sight of all those hard muscles nearly took her breath away. Indeed they did. And shame on her. What would Elizabeth say if she knew? A lady didn't think about such things, much less stare as if she were starved and feasting her eyes upon a banquet.

"You aren't going to sleep like that, are you? Don't tell me that lady tutor of yours taught you to sleep in a corset."

"Don't be stupid."

He grinned. "Want me to get your buttons?"

"Touch my buttons and you'll lose a finger or two. I managed to do them up. I can undo them."

"Should I turn my back?"

Which would have him facing the mirror, the sneaky weasel.

"Just blow out the lamp and go to sleep. Fast asleep."

"I never sleep so hard that I can't hear everything that goes on around me, Georgie girl. If you head for either the window or the door any time during the night, you're going to find me on you like sap on a pine tree."

It was an image that started her imagination humming, much to her distress. "Just blow out the damned lamp!"

Once the room was pitch dark, Georgie struggled with buttons, laces, and ties, until her dress and petticoats were a puddle at her feet, her corset lay in a stiff heap in the corner, and she could once again draw a free breath. Standing there in chemise, drawers, and cotton stockings, she felt naked to the skin, somehow, and hot all over, as if Cougar's eyes burned a slow fire over her indecent exposure. Before she'd gone to Chicago, Georgia wouldn't have given her undress much thought, but Elizabeth had pounded the notion of modesty clear down to her bone. Layers of clothing gave protection as well as warmth, protection from leers, masculine smirks, and lascivious thoughts. Protection from

Cougar Barnes, who was the last person in the world Georgie had expected to be a danger.

Threats from Apaches, wild animals, and the elements Georgie could take in stride, even after growing soft on city living. Cougar didn't pose that kind of threat. He invaded her peace of mind, robbed her of pride, inspired strange heats and quivers just by a smile or the flex of a muscle or worse, sitting in his chair half naked watching her in the dark. She knew he watched, could feel his gaze even though she couldn't see it. She wondered if he had the eyes of his namesake, probing the dark with catlike keenness.

"Quit it," she growled.

"Quit what?"

"Looking at me."

She could feel his smile. "It's dark," he said innocently.

"Just quit it." She ripped back the bedclothes, climbed in, and pulled the blankets up to her chin. It was a big bed, more than big enough for two. A man as big as Cougar would take the lion's share of the mattress, though. Georgie pictured them lying there together. She would have to squeeze right up against him just to stay on the bed. They would fit together like two spoons in a drawer, his arms wrapped around her like steel bands, his heart beating against her back, her backside snuggled into his . . . damn!

Quit it! Just quit it!!

What worm in her brain forced her to think such thoughts? She wanted to squirm against strange aches in private places. She wanted to throw off the blankets to ease the throbbing heat. She wanted to saunter over to that chair where Cougar sat and . . .

Get your mind away from there, you little hussy!

Alexander didn't do this to her. He made her smile, made her stomach flutter a bit, but he didn't get inside her with every twitch of his mouth and stab of his eyes. He didn't make her want to explode from the pressure building inside her. The feeling scared her more than rattlesnakes, more than dust storms, more than Indians lurking in the trees. This enemy lurked in her heart—and several less poetic places she didn't even want to think about.

Georgie didn't understand it. She had always admired Cougar. Maybe she entertained a yearning or two in his direction. He was a good-looking cuss, and mannerly, when he wanted to be. His strength tempted a woman to feel safe when he was around. His smile made a woman feel a lot more than safe.

And yes, maybe Georgie had experienced a few tingles for Cougar in her old life, but those tingles were like gentle summer breezes compared to the cyclone that possessed her now. Maybe that whirlwind caught her up because she had felt the power of being a woman. She knew that she could be a woman. A real woman. And that new womanly part of herself appreciated Cougar Barnes in a way that scared Georgie half to death.

Good thing, she told herself, that the new woman in her didn't get so riled up over Alexander, or her life would never know peace. Alexander could give her respect, safety, and warm caring. Cougar would give her toil, tumult, and an itch that needed constantly to be scratched.

That itch was a bad thing, she told herself. A very bad thing.

But lying there in bed, feeling Cougar's presence like a hot spot in the room, Georgie couldn't quite convince herself of how bad a thing it really was.

Chapter 17

"They were here at this same hotel two days ago," Alex told Elizabeth as he sat down opposite her in the dining room.

This place wasn't an establishment that he would have patronized, given a choice, but it was close to the railroad station and inexpensive. He deduced that if Barnes and Georgia had stopped in Omaha, this hotel was a likely place where they would stay, and he'd been right. He had also been lucky. The fleeing couple could have ridden the train straight through without stopping for a night's rest. Or they could have easily chosen another hotel.

But they hadn't. The proprietor had recognized them immediately from Alex's description, even pointed out the phony name Barnes had used to sign the register. How many ox-sized blond gentlemen and fire-haired ladies passed through his lobby in a year? the innkeeper had asked with a chuckle. It had to be them. He remembered them especially well because of the squabbling that had inspired a couple of complaints from the neighboring room.

"That lady doesn't take any guff from her man, that's for sure," the man had told Alex. "I wouldn't want to get on her bad side, that's for sure. But her mister was big enough to take care of himself, I suppose."

Not big enough, Alex reflected, to take care of himself once Alex caught up to him. The idea of Barnes dragging Georgia halfway across the country, humiliating and compromising her by pretending to be man and wife, infuriated him beyond measure. The proprietor's description of the two of them together convinced Alex that Elizabeth was right. Georgia did not participate willingly in this flight back to the frontier.

"They were here in this very hotel?" Elizabeth asked.

"They left two days ago. By now they're halfway to San Francisco, if that's where they're going."

"But they're headed for Arizona, don't you think?"

"I would think. But the most common way to get there since the railroad crossed the country is to take a steamer from San Francisco down the coast, around the southernmost point of Baja California, then north to the mouth of the Colorado River. From there you can take a flat-bottomed stern-wheeler up the river to some point that puts you as close as possible to where you want to go in the interior."

She swallowed hard. "Oh."

Alex gave his companion a small smile. "It's not so bad, at least not at this time of year. During the summer the temperatures going up the Colorado River reach well over a hundred degrees—as much as a hundred forty, I've heard. But it's much cooler now. The worst we might meet is a little rough weather going down the Pacific Coast on the steamer. With luck even that won't be a problem."

"Of course. How bad could it be? People do it every day."

He chuckled at her attempt at nonchalance, when she was so obviously frightened as a mouse. "Elizabeth, you could very easily return from here to Chicago, if you want. I promise I will bring Georgia back in one piece. You needn't worry about her reputation. It's already in shreds, and once she's my wife, no one will dare give her insult."

"You say her reputation is already in shreds, yet you will still marry her?"

"Of course I will. This misadventure is not her fault. A woman's reputation can be a very artificial thing, not at all a reflection of character. I know Georgia's character, and so do you. She is beyond being damaged by petty tongues."

She smiled slowly, and he thought, a bit sadly. "You are an exceptional man, Mr. Stanford. Not many men are so generous or open-minded."

Their conversation was interrupted by a waiter, who asked for their dinner order. Alex ordered a beefsteak for both of them. There wasn't much choice on the menu, but this far west, one was lucky not to be required to hunt and kill the meal yourself.

"And would you and your wife like something to drink?"

Elizabeth's face flushed, but she kept her composure. "Just water," she said.

"And I'll have a beer."

The waiter left, and Elizabeth's tight expression eased a bit.

"I'm sorry you were subject to that embarrassment. I saw no reason to correct the man, though, considering that we're traveling together unchaperoned."

"That's quite all right. When I proposed to come with you, I assured you that I was entirely prepared for any consequences that might arise, and I am. As you say, a woman's reputation can be an artificial measure of character. I know who and what I am, and that should be enough. Raised eyebrows should not bother me."

Alex smiled at the brave front that was so obviously a front. He had to give Elizabeth credit, though. So far she had endured with a cheerful steadiness and composure that surprised him. When he had called at Graystone House in the gray of early dawn two days ago, she met him with an economically and sensibly packed carpetbag and a determination to be as little trouble to him as possible. She didn't complain of the cold on the train, nor the soot, the smoke, nor the rocking motion which discomposed some ladies and men as well. Instead, she showed great curiosity about the countryside through which they sped. Her questions about the frontier, the newly completed tracks that now stretched from coast to coast, and the difficulties ahead showed intelligence and thoughtfulness. Even the freighting business which had brought him West many times was subject to her inquiry. Her comments about the probable effect of the expanding railroads on Stanford Shipping demonstrated surprising insight.

Elizabeth Whitman was an interesting woman as well as a very attractive one. Alex found himself wishing that she weren't quite so attractive, that her brown hair was mousy instead of glistening, gentle fawn, her eyes insipid rather than pure, golden hazel, her figure pudgy instead of supple and willow-slim. After all, he had a mission to perform and a commitment to honor. Distractions were unwelcome, and Elizabeth was proving to be an extraordinary distraction.

"I posted a letter to my mother when we arrived," she told him. "I fear that she and both my sisters believe I've taken leave of my senses."

"I'm not sure that I don't agree. I'm very grateful for your concern about Georgia, but when we return, your reputation will be destroyed. There's no help for that, given the circumstances. And though I've said that reputation can be an artificial thing, it is still of paramount importance in our world, especially to an unmarried woman."

She smiled quietly. "You're right, of course, but it really doesn't matter. I will never marry. I'm much too old and firmly on the shelf, so loss of my good name doesn't rob me of my marriage prospects. And since Mr. Kennedy most generously offered me the position of housekeeper, I don't need a spotless character for the sake of obtaining employment."

Alex thought again what a shame it was that such a lovely woman should be put on the shelf simply because of her father's sins. He didn't like to think of Elizabeth Whitman spending her days as an old man's housekeeper.

"Actually, I'm quite enjoying myself"—her eyes twinkled merrily—"in spite of the scandalous nature of our journey. All my life I've been entirely too meek and conventional. I followed the rules without really thinking about them. I concerned myself only with what was proper and acceptable, not with what was good or right. But Georgia inspired me, bless her. She showed me that decent women do not have to sit at home in the narrow little box where men would put them. Georgia has fended for herself, thought for herself, done what many men would quail at doing, and her decency survives. She is truly all the things a woman should be—generous, caring, unselfish, and a true friend. Yet she has never followed the rules or done what the world believes a woman should do."

"I'll admit that Georgia is an exceptional woman."

"She truly is. When I first met her, I thought her an uncivilized hoyden"—she gave him a sharp glance—"as did you, Mr. Stanford. But I soon learned that in strength of spirit she measures far above most women of my acquaintance, including myself. If I could be half the woman Georgia is, I would be grateful."

"You give yourself far too little credit." Alex found himself wanting to reach out and take Elizabeth's hand, but of course he didn't. "You have a good share of stamina and courage yourself, Miss Whitman, or you would never have left Chicago. Everyone displays character in his own way. Georgia has led a life that demands overt courage and resourcefulness. Your life has been different, but I think you have shown as much strength and courage as she has."

"I have sat home all my life, sir."

"Adventure is not the only thing that requires courage."

The steaks arrived, still sizzling from the stove, with goodly portions of potatoes, gravy, hot brown bread, boiled peas, and a custard for dessert, all served at the same time. Dining got less dainty the farther west one traveled.

"Oh, my! I don't think I can eat all this."

"It's going to be a very tiring trip from here on out," Alex told her. "You'd better tell your appetite to expand. You'll need to keep up your energy for the journey ahead. If you want a test of stamina and resourcefulness, my dear, the way west may give it to you." He caught her full attention with a grave look. "Miss Whitman, be very sure before we leave Omaha tomorrow morning that you truly want to go on. Give what you are doing serious thought. No one, least of all myself, would fault you for turning back. In fact, I would consider it a decision of exceptional good sense. The farther West we go, the more primitive the conditions, but I don't intend to stop until I've found Georgia and dealt with Cooper Barnes."

She met his seriousness with a gravity of her own. "What will you do to Mr. Barnes when you find him?"

"Cooper Barnes is going to get exactly what he deserves, the scoundrel. I've already sent word to the authorities in Prescott. If he and Georgia get to Arizona before us, the man will find an unpleasant surprise waiting for him."

The clear October sky, bright with the dawn, made a perfect backdrop for the soaring Rocky Mountains. The new-risen sun touched the peaks with rose and left the lower heights dark with purple shadow. Slowly the morning light crept downward. Soon the whole Front Range would blaze with the new day.

Already the town of Denver was awake. Shops were opening their doors. People hurried along the streets, intent on getting wherever it was they were going. They gave neither Cougar nor Georgia a second glance where they stood at Satler's Livery Barn.

"Check that pack load good," Cougar told Georgia. "That mule looks a bit fractious."

Georgia was feeling a bit fractious herself. "I know how to load a mule."

"Just checking."

Somewhere along about Wyoming, Georgia had stopped trying to escape. She might have been able to bolt if just Cougar stood in her way, but her own stubborn self made things more difficult. A good part of her wanted to stretch out this interlude as long as she could. The clear, crisp western air invigorated her, and the bright sun warmed her blood. She hadn't realized how much she had hated being trapped in those hazy, damp Chicago days. The mountains themselves reached out seductively, wooing her spirit, making her feel as though she could take wing and fly up to those craggy heights.

The mountains, however, didn't have the market cornered on seduction. Cougar's presence gave a certain tension to every nerve in her body. Not that he did anything overt—no kisses, few touches, no more honeyed words of romance. He'd stated his case and expected her to think on it, Georgia knew. Cougar was that sort of fellow. When he spoke, he expected people to listen.

Georgia had listened all right. Cougar wanted to marry her. He thought she was a damn fool for playing at polite society. He believed her too much a damn fool to make her own decision about Alex Stanford. He wanted to marry her . . . marry her . . . marry her. Cougar didn't need to nag when her mind did the job for him.

She didn't believe him, of course. Damn fool she might be in some things, but she hadn't been born yesterday. In spite of his protestations, Cougar would probably marry a long-eared mule if he thought it would get him cows grazing in Chino Valley.

But what would she do, asked the pesky voice in the back of her head, if Cougar really did love her? Suppose he truly wanted her to share his life, stand beside him in the adventure of starting a ranch in Chino, lie beside him in his bed, give him her body, bear his children? Could she bear the belief that Cougar truly loved her when she had committed herself to Alexander Stanford and life in Chicago?

She wouldn't think about that, Georgia told herself firmly, because she didn't believe Cougar for one minute. Not one frigging minute did she believe him.

"Are you ready?" he asked.

"Hold on. You were the one who wanted the pack checked."

"How long does it take to check a few knots?"

She tsked. "What a nag you are. No wonder you can't find a woman to marry you."

He just looked at her until she flushed.

They trotted out of Denver, leading a pack mule and riding horses they'd bought at the livery. Cougar rode a big gray gelding, and Georgia sat astride an agile little chestnut mare. When Cougar had facetiously inquired if she required a sidesaddle, she had fired back: "You want to buy a sidesaddle, buster, then you ride it." She had been grateful to use the excuse to once again don trousers—stiff new denims she'd bought, or rather Cougar had bought, at a dry goods store in Denver. Stiff as they were, the trousers were heaven compared to her feminine attire. The corset she had discarded in Cheyenne, hoping Cougar wouldn't notice. But she'd had no excuse to dump the dress and mounds of petticoats until now.

They rode south toward Santa Fe with the mountains on their right and the rolling plains on their left. The chill of fall spiced the air, but the sun was warm and comfortable. With every stride of her spirited mare, Georgia's heart lifted. She had forgotten the bliss of freedom. Caging her soul inside the confines of her grandfather's dreary stone mansion had made life seem dull and gray. Was that why she had finally buckled under to the notion of marrying Alexander? Had her spirit been so crimped and cowed in that lackluster life that she had come to think of comfort and security was better than freedom? Or had she just thought she was no longer tough enough for the frontier?

She couldn't guess at the answer. Georgie was overthrowing Georgia so thoroughly that she scarcely remembered the reasons for anything that she had done in Chicago. Compared to the exhilaration of being once again in her own world, her supposed triumphs in a far-off city seemed petty.

"Keep an eye out," Cougar warned her. "The Indians around here aren't much friendlier than the ones at home."

"You don't need to talk like I'm a greenhorn," she snapped.

"Just wanted to let you know, so you don't get any ideas about taking off by yourself when I'm not looking."

Georgia refused to be civil to him, to give him the slightest hint of her happiness to be back where a person could see for a hundred miles and every square foot of space wasn't crowded with homes, shops, offices, and scurrying people. He might begin to think he had succeeded in bringing her to her senses, as if she needed someone to set her on the straight path. He might think she believed his story about loving her. He might catch on to the fact that watching him ride tall and powerful in the saddle, one with his horse, the sun burnishing his skin to warm copper, made her stomach melt. He might think that he crept into her daydreams and made her sleep far more entertaining than restful.

She didn't want him to think those things, even if they were true.

Their first day out was an easy one. They bought a midday dinner at a stage posting house along with a stagecoach full of passengers bound from Denver to Santa Fe. The group included two women, a mother and daughter traveling with the menfolk of their family. Both gave Georgie curious looks. The older woman regarded her with a look of near horror before she managed to hide the expression behind a blank face and pointedly turned her back. The daughter, a girl of perhaps fourteen or fifteen, simply stared.

Georgia surprised herself by smiling at the both of them. She didn't care what they thought. In her old life she had thought that such snubs didn't bother her, but now she realized that they had. The contempt of women who saw her as a freak or a hoyden had convinced her that she was somehow different, that she could never aspire to the pedestal of being a true woman.

But Georgia Kennedy was every bit a woman, no matter what she wore or how she spoke, walked, or lived. Underneath it all was a woman who could be the belle of the ball and charm the socks off anyone she pleased. Georgia knew that now, and the knowledge made her strong. She could smile in the face of narrow-minded contempt and simply feel superior.

The thought made her laugh aloud as they walked into the posting house. The laugh earned her some wary looks from the stage passengers, but only a grin from Cougar. The laugh lines around his eyes deepened in what seemed to be amused understanding. Yet he couldn't read her mind, couldn't understand. Could he?

They rode on through the afternoon until the sun had sunk well below the mountains. A rough homestead squatting in the lee of pine-clad ridge offered the chance of shelter for the night, and the family there welcomed them as if they were good friends. The homesteader himself introduced himself as Henry Macon. His wife was Sarah. Four children crowded around them, their names spoken but lost in the exuberant welcome.

"Don't see many traveling by theirselves anymore," Henry told them. "Most everyone takes the stage nowadays. Safer, I gotta say."

The stage trip would have been faster than traveling by horse and leading a mule. But the stage was crowded and dusty. People were squeezed shoulder to shoulder, coughing, sweating, queasy from the rocking motion, and trying to dodge the tobacco juice spit out the window by the men. Neither Cougar nor Georgia had even mentioned taking the stage.

They ate a hearty meal with the family in the dirt-floored log cabin they called home—not much bigger, Georgia noticed, than her cabin on the Lynx, even though it housed Henry, Sarah, and four rowdy children. The two girls were as rowdy and talkative as their brothers, all pumped up by the rare treat of having strangers in the house, people who hadn't seen the oldest boy's pet garter snake, who hadn't yet admired the poem that the youngest little girl had made up all on her own, as she proudly told them after reciting two verses. The older girl jumped in to show how she could do fractions, and the smallest boy, who trailed after all of them in size and age, insisted on taking Cougar and Georgia out into the yard to introduce them to a rooster by the name of Clyde.

Sarah, rosy cheeked and rather dumpy, worked together with her husband to manage both house and brood. They were a cheerful couple, obviously still in love after years of marriage.

As they sat down to supper, Henry boasted, "My Sarah here was the best cook in the whole state of Pennsylvania before we left and came out here."

Sarah chortled. "Not in the whole state, Henry."

"Sure thing in the whole state. Wait'll you taste her berry pie. We've got berries galore up on the ridge here, and the kids will spend the whole day hunting them just so

Ma can make a pie every night of the week. And her biscuits plumb melt in your mouth."

"Oh, go on!" Sarah flushed equally with embarrassment and pleasure. The flush deepened when Henry leaned over the table and gave her a smack on the cheek, something that would have horrified the arbiters of manners in Chicago society. Mannerly people reserved displays of affection for times when they were alone. Even then such things were expected to be ritualized and formal.

But Henry and Sarah made their own rules, it seemed. Neither looked askance at Georgia in her denim trousers, boots, broadcloth shirt, and floppy felt hat. And if they were shocked at her riding astride like a man, they didn't utter a word about it.

"Ma!" the youngest boy cried. "Emily took all the biscuits! Make her share."

"There were only two left," Emily said smugly. "I'm bigger than you, so I need to eat more."

"I'm growing faster than you, so *I* need to eat more."

"Emily, give Chester one of the biscuits. If you want to be a hog, then go into the kitchen and stir up another batch yourself." Sarah didn't raise her voice one bit, but Emily promptly handed over one of the biscuits. Chester gave her a smirk, but turned it into a polite smile when his mother's eye fell upon him.

After the meal everyone helped clean up the mess, not only the females. Jane and Toby, the oldest two children, brought in more firewood while Emily set the table for breakfast and Chester dried the dishes, with help from Georgia. Cougar chatted with Henry, comparing their firearms. Henry showed off his new Winchester repeating rifle. Cougar stood by the proven reliability of his old Henry rifle and Colt .44-caliber single-action revolver.

In the kitchen Georgia and Sarah laughed at stories Sarah told about their journey west. "I'll take a good sturdy wagon over that monster of steel and steam any day," she said, shaking her head. "Back in '60, when we came out, that was the way most folks came out here. We took the train for a ways from Pittsburgh. That was bad enough. Then the steamer down to Council Bluffs, where we formed up a big wagon train. We had fifty wagons and more, I'd guess. Some real characters, too. There was one old gal who was seventy if she was a day. She could walk the rest of us plumb into the ground, rain, wind, or shine."

"Why did you come West, Sarah?"

Georgia expected the woman to tell her that her husband had gotten the wanderlust, or that their farm had failed, or some other such excuse. She was surprised when Sarah got a big smile on her face. "It was my idea. Pennsylvania's getting too crowded for my taste. We saw the war was coming and wanted no part of it. We all needed some fresh air and a new life, I thought. Henry kind of had a hankering to pull up stakes for a while, but he didn't think me and the kids could manage the trip. I set him straight on that right quick. So we sold out our store and used the money to come out here. Haven't ever regretted it, either. Here's where a body can do what he pleases without nosy neighbors sticking their noses into your business. And if it's a harder life than we had back East, well, my Henry and I like working together to make something where there wasn't anything before. We all pitch in, me and my man and the kids, and so this place, this life, it belongs to all of us."

Henry ambled over to the kitchen area. "Are you two females through gabbing here?"

"I'm not a female," Chester told him indignantly.

His father grinned. "No, little man, you certainly aren't."

"And I'm not gabbing!"

"That because you aren't a female, eh?"

Sarah leveled a look at him that included as much affection as exasperation.

He merely smiled at his wife. "Jane wants to read to us from her book of poems. And she wants everybody in the audience."

"Well, in that case, Chester—you run along. I'll be along when these last pots are washed. And we'll bring some hot cider."

Chester happily went with his father while Sarah's gaze fondly followed. "My Henry's such a good man. Last time he went up to Denver, he brought our Janey down a whole load of books right along with the flour, sugar, and saleratus. She's a smart one, that girl, and a real deep thinker. Reads to the family almost every night. Her father does everything he can to make sure that sharp mind of hers always has something to chew on. Not every man would care about such things."

Georgia agreed. "That's true. You must be very proud of your whole family. They're wonderful."

"I am proud. Proud of every last one of them. Put that cider on to heat, would you, please?" The woman gave Georgia a canny look. "Seems to me, that's a pretty good man you've got for yourself, too. Looks like he could break a fencepost in two with his bare hands, but he's got a gentle look to his eye. He's obviously head over heels for you. I'm sure when you two have a family, you'll be as proud of them as I am of mine."

Georgia opened her mouth to deny that Cougar was "her man," then closed it. No one here had bothered to ask if she and Cougar were a married couple. These good people simply assumed that a man and woman traveling together alone would be husband and wife. Big-hearted and hospitable as they were, Henry and Sarah probably wouldn't throw them out if they knew the truth. But Georgia found herself reluctant to disappoint them.

A picture took form in her mind, inspired by Sarah's words. Cougar head over heels in love with her. Children gathered at their feet just as Sarah and Henry's four were gathered by the fireplace, waiting for their mother to join them for Jane's reading. There would be a boy with Cougar's sunlight-colored hair, and in time he would grow in size and muscle until he was big and strong as his father. But no woman would ever be afraid of him, because he would have his father's "gentle eye." And the girl would have Georgia's red-gold hair and green eyes. From the first, Georgia would make sure she had the manners of a lady and knew beyond a doubt that being a woman was a powerful and good thing. But she would also learn to shoot, ride, hunt, build a cabin, and ear-down an ornery mule. Cougar could teach her to wrestle. Georgia had once seen him wrestle a man half again his size—though it was difficult to believe any man could be that big—and win.

"You ladies coming?" Henry called from across the cabin.

Georgia had to shake herself out of her mental ramblings. Such imaginings were a bunch of hooey. She and Cougar weren't married, would never have that boy with gold hair and a girl who could shoot as well as serve tea. Because Georgia had promised herself to Alexander, and any children she bore Alexander would suffer being raised in Chicago. Because Cougar didn't really love her; he loved her stupid gold. Not to mention he was a stubborn, arrogant, kidnapping jackass.

But, as Sarah had said, he probably could break a fencepost in two with his bare hands, if he had a mind to—a thing to admire in any man. And he did have a gentle eye.

They spent the evening very pleasantly in front of the fireplace listening to Jane read from Keats and Longfellow. Later, the whole family listened to Henry tell stories his grandfather had told about early days in Pennsylvania. Georgia sat with Cougar on a homemade bench that Toby, the older boy, had made with his two own hands, and he was mighty proud of it, he informed them. She didn't object when Cougar's arm stole around her shoulders. It seemed right, somehow. She told herself it was an act for the benefit of their hosts, but still it felt right.

The family retired early, the parents to the cabin's one private room, the girls to their beds in the loft, and the boys to straw mattresses in front of the fireplace. Georgia and Cougar took their bedrolls to the barn.

The barn had every comfort they needed: straw to sleep on, four walls and a roof for shelter, and two plowhorses and one milk cow to make things cozy. A cold wind blew down the ridge from the higher mountains, and Georgia was grateful for the shelter. Sleeping in a barn couldn't compare to her bedchamber in Greystone House, where a feather mattress pampered her, a fireplace warmed all the hours of the night, and Rachel, her own personal maid, slept close by. But Georgia felt more comfortable in the barn than she ever had in her grandfather's house.

"These are nice people," she told Cougar as she spread out her share of the blankets. "Those children are sweet."

"Our children will be just as sweet."

Georgia flushed as the children she'd imagined as Cougar's—hers and Cougar's—jumped back into her mind. She turned away from the light of the lantern to hide her embarrassment. Imagination could certainly get a person in trouble.

"You ready for the lantern to go out?"

"Sure." She settled into her blankets, trying to think warm thoughts to keep out the cold. City living had indeed made her soft. She used to be able to fall asleep instantly in her cold drafty cabin with a blizzard raging outside.

Not many minutes passed before she heard the straw rustle as Cougar moved. Then extra blankets landed on top of her.

"Move over, Georgie. It's too cold to waste heat sleeping apart."

She should object, Georgia told herself as he settled in beside her and tucked the blankets around them. His arm snaked around her waist and pulled her back against him. Rock hard male flesh warmed her back, and blankets warmed her front. They fit together perfectly, his knees bent into the curve of hers, her backside snuggled into his . . . his . . . she really, really should object.

His voice rumbled in her ear. "Are you all right?"

She sighed in bliss and snuggled closer, so all right was she. Objection didn't stand a chance. His arm about her, thick with muscle and warm with his heat, made her feel safe, secure, wanted, cared for. Whether those things were true or not, Georgia decided, she owed herself one night to simply enjoy the feelings. His breath ruffled her hair, his heartbeat pulsed against her back in a rhythm that could so easily become a familiar part of her nights.

Don't think about it, she warned herself. Don't think at all.

Before her conscience had time to scold her, she surrendered to blissful sleep.

Chapter 18

The docks of San Francisco were no place for a lady, but Elizabeth had been a number of places the last week or so that would have made a true lady swoon. There had been the little mercantile in Rock Springs, Wyoming, where she and a rather slatternly woman had admired the same sewing kit. It was the last of its kind on the shelf, and they had both reached for it at the same time. The woman's eyes had swept Elizabeth up and down in surprise, then she had bellowed out a laugh. "You take the thing, honey. If a busted seam shows a little more of my skin, it'll just be good for business."

With a start Elizabeth had realized that she occupied the same room and breathed the same air as an actual soiled dove. Astonishment had left her speechless, so she had simply stood there like an idiot with the sewing kit in her hand while the woman continued to chuckle and wandered away.

But she hadn't fainted, or screamed, or even felt particularly soiled. More than anything else she had felt sorry for a woman who had to sell herself in order to survive. How did she maintain such a jolly laugh while leading such a life?

Then Mirage, Nevada, had happened. She still thought

of the little place and its train depot as an incident, not a town. The train locomotive had required some sort of repair before continuing, so she and Alexander had been stuck overnight in the depot. They had obtained food, if one considered greasy hunks of meat swimming in a stew with limp onions and something unidentifiably green to be food. But only a few rooms were available, and they were all taken. Along with most of the other passengers, Alexander and Elizabeth spent the night in the depot, which at least had a cast-iron stove that provided heat. Some passengers tried to sleep in the train but soon gave up because of the cold.

What lady of any reputation would dream of spending the night sitting on a bench, leaning against the shoulder of a man who was not her husband? Unthinkable. Not only that—she had to sleep, if she were to sleep at all, in full view of at least fifty pairs of eyes, many of whom belonged to rather rough-cut men. One other woman besides Elizabeth had graced the room, and she was a woman who spoke in overloud tones and rather coarse language.

Now Elizabeth found herself in San Francisco, perusing the dockyard where she and Alexander would soon board a steamship that would take them down the Pacific Coast and back up the Gulf of California to the mouth of the Colorado River. Elizabeth was temporarily alone among the crowd waiting to board the *Dolphin* while Alexander had gone to check on their steamer trunk. They had both purchased several items of additional clothing during the two days spent waiting for the steamer to sail, so Alexander had found a roomy trunk to hold the bulk of their things. Of course she could never tell her friends or family that she had packed her clothes with a man's in the same piece of baggage. Dresses, hats, shoes, and heaven forbid, unmentionables all lying intimately with his. Scandalous! But practical.

Elizabeth wondered if she would ever again be the same woman who had begun this journey. Or would she return to her humble position in Chicago restless with the knowledge that the world encompassed more than she had realized, and she was made of sterner stuff than she had imagined. She had endured dust, smoke, hot cinders, cold, and squalid stopovers without complaint—well, at least not much complaint. She had crossed mountains, deserts, and plains that stretched forever without a house in sight, hobnobbed with people from all walks of life, few of whom the humblest member of Chicago society would have received into her parlor. Indeed, Elizabeth was coming to realize that the slice of society she and her family occupied was a very narrow slice, and the rules they followed would seem as strange to the rest of the world as the rest of the world seemed to her.

"Well, lookee what we have here!" A coarse masculine voice interrupted Elizabeth's appreciation of her expanded horizons. "Hello, little lady. All alone, are ya? You need a man to keep you company?"

The man was dressed like a stevedore, and he had two companions who looked as though they lifted steel girders for entertainment. All three grinned at her in a most unsavory fashion. Elizabeth lofted her chin, gave them her back, and moved in the direction of the swarm of passengers. She had allowed herself to drift apart from the crowd, not wanting to endure the crush of so many bodies, but now she realized that protection came with numbers.

"Wait a minute, there, sweetheart! Don't go being rude to Davy and his friends. We don't like rude women, but if you was to be real nice to us, we might forgive ya, eh, boys? There's plenty of places around here you could apologize to all three of us."

Dark warehouses and labyrinthine alleyways between piles of freight loomed all too close. Daylight was no protection, and apparently the bustling population around them gave these beasts no pause. Indeed, no one seemed particularly interested in what went on around them, so intent were they upon their own concerns. Elizabeth wondered if she should scream. Making such a fuss would be unladylike in the extreme, but as a last resort, it might bring help.

"Leave me alone," she demanded while moving ever closer to the crowd, "or I shall call for help."

The chief beast mocked her cultured tone. "'I shall call for help!' Horrors! We're afraid!" He grabbed her arm.

Without thinking about it, she brought up her parasol and whacked him on the side of the head. He grunted, releasing her, as his two companions laughed. Now the people hurrying by began to take note of what was happening.

In spite of the dire circumstances Elizabeth swelled with pride. She had actually struck a blow in her own defense without calling for someone else to help her. Wonder of wonders!

"You little bitch!" the wounded man growled. "I'll teach you."

But others were taking note. "Here now," a man in overalls said. "What's this?"

And then a welcome voice made Elizabeth forget the pride of handling matters on her own. "Elizabeth, what the . . . ?" Alexander took her arm and pulled her behind the barrier of his broad, strong body. It was all she could do not to wrap her arms around him and plaster herself against his back, more than willing to give up her brief foray into self-defense.

"They wanted to . . . to . . ."

"Never mind. I can guess." He pointed an accusing finger at the men who had accosted her. "You want to take on someone your own size, you scoundrels? One at a time or all three. It makes little difference."

Elizabeth had never before heard that note of angry challenge in Alexander's voice. She was very glad that he was on her side.

The miscreants wanted no part of Alexander Stanford. Stumbling over each other in their haste to disappear, they melted back into the crowd.

Forgetting her pride, Elizabeth gushed, "Oh, Mr. Stanford! I'm so glad you came."

He turned around to face her, his eyes shadowed by concern. "Are you hurt?"

"No. Just . . . just a bit . . . discomfited."

"I should never have left you alone for even a minute. A woman as attractive as you are—well, I shouldn't have left you alone."

As attractive as she was? What a novel idea! "You mustn't blame yourself. You don't have to watch out for me every minute. I vowed that I would be as little trouble to you as possible."

"You haven't been any trouble to me. You have been stoic beyond all expectations, and courageous as well. But in some things a woman still needs a man's protection."

The smile he gave her melted her insides so thoroughly she could scarcely stand. *Foolish, foolish girl*, she chided. *Don't do this to yourself.*

"And please, Elizabeth, don't continue to call me Mr. Stanford. After these last days we've been together, I think we may safely relax the formalities."

Alexander! What a lovely name. A strong, masculine, yet sensitive name. She lowered her eyes, flushing. "All right, Alexander."

"It looks as if the *Dolphin* is finally boarding. We'd better go."

She looked up to where the steamer's deck floated high above the dock. A gangway climbed up to where a uniformed crewman stood allowing the passengers to pass, one by one—men laden with huge packs carried on their backs, women with children hanging on their skirts, a few gentlemen and ladies with trains of attendants, and a whole troop of military men shepherded up the gangway by their officers.

What an odd assortment, Elizabeth mused with a smile. Adventures upon adventures. What memories she would have to take back to her dull life in Chicago.

Not until late afternoon, hours after they climbed the gangplank and boarded the steamer, did a blast of the ship's stack signal them getting under way. Elizabeth stood with Alexander at the rail, along with crowds of others, to see the ropes cast off and the ship inch slowly from the dock. Then they went to the other side to gaze out over the water and the traffic of boats, large and small.

Elizabeth found herself entranced. "I've never seen the sea," she confided to Alexander. "It looks much the same as Lake Michigan, but the smell is different. And somehow I get the feeling of how very huge it is."

"This isn't really the sea," Alexander told her. "Where we are now is San Francisco Bay, which is protected against the great rollers that come in from the Pacific. When we leave the bay the water may be much rougher."

Elizabeth's heart leapt in exhilaration, not apprehension. She would ride this great hulking steamer upon the briny sea, over the great Pacific rollers to the very southern tip of Baja California and around, then up the Mexican Gulf of California, in an actual foreign country. When she and Alexander had embarked upon the train in Chicago, she had been so frightened that her knees were water, but now, launching out onto the great ocean, fear was the farthest thing from her mind.

What a different person she had become. The frail-hearted Elizabeth Whitman who had retired in shame from the censure of Chicago society, who had faced each day with a measure of dread for the future of herself and her family, who had quailed at braving the unknown for her dearest friend—that Elizabeth Whitman was no longer and never would be again. She would return to a humble life in Chicago as Alvin Kennedy's housekeeper, she would still worry about her family and wince at reminders of her father's tragedy, but within her heart she would know that she was strong enough to meet challenge and adventure, if need be. She was not fragile. She was not helpless. And she could survive more than anyone would ever have thought.

Elizabeth soon proved that she could survive more than most of the passengers on the *Dolphin*. From the moment the big steamer exited the bay, rough water tossed them to and fro with a peculiar rolling motion that turned many a face green. As they progressed down the coast, the waves grew bigger and the motion of the ship more chaotic, until almost everyone was lying in a bunk wishing he or she could die or hanging over the rail heaving into the sea. Elizabeth was one of those iron-stomached people unaffected by the motion.

Alexander was not so fortunate. After mere hours in turbulent water he surrendered to his malady and holed up in his stateroom, his face a ghastly green and his stomach in a state of constant rebellion.

As one of the last passengers left standing, Elizabeth of

necessity nursed those less fortunate than she. There was simply no one else to do it. The crew were busy with their duties. The ship's physician was overwhelmed. A few other healthy passengers tried to be of help, but too often the distasteful sights and smells of seasickness pushed them over the edge into sickness themselves. Elizabeth, strangely enough, had the strongest stomach of all.

Alexander, of course, was her primary concern. When he objected to her care, she brushed his objections aside. At first he endured mortal embarrassment when he had to suffer Elizabeth to clean up both his messes and his person. But soon the very misery of illness banished all concerns except survival, and at times he cursed survival itself. Elizabeth spent every moment she had free sitting at Alexander's side, bathing his face and throat in cool water, and keeping his person, his clothing, and his bedding as clean as she could. Yes, she even changed his clothes for him and found that the task was impossible to accomplish with averted eyes. He was too sick to be embarrassed, but she wasn't.

"You should go," he groaned in one of his more lucid moments. "This isn't right."

"Of course it's right," she told him gently. "We are friends, are we not? And friends help each other through times like these."

"This isn't right," he repeated in a mumble.

"Don't be silly. I've mopped up after almost every passenger on this benighted ship, so I might as well perform the same service for you."

"Not the same . . ."

"No, it's not the same, I'll admit. I like you better than I like any of them, so the task is easier here. Don't give me trouble, Alexander. Just do as you're told."

On day five of the voyage the vessel's captain himself took time to thank Elizabeth for her service. "You're a brave lass," the red-haired, burly Scot told her. "Most lassies would be looking the other way with the mess we have aboard the old *Dolphin* this trip. Everyone on the ship owes you thanks."

"No thanks are needed, Captain. In this case I feel fortunate to be the one serving instead of the one who needs the service."

"It's a nasty sea we're plowing through right now. Even your man is down, is he?"

She scarcely had the energy to blush at the captain's assumption that Alexander was "her man." Dear Alexander. This messy business had dissolved any masculine mystique surrounding him, reducing him from the status of near god to mortal man. She loved him even more for it.

The thought caught her by surprise, her first admission that she did actually love Alex Stanford. Fool that she was, she loved him heart and soul, ill or whole. He was the sun to her days and balm of her nights.

And he belonged to another woman, a beautiful, unique woman who was not Elizabeth's rival but her friend. Of course, if he got much weaker, Alex would belong to neither of them.

"He's very ill, I fear. He looks just ghastly. I only wish I could do something to relieve him."

The Scot merely smiled. "Sometimes it's the big, braw lads that crash the hardest, queer thing though it is. Try giving him a bit of sea biscuit. Sometimes it can sit on a stomach when nothing else can. Tell Otto in the galley that he is to give you as much as you need."

"Thank you. I will try it."

She tried the sea biscuit. The results were spectacularly bad.

"I'm sorry," Alexander said weakly between bouts of retching. "So sorry."

Elizabeth sighed wearily. "So much for the captain's sea biscuit."

The very mention of the stuff brought on another unpleasant spasm. Elizabeth held Alexander's head while he tried to heave his already empty stomach into a basin. When it was over, she bathed his face in cold water, peeled the soiled shirt from his torso, and patiently helped him don a clean one—only to have her work undone by another fit of sickness.

Purgatory couldn't be worse than this, Elizabeth decided as she sat beside Alexander and cleaned him once again. If she didn't get some relief from the everlasting round of nursing, she was going to fall ill herself. She felt like a limp piece of seaweed. Oh, how tempting it would be just to collapse, to let someone else care for the sick, care for her. . . .

A touch on her face roused her from near stupor. Alexander's finger trailed gently along her cheek. "You are an angel," he said hoarsely. "Such strength in that slender form."

She tried to summon a smile. "That's me—an angel." She folded his clammy fingers in her hand. "You rest. I have a few others I need to check on."

More than a few others, if the truth be known. The messes and moaning, soiled linen and soiled bodies never ended.

A day later the sea calmed somewhat. Alex acquired his sea legs, and many others recovered as well. Enough remained ill to keep Elizabeth busy, however. Alexander urged her to leave the nursing to someone else and get some rest.

"You are not the only one who was sick," she snapped at him the seventh day out. Her brittle temper dictated her tone. "There are others still sick."

"There are also others to care for them."

Her days had become a gray haze, and she moved through them on nervous energy alone, automatically going about her chores, unable to think past putting one foot in front of the other.

"Others seem to lapse back into sickness the moment they smell . . . they smell . . ." A chill gripped her in spite of the warm southern breeze coming off the sea, and the grayness in her head became even grayer. "Oh, Alexander . . ."

His face swam above hers. The strength of his arms closed around her as she collapsed.

Georgia was bone tired, but it was a good kind of tired that a body suffers from too much sun, wind, and too many hours in the saddle. This kind of tired didn't wear a person down like the weariness that resulted from boredom, tension, and too much time spent in useless chatter with people one didn't really like. The good kind of tired disappeared after a night's sleep. The other kind could stick with a person for weeks. Maybe even years.

"Quite a sight, isn't it?" Cougar said.

They had topped a ridge a day's ride north of Santa Fe, and spread out before them was New Mexico's pine-clad high country. Tomorrow they would stay in a Santa Fe hotel, soak in a hot bath, eat food that wasn't cooked over an open fire, and sleep on something softer than the ground. Then they would turn west and head for Arizona.

"It is a sight," Georgia confirmed. Her heart sang. Ever since they'd mounted up in Denver, she had felt as though she had come home. The scent of pine and juniper was something she had grown up with. And every autumn she could remember the mountain heights turning gold with the changing aspen colors. It was a ritual that had marked each passing year of her life, familiar and dear.

She owed Cougar thanks, Georgia admitted, though only to herself. Chicago had confused her. Maybe that hideous corset had stopped the blood flow to her brain. Maybe the damp air had molded her thinking process. Such excuses were the only explanation for some of the decisions she had made. But she had made them, for better or worse, and now what was she going to do about them? Right now with the fresh breeze in her face and the sun setting in a glorious display of red, she didn't want to think about it.

They camped halfway down the ridge, out of the wind. Georgia set a snare for a rabbit while Cougar brought in firewood, and as the stars came out they dined on hot rabbit stew and a loaf of bread they had bought from a farmer two days past. As the sky darkened to black velvet, the stars grew brighter. The Milky Way stretched in a jeweled trail from horizon to horizon.

Directly after dinner they retired to their separate bedrolls on either side of the fire. Georgia watched the glow of the coals, her mind active even though her body was melting-into-the-ground tired. She wondered if her grandfather and Elizabeth had believed that stupid note Cougar had forced her to leave—that she and Cougar had eloped to New York. They wouldn't have, she decided. Elizabeth knew her much too well to think she would back out on Alexander without so much as a word. Georgia hoped she wasn't awfully worried, but maybe a little bit worried. No one had worried about her in a long time. Even her father had always assumed she could take care of herself. She could, most times. But having someone worry meant someone cared. That was nice. Georgia figured that of all the people she knew, probably Elizabeth was the one most likely to care. She wouldn't believe that Georgia had eloped, and she was probably worried about what had actually happened.

Her granddad—well, Alvin was a manipulating, stubborn old coot, and he might be willing to believe the worst of her. They had gotten to know each other a bit, though, and she couldn't help but have a fondness for him, in spite of everything. She couldn't stay mad at a man who was so easily beat at chess. Alvin was no gamester. How she would have loved to have gotten him into a game of poker. She could have won back her claims without going to the trouble of getting hitched.

Well, she had the claims back now, and she wasn't hitched yet. She had promised, though. A promise was a promise. Alexander Stanford was a good, honest man, and she liked him a lot. He made her laugh. He kissed nice. He made her stomach flutter. What more could a woman ask?

She glanced across the fire at the other bedroll. Cougar... No, she didn't even want to think about it. Cougar couldn't really love her. He'd known her when she was an ox in pigtails. She'd beat him at arm wrestling. None of her lady posturing had fooled him.

All that didn't matter, Georgia told herself. She would enjoy this visit to her old world, and then she would decide what to do about Alexander and her granddad. Life was so complicated.

With those restless thoughts on her mind, she finally surrendered to sleep.

Sometime later she woke shivering. The fire had

burned down to coals, and stars no longer spangled the heavens. Only a few peeked through ragged tears in the low cloud cover that now dominated the sky. A dampness to the air made her think that snow was coming, and even as she thought it, the first flakes of white blew in on a cold wind.

Cougar's bedroll was empty. When Georgia raised up and looked around, she saw him in the unsteady glow of the coals cutting branches from a juniper tree.

"No telling how much it might snow," he told her when he saw she was awake. "We need some shelter."

With a groan of weariness, Georgia climbed out of her blankets to help.

The shelter went up quickly. Both of them had built the same sort of lean-to many times before—branches tied together and propped against a tree trunk, wedged into the lower branches of the tree for sturdiness. Smaller branches strewn over the shelter's floor added both comfort and warmth, and rocks hot from the fire, set in a cast-iron skillet, kept the cold at bay. Last of all they stowed the packs under shelter to keep them dry, picketed the animals beneath the branches of a big tree, and built a new fire close to the door of the lean-to.

They were set for the night or for a few days, if the need arose.

"This better not turn into a blizzard," Georgia grumbled as she resettled into her blankets in the lean-to. "I was really looking forward to a real bed in Santa Fe tomorrow night."

"This lean-to is cozier than most hotels I've been in," Cougar said.

"I was wanting a bath, too. Bathing sort of gets to be a habit after you get used to it."

He grinned. "I can't help you there. I can offer some built-in heat, though." He lifted his blankets invitingly. "It's a waste on a night like this to sleep alone when two sleep so much warmer."

That was the truth, and everyone who wintered on the frontier knew it. In Henry and Sarah's barn she hadn't hesitated to jump into Cougar Barnes's bedroll, but somehow having those kind people and their children sleeping just a holler away had made a shared bed all right, though she had awakened with the strangest urges gripping her body. She had wanted to turn toward Cougar, wrap herself around him, and . . .

Nope! She didn't want to think about that! For much of her adult life she hadn't given a thought to being a woman. Now she did. She might not be totally a lady, but being a woman, Georgia had discovered, wasn't something a body had to learn. All along she'd been as much a woman as Evie Perkins or Louisa Rawlins or the girls working at Mattie Bee's. The woman in her had simply waited for the right time and place to come out of hiding.

Climbing in the bedroll with Cougar, in the middle of nowhere, with only the trees and animals to watch or listen, might just make that woman in her take the bit in her teeth and gallop somewhere that Georgia would regret.

Then again, since when had she grown so cautious? Since when had she been afraid, not of Apaches, snakes, or scorpions, but of herself? Had Chicago done that to her? Georgia sighed, not liking this new image of timidity.

"Share blankets, eh?"

"It's sensible."

Was that a gleam in Cougar's eye or a reflection of the fire?

"All this would surely raise a pack of eyebrows back in Chicago," she said.

"Do you care what the eyebrows in Chicago do?"

It was a question that went beyond just huddling together for warmth, Georgia realized. It went to the heart of what she didn't want to think about.

"I don't know anymore."

He smiled, the devil himself. "Come share my blankets, Georgia. It's cold."

Cougar also knew that sharing blankets here was something more than sharing blankets in Henry and Sarah's barn. He had to know. His eyes tangled with hers, and an irresistible urge to be close to him rose up and almost clogged Georgia's breathing. The snow and wind outside cocooned them in their own little world, and in this world,

Georgia wanted to sleep in his arms. To hell with Chicago's eyebrows. To hell with her own conscience shaking a finger at her.

"That's better," he said as he wrapped both their blankets around them, sealing them together. "I'm warmer already."

So was Georgia, and not purely from body heat. Cougar was a hunk of temptation walking around on two legs. Even before she'd become a woman, Georgia had noticed that. Now that she was a woman, well, she noticed it a lot more. Unfamiliar longings washed through her, making her heart pound. Lying in these blankets in the circle of Cougar's arms felt so nice, so safe, but so . . . so frustrating!

"Are you comfortable?"

Too comfortable. "Yup."

"You feel jumpy."

Was that what it was called? "I'm not jumpy."

One of his hands started to move up and down her spine in a soothing rhythm. "Relax, Georgie. How many times have I told you I love you? You think I would do anything to hurt you? Ever?"

She managed a snort, though it wasn't all that convincing. "Love! Tell me as many times as you want. I still don't believe you."

His breath was warm in her ear. "You should."

Tingles ran up and down her spine along with his caressing hand. Georgia was fast losing track of should and shouldn't, ought to and ought not. "Cougar . . ."

"You want me to stop?"

She couldn't make herself say yes. Instead she turned toward him, bracing her hands against his broad chest. She had meant to keep him at a distance, but those hands of hers wanted to move over the expanse of muscle in front of her, wanted to caress, warm, and soothe. She had to clench her teeth to keep the unruly hands still.

Cougar placed a hand over one of hers and moved it above his heart. "You're in here, Georgie girl. You can disbelieve me all you want, but you're still in here. I think you always will be. You are the right woman. The only woman."

If Cougar was truly lying, he was a better liar than Georgia thought he was. Or maybe she just wanted to believe him. To be truly loved—that would be sweeter than pure water in the desert or gold gleaming on a hillside.

"I want to be loved." She surprised herself by her words, but Cougar didn't look surprised. "Do you really love me, Cougar? Me? Not the claims on the Lynx? Not anything I have or will have?"

"I love you." He made the words into a promise and sealed the promise with a gentle kiss on her brow, each cheek, then her mouth. Georgia's insides started to melt. The night might be cold enough to freeze beer, but she was steaming inside.

"You're a good man, Cougar," she said against his mouth. No matter the right or wrong of it, the wise or foolish, she loved Cougar Barnes. Maybe she had loved him long before she left Arizona.

Warm breath caressed her neck. "My Georgie. We are going to be so good together."

She refused to think, only feel. And when he slipped a hand inside her shirt, his touch felt very, very good.

"There *is* something of yours that I want."

She scarcely heard him, so wonderful did that hand feel.

"I want all of this." Calloused fingers toyed with her breast. The other hand traveled lower, to where her legs joined, and caressed gently, so gently. "And this, too."

She sucked in a breath. "Yes. Please. Keep doing that."

"I'm not about to stop. We have all the long cold night."

Georgia helped him peel down her shirt at the same time she attacked his. She had never been one for proceeding slowly, no matter what the task. When his chest was bare, she wanted to explore every slab of muscle, every ridge, every hollow, but he distracted her with his mouth on her breasts.

She retaliated by unfastening his belt. He struck back, sliding her trousers from her hips, the longhandles with them. They ended up around her knees. When his hand found the softest of her skin, the most private warmth she had to offer, Georgia gasped. "Are you supposed to do that?"

"Trust me, yes."

She could hardly breathe, and thinking was out of the question. A great tension gripped her, shook her, then suddenly released her with a shuddering warm thrill. She didn't know what had happened, but whatever it was made her want more. He kissed her gently as utter relaxation threatened to float her right out of the blankets.

"I . . . I . . ."

"I know," he breathed.

She cupped the hard length of him through his trousers. "You don't want to keep these on, do you?"

"Hell, no."

"Then lets get rid of them."

Moments later they were both peeled down to skin, but no hint of cold bothered them, despite the storm outside. Georgia's curious hands explored him while Cougar visibly gritted his teeth. "Does that hurt?" she asked impishly.

"You're a tease."

"You have a very interesting body."

His breath came hard. "Thank you."

She had no idea men were so big. But then, Cougar was big all over. Just touching his nakedness made that lovely tension start up again.

"Enough is enough," he gritted out.

"I thought you said we had all night."

"I overestimated myself."

He rose above her, parting her knees with his thigh and kissing her fiercely. When she felt him probe that most intimate place, she tensed in spite of herself.

"I would never hurt you," he promised. "Let me do this, my love."

He promised truly. So gentle was he that the only thing she felt was bliss. Having him inside her body seemed natural and right, like two halves coming together as a whole. It was right, so right, and got righter as he moved faster and deeper. She forgot the shelter, the storm, the past and the future. Only now mattered. And then now exploded into a million bright shards, raining rapture. Georgia wrapped herself around him and clung while the shards slowly drifted, darkened, and became warm, welcome sleep.

Chapter 19

Compared to the houses Elizabeth was accustomed to, the so-called house that Alexander arranged for their stay in Prescott was hardly a house at all. It was nothing more than a two-room log cabin with a plank floor and a fireplace that served for cooking as well as heat. A rude table with equally rude chairs was the only furniture along with a rope-sprung bed in the tiny bedroom.

When Elizabeth first walked through the door, however, she thought she'd entered the gates of Heaven. "This is wonderful," she told Alexander. "How did you find it?"

"This is Georgia's house. The marshal directed me to it."

"Oh, my! I thought Georgia lived on some mining claim in the middle of nowhere."

Alex laughed. "You call this the middle of somewhere?"

"After days steaming up the Colorado and more days bouncing along in that wagon through country that I vow God has never touched—yes, Prescott and this little house are seats of luxury."

One corner of Alexander's mouth lifted in a half smile. "You are a remarkable woman, Elizabeth. I seem to be repeating that phrase endlessly on this journey, but it's true."

Elizabeth turned her head away, deliberately not looking at him. Their eyes had tangled too often of late, and each time it was more difficult to untangle. This journey had removed the niceties of him being a gentleman and her a gentlewoman. It had also removed any illusions each held about the other. Half the time traveling down the Pacific Coast on the *Dolphin*, she had engaged in the intimate duties of nursing him back to health. The other half he had performed the same service for her after she had collapsed in his very arms—such a forward thing to do!—of exhaustion. No woman had been available to tend her, so Alexander had done the job.

Such intimacies of the body produced intimacies of the soul as well. The attraction she had felt for Alexander back in Chicago was a mere shadow compared to the soul-deep connection between them now. The connection existed for him as well. Elizabeth saw it in his eyes, heard it in his voice, felt it in the small touches that were inevitable in the forced close association of their journey.

But all that didn't change the fact that Alexander was committed to Georgia. No true gentleman reneged on a betrothal, not if he were honorable and true as Alexander was honorable and true. Elizabeth wouldn't want him to throw over Georgia for her. She loved Georgia as she might love a sister and wanted only the best for both her and Alexander.

But her eyes spoke something entirely different every time they met Alexander's, so she avoided getting caught in his gaze. The sooner they found Georgia and the scoundrel who had taken her, the better.

"Since we are staying in Georgia's house, I assume she has not yet arrived in the area."

"Not so far as the marshal knows. He's had a watch on Georgia's claims. If they get here, we'll know it."

Her head swung sharply in his direction. "If they get here?"

His mouth tightened. "We never knew for certain that this was their destination."

"They were in Omaha before us."

"The west is a big place."

"They have to come here."

And this had to end. Elizabeth had to see Georgia rescued and Alexander settled before she could get on with the rest of her life, before she could forget looking into Alexander Stanford's eyes and knowing that he returned her love.

The tone of her voice made him reach out to give her comfort, but with a shadow of regret in his eyes, he dropped his hand before they touched.

Georgia looked southwest to the end of their journey, shading her eyes with one hand. There in the distance stood the granite hills that were the southern boundary of Chino Valley, gleaming pink in the sinking sun. Farther south lay Prescott, the Lynx, and Georgia's claims.

"Home," Cougar said.

"Home," she echoed. Even to Georgia's own ears her voice rang with longing. She wanted to be home, to sleep in her own humble little cabin on the Lynx, luxuriating in familiar sounds, scents, and sights. She wanted to give Essie a huge hug and tell her of the wonders she had seen, the unbelievable things she had done. She wanted to ride into town and greet old friends, show off new manners and new confidence.

But right then confidence was faltering. Her life and future were all questions and no answers. Or perhaps the answers sat there in her head, but she simply didn't like them. She didn't want to leave this splendid country of mountains and blue sky, but she had committed herself to Alexander and Chicago. She didn't want to leave Cougar Barnes, and yet she'd given her word. Her word was important. Alexander, his father, Georgia's grandfather, Elizabeth, and everyone who had read the engagement announcement in the newspaper would expect her to keep it.

"If we push hard," Cougar said, "we can make your place on the Lynx tonight. If we push hard."

His voice was flat and unenthused. Clearly, Cougar also wanted the journey to end. These past weeks they'd traveled through a world that was theirs alone. They had argued and sniped—well, truthfully, Georgia admitted, she was the one who had argued and sniped, but Cougar had given back everything she'd thrown his way and then some. Despite hot words and occasional insults, a bond linked them. It had grown stronger every day. Maybe it had always been there, even during the days before she'd awakened to the fact that she was a woman in spite of herself. But these past weeks had wound strand after strand of that bond around her heart.

And then they had done the unthinkable. Unthinkable, yet irresistible. They'd made love. Not just once, but every time they had wakened during that snowy night on the ridge north of Santa Fe. Georgia had forgotten her promise to Alexander, forgotten her honor, forgotten everything, in fact, except Cougar loving her. She had sunk lower than a weasel and soared to heights higher than the Rockies themselves.

The one night stood alone, unrepeated. Since then conversation had been constrained by an uneasiness that sat on both their consciences. Deep in her gut, Georgia wanted to make love to Cougar every night, but she told herself the desire was wrong and wanton. Cougar must have thought so, too, because in a tight voice he had apologized for that splendiferous, disgraceful night, saying that he wouldn't take advantage of her again. Not until they had straightened things out—as if anything would ever be straight again.

They sat there on their horses looking out into the distance until the delay became ridiculous.

"Guess we should move on," Cougar muttered.

"Guess so."

Cougar kneed his mount and started slowly down the slope before them. Georgia followed, and the pack mule fell into line behind them. The mule wheezed out a weary sigh, and Georgia's heart echoed the sentiment.

For an hour they rode through the warm autumn day. The peaks to the northeast blazed in glory with swathes of aspen gold. The trail ahead led to gold as well, gold that hid in streambeds and veined hillsides, the gold of lush green pastures where cattle might one day graze. That was Cougar's dream of gold, and for all that she had pooh-poohed it to his face, Georgia admitted that in the long run, his dream was likely to serve him better than the elusive glitter in a quartz vein or the sparkle of gold flakes in the bottom of a sluice. She could almost picture him on the ranch he would someday have, cattle grazing in the distance, children around him, wife smiling up at him from the circle of his strong arm.

Georgia almost choked, so badly did she want to be in that picture. As if sensing her wash of feeling, her horse stopped in the middle of the path. Georgia bit her lip hard, telling herself all the reasons she had to sit on that bench in Prescott's town square and tell Cougar right out loud that she wanted to go back to Chicago, that she wanted to marry Alexander Stanford. Tell me that's what you want, he had said, and you're free to go, to do what she had to do.

He didn't really love her anyway, she reminded herself. Her gold was the key to his ranch. Maybe if she kept repeating that she might start believing it again. That would make things so much easier.

"What's wrong?" Cougar demanded testily. He wasn't exactly in the best of humors, either.

"What?"

"You stopped."

"Did I? I guess I wasn't paying attention."

He turned his horse so that it was crosswise to the trail, then just sat there, looking at her with a shuttered expression. His mount shifted uneasily, responding to his mood.

"You know something?" he queried tightly.

"What?"

"We should be paying attention to the trail, to where we're going, to what might be around the next bend or hidden in the brush. An Apache raiding party could be watching us right now, and we wouldn't know it, because we've been preoccupied with you and me and what's going on in our own stupid heads. We're going to get ourselves killed."

"All right," she said, chastened.

"Not all right, dammit! Forget going to Prescott, sitting in the goddamned town square, and bringing everything to a nice, neat ending where you make up your goddamned mind."

His tone made her bristle. After all, the situation wasn't all her fault. In fact, it wasn't her fault at all. Well, some, maybe. Just a little. "What do you want, Cougar?"

"What do I want?"

"That's what I asked."

"I'll tell you what I want. I want to know if you really think I did all of this—snatched you from your grandfather's place in Chicago and dragged you all the way back to Arizona—just to get my hands on your frigging gold. I want to know if you truly believe I would ask you to marry me, to share my life, not because I love you, but so I could sink everything you had into my own dream. I want to know if that night outside of Santa Fe meant nothing to you. Do you really believe I'm the kind of man who would make love to you just because you had something I want? Do you?"

This particular fuse had been burning awhile, Georgia thought. Fine. She had a few sticks of her own dynamite that were ready to blow. "You're not the one with all the bones to pick here, mister. I didn't follow you around the town of Chicago moaning and groaning about you tarnishing your sterling self just because you were trying to do right by everyone. I didn't laugh in your face when you were trying to be what nature intended you to be. And I certainly didn't sling you over my shoulder and toss you into a freight car headed west just because I thought that I was right and you were a goddamned fool. Don't get me started, you blockheaded, ox-brained jackass."

"Don't change the subject!"

"If you're going to yell at me, then I have twice as much reason to yell at you."

"I'm not yelling at you. I'm asking a goddamned question!"

"What goddamned question?"

"Do you think I'm after your stupid claims and your stupid gold?"

"And not really after my stupid self?" she queried with narrowed eyes.

"And not after your stubborn, wayward, wonderful self."

They glared at each other for the space of ten long heartbeats. Then Georgia heaved a sigh. "No," she said simply.

"No, what?"

"No, I don't believe that."

His eyes narrowed suspiciously.

"I did," she admitted. "You gave me enough reason to believe the worst, you moron, following me to Chicago, threatening to talk to my grandfather, telling me I could never be a lady."

"I never said you couldn't be a lady. I said you didn't have to be a lady. You shouldn't have to follow somebody else's rules to be loved."

"That's not what you said."

"That's what I meant."

"Doesn't count."

He sighed and looked down at his hands resting on the saddle horn. Then he looked up and locked his eyes onto hers. "But you don't think any more that I'm a frigging mercenary who's after your gold."

She hesitated just a moment, then eased into the beginnings of a smile. "No."

"Instead, you think I'm a blockheaded, ox-brained jackass."

Her smile grew broader.

"And you know that I love you."

The smile faltered a bit. "Do you?"

He ignored the question. "And you love me."

She stuck her nose into the air. "What makes you think that?"

He chuckled, much more relaxed since her admission that he was not, indeed, a frigging mercenary. "You told me that, on a ridge north of Santa Fe."

"I didn't say I loved you."

"Georgie, some things are said much better without words."

Heat rushed to her cheeks, because she knew exactly what he meant. Their long night of loving still lay fresh in her mind, perhaps because it was the subject of her daydreams and often replayed in night dreams as well.

"So why don't we settle this right here, Georgie. I'm telling you straight out from the heart, I want you more than I want that claim you sold me. I want you more even than I want a ranch in Chino Valley. I can't promise you the world if you marry me, but I can promise you whatever part of the world is mine. Will you marry me?"

Oh, the temptation! She tried to remind herself that doing what was right was more important than doing what she wanted. She tried not to think of having Cougar Barnes by her side and in her bed for the rest of her life. She tried not to think of children, some with hair of gold-red, some with Cougar's mane of burnished wheat, all with Cougar's crooked grin and dancing eyes.

"Georgie?"

She couldn't meet his gaze. She didn't dare.

"Do you want me to get off this horse and drop down on one knee? Do you want fancy words?"

"No," she said in a small voice.

"Then what?"

She took a deep, fortifying breath. "Cougar, you keep forgetting that I'm an engaged woman. What about Alexander? What about the promise I made to him? I can't just traipse off and marry one fellow when I'm practically hitched to another one."

"All things considered, you're much closer to being hitched to me than to Alexander."

She blinked. That was true, considering the things they'd done.

"Georgie, you said yes to Stanford. You made a promise, and that's important. But sometimes promises can't be kept. Sometimes they shouldn't be kept. Things change. People change. More important than being an engaged woman, you're a beloved woman. And it isn't Alex Stanford who loves you. It's me. Alex is a good man, and he would give you an easier life than I can. But he will never love you like I love you. I've loved you since I first saw you shoveling gravel beside your daddy. You were wearing those goddamned overalls and the sorriest hat in the world, and I thought to myself, now there's a sight to see. I guess I had it hidden in the back of my mind that someday I would get smart and ask you to settle down with me, but it didn't seem a real urgent thing to do until you left. Then it pushed right up from the back of my mind to the front, and I realized what I'd let slip through my fingers.

"Then when I saw you in Chicago looking like every man's dream, looking like you were enjoying yourself in a world that I despised, I got scared mad. Georgie, I never meant to hurt you with the things I said—or maybe I did, because seeing you soaking up the attention of all those other men hurt. I'm sorry. You were beautiful in Chicago. You're beautiful now, with that smudge of dirt on your nose and the streak of mule slobber on your sleeve. You have it in you to be a fine lady. Hell, you could probably be the toast of Chicago or New York. But I love you just the way you are now, with no airs or frills. Just Georgie. The best thing I can offer you is love that's going to last a lifetime."

She'd never known Cougar to run off at the mouth so. Love did amazing things to a man. It did amazing things to a woman as well, made her trade a secure, comfortable future for one with no certainties at all.

"So, Georgie, will you marry me?"

"Yes."

"This is the last time I'll ask. If you want to go on back to Chicago and spend your life—what did you say?"

She smirked. "I said yes. Don't you ever listen?"

He just looked at her, one corner of his mouth twitching upward into his trademark grin.

Everything settled into place inside her. This was right, Georgia knew. Somehow she would explain to Alexander and her grandfather. And Elizabeth—she would understand perfectly. Elizabeth was a woman who understood other women's hearts. "We're not going to make Prescott tonight," she said casually, as if every day she sent her life spinning tail over teeth. "The sun is setting."

Cougar sent a quick glance west, as if tearing his eyes away from her were an effort. The molten half-disk of the sun was sinking behind the hills. He grinned. "So it is. Good."

"Good? I thought you wanted to make it in tonight."

"I'd rather ride up that little valley over there and find a nice cozy place to camp."

The look he gave her made Georgia's face grow warm. "We could do that," she said softly.

They did that. A leaf-blanketed stream bank beneath spreading cottonwood trees was about as cozy and comfortable as any campsite could be. The streambed was dry, but digging in the sand produced plenty of clean, cold water for both humans and animals. Soon the horses and mule were safely hobbled and set to graze on knee-high brownish grass, the bedrolls were laid out on a mattress of yellow leaves, and Cougar and Georgia made a supper of jerked rabbit meat, dried apples, and cold corn tortillas. Both wrapped in thoughts of their own, they said very little. Georgia's mind hummed happily along with speculations about the future, neatly dodging around any difficulties with her grandfather or Alexander. Now that she had stopped resisting her heart, the world felt lighter. How could she have believed for one moment that she could live her life in drab Chicago, content to live with a man who freely admitted that he didn't love her?

But she didn't want to think about Chicago and Alexander. She wanted to revel in the new picture in her head—the one with Cougar surrounded by his children on his Chino Valley ranch, his wife tucked securely in the curve of one arm. That wife now had a face, and it was Georgia's. It was Georgia smiling up at him, with their children jumping happily about the place. It was Georgia tucking her head beneath his strong, square chin when he moved her into an embrace, and it was Georgia who strolled at his side toward their house, toward a cozy fire and their bed, where every night she slept in Cougar's arms.

Indeed, her thoughts had no room for Chicago, Alexander, or anyone but Cougar.

"Georgie? Did you hear what I said?"

She jerked her head up sharply, as if awakened suddenly from sleep. "What?"

His eyes sparkled with amusement. "Where were you?"

She wasn't about to tell him about the scene she'd invented for them. In good time he would be there himself. "I . . . just . . . things."

One eyebrow cocked upward. "I said that we should get married."

"Cougar, I thought we settled that already. You proposed. I said yes." She couldn't help but smile at the thought.

"I mean now. Here."

"Now?"

"Yup."

"Here?"

"Right here."

"There's no preacher."

"We'll do it later with a preacher. But we can make the vows to each other. We're the ones who count the most, anyway. Then we'll be married in our eyes and in God's eyes, married enough to act married, for you to know I'm your husband and me to know that you're my wife. No more questions. A done deal."

Married enough to act married. Georgia's heart began to pound. On the frontier, where preaching men could be few and far between, do-it-yourself weddings were common. Among the people who braved this barely civilized land, they were considered as legitimate as vows taken before a minister.

She had said she would marry the man, and now the man was calling upon her to pony-up. Suddenly a rush of elation crowded every doubt from Georgia's mind. This very night Cougar Barnes and she could be husband and wife. She grinned. "Let's do it."

Cougar took her hand and pulled her up from where she sat on a rock.

"Shouldn't we kneel or something?" she said uncertainly.

"I don't expect you to kneel for me, Georgie girl. I figure we can take our vows standing like the two adult people we are."

She liked the sound of that.

Cougar started. In a strong voice he promised, "I, Cooper David Barnes, take you, Georgia Kennedy, to be my wife under the laws of God and man. I'll look after you, when need be. I'll love you. I'll share whatever worldly goods I have, and I won't so much as look at another woman as long as you're alive." His eyes sparkled in the light of the rising moon, and he grinned.

"That sounds pretty good," Georgia said.

"Your turn."

Georgia bit her lip. This was so much more important than some ritual read from a book. "I, Georgia Kennedy, take you, Cooper David Barnes, to be my husband under the laws of God and man. I'll watch your back. I'll tend you when you need tending. I'll share whatever I have, and I'll try not to give you too much lip when you act like a jackass."

That earned her a raised brow, but she only smiled.

"If I have to, I'll clean your house and do your laundry, but you'll be sorry if you eat my cooking. I'll give you children, if I can. I'll keep myself for you alone, and I'll stick with you until the end, either yours or mine." Her smile broadened. "And I'll love you the rest of my days."

"We both promise this in good faith," Cougar said.

"We do," Georgia confirmed.

"And so now I pronounce that I'm your husband."

"And I pronounce that I'm your wife."

"I think that brings us to the part where somebody says I can kiss my bride."

He took her in his arms and did just that, not a chaste self-conscious kiss that a groom might give his bride, but a hungry, possessive, thorough kiss of a man long in need of a woman. His woman. Georgia.

Georgia's knees melted as heat flooded through her veins. Cougar tasted of sun, wind, dust, and desire, and she wanted him so much that she wanted to drag him down to the ground and wrap herself around him. How did she ever believe that she could be a quiet and well-mannered lady?

"God . . . Georgie!"

"Is this acting like married folks?"

"Only the very lucky ones. Whoa! That belt has a buckle. You don't have to rip it off."

But he was treating her clothing in much the same way.

Still kissing, they stumbled toward the blankets. By the time they got there, clothes no longer separated them.

Tumbling with her new husband onto the bedrolls, Georgia instinctively wrapped her legs around his hips. This marriage thing stoked a woman's needs, that was for sure. She ached, she burned, she needed him so much she could scarcely think.

"Slow down, Mrs. Barnes. I want to make this so right for you."

"Then make it . . . oh, jeez!"

His hand slipped between their bodies and stroked the very center of her desire. The caress soothed at the same time it made her want him even more.

"Relax," he whispered against her throat. "Let me build you a fire that will last all night."

She gave herself over to him. "I love you," she sighed.

"I love you right back." He kissed her forehead. "And love you." The tip of her nose. "And love you." Her lips. "And love you forever, wife of mine."

An expert flick of his thumb sent her over the edge into bliss, but no sooner had that explosion started to calm than he started another fire, this time rolling her beneath him and claiming her for his own. Pent-up desire showed in the tension of every muscle, the tight control of every movement, yet he rode her gently, thrusting to his full length only when she grasped his buttocks and urged him forward.

Georgie was not gentle in her passion. She was not quiet, and she was certainly not refined. Later, as she lay replete and happy with Cougar still cradled between her legs, she reflected wonderingly upon her efforts to confine herself within the strictures of ladyhood. She never would have made it, and wasn't that a stroke of luck?

Chapter 20

Cougar tied his horse to the hitching rail outside Big Mike's Tavern and looked around him in satisfaction. Prescott hadn't changed. The streets were still dirt. A haze of wood smoke still hung over the town. The men walking down Gurley Street still wore everything from fancy suits to denims to clothes made from old flour sacks.

Homecoming had never been so good. Life itself had never been so good, not because he was back in Prescott, but because Georgie Kennedy—hotheaded, mercurial, beautiful, sweet, courageous, stubborn, and sometimes downright dangerous Georgie Kennedy—was now his wife. And what a wife, what a lover! He hadn't slept a wink the night before, yet this morning so much energy coursed through his veins that he hardly needed a horse to cover the remaining miles to town. He could have flown. But what he had really wanted to do was spend all day beneath those cottonwoods on their bed of leaves and blankets, loving Georgie.

Things waited to be done, however, and the sooner they were done, the sooner they could start building a life together. Cougar had come into town to send word to Alvin Kennedy about their safe arrival and their marriage. He hoped the old man didn't get cranky about things and try to get Georgie's claims back. For himself, he no longer cared so much about the gold. He could find some other way to earn seed money for his ranch. But Georgie had sunk her heart into her father's mine on the Lynx.

Georgie had headed straight to her place on the Lynx. She was eager to see Essie and recount her adventures. After he'd sent word to Chicago and picked up some provisions, Cougar would meet her at her cabin. But first—he intended to wet his whistle and catch up on the local gossip after weeks on the trail, and Big Mike's Tavern was the best place to do it.

"Holy moly!" Skillet Mahoney greeted Cougar. "Lookee who the wind blowed in!"

"Howdy, Skillet, Dooley, Cal." Cougar figured he would find those three at Mikes. They always spent more time lifting a glass than a shovel. "Mike, give me a nice cold beer."

From behind the rough-hewn bar, Big Mike looked a bit surprised. "Didn't expect to see you back, Cougar."

"Said I'd be back."

The bartender slid him a beer. "Been hearing strange tales."

"What would that be?"

"Tol' ya that was a pile of bullshit," Skillet told Mike. "If Cougar's gonna make off with some female, it fer sure ain't gonna be ol' George."

Before Cougar could decide whether or not to take offense, Marshal Colin Tate walked through the swinging doors. He did not look happy.

Cougar greeted him with an easy grin. "Howdy, Colin."

"Cougar. Didn't really expect to see you back any time soon."

"Why is that?" Cougar began to get a bad feeling about all of this.

"Kinda wish you hadn't just ridden into town bold as brass like that, letting everyone under the sun get a good look at you."

"Why shouldn't I ride into town bold as brass?"

"'Cause now I have to arrest you. Everyone knows you're here, so I can't shirk my duty."

"Arrest me?"

"Surefire. Got word weeks ago, said you'd kidnapped one Georgia Kennedy." He gave Cougar a look. "They're kidding, right? Georgie?"

"Shit!" Cougar took a long pull on his beer. "It's a misunderstanding. And I wish to hell you jackasses would stop talking about my wife as if she were some kind of joke."

"Yer wife?" Skillet chortled.

"Yes, my wife. And anyone who doesn't give her the respect due will meet with the business end of my fist."

"You married Georgie? Our Georgie?" Colin shook his head. "I swear the world gets stranger every day. But I still have to haul your ass in. There's a fellow from Chicago here in town who's itching to get a piece of you, and I'd say right now you're safer in jail than wandering around town."

"You're going to put me in jail?" Cougar let an edge slide into his voice.

"Now, don't be putting up a fight, Cougar. You and me, we been friends a long time. If this is a misunderstanding, like you say, we'll get it straightened out. Where the hell is Georgie, anyway?"

"Where do you think she is?"

Dooley chuckled. "Coug, if you married her for that mine of hers, you made a bad bargain."

Georgia nearly wept. Essie couldn't let her go, but hugged her and hugged her until Georgia thought her eyes might pop right out of her head. It was indescribably good to see Essie again, to finally lay eyes on the familiar hills, streambed, and the ratty old rocker she had fed shovels full of gravel—endless backbreaking shovels full—in order to add to the nest egg her father had built and had never been able to enjoy. She wanted to weep when she first stepped into the cozy little cabin that she and her father had built together, when she sat down upon the bed where she had, so many nights, dropped into exhausted slumber listening to the wind through the pines and the babble of the stream.

The stream wasn't babbling at this homecoming, however. The Mexican helpers whom Essie had found to work the diggings were gone, and the rocker was clean of gravel.

Georgia scarcely noticed these things when she rode up, so eager was she to relate her adventures and to break the astounding news of her marriage. But Essie started in before Georgia could get a word in edgewise.

"Look at you, *chica*!" Essie surveyed her approvingly as they stepped from the cabin into the bright October sunlight. "You look like a lady, even in those denims and that ugly hat. You look different!"

It was true that she took more care with her appearance. Her clothes fit, even if they were improper female attire. Her hair was pinned neatly beneath her hat instead of bouncing down her back in two scraggly braids. She kept her nails trimmed smooth instead of letting them deteriorate to a ragged mess, and treated her face with lard most nights to heal the dryness of sun and wind.

Georgia was gratified Essie noticed the difference. She didn't want to go back to being the ragamuffin she'd been before Elizabeth had taught her how to be a woman.

She almost giggled at the thought. Elizabeth hadn't taught her the most important thing about being a woman. Cougar had done that. Her heart jumped at the thought of him, of the vows they had taken beneath the moon and stars. Even now he would be sending word to Chicago that they were married. Whatever her granddad's reaction might be, they would deal with it together. And Alexander, well, she would carry a bit of guilt on her conscience concerning Alexander, but at least she wasn't breaking his heart.

Georgia opened her mouth to tell Essie about Cougar, but Essie cut her off with a sternly waving finger. "I got to tell you, *chica*, before we start gabbing, because I been waiting and waiting for you to come home and wondering what we're going to do. Things aren't good here. We got hardly any rain after June—just a few spotty storms here and there that didn't do anybody any good. The stream is dry, and God only knows when it will run again. Jose and Luis left because we couldn't work the gravel without water, and *chica*, when we were working the gravel, we weren't getting much color."

"Did you move the pit? Dig somewhere else?"

"We dug three new pits. The one up by that big granite boulder looked good for a few days, but it petered out fast. The others were worse."

Georgia sat on a stump that had often cradled her backside in the past when she was resting from her labors, eating meals, or simply gazing up the valley to admire the beauty of the Lynx. Now it was familiar and comforting. But familiarity and comfort couldn't change Essie's news—the claim was played out. It had been a good run, better than most on the Lynx, but it was done. Even if winter rain and snow gave new life to the stream, nothing could put gold back into the ground once it was gone.

She looked up the hillside to the second claim, where the gold was locked into a quartz vein. There was still that. Essie followed the direction of her gaze.

"The men hacked away at the vein and sent the ore in for assay. It's got gold, but these assays weren't as good as the first ones. Jose said if Cougar used dynamite and got farther into the vein, it might get better."

At the mention of Jose, Essie's brown face actually turned pink.

"You're coloring up!" Georgia accused.

The older woman nodded almost shyly. "Jose and me, we got married two weeks ago. He wants us to go down to Tucson. His brother there has a good farm on the San Pedro River."

Georgia's mouth fell open. Even while she had been changing herself, everything she had left, everything that she'd thought would stay the same, waiting for her return, had changed as well. She sighed. "We might as well go in out of the sun, because I can see we both have a lot of things to tell."

Cougar didn't like jail. He didn't like the smell, the cold, the lice-infested mattress, the dirt that crusted the walls. He didn't like staring between the bars, counting the nails that held together the rough plank wall of the jail room. But what he liked least of all was staring through the bars at Alexander Stanford.

"Where is she?" Alexander didn't waste time getting to

the point, just as he'd wasted no time getting to the jail when Colin had sent a boy to let him know Cougar had been arrested.

"She's exactly where she wants to be. At her mine." Cougar had toyed with the notion of refusing to answer, but anyone in town could tell him where the Kennedy claims were, and if Alexander had a brain in his head, that would be the first place he would search for Georgia.

"If you've harmed one hair on her head, Barnes, I'll roast you over a slow fire. I swear I will."

"You must be out of your mind to think I would hurt Georgie. And if you think she's that easy to get the best of, you certainly don't know her very well."

"It turned out that I didn't know you very well, didn't it? We were friends once. Those school days were a long time ago, but I would have sworn no amount of time or adventuring could turn Cooper Barnes into a man who would kidnap a woman and carry her off against her will. Did you really think anyone would believe that she would promise herself to me one moment and elope with you the next?"

Cougar snorted, thinking that Stanford was in for an unpleasant surprise. "Again, you don't know Georgie very well. Nobody holds that woman against her will for very long. If she hadn't wanted to be with me, she would have found a way to leave. I didn't kidnap Georgie. I just escorted her home to remind her of who she really was. She'll tell you that herself."

He almost told Alexander that he had lost. Georgie loved Cougar, had married Cougar, and a twenty-mule team couldn't drag her back to Chicago. But a small niggling doubt kept his mouth shut. Making their vows under the night sky with only the coyotes to listen was all very well, but it wasn't as legal as a wedding with a real preacher. Confronted by Alexander and the life he offered in Chicago, would Georgie regret those informal vows? He had to let Georgie make that decision. He couldn't make it for her.

"I mean to ask her. You can be sure of that."

"We can ask her together. I'll personally show you the way to her cabin."

Alexander chuckled and shook his head. "I don't think so, since I'm going to do my best to see you rot in that jail, and then in prison, if I can manage it. Men who commit crimes against women are about the lowest thing on this earth, as far as I'm concerned. So enjoy yourself thinking of the future."

Cougar ground his teeth in frustration as Alexander walked out the door. "Colin!" he demanded. "Colin, goddammit, get in here."

Colin obediently appeared in the doorway. "Good thing you're a friend, Cougar, because usually I'd put a prisoner on bread and water for using a tone like that."

"Stuff it, Colin. You go out to Georgie's mine with Stanford and make sure he doesn't get out of line. Either that, or let me out of this hole."

"Can't do that, Cougar. Not until this is settled."

"Then go with him, dammit, and tell Georgie what's happened."

"Go easy on those bars, friend. You're about to bend them."

"Just go!"

Essie shaded her eyes with her hand and squinted downstream at the rough track that led from the diggings to the wagon road. "There's a regular parade coming up the trail."

Georgia's head jerked around from where she was repairing the latch on the cabin door. "Is it Cougar?"

"Not Cougar. I don't know these folks. There's a woman with them. No, wait. One of them is Colin."

Curiosity mixed with hope in Georgia's heart. All afternoon she had fretted and worried. Cougar and she had agreed to meet at the claim before sunset, and even now the sun rested on the hills to the west. Every noise had made her look up in hope, thinking it was him, but he hadn't come. Georgia tried not to heed the awful thoughts that sneaked into her mind—that he had heard in town about the stream gravel playing out, about the disappointing assays on the claim she'd sold him. She'd been wrong in trusting him. He had wanted her for the claims after all, and once he discovered the claims wouldn't do him much good, he didn't want her anymore.

She tried to dismiss such mutterings in her head. Cougar loved her. They'd taken vows, even though they weren't strictly legal and binding. He didn't want her for what she had. There was a good reason why he hadn't shown up when he was supposed to.

Essie had tried to talk Georgia out of worrying. "Cougar Barnes is a good man," she'd said emphatically. "I never yet heard of him cheating, lying, or letting down a friend. If he took vows with you, you're as hitched as two mules in harness. So you just settle down, *chica*. You picked yourself a good man, and he'll be out here before you know it."

And he still hadn't come. Now there was this strange party with Colin Tate in the lead, and—she shaded her eyes so that she could see better, and her heart began to thunder. She recognized the man and woman with Colin. Looking strangely at home riding astride, her skirt riding up to mid-calf to expose a very improper amount of stocking-clad leg, was none other than Elizabeth Whitman, and with her, tall, handsome, and bronzed from the sun, was Alexander Stanford.

"Oh, damn," she breathed. So much for sending word back to Chicago. Chicago had followed them.

Elizabeth was the first to jump off her horse. She ran to Georgia and wrapped her in an ecstatic hug.

"Georgia! Oh, Georgia! We were so worried about you! When I found that note, I knew you'd been forced to write it. I kept imagining all these horrible things happening to you, but look at you! You're in one piece, aren't you?"

"Of course I am." Georgia regarded Elizabeth in amazement. "Forget looking at me. Look at you! You traveled all this way? With . . ." She glanced at Alexander, who hung back somewhat awkwardly, and Elizabeth actually turned pink in the cheeks.

"I had to find you, to help you. . . . I knew you would do the same for me, and how could I be less of a friend?"

The idea of making the rugged journey West must have been a daunting one to Elizabeth, who had never ventured beyond the civilized confines of Chicago. Georgia could appreciate the magnitude of caring that Elizabeth had shown by coming after her. The thought of having a friend so dear almost brought tears to her eyes.

Alexander must have seen the concern on her face, because he finally stepped forward. "You don't need to be afraid of anything now, Georgia dear. That miscreant who kidnapped you is behind bars. God and the justice system willing, he will remain there for a good long time."

That got Georgia's attention fast. She set Elizabeth aside. "Cougar is in jail?"

"I sent word ahead when we discovered you two had passed through Omaha. The scoundrel was arrested the minute he got into town."

"You had Cougar *arrested*?"

"Of course!"

Horror mixed with relief. Now she knew why Cougar hadn't met her as he'd promised. She looked toward Colin for explanation, but the marshal gave her only a sheepish shrug. She could imagine Cougar in Prescott's tiny jail cell, penned like a frustrated wild animal. Colin would be lucky if he didn't rip the bars down. The image summoned a tide of fury that rose and nearly choked her. Before she quite thought about it, she drew back her fist and delivered a right hook to Alexander's jaw.

Alexander staggered under the force of her unexpected blow. He might have actually fallen if the marshal hadn't caught him.

Elizabeth's jaw dropped. "Georgia!"

Essie threw up her hands and retreated to the cabin, muttering.

Georgia shook her hand to relieve the sting. "Sorry, Elizabeth. I know punching someone in the jaw isn't ladylike, but he deserves it."

Back on his feet, Alexander regarded Georgia warily. "Are you telling me you went with Barnes willingly?"

"As if some ox-sized clod could sneak up on me and cart me off without my wanting to be carted off! Do you think I would have come all the way back here with him if I hadn't wanted to?"

Colin slid Alexander an amused look. "She packs a mule's kick in that right hook, doesn't she?"

He rubbed his jaw and chuckled. "You are indeed a unique woman. I always knew that."

Georgia laughed. She did like the man. "I'm sorry, Alexander. I promise I'll tell Cougar that you've already gotten your just desserts, so he doesn't feel obligated to punch you out again."

"I take it you're jilting me."

"I can't marry you, because I love Cougar, and I didn't realize it until he helped me get back to who I really am. I'm sorry that I have to break a promise, but I wouldn't make a good wife for you anyway."

"Georgia, I have a feeling you would make a terrific wife for anyone you loved, which obviously isn't me. Don't let our engagement rest on your conscience. Sometimes a promise has to be broken for the benefit of both parties involved." He sent a peculiar smile in Elizabeth's direction. She immediately ducked her head and looked away, but not before Georgia caught the flame on her cheeks.

While Alexander and Colin watered the horses at the well Jose had dug when the stream dried up, Georgia took Elizabeth in to formally meet Essie.

"I've heard so much about you, Esperanza. Georgia talked about you almost as if you were her mother."

Essie sniffed. "I am the closest thing to a mother that she has." She turned a jaundiced eye on her "daughter." "And if I catch her throwing any more punches and acting like a drunken prospector in a saloon, I'll turn her over my knee."

"I didn't hurt him," Georgia insisted, chagrined.

Elizabeth took up Essie's side. "That's not the point, dear."

"Don't gang up on me, you two."

Elizabeth couldn't manage a good scold. She gave Georgia an impulsive hug. "I was so worried about you. So was Alexander."

Georgia grimaced guiltily.

"Oh, Georgia! Don't feel bad about breaking off your

engagement to Alexander. I . . . we . . . got to know each other so well on this incredible journey that, well . . ."

"Yes?" Georgia and Essie both prompted.

"Well, we . . . of course he hasn't said anything, because he was engaged to you, Georgia, and no gentleman worth his salt would dream of backing out of an engagement."

Georgia frowned.

"Though, of course," Elizabeth said hastily, "it's much more acceptable for a woman to change her mind. Oh, Georgia, I'm just sure that Alexander loves me, and now that you've freed him from his obligation to you, I can at least hope for a declaration. He's such a good man, and since your grandfather and his father talked him into courting you, he's started living again. He even talked about moving out to San Francisco to oversee the western part of Stanford Shipping."

Georgia felt almost dizzy with relief. She hadn't realized how heavily her promise to Alexander had rested on her conscience. Elizabeth would make him a much better wife than Georgia ever could.

"And I have you to thank for everything, dear friend," Elizabeth said with a smile. "You inspired me to become my own woman, to step out of the boundaries that society dictates for proper women." She dimpled impishly. "And then you jilted the man I love so that perhaps I can have him."

Georgia laughed. "What a friend I am!"

Georgia rode back to town with Colin, Alexander, and Elizabeth. The buoyancy that had lifted her when she'd learned the reason for Cougar's absence had disappeared, replaced by a carping worry that she couldn't banish. Elizabeth's statement haunted her. No man worth his salt would back out of an engagement, and that probably went double for solemn but not quite legally binding vows spoken with only the moon and stars officiating. Maybe Cougar hadn't wanted her only because of her formerly rich gold claims, but if he'd heard the news, he was bound to be disappointed. The gold might have fizzled out, but

Cougar was still stuck with her. Had she been right in believing that he loved her for herself?

And how much did Georgia really love Cougar? Enough to give him a chance to back out of their marriage with a clear conscience? The very thought made her want to throw up. But so did the prospect of never being sure of what he would have done, given the chance.

"Coug, if you don't stop pacing that cell, you're going to be worn to a stick before the circuit judge comes around." The part-time deputy marshal, Pig Dawber by name, lounged against the frame of the jail-room door and goaded Cougar with a grin. Ever since Cougar had won his pig in a game of five-card stud and then sold it back to him for five bucks, he'd wanted to get a couple of ounces of his flesh. These past few hours had been his chance.

"I'm not waiting for any damned circuit judge! Pig, let me out of here. If you think I'm going to spend the night sleeping on that bug-ridden mattress just because of some trumped-up, ridiculous charge, you've got another think coming. And I'll tell Colin the same thing when he comes back. And where the hell is he, anyway? He could have ridden out and back to Georgie's twice by now."

"Cougar, you ain't in no position to say nothin', so just keep your flytrap shut." With that, the deputy sauntered off, shutting the jail-room door tight and blocking Cougar's view of the outer office and, through the window, the outside world.

Cougar grabbed the bars in aggravation, wondering what Georgia had felt when she saw Alexander, what she'd thought hearing he'd been tossed into jail. Did Alexander remind her of the wealth and comfort she'd be missing as Cougar's wife? Did she have second thoughts about the vows they'd taken the night before?

Those thoughts ate at him, increasing his frustration. He delivered a painful kick to the cell bars—painful to his foot, not to the bars.

"Settle down in there, Coug! Marshal's here."

Only a moment passed before Colin Tate poked his head through the door. "Got a visitor for you."

Georgia pushed through the doorway behind him. Cougar's heart did a back flip.

"Georgia! Thank God!"

"Howdy, Cougar."

"Now will you let me out?" Cougar called to the marshal, who had retreated to the outer office.

"It's up to the lady, Coug. She said she wanted to talk to you while you had to stay put and listen."

Cougar questioned Georgia with a wary look. Green eyes sparkled wickedly through the bars at him.

"Nice accommodations," she noted with a smile. "Bed's a little small for someone your size, but it beats sleeping hog-tied on the floor of a moving freight car."

"Goddammit!" Cougar groaned. "You're going to take advantage of this, aren't you?"

"Such language!" she said primly.

"Georgia, honey, get the keys from Colin and let me out."

She ran one finger thoughtfully over the bars. "Let's see . . . there was the time you stole all my clothes in Omaha. That wasn't nice, Cougar."

"Come on, Georgie girl, we've moved past that. You know my intentions were good."

"The food good in here?"

"It stinks. Let me out, honey girl."

"Well, let me think. You did tell that nice shop lady in Galesburg that I was touched in the head. That wasn't nice, Cougar."

"Neither is this. Come on, Georgie! What do you want me to do? Will you please tell Colin that I didn't kidnap you, that we're married, that he needs to open this door and let me out of here?"

She shook her head, serious now. "This has been a bad day for us both, Cougar. I suppose you heard about the claims."

The cloud in her eyes made him moderate his tone. "Yeah. I did. I'm sorry, Georgia. You had a good run."

"Yeah. And here you are, stuck with me."

"No more than you're stuck with me."

From the look on her face, Cougar gathered that wasn't

the answer she was looking for. He'd never been good at understanding the nuances of what women wanted to hear.

"I know you'll stick by me because you said you would, Cougar. Even though no one saw the vows we made."

He didn't say a thing. This was dangerous territory for a man.

"But I want to be fair and give you a sporting chance to go your own way. I propose a shoot-out."

Very dangerous. "You want to shoot me now? Hell, Georgie, I thought we were doing better than that."

She grinned. "A marksmanship contest, blockhead. First light tomorrow morning. And you can't use me as a target. If you win, you're a free man. You can do whatever you please and just forget about me. If I win, though, you stick by me in spite of the failing claims."

Cougar told himself to be careful. Georgie was in a mood, and that could lead to all kinds of trouble. "Done!" he declared.

A frown creased her brow. "Well, all right, then. Done."

Her tone said he hadn't given the right answer. Maybe she had been hoping he would turn down this chance and declare his undying love—as if she would believe him. Let the little troublemaker stew, Cougar decided. This was her idea, and she could just live with it.

First light the next morning, Skillet Mahoney and Dooley Peters set out a target in the town square in the same spot that the Fourth of July marksmanship contests were held. A good part of the town turned out to watch. News of Georgia's return and Cougar's arrest had spread like wildfire. In a town where most news concerned Apache attacks, drought, or other disasters, this was just downright fun.

Georgia arrived at the square weary and cranky. She'd spent the night in her "town house" with Elizabeth and Alexander, crowded with Elizabeth on the bed, staring into the dark instead of sleeping.

She'd not seen hide nor hair of Cougar since she'd okayed his release from Colin's jail. But he showed up at the square looking cocky and confident. Georgia wanted to hit him when he gave her a cheerful greeting.

"Morning, Georgie."

She just glared.

"Yeah, morning, Georgie," Skillet echoed. "How's your trigger finger?"

"Stuff it, Skillet."

"Well, lookee who got up cranky as an ol' sow bear."

Georgia was not pleased to have everyone looking at her, even though quite a few people had come up to her to comment upon what a change Chicago had wrought.

"Yer downright pretty," Cal Newman allowed. "Who woulda' thunk it?"

"I always knew you was a looker under those coveralls," Starlight Sadie, who worked at Mattie Bee's, told her.

Even the preacher's wife ventured forward. "I have some dress patterns you might look at," she hinted. "Your friend Miss Whitman told me at church Sunday that you were the absolute belle of society in Chicago. I think it's wonderful, dear. And now that your long journey is over, I'm sure you'll want to be getting out of those trousers."

Getting out of her trousers was the least of Georgia's problems, unless she was getting out of them for Cougar Barnes. What a stupid idea it had been to give the man any kind of slack at all. If he didn't really love her now, she could have made him love her eventually. Now she might not have the chance, thanks to stupidity brought on, no doubt, by all the gushy emotion of seeing Elizabeth and Alexander again.

"Contestants ready?" Dooley asked.

Cougar had volunteered to let Georgia use his Henry. What could be more generous than that? It was a good rifle, and Georgia was used to the feel and sighting, because she'd used it many a time since they'd gotten off the train in Denver. She ran her hand along the wooden stock in a caress. She had to win. She just had to win.

"Ready," Cougar said, patting the Remington he had borrowed from Cal Newman.

"Ready," Georgia echoed.

Elizabeth dithered a few feet away. She had insisted on trailing along as "second," as she put it. "I don't understand why you're doing this," she whispered. "Can't you and Mr. Barnes simply discuss things in a civilized fashion?"

"No."

"And I don't understand the issue, either. Didn't you say that you came with him willingly?"

"Elizabeth . . . Please go keep Alexander company."

Elizabeth sighed. "You will explain all this to me when it's over, won't you?"

Someone should explain it to me, Georgia thought disconsolately.

Cougar was first to fire. He sent a slug square into the center of the bull's-eye Skillet had painted on a flour sack pinned to a bale of straw. The crowd murmured appreciatively.

So much for the hope that he might throw the contest. Her son-of-a-bitch husband was actually trying to win!

Georgia raised the Henry and fired. Her hands must have shaken for some reason, because she hit the target just a hair off center.

"The first round goes to Cougar!" Skillet crowed. He was a man, so naturally he was on Cougar's side.

The contest was set for the best two out of three. Georgia still had two more chances.

Cougar looked annoyingly relaxed as he fired off his second shot, but the slug entered the target just to the side of center. He frowned mightily, obviously upset with himself.

Georgia sighed and patted the stock of the Henry. "Come on, you faithful old thing. Fire straight and fire true."

She hit dead center.

"The second round goes to George . . . ahem . . . ah . . . Miss Kennedy!"

It was tempting to give Cougar a triumphant smirk, but she didn't dare look at him. He looked at her, though. She could feel the weight of his eyes.

"Nice shooting," he said.

She smiled tightly.

Cougar raised his rifle for the third time. He could throw this shot and still be her husband, if he wanted.

Georgia held her breath as the rifle cracked. Skillet marched officiously to the target to declare, "Dead center!"

So much for that. If her shot didn't go true, she would lose. If she tied up the contest, they would shoot again. That was the best she could hope for.

Georgia hesitated, chewing on her lower lip as her conscience began to nag. Was it fair, really, to shackle the man to her if he wanted his freedom? Never mind that he had carted her off from Chicago kicking and screaming and vowed to marry her. Never mind that he had sworn that he loved her, that the gold didn't matter, until she had been stupid enough to believe him, until she had abandoned good sense and fallen in love with him even more than she'd loved him before. And she had loved him before. Before Chicago. Before her father died, either. She'd just been scared to admit to such a thing.

She raised the Henry and fired. Skillet marched to the target and examined the result.

"Third round goes to Cougar! Contest winner—Cougar Barnes!"

Even Georgia didn't know if she had meant to hit center. She would probably wonder about it a long time.

"I won," Cougar said.

"You won," she agreed, her heart sinking into her stomach like a big lead ball.

He propped his rifle against a tree. "I have something to say to you."

Would he embarrass her in front of all of these people, all her friends, Alex and Elizabeth, too? She steeled her jaw. "Yes?"

He dropped onto one knee.

"What are you doing?"

"Proposing, right here for everyone to see."

"Proposing?"

"Yes, proposing. The last time I proposed, you said yes, so I figured that I didn't have to do this anymore. But I guess I owe you another chance to say no, since you did the same for me. And I can see the only way to convince you that I really love you is to get down on bended knee in front of everybody, with everybody here knowing your two claims aren't worth the dynamite to blow them to hell, and ask you to marry me. So I set about to win that freedom you offered and then give it up again.

"Georgie girl, you're the only thing I really want. Marry me."

An audible sigh came from Elizabeth, who watched raptly with folded hands.

"You didn't really want to back out, then?"

"Nope. How long do I have to stay down here?"

Georgia grinned. "Get up, you jackass. This time can we have a real wedding?"

"No more talk of gold claims?"

"To hell with the claims. I'm going to have a ranch, and I'm going to punch cows right alongside you. That's when I'm not busy impressing the good ladies of Prescott with my dainty manners and genteel conversation."

Alexander interrupted, Elizabeth on his arm. "The preacher just mentioned he has time for a wedding tomorrow morning." He glanced down at Elizabeth with his heart in his eyes. "Actually, a double wedding, if you don't mind, Barnes."

Georgia looked at Elizabeth, her heart suddenly so full she was sure the sun had come to roost in her chest. Elizabeth patted Alexander's arm and broke free, threading her arm through Georgia's and sighing happily. "We must discuss what we will wear tomorrow. You absolutely cannot be married in trousers, Georgia. It simply won't do. And we'll want to rub lard on your face tonight, though it won't take away that sunbronzed color. Have you been going without a hat . . . ?"

Cougar watched the women disappear into a crowd of suddenly interested women. "You know?" he confided to Alexander. "I once fought a mountain lion with my bare hands and won, but this time I might have bitten off more than I can chew."

Epilogue

Georgia squatted by the gate of the corral, hammer in hand and nails protruding from her mouth like long iron teeth. She shoved the broken crossbar back into its slot, selected a nail, and then almost swallowed all the rest when a voice piped from behind her.

"You shouldn't hold nails in your teeth, Ma, 'cause you'll swallow them. That's what Pa told me."

Georgia removed the nails from her mouth and looked around at the redheaded four-year-old who watched intently. "Your pa's right, Nathan."

"Can I hammer the nail?"

"Will you be careful not to squash your thumb?"

"You hold the nail."

"Then will you be careful not to squash *my* thumb?"

He grinned his father's trademark crooked grin because he knew it generally got him what he wanted. "I promise."

She couldn't resist that smile. He was so like his father, so like the child in the picture of Cougar's ranch that she'd imagined six years ago. She handed the hammer to her son.

No sooner had Nathan taken the hammer than a little black-haired, brown-faced girl bounced up. "I *want* to help!"

Maria was the eldest of Essie and Jose's brood of three.

The Mexican couple hadn't lasted long on the San Pedro farm south of Tucson. Farming just wasn't in Jose's blood, and Esperanza had hated the heat and the dry of southeastern Arizona. A year after Cougar had brought his first herd to Chino, Essie and Jose had returned to work on the BK Ranch—B for Barnes, K for Kennedy, because Alvin had helped fund that first herd. With the money Cougar had saved over the years and Alvin's investment, the BK had started with a respectable herd of cattle. The profits that Georgia and her father had banked over the years from the Lynx Creek claim had seen them through the first couple of hard years until the ranch could stand on its own.

"Girls can't hammer," Nathan told Maria.

"Your mother hammers."

"She's not a girl, she's a—" He looked at Georgia doubtfully.

"A lady," she finished for him, "which is simply a grown-up sort of girl. Girls and ladies can do whatever they like, and don't either of you forget it."

That was a lesson Georgia had learned the hard way, that she didn't have to choose one role over the other. When she worked at ranch chores, she donned sturdy denim trousers and a floppy hat. The next day she might put on her lady manners along with her best dress and prettiest bonnet for a visit to Fort Whipple to have tea with the military wives or into Prescott to go to a Sunday social. Since General Crook's successful campaign against the Apaches in 1872, Arizona Territory had become both more populous and more civilized, and the influx of farmers, ranchers, cowboys, and shopkeepers had brought some of the strictures of society that prevailed farther east. But no one laughed at Georgia anymore, and the good women of the area didn't pull aside their skirts when she passed. Rather they called out a greeting or invited her to stop and visit. Georgia had proved she was a lady and more.

Maria smirked at the boy, then asked Georgia, "Can I hammer?"

"You can have a turn." She sighed. At this rate the gate would never get repaired.

A call from the house interrupted the hammering lesson. Essie sat on the wraparound covered porch with the gold-haired three-year-old girl that was Georgia's youngest—temporarily. From the way her stomach was heaving most mornings, Georgia suspected that another was on the way. "They're coming!" Essie yelled. "I can see them way up the road!"

Georgia immediately gathered up hammer, nails, and children and hurried toward the house. Her heart gave the familiar ecstatic lurch that six years of marriage to Cougar Barnes hadn't cured. Cougar was coming back. No matter that he'd been gone only half a day. Her heart reacted as if he'd been gone a month.

"You'd better put on a dress to greet your grandpa," Essie scolded. "You don't want him to see you looking like a ranch hand."

Essie would never give up mothering Georgia, even though Georgia had a husband and children of her own. "Yes, ma'am. If you'll wash these urchins and get them fit for company."

Twenty minutes later Georgia, dressed as properly as even Elizabeth could have hoped, stepped demurely from the front porch to greet her guests. It was a good thing she had put on her Sunday best, because one of those guests was Elizabeth herself, dressed as a wealthy San Francisco matron should be, with Alexander, their five-year-old curly-headed, raven-haired boy, and Elizabeth's sister Chloe, who had come along to help with the little boy. Georgia kissed Elizabeth and Chloe, hugged Alexander, asked after Phoebe and Claudia, who both lived in San Francisco, and then took her grandfather's hand.

"I'm so glad you finally came."

Alvin gave the house, corrals, barn, and rolling green pastures an approving look. "So this is what you've been raving about in your letters for these past years. I can see my partnership in this will be as profitable as my partnership in Stanford-Kennedy." He smiled at Alexander, who nodded equably. "The junior side of the partnership has done a very nice job in San Francisco beefing up the West Coast side of the business. Bigger is better, I always say. I don't put my money where it won't grow."

Georgia didn't quibble. Let her grandfather pretend that he'd invested in the BK to make a profit. She knew he'd done it out of love for her. Alvin was a remarkable man. He had talked Robert Stanford into going through with their business merger even though Georgia had jilted Alexander. Robert had gotten what he wanted, after all. Alexander had married a fine woman and started a new generation of Stanfords to carry on the line. The old man had then managed to survive the great fire of 1870 that had devastated Chicago, including Greystone House, and rebuilt an even bigger mansion. Now he was touring the West to see where his son had wandered and worked—no easy feat for a man getting on in his seventies. The last two months he had visited Alexander and Elizabeth in San Francisco, and now that the summer heat had moderated, they had traveled together to Arizona for a good long visit here.

"We've had a nice profit for three years in a row," Georgia told him.

"That's what I like to hear."

Georgia saved the best greeting for last, giving her husband a kiss that was fit for public consumption but promised privately of joys to come. He smiled down at her with the cocky smile she loved so well.

"Miss me?" he asked, taking her loosely into his arms.

"You were only gone for a half day."

"So I was. Their stage was bang on time. The trip isn't what it used to be."

"A lot of things aren't what they used to be," she commented, leaning her head against his shoulder as they followed their guests inside. Then she grinned. "But I still missed you. That's never going to change."

As the adults filed through the door into the big two-story house, five-year-old Robbie Stanford stayed behind, sidling up to three-year-old Lucy Barnes under Essie's watchful eye. He looked the little girl up and down and decided she was worthy of his attention. "My father's richer than your father," seemed a good opening line. It was always good for a man to establish superiority over a female at the very start.

Lucy gave him a wicked grin. "So? My pa can beat yours in a fight."

"No, he can't."

"My ma can, too."

"That's a lie."

"Is not."

"Is, too."

"Is not."

"You're just a dumb girl! What do you know?"

To show him what she knew, little Lucy hooked her foot around his heel and flipped him tail over teeth onto the ground. Satisfied, she dusted her hands and marched into the house after the adults.

Essie stood with hands on Marie's shoulders and watched the scene play out without intervening. She figured it was kinder for the boy to learn firsthand that a man didn't mess with a female who had Georgie Barnes's blood running through her veins.

She patted Marie's little shoulder. "We have a whole new generation of little Georgies to look forward to. God save us."

But she smiled as she said it.

National bestselling author
EMILY CARMICHAEL
JEZEBEL'S SISTER
0-515-12996-8

Take an innocent girl, a wagon full of prostitutes, and a devilishly handsome preacher, and you've got a wild Western romance.

"Emily Carmichael writes witty fare for romantic readers."
—Literary Times

"One of the most imaginative writers working in romance."
—Affaire de Coeur

Available wherever books are sold or
to order call 1-800-788-6262

*More entertaining romance Texas-style
from USA Today bestselling author*

Jodi Thomas

FEATURING THE MCLAIN BROTHERS:

TWILIGHT IN TEXAS	0-515-13027
THE TEXAN'S TOUCH	0-515-12299-8
TO KISS A TEXAN	0-515-12503-2
TO WED IN TEXAS	0-515-17516-2

ALSO AVAILABLE:

TWO TEXAS HEARTS	0-515-12099-5
TEXAS LOVE SONG	0-515-11953-9
THE TEXAN'S DREAM	0-515-13176-8
THE TEXAN'S WAGER	0-515-13400-7

*"Jodi draws the reader into her stories from the first page...
She's one of my favorites."*
—Debbie Macomber

*Available wherever books are sold or
to order call 1-800-788-6262*

Your personal invitation to a
very private affair...

MEET ME AT MIDNIGHT

Jacqueline Navin

0-515-13054-0

As part of a devious wager, Raphael Giscard is
planning to seduce pretty Julia Brodie.
But he never counted on falling in love with her.

"Ms. Navin's style is exhilarating...
she plots like a master." —*Rendezvous*

Available wherever books are sold or
to order call 1-800-788-6262

Berkley Books proudly introduces

Berkley Sensation

a **brand-new** romance line featuring today's **best-loved** authors—and tomorrow's **hottest** up-and-comers!

Every month...
Four sensational writers

Every month...
Four sensational new romances
from historical to contemporary, suspense to cozy.

Now that Berkley Sensation is around...

This summer is going to be a scorcher!

B072

PENGUIN GROUP (USA) INC.
Online

Your Internet gateway to a virtual environment with hundreds of entertaining and enlightening books from Penguin Group (USA) Inc.

While you're there, get the latest buzz on the best authors and books around—

Tom Clancy, Patricia Cornwell, W.E.B. Griffin, Nora Roberts, William Gibson, Robin Cook, Brian Jacques, Catherine Coulter, Stephen King, Ken Follett, Terry McMillan, and many more!

Penguin Group (USA) Inc. Online is located at http://www.penguin.com

PENGUIN GROUP (USA) Inc. NEWS

Every month you'll get an inside look at our upcoming books and new features on our site. This is an ongoing effort to provide you with the most up-to-date information about our books and authors.

Subscribe to Penguin Group (USA) Inc. News at http://www.penguin.com/newsletters